MW00352145

CAESAR OBSESSED

PASSION, CONQUEST, AND TRAGEDY IN GAUL

CAESAR OBSESSED

PASSION, CONQUEST, AND TRAGEDY IN GAUL

ANTHONY R. LICATA

G. ANTON
Publisher

Chicago

Copyright © 2022 by Anthony R. Licata

All rights reserved. Printed in the United States of America. No part of this publication may be used or reproduced in any manner whatsoever without the prior written permission of the publisher, except in the case of brief quotations embodied in critical articles and reviews.

Published in the U.S.A. by
G. Anton Publishing, LLC
Chicago, Illinois
Vivian Craig – General Manager
vcraig@gantonpublishing.com
www.gantonpublishing.com

First Edition

ISBN 978-0-9966799-6-1 (Hardback)
ISBN 978-0-9966799-7-8 (Paperback)
ISBN 978-0-9966799-8-5 (eBook)
Library of Congress Control Number: 2022940097

Cover Design: Stephanie Rocha

Cover Design Contributor: Tanja Prokop

Maps and Illustrations: James Swanson

Interior Design: Tracy Atkins, The Book Makers

Back Cover/Title Page Art: View of Caesar's Bridge Over the Rhine © Sir John Soane's Museum, London

Cover Images: iStock; Shutterstock; Dreamstime/Luis Louro; Unsplash/Jasper Boer; Unsplash/Faith Crabtree

For the great lawyers Newton N. Minow and Jack Guthman,
to whom I owe it all

A Special Dedication

G. A. Beller and Vivian Craig of G. Anton Publishing have been tireless in pushing me to improve this book to its final form. Not only were they unwavering in their support throughout the years of manuscript development, but their creative input into the storyline has been invaluable. I am immensely indebted to them, and I sincerely thank them for their contributions, support, and friendship.

DRAMATIS PERSONAE
(IN ORDER OF APPEARANCE)

Curio	Adjutant and confidant to Caesar
Marcus Vitruvius Mamurra	Prefect of engineers
Dominicus	Mamurra's slave
Gaius Julius Caesar	General of the Roman army in Gaul, member of the Triumvirate with Pompey and Crassus
Titus Labienus	Senior legate (second-in-command)
Gordianus	Tribune of the Tenth Legion
Ariovistus	King of the Suebi Tribe of Germania
Nofio	Chief blacksmith
Hortensius	Tribune of the Twelfth Legion
Lentulus	Flank officer of the Twelfth Legion
Boduognatus	Leader of the Nervii Tribe of Belgae
Trolianus	Predecessor to Mamurra as prefect of engineers
Devorra	Daughter of Boduognatus
Aloucca	Devorra's slave
Gabinier	Warrior of the Nervii Tribe
Luca	Mamurra's father
Rotollo	Mamurra's first mentor
Catullus	Senator of Rome
Giacomo	First assistant to Mamurra
Correus	Leader of the Bellovaci Tribe of Belgae
Maccheor	Son of Correus
Pomorro	Warrior and confidant of Boduognatus

Vatteus	*Roman army doctor*
Molena	*Belgic slave, sister of Elliandro*
Elliandro	*Belgic slave, brother of Molena*
Flavius	*Tribune of the Roman Cavalry*
Metellus	*Tribune of the Twenty-Fourth Legion*
Pompeius Magnus (Pompey)	*Former consul of Rome, member of the Triumvirate with Caesar and Crassus*
Julia	*Caesar's daughter*
Garibus	*Staff engineer, formerly for Pompey*
Decimus Junius Brutus	*Roman admiral, Caesar's cousin*
Young Crassus	*Son of Marcus Licinius Crassus*
Calpurnia	*Caesar's wife*
Rabanus	*Belgic peasant farmer*
Berhta	*Wife of Rabanus*
Gustavus	*Nervii warrior*
Giovanus	*Nervii warrior*
Gregarus	*Nervii warrior*
Othon	*Farmer in Gaul*
Marcus Licinius Crassus	*Member of the Triumvirate with Caesar and Pompey*
Octavius Caesar	*Caesar's nephew*
Marcus Vitruvius Agrippa	*General of Octavius's forces*

THE ROMAN WORLD 55 BC

TRIBES OF GAUL

THE ROMAN HIERARCHY

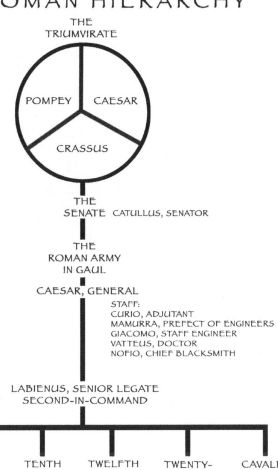

THE
TRIUMVIRATE

POMPEY | CAESAR

CRASSUS

THE
SENATE CATULLUS, SENATOR

THE
ROMAN ARMY
IN GAUL

CAESAR, GENERAL

STAFF:
CURIO, ADJUTANT
MAMURRA, PREFECT OF ENGINEERS
GIACOMO, STAFF ENGINEER
VATTEUS, DOCTOR
NOFIO, CHIEF BLACKSMITH

LABIENUS, SENIOR LEGATE
SECOND-IN-COMMAND

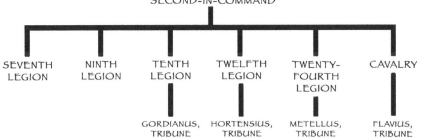

SEVENTH LEGION	NINTH LEGION	TENTH LEGION	TWELFTH LEGION	TWENTY-FOURTH LEGION	CAVALRY
		GORDIANUS, TRIBUNE	HORTENSIUS, TRIBUNE	METELLUS, TRIBUNE	FLAVIUS, TRIBUNE

Prologue

Rome, 44 bc

"It's your move, Curio."

The older man snapped out of his reverie. He fixed his attention on the inlaid squares of the game board before him. The two men were locked in a pitched battle of latrones, moving polished stone pieces over the squares, each trying to surround his opponent's pieces. Curio had never lost to this challenger. In fact, he had never lost to *anyone*. Except Caesar.

"You seem preoccupied," Mamurra said in an amused tone. "Thinking about Caesar at the Forum today?"

Curio studied the pumice-stone table holding the game board. The table base was unusual: it was a detailed sculpture of a massively muscled man—Heracles, perhaps?—holding the flat surface above his grimacing bearded face. Curio's thin lips pressed together in a scowl. The expression brought a slight wince of pain; the mauve ruined skin of his burn-ravaged cheek protested at being stretched, even after all these years. As was his habit, he tugged at the scar, trying to make it more pliable. "So, you've taken up mind reading now that you're retired?"

If Mamurra even noticed the scar after all their years together, he gave no sign of it. Instead, he pointed at the table pedestal and said, "Atlas—who else?" Then, with a trace of jest in his voice: "You spent your entire career protecting Caesar's back; it doesn't take a mind reader to guess you're thinking about him."

The two sat on the veranda of Mamurra's magnificent home on the northernmost bulge of the Caelian Hill, near the very pinnacle of the rise. It faced west, to provide a sweeping view of the fashionable houses nestled into the nearby Palatine Hill, and farther away, just to the north, the Forum itself, meeting place of the Roman Senate, the seat of all power. Looming over it from atop the Capitoline Hill, just behind the Forum, stood the

1

monumental Temple of Jupiter, Optimus Maximus, one of the wonders of the world.

Curio pulled his lambskin cloak around him, seeking warmth against the chilly March air. The undyed cloth was a dull gray, matching the slate sky overhead. He cast a sweeping look at Mamurra's spectacular manse, fully clad in rare Numidian Giallo Antico marble, the first residence in Rome to be so adorned. Curio marveled at the underlying structure required to hold the massive weight of the stone overlay. Only Mamurra, Caesar's prefect of engineers, could have designed it.

"I'm unable to free my mind of him," Curio said wearily. "Calpurnia begged him not to go to the Senate today. She had a horrible nightmare last night. The gods were telling her to persuade him to stay at home."

Mamurra grinned. "When did Caesar ever listen to a woman?"

Curio managed a wan smile. "He often didn't listen to *me*."

"Hmph," Mamurra grunted. Curio and Caesar had been together since they were boys. Curio's father had been a farmer on the Julian estate— Curio grew up idolizing the older Gaius, following him around like a puppy, even when Caesar entered the army. While he was not much good at handling weapons, young Curio had proved himself exceptionally adept at managing the never-ending barrage of details inherent in running a Roman army in the field. He had toiled relentlessly in Caesar's shadow as the great man rose through the ranks, always happily staying in the background, cranking out the orders issued by Caesar, solving his problems, writing his letters, even serving as scribe while Caesar dictated his celebrated account of the war in Gaul. And it was well known that Curio had enlisted another boyhood friend, Vatteus, to serve as an army doctor, to help care for Caesar's ailments, however much the general had tried to keep his frailties hidden from the men. Whatever Caesar needed done, Curio took care of it.

Curio suddenly reached out and slid a stone on the board to flank one of Mamurra's pieces, capturing it.

The engineer erupted in frustration. "Curio, you spent too many years at Caesar's elbow—you've mastered his tactics!"

Curio gave the engineer a cynical look. "Perhaps it was Caesar who acquired his tactics from me."

Mamurra looked shocked. Curio had never claimed credit for any of the triumphs Caesar had pulled off every time all appeared lost on the battlefield.

Curio took up one of the mugs resting on the table beside the polished wooden board. He swirled the wine, full bodied, brought back from the

Champagne region in Gaul, a deeper scarlet than the Roman army colors. It had not been watered. But the mug itself was of more interest to him. It featured a painted depiction of a Roman naval ship, a trireme, sporting three banks of oars.

"It was a gift from our general," Mamurra said.

Curio turned it delicately, admiring the craftsmanship. "In recognition of the man who built the fleet that won for him against the Veneti, no doubt. He was always generous with you in victory." He tilted the mug toward the house, the most ostentatious marker of the wealth Caesar had showered on his engineer.

"Don't cry poor to me," Mamurra retorted. "He made you rich, too. All those slaves, hauled out of Gaul and Germania."

Curio could not deny it. "Especially the slaves. We both profited greatly from our service to him," he concurred. His eye fell upon a sizeable terracotta urn on the veranda, glazed to hold the image of two naked boys painted against a background of light cyan. He knew better than to remark on that topic. "What a distance we've both come from our humble beginnings, Mamurra."

Mamurra could have taken umbrage at that; his roots were more respectable, having been born into a prosperous mercantile family. But he had not been the firstborn, and so would not have inherited the family business, leaving him . . . the army. However, Mamurra seemed not to have heard Curio's observation, seemingly intent on the board, as if trying to fathom some stroke of genius that might salvage his badly depleted pieces.

Then they heard the faint cries.

"He's dead! He's dead! Master, they've killed Caesar!"

A slave was panting as he ran up the Via Tuscolana, a winding road on the Caelian Hill, the gravel crunching beneath his boots.

Both men rose to their feet as the breathless slave staggered up the steps of the portico.

"Calm yourself, Dominicus," Mamurra said to the man, who was gasping for air. The slave had been with Mamurra for years, first assigned to him by Caesar during the campaign against the Belgae. "What is this nonsense?"

"Master, they've killed him, right there on the floor of the Senate. He's dead. Caesar is dead!"

Curio lost all color in his face, and his hands began to tremble.

Mamurra grabbed his servant by the arms. "Who? Who killed him?"

The slave, fearful, blurted out, "It was a group of senators. They say Cassius was among them. Brutus, too, and that snake Catullus."

Curio shot an acid eye at his colleague, knowing the impact Catullus's name would have on Mamurra. "A conspiracy," he said, his voice devoid of emotion. "If only Caesar had listened! I knew all his 'dictator for life' talk was going to cause trouble. May the gods curse those elite patricians!"

"You're certain?" Mamurra pressed, squeezing the slave harder.

Dominicus trembled. "I am afraid it is true, master. I went into the Forum and saw it myself. Caesar was lying there, not far from the ivory chair on the rostrum, all bled out. He was stabbed many times."

Reaching into his tunic, the slave produced an elegant dagger of highly skilled Roman metalwork, razor sharp. The handle was inlaid with a superb ivory carving of the Imperial eagle, symbol of the power of the Senate.

Both men recognized it at once, but Curio felt faint at the sight of it. "Caesar's dagger," he choked.

"I took it from his hand," Dominicus said. "He died clutching it. I did not want some stranger to have it."

Mamurra took the dagger from his slave. It was Caesar's, no question about it. He rubbed his thumb over the eagle, as if to wipe away any traces of blood it might have drawn in the struggle, then handed it to Curio. They both stood there, dumbfounded, trying to grasp the enormity of it. Caesar was dead, murdered by the old-line Roman faction, the same bastards he had pardoned for backing Pompey after they lost the civil war.

"At least he died fighting," Mamurra said, his voice cracking.

Curio thought differently but didn't say so. No point in wasting it on these two. "I told him not to trust them!" he moaned, tears forming at the corners of his bloodshot eyes. "I told him to kill them all! Now they've done him in!"

Mamurra shuddered, as if gripped by a chill not even his winter garb could stifle. He looked at Curio and said urgently, "If Caesar's enemies have murdered him, they are intent on seizing power. And when they do, they surely will take vengeance on Caesar's backers."

Taking a moment to compose himself, Mamurra turned to regard his remarkable abode. He had always told everyone the structure was his second-greatest career achievement. He clenched his jaw, a sure sign he had made up his mind.

"Summon all members of the household," Mamurra said to Dominicus with the authority he had learned as an officer under Caesar. "Set them to packing at once. We leave tonight for my villa in Formiae." It was his hometown, a lovely port village nestled along the Appian Way, between Rome and Naples. He would be safe there.

"Where will you go?" Mamurra asked Curio.

Curio had recovered his bearings and answered calmly. "I must speak to his heir," he said with conviction. "He needs to flee Rome. Once they see what Caesar has done in his will, Caesar's heir will be at grave risk."

Mamurra furrowed his brow. "How do you know what is in Caesar's will? It's sealed. Held by the Vestal Virgins for safekeeping."

Curio gave him a flat stare. "Who," he asked drily, "do you think wrote it?"

"Of course," Mamurra said. "And once that is done?"

"I shall remain in Rome. I've always stayed clear of politics, so I should have no reason to fear Caesar's enemies. I mean nothing to them."

"I pray you are right," Mamurra said, then hastily embraced his friend as he prepared to leave.

Raising his mug of wine, Curio whispered, "And to mighty Caesar, *requiescat in pace!*"

❧❧❧

HOURS LATER, as evening approached, the household was in turmoil as slaves scurried this way and that, carrying Mamurra's many valued possessions, including Mamurra's irreplaceable collection of engineering books. One book in particular was packed with exceptional care—*Bellum Gallicum*, Caesar's supposed account of the war in Gaul, authored for him by Curio, of course.

Time was short, Mamurra knew. Already, rioting had broken out all over Rome as word spread among the lower classes that Caesar, their great advocate and champion, had been slain by a cabal of elite Romans determined to restore the old order. Mobs had gathered at the Forum itself, and, more seriously, had marched to do violence to the houses of senators implicated in the plot.

Mamurra was certain that the murdering conspirators would focus first on Caesar's more highly visible lieutenants, such as Marc Antony, expected to be Caesar's heir, and perhaps Caesar's young nephew, Octavius, before getting around to the likes of dedicated Caesarian officers such as himself. By then, he intended to be long gone from the dangerous environs of Rome.

He turned his attention to his most prized possession of them all, so precious that he would die to defend it. From its hiding place behind a false panel in the wall of his study, Mamurra withdrew a long wooden tube, sealed on one end and with a removable lid at the other. The tube was expertly crafted from the rarest African teak, a treasure in itself. He opened the tube and gingerly extracted a rolled set of vellum sheets. They were beginning to yellow with age, but as he spread them out on his broad desk and weighed down the corners to keep them from curling, he could not help but smile with pride at their content.

My greatest work, he thought, with a professional's deep satisfaction of a master accomplishment. He delicately ran his fingers over the sketches: the plans for the slanted pilings, the deck, the trusses and supports, the iron brackets, the upstream buffers . . . all of it so painstakingly laid out, every contingency addressed, every stress point reinforced, every challenge resolved. It was a work of art, more so than any of the treasures already loaded on the wagons.

Mamurra's hand reached the bottom of a page. There it was . . . and on the bottom of each of the sheets. For the first time since he had heard the awful news, Mamurra wept. But he did not let his tears fall upon the priceless drawings.

"Master?"

Mamurra looked up.

Dominicus had been watching him. "What is it?"

Mamurra could not hold back a smile. "These are the plans for the bridge over the Rhine. Caesar demanded it be built in ten days. Impossible. It was madness."

Dominicus looked puzzled. "But it was done. You did it."

Mamurra pointed to the bottom of one of the sheets. "It was for him."

There, scratched on the parchment sheet, was that bold, unforgettable script:

So ordered.
Gaius Julius Caesar

He needed to hurry, Mamurra knew that. But still, with the great man's own signature right there before him, he could not help himself. His thoughts drifted back . . . back to those days in the wilderness of Gaul . . . back to where it all began.

I

VESONTIO, GAUL, 57 BC

CAESAR WAS NOT PLEASED, as his longtime second-in-command, the senior legate Titus Labienus, could easily tell. After so many years at Caesar's side, Labienus knew at a glance that the commander of all the Roman forces in Gaul was about to reprimand someone, and it was not going to be pretty.

Caesar and his deputy were standing on a tall platform, taller than any trees in the vicinity. It had been erected by the army's engineers so that the high command could have a bird's-eye view of the troops of the Twelfth Legion in their drill.

At a barked order from the legion's commander, passed on by officers down the line, the full assembly of nearly five thousand men had fallen out from marching ranks and hurriedly taken up the standard defensive posture, forming a broad arc, shields up and spears bristling. Their duty was to protect the precious baggage train, those hundreds of wagons and pack animals that carried the essential food and materials needed to sustain the army. In the upcoming campaign, the Twelfth would have the vital task of defending this lifeline.

The morning air was cool, but the sun's altitude suggested that summer was not far off, and with it, the prime campaigning season. Labienus knew that Caesar wanted his army ready for anything.

"Look yonder at their left flank, Labienus," Caesar said with disapproval. "Who commands that cohort? His legionaries would collapse if someone with the cunning of Ariovistus were to surprise them."

Labienus arched an eyebrow. "Ariovistus? I thought you were planning this campaign against the Belgae, not the tribes of Germania." Even though he was a steely veteran, Labienus shuddered at the thought of facing the Germanic hordes again. They were fearless, those Germanic barbarians, to the point of being crazy. They would charge headlong into the strongest formation, screaming and hacking like men possessed by demons, and they would not give up until their very last man was dead. And their *size*! They were giants, solid as oxen, and just as hairy and foul smelling. Even worse, ruthlessly ferocious. He wanted no part of facing them again.

Caesar's scowl turned to an impish grin, and those bright hazel eyes twinkled. "You would shy away from a rematch, Labienus?"

Labienus cast a long look at his general. Caesar seemed not to have aged at all in three years of hard fighting and even harder bargaining with all the complicated tribes and chiefs and factions that made up Gaul. He was long and lean, in excellent physical condition for a man in his forties, still capable of taking up shield and sword to wade into a fray when necessary to turn the tide of a battle. Amazingly, he bore no scars from any of his forays into combat; his face was tanned and leathery from so much exposure to the elements, but all his features were fully intact. His nose was long and straight, never having been broken, his square jaw was pronounced, a sure sign of a natural leader. And that chin! Sharp and chiseled, a window into the man himself. Labienus could easily see why men were drawn to follow him, and why so many women found him irresistible.

"I fight whomever Caesar orders me to fight," Labienus said in a sly tone. "But after we beat them here at Vesontio, Ariovistus hurried back across the Rhine to hide in his forests, and we haven't heard a whisper from him since. Why tempt the fates?"

Caesar stroked his clean-shaven jaw, his classic gesture when considering a subordinate's suggestion. As if he were seriously considering it . . . which of course he never did if he had already made up his mind. But on this topic, Labienus knew the normally decisive Caesar was torn. He had spent three years fighting in Gaul, seeking to subjugate this hostile land populated with so many different tribes, each with their own arcane laws and customs.

The territory west of the Rhine River, that great natural barrier between Gaul and Germania, had been especially nettlesome. The large and powerful Germanic tribe known as the Suebi had been encroaching into Gaul for a number of years. Led by their clever and merciless King Ariovistus, they had meddled in Gallic tribal disputes and taken considerable land in the process. Ariovistus had wasted no time in establishing large numbers of his Suebi in far eastern Gaul, especially in a rich valley through which the Doubs River coursed. The land was taken from the Aedui people. The Roman Senate, in 60 BC, had recognized this state of affairs in a decree.

However, the Senate, hoping to deter further Germanic migration into Gaul, had declared Rome to be an ally of the Aedui people.

By the time Caesar began his campaign in Gaul two years later, Ariovistus had gotten greedy and was demanding even more territory from the hapless Aedui. Caesar tried to broker a deal, but Ariovistus refused to meet. Roman honor was at stake: Caesar moved to intercept the oncoming horde. Here at Vesontio, the two armies met in an all-out showdown. Ariovistus succeeded in outmaneuvering the Romans and had them surrounded. Caesar still smarted over that. Rather than let himself be starved into surrendering, Caesar gave a rousing speech to his men and attacked. The Romans prevailed, winning a great victory and sending Ariovistus packing back across the Rhine—camp storytellers claimed the wily fox himself had swum across! But the Roman high command knew they had escaped by a whisker, and but for Caesar's own sorely tested skill at battlefield management, the result might have been a disaster for Rome.

As a gesture of his disdain for the Suebi, Caesar had established his headquarters at Vesontio. He liked the terrain, protected as it was by a huge U-shaped bend in the Doubs River, which afforded safeguarding on three sides. Within this secure refuge, Caesar had spent the winter, refitting his depleted legions and plotting his next move. He wanted to go northeast, against the territory known as the Belgae, for the loose confederation of tribes populating the land bordered on the north by the North Sea, and on the south by the Rhine. There was considerable wealth to be obtained by conquering them.

Caesar gave a weary sigh. "No, Labienus, our plan is set. We move north and east, to bring the benefits of Roman civilization to the wilds of the Belgae. But for now," he continued, moving toward the ladder at the edge of the platform, "send the legion commander and his officer of the left flank to my headquarters. I want to have a word with them."

Caesar started down the ladder, leaving Labienus to watch as the sun glinted off the balding pate of the general's head. His adjutant, Curio, was waiting at the base of the ladder. Labienus disliked Curio—he knew that the two had grown up together, Curio always in the shadow of the older and more accomplished Caesar, but he carried a self-important air, no doubt drawn from his regular and close access to the general. *Rather arrogant*, Labienus thought, *for a fellow whose face was so marred.* Labienus was always distrustful of those who would seek to curry favor with the general.

He waved to the legion commander on the ground, indicating he wanted to see the man, so he could tell him to report to the general's headquarters.

He grinned, knowing full well that Caesar never reprimanded officers in the sight of their men. *Praise in public, criticize in private* was one of Caesar's favorite sayings. Those poor fellows down on the field were going to get chewed out by an expert.

⁂

CAESAR ACCEPTED his assistant's salute as he set foot on terra firma, relieved to be back on solid ground.

"Were you pleased with the drill?" the younger man asked as Caesar made his way to the waiting horses, surrounded by his cavalry guard.

"Pahh," Caesar snorted. "Totally unacceptable. But nothing a little tongue-lashing can't correct."

Curio knew what that meant: someone was going to catch hell, maybe even get demoted. "What do you want to do next?" he asked the general in an even tone.

Caesar was hauling himself onto his mount, a handsome chestnut mare. "I want to see how Nofio is coming along with the coffles," he said, and gave the animal a sharp kick.

Some minutes later, dust swirling all about them, the riders descended on a cluster of firepits, each fed by a large bellows being worked furiously by the sweat-drenched slaves chained to the apparatus. Farther beyond, the tents housing the blacksmiths were lined up in good Roman order. The air was full of the clanking sounds of the laboring blacksmiths and the acrid odor of coking coal.

Caesar pulled up before a grime-covered bull of a man standing at a battered anvil and pounding a piece of metal into a curve. The smith was so intent upon his task that he did not even look up as the general approached.

"Nofio," Caesar said in a voice loud enough to penetrate the din, "I gave you command of the smiths because you told me you could meet my quotas. So, how go your preparations?"

Startled from his concentration, Nofio looked up and dropped his hammer. "Sir, as you can see, we are working night and day to provide what you will need for the campaign."

Caesar studied the man. He was so solid he might have been made from the same iron with which he toiled. His head was shaved completely bald, the better to cope with the relentless heat of the forge. Endless toil with the hammer and tongs, staples of the trade, had made ham hocks of his gnarled hands.

Caesar's face twisted into a skeptical countenance and he dismounted. "Show me."

Nofio took a burlap cloth from the table and wiped his hands and face. As he passed by the slave tending the bellows, he handed the rag to him. "Keep the fire hot," he barked to the slave, "or I'll skin your hide when I get back."

He led the general, accompanied by Curio and several other staff officers, to an enormous pile of long iron chains massed between the working forges and the tents.

The blacksmith lifted one, the heavy metal clanking. He pointed to the cuffs: one every three feet, bonded to the chain, each with a simple locking mechanism.

"Ten slaves to a coffle." Nofio beamed with pride. "None will escape, nor do harm to any guard, with one hand locked in the cuff and chained to the others. You can march them all the way to Rome like that if you like."

Caesar gave no sign of his approval. Instead, he pointed at the pile of metal. "It's not nearly enough," he said to the blacksmith. "Not for the numbers we plan to take out of the Belgae."

Nofio was offended. "Sir, this is only today's production! The rest are already packed with the baggage train."

Caesar tilted his head to show his pleasure. He reached out and shook the man's hand, saying, "Well done, Nofio. Your men will share in the bounty from the sale of the slaves." He turned to Curio and said in a low voice, "Now, let's attend to the protection of the baggage train."

LABIENUS ESCORTED THE TRIBUNE of the Twelfth Legion, a sturdy veteran named Hortensius, and a much younger officer, Lentulus, who was clearly terrified, into Caesar's inner sanctum. The Roman general had established a suite of offices for himself and his staff in a large stone fortification that had been erected at Vesontio by Ariovistus himself. The rooms were stark and drafty. They were dimly lit, too: Caesar's fear of fire was well known, and he allowed only a handful of candles and oil lamps spread about the room. For warmth against the chill, Caesar had donned a thick cape woven from the best astrakhan fleece, shipped all the way from the territory of the unconquerable Afghans, dyed all scarlet but for gold piping about the neckline.

Caesar was seated at his large desk, built for him with oak from the nearby forest as soon as he had set up shop in the gloomy but exceptionally well-protected fortress. Beside him sat Curio, responsible for keeping all the records straight, no small task when considering the bureaucracy of the Roman army. They were working on a report, answering another idiotic request for information from the Roman Senate.

As Labienus and the men from the Twelfth came in, Curio looked up and moved a respectful distance away from the desk, knowing the men were about to be reprimanded.

Labienus struggled to keep a straight face while the men waited. He could virtually read their minds. *What does he want with us? What have we done wrong?* They knew only that the general had summoned them—Labienus gave them no clue about what Caesar was thinking.

Caesar kept the men waiting in silence as he perused the report, allowing their tension to mount. This was purely for dramatic effect: Caesar loved to let his junior officers stew as they awaited their fate, much like an accused criminal awaiting the jury's verdict.

After several minutes of this torture, Caesar finally made a show of handing the report to Curio, then stood to face them.

"Can you give me any good reason why I should not have the two of you relieved of your commands and relegated back to the ranks?" he asked sharply.

The men turned ashen.

"Well?" he demanded. "Do you not understand the seriousness of my dissatisfaction?"

Hortensius, as the senior of the two, stammered, "M-m-mighty Caesar, sir, we serve you most faithfully, with all dedication. What have we done to offend you?"

Caesar looked at Curio in disbelief. He narrowed his eyes and gave them his harshest glare. Survivors of that look often told stories about how he could knock over an armored warhorse with it. "I have put you in charge of defending the baggage train. The baggage train! With our food, livestock, all our weapons, the artillery, our siege machines, payroll for the men—everything we need to survive in this wretched place they call Gaul. And today, out there, you gave me no confidence whatsoever that you or your men are ready to defend it."

The legion commander's craggy face turned florid with anger, but he kept his wits. "Sir, to a man we are ready to die in defense of the train. It is the lifeblood of the entire army on the march. We are very clear about that."

"Oh, you'll die, all right." Caesar laughed with contempt. He pointed at the younger man. "Especially with this sorry excuse of a flank commander holding your left side. What I saw today made my blood run cold. A savvy opponent, someone like Ariovistus, would have punched through that leaky formation in a heartbeat. He'd roll up your entire line like it was baker's dough."

At this, the younger man hung his head in shame.

"Well, Hortensius, what say you?"

The soldier, a veteran of many battles, drew himself to his full height. "Sir, if any blame is to attach to the effort today, it is mine alone. This young man is newly appointed to his post, by me. Sack me if you must, but he shows promise and deserves a second chance to acquit himself in your eyes."

How refreshing, Labienus thought. *A commander who takes responsibility for the failure of his men and pleads on their behalf, rather than making excuses.*

Caesar turned his gaze to the luckless flank officer, barely more than a boy. He studied the young man's handsome features, his unblemished skin, and his manly build. He was an outstanding specimen of Rome. "What is your name, soldier?" he asked the lad.

Labienus shifted his weight, uncomfortable whenever Caesar looked at a fellow like that.

The young man summoned up all his courage, swallowed hard, and said in a firm voice, "Lentulus, sir. Of the town of Milan."

"Well, Lentulus of Milan, do you understand what was wrong with your formation today? Your men were spaced too far apart; their shields were resting on the ground rather than held high; their spears too were resting on the ground, upright. They must be horizontal, extending out, to ward off the attackers. Your men were lazy today, Lentulus. Do you know why that means death for us all?"

Poor Lentulus gave him a hangdog look.

"How we drill is how we will fight!" Caesar snapped. He looked at Curio, then sighed and put his hand on the boy's shoulder. "Your commander has faith in you, soldier. Should I?"

Lentulus threw his shoulders back and pleaded, "Sir, I understand your expectations now. I beg of you, give me another chance. I will not let you down again."

Caesar turned to his senior legate, who had maintained a bored expression throughout this little comedy, and asked, "Labienus?"

Labienus, of course, knew from long experience what Caesar had already decided. "I say that we write off today as training for our inexperienced colleague," he said with a shrug. "But tomorrow we cannot be so forgiving."

Caesar picked up a scroll from his desk and brandished it before them. "Especially not after this report today, gentlemen."

He unrolled the sheet. "The Belgae are attempting to steal the march on us. They have moved, in large numbers, into northeast Gaul, against the Aedui. A good ten days of marching from here."

In a flash, Labienus knew what this meant. But the legionaries had no clue.

"Curio, tell these fellows the implications of this news."

Curio did not hesitate. "The Senate has declared the Aedui to be our ally. We are honor bound to come to their aid, just as we did against Ariovistus."

Caesar agreed. "The Nervii tribe of the Belgae is led by a fierce loutish fellow named Boduognatus. Our sources tell us he is strong and fearless, but not the smartest of the tribal chiefs."

Looking up at the two men from the Twelfth, Caesar pointed toward the door. "Run your drill again this afternoon, gentlemen. Do not disappoint me this time. We march in two days, and I do not want to spend time finding someone else to guard the baggage train."

After the pair had exited, Labienus faced his general. "There is one other matter, Caesar, which came to my attention just before I brought those two in to see you."

Caesar walked around the desk and plopped himself heavily onto his chair, ever weary of the incessant demands of being in command. He gathered up a sheaf of documents and handed them to Curio.

"Do with them whatever you will," Caesar said. "Just keep the Senate dogs from nipping at my heels." He turned his attention to Labienus.

"Your prefect of engineers has lost his battle with the consumption," Labienus said sadly. "He died this morning while we were on the tower." Caesar's fondness for the man who supervised the engineers was legendary. And with good cause: it was the engineers whose skill had provided the roads and bridges, the earthworks and fortifications, the placement of siege operations, and so much more for many of Caesar's greatest victories.

"Poor Trolianus," Caesar moaned, resting his forehead on the palm of his hand. "I saw him just yesterday; he was a mere skeleton."

"Yes," agreed Labienus, fully aware of the awful pain the consumption had wrought upon their longtime comrade. "The timing couldn't be worse."

"Boduognatus has chosen an opportune time to make his strike," Caesar said glumly. "We cannot delay our departure."

Labienus replied, "I have my eye on a possible replacement."

This stirred Caesar's attention. It was a critical selection; the engineers were the key to every successful campaign.

"He's with the Tenth," Labienus said with intent, knowing the soft spot in Caesar's heart for the men of his most stalwart legion, who had saved his hide on the battlefield so many times. In fact, in his speech to the troops before the battle with Ariovistus, he had held up the Tenth as the role model for all the army.

"Really, now," Caesar ruminated, his interest evidently aroused. "The Tenth can outfight anyone, but an engineer?"

"He's rather young, but supposedly quite talented, according to Gordianus," Labienus said, referring to the tribune of the Tenth. Other than himself, there was no one Caesar trusted more in the whole army than Gordianus. *Well, maybe this young staff fellow, Curio . . .*

"I care not about young; I must have staff who are smart." Caesar tilted his head toward Curio, who appeared immensely gratified by the gesture. "My senior engineering officer is the driver of our entire enterprise."

Labienus knew this. "This lad was put in charge of building the bridge over the Doubs River by Trolianus himself."

His words had the desired effect: Caesar was clearly impressed. The bridge project was one of his top priorities. He had pitched his headquarters at the bottom of the U river bend, which left him trapped against the water if a sizeable-enough force ever got past the two legions encamped at the top of the U to protect the high command. Caesar ordered that a bridge be built at the bottom of the U to give him a way out if ever he might need it.

"Trolianus knew my thoughts regarding the importance of the bridge," Caesar reflected, and then said with his customary authority, "Fetch this young fellow and let me have a look at him."

Labienus turned to go, but Caesar asked with just a hint of impatience, "Does he have a name?"

Without turning, Labienus replied, "His name is Mamurra. We shall see if you like him."

II

SPIENNES, IN THE TERRITORY OF THE BELGAE

"ALOUCCA, THERE HE IS!"

The Belgic maiden Devorra nudged the older woman next to her and whispered excitedly, "He probably came to the market just to see me!" She reached a hand up to smooth her straight flaxen hair, tucking it behind her ear.

"Careful," Aloucca warned, "you must not seem too eager."

Devorra pretended to be preoccupied with selecting apples from a table full of them in a market stall in the fortified town of Spiennes, located along the Trouille River, in the heart of Nervii territory. Her father, Boduognatus, had chosen to make the town his gathering point for the alliance of the Belgae tribes he was assembling to prevent the Romans from making all of Gaul into a Roman province. The town's modest fortifications would never withstand a determined Roman assault, but its placement on the river, with its plentiful water and rich farm produce, made the site a good place for the anticipated hordes of warriors arriving daily in response to Boduognatus's call for an offensive against the Roman invaders.

The apples did not look good—it was too early in the spring to expect much—but she held one up as if to study it. Her real purpose was to scan the crowd for the powerful warrior Gabinier, who always seemed to show up whenever she was out and about. But she could not find him.

A strong, deep voice startled her from behind. "The apples are not to your liking?"

Devorra whirled around, her simple peasant dress flaring up to allow just the briefest glimpse of her legs—enough to bring a grin to the young man's eager face, framed by a thick mane of wavy locks, the color of sand on a beach.

"Gabinier!" she exclaimed. "Why do you sneak up behind me like that?

You scared me!"

He did not answer right away, and she felt herself flushing as she realized he was studying her.

Devorra's face was a slender oval, framed by long tresses of straight, flaxen hair. Above her rosy cheeks, she had sparkling green eyes that shone to him like stars on a clear night. Her full, sensuous lips curled in a broad, sweet smile, showing him dazzling teeth. Even in the loose-fitting shift dress she was wearing, her shapely body was alluring. Best of all, she had a carefree manner that immediately put at ease anyone who met her.

She gave him a broad, sweet smile.

"I wanted to surprise you," Gabinier said to her, laughing. "I feared you might have forgotten me while I was off looking for Romans."

Her smile turned to a frown. "I wondered why I have not seen you at Father's tribal council," she said. "I dared not ask where you might be."

"Your father expects that his attacks on the Aedui will have their desired effect, and the Romans will march to the aid of their ally," the warrior explained. "He wants to have plenty of warning before they get here. I am just back from a scouting mission."

Devorra was fully aware of her father's master plan, having served food and drink during many of the deliberations of the tribal leaders. Boduognatus had watched with alarm as Caesar had systematically brought the various tribes of Gaul under his Roman thumb over the last three years. Her father believed it was only a matter of time before the rapacious Romans extended their reach to the tribes of the Belgae, and he was determined not to sit around and wait for the attack.

"But that's so dangerous!" she said. "What if the Romans were to catch you?"

Gabinier waved her concern away. "Have no fear, my lady. Nothing could keep me from making my way back to you!"

Devorra felt her heart skip a beat. His words were exactly what she had been dreaming of. She took in his muscled frame, clad in crude leather britches and a loose-fitting jacket of plain linen, cinched tight with a cord belt that held a long, unsheathed sword. She lingered upon his handsome face. He was clean-shaven, affording her a full appreciation of his bronzed skin and prominent chin with an endearing dimple at its center.

"Well," she said airily, "I am most pleased you have made it back to us. Did you see any Romans?"

He shook his head, and she loved the way his flowing hair moved with him. "Not this time," he said determinedly. "But I will soon head out again."

A chill passed through her. "Must you go?" she asked. "Surely my father can find others who should take a turn."

Gabinier put his hand on her arm, a potentially scandalous act in a public market, but he did it so lightly she did not shy away. "Will I see you at the council tonight?" he asked.

It was her turn to be flirtatious. "Perhaps," she said coyly, her green eyes sparkling, "if you bother to look."

Devorra noticed that her attendant was frowning. *Why*, she wondered, *is Aloucca so concerned about our talking here in the public marketplace?* She dismissed the thought.

"Come, Aloucca," she said, remembering the woman's warning not to seem too eager. "We must make ready for our work tonight."

III

VESONTIO

RIVER WORK IS THE WORST, Mamurra thought as he watched a team of slaves pulling on ropes, trying to muscle a massive wooden pole into position without themselves falling into the murky water. The pole was dangling from a hand-operated crane mounted on a barge anchored in the middle of the Doubs River. The young engineer had taken up a position on the barge to supervise this critical portion of the work. Several smaller boats were clustered nearby, each with slaves leaning over the gunwales, seeking to fix the pole tight against another pole already driven into the riverbed below. The team was tasked with building a cofferdam, a series of long poles driven to form a ring in the midst of the strong current, swollen from the spring rains. Once the ring was firmly in place, a crew would be set to the chore of pumping out the water inside the ring, creating, in effect, a working area on the actual floor of the riverbed. Within this man-made void, once the riverbed had dried out, foundations would be dug and a masonry pier erected. Similar efforts were underway on either side of the midstream cofferdam, closer to the respective banks; the three piers would provide the structural base upon which the bridge deck ultimately would rest.

Mamurra was keenly aware that the tribune Gordianus, commander of the Tenth Legion, and several of his staff officers were watching this operation from the riverbank. Gordianus had made it clear that the bridge was very important to Caesar himself—it was a major assignment to be entrusted to one of the youngest members of the Tenth's engineering complement. Mamurra had been amazed when Gordianus had told him that the chief engineer, Trolianus, had recommended him for the task from his sickbed. Mamurra had hoped that Trolianus would survive long enough to see it completed, but word had arrived earlier in the morning that his mentor had succumbed to the wasting effects of the horrible consumption. Mamurra was determined to show everyone in the army that the senior engineer's trust in him had been well deserved.

When he was satisfied that the second pole was properly snug against the first, held in place by the slaves pulling their ropes tight, Mamurra gave a signal to release the pole from the crane. When this was done, the men swung the crane back over the barge and quickly hoisted a tremendously heavy iron mallet. They swung it back over the pole, intending to use the mallet to pound the pole deep into the riverbed.

Just as they were about to strike the first blow, bad luck intervened: the river current slammed one of the adjoining boats against the target pole, dislodging it and knocking several of the unfortunate laborers into the water. As the crews scurried furiously to rescue their comrades, the entire situation dissolved into chaos. Even worse, the current pulled the pole out of alignment, ripping it away from the remaining handful of men who were trying to hang on to their ropes. Mamurra watched in anger as the pole floated away. He shouted at several of the boats not engaged in the rescue operations to give chase and bring it back. His frustration turned to horror as he watched the runaway pole slam into the nearby cofferdam, ripping away a portion of that construction as well. It was an unmitigated disaster.

Damn it all! We've fallen behind schedule! Mamurra fumed as he watched the workers trying to get things back under control. He looked at the bank, in the direction of the officers surrounding Gordianus.

They were all laughing at him.

LATER, AS THE CREW was making another attempt to drive the pole into place, Mamurra saw Gordianus motioning him to return to the shore.

Mamurra's blood ran cold. *I'm done,* he thought miserably. *He's going to put me in charge of digging the latrines.*

Heartsick at his failure, he transferred to one of the smaller boats and had himself rowed over to the waiting knot of officers. Gordianus, a crusty veteran officer, was inscrutable.

"You wanted me, sir?" Mamurra asked, nearly trembling.

"I have an order that you are to report to Caesar's headquarters. The old man himself wants to see you," Gordianus growled.

Mamurra went weak in the knees. "Me? Caesar wants to see me? But—but, why?"

"He's probably heard about your great success at bridge building," Gordianus cracked, eliciting a laugh from the assembled staff.

Mamurra slumped in shame.

"Get yourself a horse and get over there to see him," Gordianus snapped. "Caesar doesn't like to be kept waiting."

All the way to Caesar's headquarters, Mamurra racked his brain, trying to imagine how Caesar could have learned of the disaster in the river so quickly. *He must have spies everywhere!* Mamurra thought glumly. *To be sacked by the general himself—how humiliating! Why wouldn't he just have Gordianus do it? Maybe he's going to have me arrested!*

Mamurra tried to get his fears under control. He, of course, had never actually spoken with Caesar, and in fact had rarely seen him except when Caesar would address the troops, as he had on the eve of the battle at Vesontio. But Trolianus had often told him how unforgiving the man could be in discharging any officer he found wanting in performance.

As his horse clopped along the narrow, muddy path toward the brooding fortress in the distance, the young man's gloomy thoughts turned to his relatives in Formiae. The family was prominent there, so much so that the community, not far from the border of the Campania region, often was called "the city of the Mamurrae." They were a prosperous mercantile family, with interests in shipping and trading based on the town's natural harbor along the edge of the Tyrrhenian Sea, part of the Mediterranean, or the *Mare Nostrum*, as the Romans called it.

Mamurra's father, Luca, was a no-nonsense disciplinarian who'd pushed his four sons to work hard and live frugally. He explained the realities of life to Mamurra at a relatively early age. "You are the second-born," his father told him one day. "That means you will not inherit the family business. That will fall to your older brother. You must seek your fortune elsewhere." It did not occur to Mamurra to take offense at this outcome— it was just the way things were.

Not long after that eye-opening talk, Mamurra's father put him to work shoveling dirt for a project to install a culvert needed to alleviate flooding of the road near the family compound. The boy badgered the crew with constant questions about the project design and its execution. Mamurra was fascinated by the utter practicality of the whole situation, the logical way one feature was inexorably connected to another, and how one small thing, badly planned, could cause so much havoc.

That evening, Mamurra eagerly explained the day's activities to his parents. His mother, a lively woman who shrewdly allowed her husband to imagine he was master of the household, suggested that the boy should perhaps consider engineering as a trade, given his apparent interest in the topic. A few days later, Luca arranged for his second son to be apprenticed out to a friendly local engineer named Rotollo, and the lad was soon immersed in the intricacies of structure and support, of water flow and drainage, of slopes and grades, the elevation of roadways, and the like.

Mamurra quickly proved himself to be something of a prodigy, easily grasping the complex problems of engineering and design, and the mathematics that underpinned it all. Before long, he was spotting the occasional errors in Rotollo's work, suggesting enhancements, and generally impressing all the engineers with whom he came into contact. To his credit, Rotollo recognized that he had taught the young man all he could, and he went to see Luca.

"Your son is blessed by the gods," Rotollo told him. "He is an extraordinary talent. We must give him the chance to make his name."

Luca, with the bemusement that any father feels when he learns his son has a talent he never would have imagined, asked, "What do you mean?"

Rotollo was candid. "There is no more certain path to success in this trade than to serve in the army."

Luca recoiled—the horrors of war and soldiering were well known. "His mother will have my hide if I suggest that!"

"Army life for engineers is not like being in the infantry," Rotollo insisted. "The slogs on the front line take all the arrows—the engineers just build the roads and the bridges, and when a siege is needed, the engineers supervise the details."

Luca was not convinced. "Anybody in the army can get killed."

"Allow me to do one thing," Rotollo suggested. "I am longtime friends with one of the top engineers in the whole Roman army. His name is Trolianus. He has made a fortune in service to that up-and-coming consul, Julius Caesar. Let me arrange for Mamurra to meet him. If Trolianus offers him a place on his staff, it will be too good to pass up."

The gods had indeed smiled upon him, for the pieces fell into place like a child's puzzle. Mamurra breezed through Trolianus's incisive questioning. The senior engineer offered him a position right on the spot, for the upcoming campaign with Caesar in Gaul. Luca managed to convince his dubious wife that their boy's candle was far too bright to be kept under Formiae's basket.

After a tearful parting from his parents and brothers, Mamurra reported for duty. Basic training was a nightmare, but Mamurra suffered through it, and then was put through the paces under the watchful eye of Trolianus himself. Mamurra did not care for the hardships of military life, but he reveled in the challenges posed by the work. He was a rising star, receiving promotion after promotion for his outstanding efforts during Caesar's campaign in Gaul, culminating in his biggest challenge yet, the bridge over the Doubs River.

And now, he thought as he passed through a guard post on the approach to Caesar's headquarters, *it's all turned to shit. Trolianus is dead, and I have failed on the bridge. What am I going to say to my parents? They will be so disappointed!*

A shriek of agony interrupted his reverie. Mamurra jerked his head, looking for the source of the hideous sound. A short distance away, a bloody pulp of a man was fixed to a tall cross, the thick nails penetrating his flesh and the wooden beams. The poor wretch was squirming, seeking a moment of relief from the relentless pain. It was hopeless—the man was begging to be put to death.

"What's that about?" Mamurra asked the guard.

"Slave tried to escape," the man replied. "Been up there for two days."

Mamurra winced.

With a toothless grin, the guard held up a scourge, dried blood still caked on the shards of glass and nails embedded in the leather thongs.

"Skinned him myself," the guard said, proud of his handiwork. "The trick is not to kill him before they nail him up there. Got to make an example of him in case any of the others are thinking about running off. I'm trying to keep him alive for at least three days."

"Why bother?" Mamurra asked.

"The other guards have made bets on how long we can keep him alive. I win the pot if he makes it another day."

The dying slave emitted a long, low moan of anguish, and Mamurra's mood darkened further.

As he was directed to Caesar's offices, he steeled himself for the humiliation of spending the rest of his enlistment assigned to the latrines.

IV

SPIENNES

HOT GREASE DRIPPED DOWN the sides of Boduognatus's mouth onto his unkempt beard. He chewed deliberately on the rib of a roasted pig, working the meat slowly. He was savoring not only the juices, but also the terror of the trembling woman standing before him.

"So, slave, what news of my beautiful daughter do you have for me today?"

Even for someone accustomed to being around raw and barbaric men, Aloucca found herself revolted whenever she was in the presence of the huge, shaggy, smelly Boduognatus, a man whose ferocity was matched only by his cruelty. More than once, she had wondered how so lovely and delicate a child as Devorra could have sprung from the loins of such a heathen—without question, the girl had gotten her beauty and grace from her mother. It was a pity the poor girl's mother had died in childbirth, with Aloucca attending her as midwife, nineteen years ago. Perhaps it was for the better—how could anyone put up with this horrible beast while trying to raise a child?

"This young warrior, Gabinier, has feelings for your daughter," she said carefully, as if juggling eggs.

Boduognatus grunted. "Why shouldn't he? She's a prize. She will fetch a great tribal lord in an alliance, to win her hand. And the rest of her, too."

Aloucca was disgusted. *How could he be so lewd about his own daughter?* But she simply said quietly, "I fear she may feel the same toward him."

Anger flared in Boduognatus's wild eyes. With great care, he set the rib, picked clean of its meat, on the platter before him. Then he lashed out, cuffing her viciously on the side of her graying head with the back of his hand. With a shriek, Aloucca fell backward onto the stone floor of the great room.

She rubbed her left temple as she righted herself, tears gushing from her eyes. "Why do you punish me, Lord? How have I offended you?"

"Your task is to care for my daughter. You must keep her inviolate so that I can use her to make a useful alliance," Boduognatus snarled. "You should not have let her near this young buck who would ruin her."

How am I to do that? The girl is headstrong, and I am a mere slave! Aloucca's thoughts raced through her throbbing head, but she dared not speak. She climbed slowly back to her feet.

Boduognatus took a rag and wiped his face. She tried not to stare at the jagged scar that ran from under his left eye across the base of his nose, a badge of the fatal duel he'd fought years earlier with the tribe's previous leader to seize leadership of the Nervii. The nose itself was purpled with veins, proof of his fondness for the grape.

"Say nothing to her of our talk," the chieftain warned her. "She must not learn that you are my informant. But make her see that she must obey me. If you fail, I will have you boiled alive."

Aloucca blanched. Years ago, she had seen a captured raider bound and slowly lowered into a great vat of boiling water, up to his neck. Even now, she could hear his hideous screams.

With a curt flick of his head, Boduognatus dismissed her.

As she made her way from his presence, still dizzy from the vicious blow, Aloucca passed a throng of warriors, waiting to see their leader. She was so upset from the conversation and in such a hurry to get away that she did not notice one man in particular, standing at the back of the group.

But Gabinier recognized her.

V

VESONTIO

LABIENUS GRINNED when the nervous young engineer was shown into his quarters, just down the corridor from Caesar's own chamber. The poor fellow had obviously come straight from his work on the bridge—his plain red tunic was spattered with mud, and his boots were not polished.

"I see that you can at least follow orders," Labienus said lightly.

When Mamurra looked at him blankly, Labienus laughed. "Your orders were to report immediately. You did not dally to make yourself properly presentable to the commanding general."

Self-conscious, Mamurra looked down at himself and turned scarlet, matching the color of his work clothes. He was handsome in the sensuous way of many Italians, with alert gray eyes and the close-cropped black hair typical of a low-ranking legionary. Labienus knew Caesar would approve of the firm set of his mouth—he considered it a sign of strength, imperative for someone he expected to oversee all his engineering operations. Like Lentulus, the poor left-flank commander who had earlier felt Caesar's wrath, Mamurra was blessed with clear skin and good teeth.

Labienus worried, in fact, that Mamurra might be a touch *too* handsome. There had been rumors over the years that Caesar in his younger days had sampled the pleasure of male lovers, or as it was described in polite Roman society, indulged in the Greek habit. Although Labienus had never actually witnessed any such conduct by his general, the rumors never left the back of his mind.

"Put yourself at ease," Labienus said, seeing the fellow's discomfort. "You're here to talk engineering, not march in a triumphal parade in Rome."

Mamurra cleared his throat. "Well, sir, that incident today in the river, it was an unfortunate accident, and I can assure you I won't let it happen again."

It was Labienus's turn to go blank. "What are you talking about?"

"The accident today in the river, sir, when the pole broke loose from its mooring and struck the other cofferdam—"

Labienus shot a look at him that silenced the young engineer. "You think we would bring you in to see the commanding general over something so minor?"

Mamurra looked nonplussed. "Sir, I'm afraid I don't understand."

Labienus rubbed his eyes with his hand. *Perhaps this lad isn't as smart as Trolianus and Gordianus have said.* He asked curtly, "Are you aware that the prefect of engineers is dead?"

"Yes, sir."

Labienus could see the lines of grief on the young man's face. "You will miss him?"

Mamurra blinked away a tear. "He taught me everything I know, sir. There will never be anyone as good as Trolianus."

"Interesting that you would say that," Labienus said with a smile. "He told Gordianus that he had never seen anybody as good as you are."

Several long moments passed before Mamurra could recover enough to speak. "Trolianus said that? About me?" *After all those times he chewed me out for making mistakes?* Mamurra shook his head, then finally stammered, "I—I don't know what to say, sir."

Labienus was pleased. *At last, a young pup with some humility! Not like that smug Curio.* "We are about to embark upon a campaign to northeast Gaul, where the Belgae have been raiding. Caesar must have roads cut through the forests; he must find fords to cross the streams we will encounter; he must have camps built daily."

This was not news to Mamurra. Rumors had been circulating for weeks that such a move might be in the offing. "Sir, I will serve the next prefect of engineers as loyally as I have served Trolianus. I give you my word."

By Jupiter, the boy still doesn't get it! Well, let Caesar tell him.

"Come with me," he said to Mamurra.

MAMURRA WAS INTIMIDATED by Caesar's spacious quarters, awed to be in the presence of the great man himself. Caesar's desk, covered with scrolls, wax tablets, and sheaves of vellum, was at one end of the chamber, lit by several oil lamps encased in glass atop a clay base. One of Caesar's personal battle standards, the vexillum, was fixed to the wall behind the desk. It was a large white flag, embroidered with a garland of leaves wrapped about the letters *SPQR*, signifying the Senate and people of Rome. Below the flag was a simple cupboard, hosting a pitcher and a bowl, presumably for washing. At the other end, adjacent to a second door, was a large hearth with a vigorous fire burning, attended by a slave. Mamurra assumed the door must provide access to the sleeping room. There were two comfortable chairs close by; Caesar sat in one reading a report. Another officer, unknown to Mamurra, was seated in the other chair, reviewing a raft of orders.

Caesar looked up from his chair and waited while Labienus introduced the junior engineer. He accepted the customary salute, Mamurra striking his breast with his right fist. Mamurra stood rigidly at attention, straight as a spear.

"This is Curio," Caesar said, introducing the two young men. "He is my adjutant."

Mamurra saluted him, too. But his eyes fixed on the ravaged skin of the man's right cheek. Curio did not seem unsettled by Mamurra's stare; Mamurra supposed he was inured to such attention.

"Curio will not be joining this discussion," the general said easily. Taking this cue, Curio rose to his feet and left the office.

The general gave the nervous engineer a long, penetrating look. Mamurra, unused to such scrutiny, shifted uncomfortably. He knew he was taller than most of the army men, but then, so too was Caesar.

"So," Caesar finally said, breaking the long silence, "you are Marcus Vitruvius Mamurra, of the town of Formiae?"

Mamurra blinked, stunned that the general knew his background. "Yes, sir."

"You may stand at ease, Mamurra."

Mamurra adopted a wider stance and cupped his hands behind his back.

"You were recruited to the engineers by Trolianus himself, shortly before we began our little odyssey here in Gaul?"

Mamurra kept his eyes straight ahead. "Yes, sir."

"Well, in your three years of service, you earned the respect of our beloved colleague, may he rest in peace."

Mamurra bit the inside of his lip, determined not to show weakness in front of the general.

"I loved him, too," Caesar said sadly. "His works helped make possible my greatest victories."

Mamurra, not knowing what to say, said nothing.

"Before he succumbed to his illness, Trolianus told your legion's tribune that your talent for the art surpassed that of any man he had ever seen. This made me want to meet you myself."

"Sir, I am flattered by such high praise from your prefect of engineers, but I assure you, I am most undeserving. I have much yet to learn," Mamurra said, studying the floor.

Caesar seemed pleased by this modest declaration. "It is a wise man who admits he always has more to learn," Caesar said, almost allowing himself a smile. "Tell me about your experience. Give me the specifics of your assignments."

Mamurra recited the various assignments he had been given. Caesar interrupted him often, asking him pointed questions about each one. How high was the wall? How deep was the foundation? How many pikes did it take to erect the fortified barricade surrounding the Roman camp built every night when a legion was on the march? How long did it take to clear a path wide enough for a legion to march through the forest eight abreast? What was the angle of the breastworks dug to block an enemy's advance?

As they talked, Mamurra was impressed at the extent of Caesar's in-depth knowledge of the details of these mundane operations—clearly, what Trolianus had said about the general's passion for the engineer's art was completely accurate.

"You're surprised that I am well informed about engineering matters?" Caesar noted.

Mamurra blushed, embarrassed at having been so easily read.

Caesar, expressionless, asked, "How do you think I managed to win all these victories?" Then, he subtly shifted the conversation: Could a bridge over a stream be built faster? Was there any way to improve the range of the Roman *ballista*, the artillery piece that flung spears into packed concentrations of enemy troops? Could the baggage train be lightened and thus made more maneuverable and less vulnerable?

Mamurra felt himself growing excited by this talk. He had many ideas on how to improve things, and even Trolianus, great as he was, had been conservative, old-fashioned, stuck in his ways. *This is how we do it in the Roman army* had been his standard reply to so many of Mamurra's suggestions.

Caesar appeared to be much different. The general was open to all nature of suggestions and brimming with his own ideas, several of which dazzled the junior officer with their scale and audacity. As he became less intimidated by the setting, Mamurra offered his views eagerly, whenever Caesar asked.

Caesar and Labienus exchanged a knowing look. They had been together long enough to recognize that Trolianus had been right—the lad was extraordinary.

Caesar pulled a blank sheet of vellum out of his stack and reached for a nearby brass stylus and an inkwell.

He's left-handed! Mamurra noted. *How unusual!*

Caesar roughed out a design for a tall siege tower, mounted on wheels. He was very animated in describing the concept, and particularly enthusiastic about what struck Mamurra as the oddest feature in the design: the tower was something of an inverted pyramid—wider at the top than at the base.

"Don't you see?" Caesar said excitedly. "The design allows us to place more men at the top, at the point of the attack. It gives us more soldiers in the face of the enemy!"

Mamurra was alarmed. The design was terrible—it would mean the deaths of any soldiers unfortunate enough to be assigned to the top. But Caesar was possessed; he seemed certain it would be a great advance in siege warfare. *What to say?*

"Well?" Caesar asked, boring in on the young man's uncertainty.

From somewhere deep in his mind, Mamurra remembered something his dear mother had told him the morning he took his leave of the family. *Let the truth be your guide, always,* she had said that day. *It will never lead you astray.*

Mamurra summoned every bit of his courage and looked his general straight in the eye. "Respectfully, sir, the design is flawed. If you build this tower, the men atop will all perish."

Caesar gave him that awful stare, the one that could turn a man's bones to jelly. "And why do you say that to your general, junior officer of mine?"

Mamurra took the full brunt of Caesar's caustic eyes, but oddly felt as calm as a quiet sea on a summer night, because he knew he was right. "Sir, the design is top-heavy; the base is too narrow. It would be easy for the enemy defenders on either side of the tower to snare it with grapples and pull it over."

Mamurra lowered his head, expecting both the conversation and his career to be over.

Caesar sat back in his chair and let Mamurra tremble for several long minutes. It was the worst stretch of silence Mamurra had ever endured.

Finally, Caesar said, "This is your last chance. You are prepared to stake your career on your assessment of my design?"

30

Much as he wanted to please his general, Mamurra remained true to himself. "Sir, I am most sorry, but that is my professional opinion." *Perhaps Rotollo will take me back into his employ* was all he could think.

For the first time during the interview, Caesar smiled at Mamurra. "Congratulations, engineer. You have passed the test."

Mamurra was lost. "I beg your pardon, sir?"

Caesar crumpled up the vellum sheet and tossed it into the fire. "The flaw is evident. Any engineer with half a brain in his head could see that it is hopelessly top-heavy. The test was to see if you would tell me the truth. I must have a prefect of engineers who will tell me what he really thinks, not what he thinks I want to hear. Labienus?"

The second-in-command said kindly to Mamurra, "You will come to learn with experience that the hardest part of the job is sorting out fact from what they want you to believe. And you will have only your own wits to guide you."

Caesar stood and extended his hand to Mamurra. "Congratulations. As of now, you are prefect of engineers for all legions serving under my command in Gaul. Curio will prepare a formal order of appointment for my signature, and an announcement will be issued to all the ranks."

Mamurra's head was swimming. "Prefect of engineers? But sir, I am not worthy of it!"

Caesar gave him that flinty look again. "I am a tolerably good judge of talent. You'll do well." He turned to Labienus. "Take this man to meet the senior staff of engineers." And with that, he sat back down and picked up another document to read.

Labienus took Mamurra gently by the arm and started to lead him away.

Just as they neared the door, Mamurra heard Caesar call out, "Don't you at least want to know what the job pays?"

Mamurra turned with a sincere look. "Sir, the opportunity you have given me is reward enough."

"Pahh," Caesar said with his characteristic frosty manner. "Labienus, did we not make Trolianus rich beyond his wildest dreams?"

Labienus laughed his concurrence.

"It is a pity that faithful Trolianus did not live to savor the fruits of his efforts," Caesar said without looking up. "Serve me well, give me victories, and I will make you rich, too."

THE EXITING OFFICERS passed Curio, who was waiting patiently just outside Caesar's quarters, with an armful of yet more scrolls and wax tablets for Caesar's attention.

Labienus, who could never pass up an opportunity to needle the staff officer, said, "Ah, Curio, this is the new prefect of engineers."

"Congratulations, Mamurra," Curio said, his tone betraying nothing of his thoughts.

"You should call him *sir*, Curio," Labienus observed, pushing the needle in a bit farther. "He outranks you now."

Curio did not wish to be drawn into a discussion of protocol with the second-in-command. *The young man must surely have talent and therefore be worthy of the high rank,* he thought. "Of course. Congratulations, sir," he said respectfully.

Mamurra, apparently oblivious to the rivalries that run rampant through any high command, smiled sheepishly. "I do not need such formality," he said simply. "I still can't believe it."

"Come, Mamurra," Labienus said. "We must get you established in your new post."

Curio stared daggers at Labienus as they made their way out. *The lad has no clue what he's gotten himself into,* he thought.

Curio entered Caesar's office without knocking, as he had the right to do by virtue of his staff position.

"We have a new prefect of engineers, then?" Curio said noncommittally.

"Yes," Caesar said, looking up from the wax tablet he was writing upon. "What do you think of my choice?"

"Given the importance of the position to the success of the army in the field, I am sure you have applied your usual discerning standards to this appointment, and I have learned to trust your judgment. I shall prepare the order announcing his appointment."

Caesar put down his stylus and handed the tablet to Curio.

"The latest chapter in your memoirs?" Curio asked, perusing the text.

"Just the important points regarding our battle with Ariovistus," Caesar replied. "It will want your skilled way with words in the final text."

Curio sighed. Caesar was determined to publish a book about his conquest of Gaul, thinking it would serve as propaganda in the never-ending battle for control of the Roman Senate. But, as with everything else, the actual work of writing it fell to poor Curio.

"You have omitted reference to the fact that Ariovistus had us surrounded," Curio said, reading more of it. "I think that's a mistake."

Caesar scrunched up his face. "It hardly flatters my generalship to admit that."

"With all due respect," Curio said, not meeting Caesar's glare, "your decision to fight your way out of the trap, and the inspiring speech you made, is what will impress our friends at the Forum." Curio discreetly did not remind Caesar that he himself had written the speech.

"Whatever you think is best," Caesar answered, his tone implying he was done with this topic. He gestured for Curio to drop the pile of documents he was carrying onto the desk and take a seat. He rubbed his temples, then closed his eyes. When he opened them, the hazel had taken a turn toward gray, his look distant and glassy.

Curio, ever vigilant, knew the symptom at a glance. He hurried to a cupboard and retrieved a small clay vial. He pulled the stopper as he approached. "Drink," he said, holding it to the general's lips.

A few swallows later, Curio wiped away a dribble as it rolled down that prodigious chin. He held his breath, silently praying to the gods that the elixir would take hold, yet again.

Long moments later, Caesar revived and became himself again.

"Loyal Rio," he said with a sigh, his wits returned. "What magic you pack in those bottles."

"I cannot claim the mixture as my own," Curio said, relieved Caesar had recovered. "Vatteus learned it from an apothecary down in Umbria. Thank the gods that it banishes these spells."

"Ah, Vatteus," Caesar said, fondness in his voice. "Our old chum. Who would have thought, back when we were playing our pranks at my father's estate, that we would all wind up here together?"

Curio did not reply. He shuddered to contemplate what a problem it would be to keep Caesar's issue hidden from the men without so loyal a friend serving as an army doctor.

"I often wonder why the gods have afflicted me, with no rhyme nor reason as to when the spells might strike," Caesar said bitterly. "They are a curse."

Curio placed the vial in the cupboard, then returned to take the seat opposite Caesar. "Do not think of it as a curse," he said softly. "Think of it merely as another challenge they have devised to test you."

Caesar did not smile. "What would the men think if they knew? They must never find out."

Curio did not respond. He disagreed with Caesar. *Far better*, he thought, *for them to know and be prepared than to discover it in the middle of a battle!*

"Where were we?"

"You were talking about Mamurra's promotion."

"Running an army is like being in charge of a gambling den," Caesar said pensively. "Every time you make a promotion, you are taking a chance. One learns to trust his instincts."

Curio, sensing that Caesar was in a reflective mood, remained silent. When the great man was willing to share his thoughts, it was best to let him talk. Curio unconsciously rotated his lower jaw from side to side, working his mouth in unison; it was his way of trying to keep the damaged skin of his cheek loose. He did it so often it had become second nature to him. But when he noticed Caesar studying him, he stilled his jaw. Although merely the son of a farmer, Curio had consciously developed a refinement of manner and held himself with the stature typical of a Roman patrician.

If Caesar felt any sympathy because of the fire that had left Curio damaged for life, he gave no indication of it. Curio knew he had earned himself a coveted spot on Caesar's personal staff by his keen instincts and the insight to understand both Caesar's daily engagement in the military campaign in Gaul and his part in the ongoing political intrigue in Rome, albeit conducted at long distance. Curio understood that problems in one arena tended to affect decisions in the other and was proud that Caesar had come to rely on his judicious counsel.

"It is not easy to make these critical decisions," Caesar mused. "So much is at stake; the wrong man in the wrong job can be the undoing of us all."

Curio dared to venture, "You must grow weary at times, having to carry the responsibility for so many decisions which could mean life or death for us all."

Caesar put his fingertips together, forming a pyramid with his hands. "With great power comes great responsibility." He sighed. "I am continually reminded of the Greek proverb: 'Be careful what you wish for, the gods may grant your wish.' Ha!"

And then, abruptly, he reverted to his usual businesslike military demeanor. Pointing to the new bundle on his desk, he asked, "What do you have for me in this pile?"

"Nothing of note," Curio said, sifting through the scrolls, "save for this one. A communication from Rome." He handed the document to Caesar.

Glancing at the wax seal, Caesar groaned. "It's from that weasel Catullus. What vexation can he be up to now?"

Caesar broke the seal and unfurled the sheet. He read it quickly, then tossed it toward Curio, who picked it up and scanned it.

"He's coming to see you, to discuss your plans for the summer campaign in Gaul?" Curio said. "This is most odd. You have kept the Senate advised of your overall strategy."

"That's the cover story," Caesar said, more energized now. "He's coming to see what dirt he can dig up on me."

"Well, he'll have to catch up with us on the march north where we take on the Belgae," Curio said with a grin. "He will find the accommodations rather below his customary standard of comfort."

Caesar turned to the rest of the work awaiting him on the desk. "Yes," he said lightly, "and keep it that way. The sooner he's gone, the happier we'll be."

The two of them shuffled through the morass of orders, requisitions, disciplinary reports, and other routine matters until at last they were done. Curio gathered up the material and rose to leave.

"One other item," Caesar said before Curio could exit. "Insofar as we are about to embark upon a campaign, I do not wish there to be confusion among the high command over your authority to pass along my orders."

Unsure where the general was going, Curio did not reply.

"When you write up the order appointing Mamurra as prefect of engineers, write up another, stating that you, as adjutant to the commanding general, are authorized at all times to speak in my place and stead."

Curio felt a rush of satisfaction pulse through him. With this order, no one in the chain of command could question that when he spoke, he spoke for Caesar. *If only I could be there when Labienus hears this news!*

"Sir, I am overwhelmed by the trust you place in me," Curio said, full of pride.

Caesar picked up the letter from Catullus and read it again. "Do not forget what I said earlier. Every time I make a promotion, I am taking a gamble."

VI

SPIENNES

"Ouch!"

"Sorry, mistress," Aloucca purred, but continued to run a comb, cut from the bone of an ox, through Devorra's golden hair. She was preparing the girl for another night of work serving food and wine to the council members meeting with her father in the great hall.

Devorra squirmed on her stool in the small cabin her father had granted them during their stay in Spiennes. The cabin's rightful owner had been forcibly evicted when the Nervii settled in for the gathering of the tribes. "Don't be so rough," the girl chided Aloucca, laughing. "My father will be furious if you pull out all my hair—no one at the council wants a bald bride!"

Aloucca chuckled at this image.

Devorra knew her father's motive for pressing her into this role—he was showcasing her to the several lords and chiefs who were pondering whether to join the coalition against the Romans. Never one to be accused of subtlety, he'd provided her with several dresses, each one cut daringly low to entice the crude and harsh men he was courting to throw in with his cause. Devorra was terrified that he would give her to one of these boors to enlist the support of some important tribe. But she also understood she was helpless to prevent such an alliance, should her father deem it prudent.

Normally, Devorra dreaded serving at the council meeting, knowing all the men would be ogling her. Tonight, however, she was looking forward to working the room, because Gabinier would be there. Perhaps she might even steal a few moments to talk with him!

"Do you think he will like me in this dress?" Devorra asked, adjusting the décolletage, wary of showing too much cleavage.

"Oh, they all will take notice of you," Aloucca said. "You are the very image of your mother."

Devorra's breath hitched. It was not easy, never having known her mother's love. Especially now, when she might have asked her mother about her own experience being used as a tool for a tribal alliance.

"What did my mother think about being forced into a marriage with my father?" she asked the slave. "Did she resist?"

Aloucca tread cautiously. "Your mother was a dutiful daughter to your grandfather."

"But what did she really think?" Devorra pressed. "Did she love my father?"

"She did her duty," Aloucca replied pointedly. "She harbored no foolish dreams of marrying some rambunctious warrior with no land of his own."

Devorra grew defensive. "It's not foolish to care for Gabinier! He is brave and strong, and he will win his fortune when he sends the Romans scurrying back across the Alps."

Aloucca put the comb down. She took her mistress by the shoulders and turned her. "I was midwife to your birth. I have brought hundreds of babies into the world. I have cared for you, Devorra, as if you were my own child. So believe me when I tell you that you must not let yourself think like this. It will bring you nothing but heartache. You are far too valuable to your father to be given to a mere foot soldier. You will become the wife of an important and wealthy man, who will provide us with a comfortable home."

Devorra assessed her companion sympathetically. Her skin was wrinkled, her scraggly hair showing white amid the gray. Her long, hooked nose was reminiscent of the sharp beak of an owl. This haggard old woman had been at Devorra's side for her whole life. But for some reason, Devorra sensed that her maid was more interested in her own fate than in the happiness of her mistress.

"How can any home be good if there is no love at its foundation?" she asked. "Am I to be bartered like a trinket for the support of some thug who happens to have murdered his way to the leadership of a tribe?"

Feeling ever more confined, Devorra grabbed a woolen shawl and hurried out of the cabin, leaving Aloucca looking dizzy with despair.

Still shaking with frustration, Devorra didn't really think about where she might go. She just kept walking, wanting to be alone. She soon found herself wandering along a path at the edge of the river, her mind desperately groping for a solution. She had no interest in the arcane conniving of these tribal infighters, and she certainly did not care for whatever trappings of wealth or comfort might be hers if her father married her off to one of those louts. She dreamed only of being in Gabinier's strong arms.

No matter that when he was not fighting as a warrior, Gabinier was a mere peasant, scratching out a living as a small farmer, hunting and fishing to supplement his food. She could be happy with him, whatever his circumstances might be. But her father had other things in mind for her—this was a daughter's lot, she knew, yet the unfairness chafed more with each day.

The path veered away from the river briefly, into a thicket of dense woods. She picked her way gingerly, not having changed from her slippers when she rushed out of the cabin.

She felt herself spiraling into despair as she thought of some of the oafish men she had served in the great hall, how they leered at her as she moved among them. *I would rather be dead than lie with any of them!* Devorra felt miserably frustrated as she emerged from the brush, back alongside the river.

When she lifted her eyes from her path, she stopped in her tracks.

Gabinier, naked as a baby, was washing himself in the river. His chiseled muscles rippled under his skin, made even more taut by the cold current. In the hardscrabble rustic life to which Devorra was accustomed, she had seen plenty of naked men. But never had she felt anything like the burst of desire that flooded through her at the sight of *this* man.

With a warrior's instinct, he jerked his head up. His square jaw dropped, and for several long moments, their eyes were locked on each other's, both in disbelief.

Recovering herself, Devorra spun away, and she heard splashing as Gabinier clambered onto the bank. She waited in silence, as she presumed he must be drying himself.

Moments later, he called out, laughing, "I am respectable now. You may turn again!"

She saw that he had pulled on the same leather pants he had been wearing earlier in the marketplace and was now donning his jacket. His heavy sword was on the ground, next to his simple farmer's boots.

"Whatever has brought you out here?" he asked, walking toward her. If he had any embarrassment at having been seen without his clothes, he did not show it. But as he drew nearer, he noticed her demeanor. "My lady, don't be ashamed—I was only bathing."

"Oh, it's not that," she said, dabbing at her eyes with the edge of her shawl, mortified that he had perceived her distress. "I was just . . . thinking about my mother, whom I never knew. That's all."

Gabinier's eyes narrowed, but he did not challenge her story. "She died when you were young?"

Devorra looked down. "Yes, giving birth to me."

It was not uncommon among the tribes for women to die in childbirth, yet Gabinier's face showed sympathy.

"How is it your father never remarried?" he asked.

With a touch of sarcasm, she replied, "Perhaps his bad luck with my mother made other fathers wary of offering him another match."

The truth, Devorra knew, and assumed Gabinier understood as well, was that the tribal fathers recognized Boduognatus as a vile man, and not even the most ambitious of them would trade a daughter to him.

"And besides," she added, "he has no problem warming his bed with wenches captured during his raids."

All this talk of Boduognatus made Devorra edgy. If her father knew she was out here alone with a man, he would be outraged and things would go badly for Gabinier. "I must be on my way," she said abruptly, turning to go.

"Wait!" Gabinier said, taking her arm. "Don't you like talking to me?"

Devorra looked away. "No, no—I mean yes! It's not that, not at all."

He put his finger under her chin and tilted her head back so she could not avoid his eyes. "Then what is it?" he pressed.

"My father would not approve," she whispered.

Gabinier's eyes flashed with anger. "I am a Nervii, and I fight for our people. Why would he object to me?"

She broke away from his touch. "My father intends to offer me as bait for an alliance. If he knew we were here, he'd have you strung up by your thumbs."

Gabinier pulled her back to him. "Your father has started a war with the Romans. He's going to need men like me," he said with conviction. "I will win glory on the battlefield, and then he will give me his approval."

A new fear swept over her. "No, no, promise me you'll be careful."

Gabinier was confident. "We will beat them. And then all will be well. But you're right: you should hurry back to your father before he sends out a search party."

They both laughed, and she stepped toward the path.

"Wait!" he said.

She dared to hope that he longed for her to stay just as much as she hated to leave.

"Can we meet here again?" he asked.

Devorra mulled it over. "It's so dangerous," she said. And then she had an idea. "When I think I can get away from my father's attention, I will send my handmaid to you with a message. Then we can meet here."

Gabinier frowned. "You mean the old woman you were with in the marketplace?"

She nodded. Then Gabinier said something that made her blood run cold.

"You must not trust that woman."

"Why not?"

"I saw her leaving your father's meeting room in the town hall," Gabinier said tersely. "I doubt your father is using her instead of those young girls he's been rutting with."

Devorra's eyes grew large as she was jolted by the truth. Her father was spying on her, with her own handmaid? Could she trust no one?

Gabinier remained calm. "Don't say anything to her about us. If you want to see me, I come here every morning when I'm not out scouting."

"I will come when I can," Devorra agreed.

Gabinier pulled her to him, holding her gaze before his eyes fluttered closed and he leaned in to kiss her. She had never been kissed before. It left her feeling lightheaded and wobbly in the knees.

She wanted nothing more than to kiss him again, but they had already pushed their luck to the edge with this chance meeting. "I must go."

Devorra started back toward the town, agog at the sweep of the last few minutes. Everything had changed . . . and yet nothing had changed. Her feelings for Gabinier had increased tenfold, but her father's intentions were still paramount.

Despite the futility of her hopes, a smile crept across her face as she stepped over the stones in the trail. She had gotten a good look at Gabinier in the river. And she longed for more.

VII

VESONTIO

MAMURRA FOLLOWED LABIENUS out of Caesar's headquarters and across a grassy lawn, toward a long, low structure recently constructed from roughly hewn logs. Small groups of officers huddled about the premises, all there for some item of business or another, including waiting to see Caesar. They all took care to salute Labienus as he walked by. And they wondered who this green-looking young fellow in his company might be.

"This is where the senior engineering staff is stationed," Labienus said, before he pushed open an ill-fitting door and went inside. All Mamurra's experience had been limited to the legion-level staff; he was only vaguely familiar with how the engineering corps was organized. The senior staff attached to Caesar's headquarters managed the overall planning of the army's movements, including the allocation of labor for the many projects necessary during any campaign. Within the senior staff, individual engineers were designated as liaison officers to the respective legions, each of which had their own engineering complement. When Trolianus recruited Mamurra back in Italy, he assigned his trainee to the staff of the Tenth Legion, Caesar's most reliable fighting unit, thinking in that role Mamurra would quickly have an opportunity to show what he could do.

Mamurra had expected the building's interior to be dimly lit, but he marveled at its brightness, attributable to an abundance of lamps, which were blazing heartily. Near each lamp was a large bucket of water.

Labienus, noticing the uncertainty on his young engineer's face, said simply, "We must have adequate light so these men can do their work. But we cannot allow fire to spread in this room. The plans and documents are too precious. Every man here must be constantly alert and ready to douse the flames if a lamp is knocked over. This is by order of Caesar himself."

He paused, as if debating whether to share something sensitive with the engineer. "Did you notice that second door in Caesar's quarters?"

"I assumed it led to his bedchamber," Mamurra said.

Labienus drew closer to Mamurra's ear. "It leads to a separate hallway. The old man is obsessed with always having two ways out of a space. His tents on campaign even have a second flap for egress."

Mamurra was mystified.

Labienus continued in a low voice, "When he was a boy, Caesar was in a barn when it caught fire. Curio was with him—that's how he got the scar on his face. They barely made it out. Ever since, Caesar has been terrified of being trapped by a fire. You should always make these exits part of your planning for his quarters."

By now the men in the room, seated on stools spread across a series of tall individual tables, were all gazing with curiosity at the two newcomers. Labienus, of course, they knew very well, but who was this young fellow?

"Gentlemen, your attention," Labienus called out in his most stern command voice. "This is your new prefect of engineers, Marcus Vitruvius Mamurra."

The senior legate looked over the room. To a man, their expression was one of disbelief. How could someone so obviously junior have been promoted to the command of the engineers?

"This man was recommended by Trolianus himself," Labienus told them. "And he has been thoroughly vetted by Caesar."

This seemed to satisfy them, and Labienus proceeded to walk Mamurra through the workroom, introducing him to the men at each table. The organization was completely logical. One table was staffed by the road builders, another by the bridge men, a third by the camp construction team, and so forth.

They reached the back of the room, where a single desk was piled high with scrolls and wax tablets. Atop the mass was a familiar-looking brass helmet with a white horsehair crest running from ear to ear across the top, signifying the rank of a senior officer. Labienus picked it up and handed it to Mamurra.

"This is proof of your office. Good luck to you." Labienus turned smartly and left the room.

Mamurra felt a cold bolt of terror rip through him. He had no idea where to begin.

A slender, much older man approached. His face was careworn and weather-beaten, but his eyes were alert. He had the swarthy complexion common among Sicilians. He gave his new but confused commander a sympathetic look. "I am Giacomo," he said, with a salute. "I was first assistant to Trolianus. Perhaps I can help you get settled."

Mamurra breathed a sigh of relief. "Yes," he agreed. "I don't have any idea what I need to do."

Giacomo was unruffled. "Neither did Trolianus on his first day on the job."

A few hours later, Mamurra was even more overwhelmed. There were literally dozens of projects underway in preparation for the expected march to the territory of the Belgae, and they were all interdependent. A route of march had been laid out, and advance crews dispatched to begin the Herculean effort of clearing out the trees and underbrush so that the army could pass. In swampy areas, the felled trees would be placed in the ground to make a plank road. Their expected path would cross no fewer than ten streams and tributaries, and the bridge team was mobilizing crews to follow behind the road builders so crossings over these water courses would be ready when the army reached them. Caesar hated to be delayed on a march. At another desk, a squad of mapmakers was furiously making multiple copies for distribution to the legion officers and the high command itself.

Thank the gods that these fellows have been at this so long they know what to do. The trick is for me to stay out of their way, Mamurra thought, watching the men scurry like ants devouring carrion.

Giacomo, presuming his new commander had not had anything to eat or drink since his arrival, brought over a baked bun and a cup of wine. It was the usual sour vintage army-issue brew, but Mamurra was thirsty and eagerly sipped it, screwing up his face at the bitter taste. "The privy," Giacomo said, "is behind the building, when you need it."

Just as he was biting into the bread, a courier burst into the compound and hurried back to Mamurra's desk. "The general wants to see you. Right away!" he barked.

Giacomo gave him a knowing look: *Get used to it.*

When he was admitted into Caesar's presence for the second time that day, Mamurra found not only Labienus and Curio, but also Gordianus and the other five legion commanders, all looking grim. With so much power in one room, something important must be happening.

"Gentlemen," Caesar said without any formalities, "by now you will have seen my order today appointing young Mamurra here as our prefect of engineers."

Mamurra felt self-conscious as these senior officers all took stock of him. Surely, they could sense his lack of confidence in his own qualifications for this senior post.

Gordianus spoke up. "He served on my staff," he growled. "Caesar has chosen well."

Mollified, the group turned their attention back to Caesar.

"What is the state of the planning for our march to face the Belgae?" the general asked crisply.

"Sir," Mamurra said, trying to convey a sense of assurance that he did not truly feel, "the planning is in place. All will be ready for the departure in two days, as you have ordered."

Caesar said coldly, "Unfortunately, the plan has changed."

"Ch-ch-changed?" Mamurra stammered, his heart pounding.

Caesar pointed to a map spread out on his desk. "We have reports that our old friend Ariovistus has crossed the Rhine again, in force, and is terrorizing his former allies, the Sequani. The timing of this move is most suspect. It may be that Ariovistus is conspiring with Boduognatus up north. Perhaps he hopes to draw off some of our forces, to give Boduognatus a better chance against us. If this is true, Mamurra, why is this a flawed strategy?"

Mamurra was thunderstruck. Mighty Caesar was asking *him* for advice?

Before he could respond, Caesar let him off the hook. "Because, Mamurra, I would not divide my army to face Ariovistus with a depleted force. Instead, the entire army will move east to meet him first. The Aedui will have to wait for us to get over there to help them."

"East?" Mamurra gulped. All the planning for the move north would have to be shelved and replaced with a precise plan to march to the east. He was beside himself.

"Uh, sir, when do you expect to head east?" he asked, dreading the answer.

"Tomorrow," Caesar said. "Do you see any problem with that?"

Of course he did! It was impossible! But the problem was one of logistics, not engineering. Mamurra knew better than to challenge Caesar on this.

"No, sir, as you wish." Mamurra felt that now-familiar stroke of terror coursing through himself. *How can I possibly pull this off?*

AS THE SUNRISE BROKE above the forest canopy just beyond the Roman headquarters, an exhausted Mamurra stepped outside of the engineering building for a short break. He settled onto a nearby tree stump and rubbed his bleary eyes. The entire crew had worked through the night. Mamurra knew he couldn't have made it without Giacomo, whose experience with Caesar's bold and sudden changes of course had made him a stalwart veteran of these frenzied all-night work sessions.

"If you try to do everything tonight, you will fail," Giacomo said when Mamurra returned from the meeting with Caesar and told the team what had happened. "Because it is impossible. Instead, you must concentrate only on what absolutely must be done to be able to move the army tomorrow morning. And then we will have the whole day to plan the next day's activity."

Giacomo could see Mamurra was not convinced. "Come with me," he told his superior, and led the prefect over to a long shelf with a series of wooden boxes. "These are the records of each of our movements," he explained. He scanned over them for a few minutes, and then pulled down a box. "Last year, when we were marching into this territory to fight Ariovistus, our plans anticipated a move much farther east than Vesontio."

He shuffled through a number of scrolls and maps. "Here!" He pulled out a sheaf of documents, bound with a cord, and dropped it on the table before Mamurra. "This was the plan for the original march. It will provide the basis for our work tonight."

Mamurra felt the sweetness of relief—at least they did not have to start from nothing. Within moments, Giacomo had distributed key items to the staff at the drafting desks, and without so much as a groan, the men got to work.

Now, hours later, Mamurra felt the warmth of the rising sun on his face. Giacomo had saved his sorry hide. They had pulled together enough materials to enable the six legions under Caesar's command, and the baggage train, to get underway by midmorning. Even now, the orders and maps were being distributed to the legion commanders.

Giacomo came out of the building carrying a bowl. Mamurra knew what it was: the foul-tasting soupy porridge that was standard fare for a Roman army on the march. Made from goat's milk mixed with lard and flavored with the most awful vinegar ever distilled, the concoction turned his stomach, but he took it nonetheless.

He scowled violently after taking a sip, then said to Giacomo, "This is even worse than usual!"

Giacomo laughed. "We eat well when Caesar wins. The rest of the time, we eat like common soldiers."

"There is something I must ask you," Mamurra said, taking in the man who had saved his sanity during the overnight scramble. "Why didn't Trolianus recommend you as his successor? You are obviously far more experienced than I, and you know what to do, no matter what the problem. I should go to Caesar and resign, telling him that you are more deserving."

Giacomo looked aghast. "Sir, if you did that, I would have to desert."

"But why wouldn't you want to be prefect when you are so obviously qualified?"

"I was offered the job by Trolianus's predecessor before he offered it to Trolianus," Giacomo replied. "And when Trolianus was dying, he asked if I wanted to succeed him. I said no each time."

This widened Mamurra's sleepy eyes. "But why is that? Have you no ambition?"

"Caesar is a military genius." Giacomo smirked. "That makes him a nightmare to work for. I didn't want the job because I know how demanding he is. Every man at those desks knows it."

"But why should I take it, then?"

"Because he asked you himself. And no one can deny Caesar!"

Satisfied that everything had been done that could possibly be done for the morning's start of the march, Mamurra allowed himself to be led to his new command tent for when the army was on the march. It had been pitched for him not far from the engineering building, close enough to the river so Mamurra could wash if he so desired.

He did not so desire. All he wanted was a short nap.

Slumber came immediately upon his falling onto the simple cot in the tent. But only a few minutes into his repose, a stern officer from Caesar's staff burst into the tent.

"Wake up, sir," the man said, shaking him.

Mamurra opened his eyes. "What is it?"

"I have a message from Caesar!"

Mamurra jolted off his cot. And when he finished reading it, he threw the parchment across the tent.

"Sir?" the courier asked.

Mamurra slumped back onto the cot. He buried his face in his hands.

The courier was at a loss. "But sir, what is it?"

"Caesar says that he received a report at daybreak that Ariovistus has cut short his raid and has crossed back into Germania."

"So?"

Mamurra reached for a blanket. "The march east is cancelled. We're back to yesterday's plan, to move north against Boduognatus. And he wants to leave tomorrow."

"Well, sir, what are you going to do?

Mamurra pulled the blanket up under his chin.

"Take the message to Giacomo," he said, unable to keep his eyes open. "He'll know what to do."

VIII

SPIENNES

THE RIPPLING WAVES OF THE TROUILLE RIVER caught the ascending spring sun and shimmered as if the current itself were a living creature. Devorra scanned its length, then scoured the narrow clearing in the forest, anxiously looking for her warrior.

But Gabinier was nowhere to be found.

Knowing that she might not soon have another opportunity to slip away from Aloucca's ever-watchful eye, she decided to wait. She took a blanket from the basket she was carrying and spread it in front of the humble tent where she had last seen Gabinier. Alone but for the chirping birds and the croaking frogs, her thoughts turned dreamily again to that afternoon when she had found him here, and the short kiss that had concluded that encounter. She had been able to think of little else since that day.

At a rustling in the trees behind her, she turned just in time to see Gabinier emerge from the woods, a stout bow in one hand and a wild turkey, arrow still protruding from its plump body, in the other. He bounded across the clearing as she clambered to her feet.

"My lady Devorra, how wonderful to see you," he exclaimed, dropping the bird and the bow and flashing his radiant smile. "How did you evade the clutches of your companion?"

Devorra, warmed by his greeting, returned the smile. "I sent her out to pick some flowers for our cabin. As soon as she was out of sight, I dashed over here."

He laughed. "How clever you are!" Then, suddenly cautious, he added, "You have said nothing to her about us?"

She took him by the hand. "No, of course not." As he exhaled in relief, she pointed to the bird. "No need to clean and cook that. I brought us something to eat."

She pulled him onto the blanket and reached for the basket. It yielded a loaf of bread, a wedge of soft cheese, and a leather pouch. She opened the flap. "A honeycomb. I love the sweetness of it!" She broke off a piece and gave it to him. "And to slake your thirst," she said cheerfully, "a flask of the finest mead to be had in all of Belgae."

Gabinier was delighted. "How did you ever get your hands on this?" he asked, uncorking it.

"I am a serving girl in the council chamber, remember?" she said, sounding naughty.

He laughed again and pulled a dagger from his belt. He cut the bread and cheese, first giving a portion to her before taking a slice for himself.

As they ate, he told her about his latest scouting mission, and she told him what tidbits of news she had picked up during her time keeping the Nervii leaders well lubricated. There was not much—the Romans were thought to be heading their way, but none had been spotted yet.

The lack of an imminent confrontation, aided by the potency of the brew he was sipping, put Gabinier at ease. He opened up a bit, telling her about his family. He was the youngest of four children, but the only son. His sisters had been married off, leaving him to work the small family homestead with his parents. They had taken sick one winter and did not survive it. The farm and its livestock were his, but he had sold it all, in order to join the fight against the Romans.

"It was nothing special," he said softly, but then added with pride, "but it was in our family for generations."

Devorra listened avidly, though not for any concern about his means or his station in the tribe. She cared nothing for such material matters. But she loved the sound of his voice. After a lifetime surrounded by self-important and brutish tribal chiefs, she found his humble simplicity tender and engaging. He was rugged and strong, yet gentle and sincere. So unlike her father! She began to fantasize about living in the countryside with Gabinier, far away from Boduognatus and all his plotting.

He told her about his scouting missions, regaling her with funny stories about his adventures. The more she laughed, the more completely comfortable she felt with him.

She decided to take the plunge. "I have something for you," she said easily, reaching again into the basket.

His puzzlement turned into a wide grin when she said, "I have made you a bracelet. See the little pouch on the underside? It contains a braided lock of my hair. I hope you will wear it with you on your missions so you will know I am thinking about you always and praying to the gods for your safe return."

Gabinier happily lifted his arm while Devorra wrapped the embossed leather band around his wrist. "Do you like it?" she asked.

"It is the most wonderful gift I've ever received," he said, turning his wrist as he admired her work. "I will wear it every day."

She clutched his wrist and said with urgency, "Promise me you will be careful on your missions and come back to me."

"All the Romans in Gaul can't keep me away from you," he replied.

For a long, long moment their eyes locked, and Devorra was thrilled to find a desire that matched her own. And then they collapsed into each other's arms, hungry for nothing but the taste of each other's lips.

IX

NORTHEASTERN GAUL, NEAR BELGAE TERRITORY

R OMAN SOLDIERS FROM THE TWENTIETH LEGION were going about the orderly business of erecting their fortified camp for the night. Mamurra and Giacomo, both seated on their mounts atop a short hill nearby, squinted as they faced the blazing sun, watching the exercise with confidence that the men had done this so often, they needed no engineering support.

When a Roman army was operating in hostile territory, each legion followed a rigid practice: the day's march was halted when about two hours of sunlight remained and a suitably large open area was available. On a well-planned march such as this one, the campsites had been scouted in advance, leaving nothing to chance. The camps were always situated near a river or stream, to ensure plentiful water for man and beast. Several of the cohorts, inured to the drill, broke from the line of march and took up their duties without specific orders. Some men formed a defensive perimeter to guard against an attack; another group set about excavating a long, deep trench to form a giant square.

Inside the square, other men set up tents and built fires, while still others brought the baggage train into the square and began unloading tall wooden stakes. The stakes would be pounded into the bottom of the backside of the trench, thus erecting a daunting stockade behind the trench itself. Moreover, the excavated dirt was piled up outside the trench along the entire span, making an outer barrier that an attacker would have to breach before reaching the trench, let alone the stockade wall. Prefabricated gates were also unloaded and positioned in the middle of each side of the square walls, so that the camp might be easily evacuated if a fire broke out. Because the gates were opposite each other on the respective sides, the tents were erected in lines to create two long lanes connecting the opposite gates. The

51

lanes formed a cross in the center of the camp, and at their intersection, the commanders' tents were established, so they could respond to any threat. In this manner, an easily defended camp was built in short order at the end of every day. It all happened swiftly and with a minimum of oversight from the officers of the legion because the routine was so well established. With five thousand soldiers available in a legion, it was amazing what could be done in just two hours.

"Come, Giacomo," Mamurra said to his deputy. "We're not needed here." He nudged his horse in the ribs, and the beast hesitantly began its way down the hill.

"Where to now, sir?" Giacomo asked.

"I must report to Caesar on the day's progress," Mamurra replied. "He is in camp tonight with the Tenth."

"Nothing unusual there," Giacomo acknowledged. Caesar's affection for the Tenth was legendary, and he often billeted with them when his army was on the march.

"Yes," Mamurra said, and then noted with evident pride in his voice, "He has invited me to dine with him tonight." *If only my father could see me now, in command of the engineers and dining with Caesar himself!* He could not help but feel as though he had made something of himself in the army.

"Just the two of you?" Giacomo asked, giving him an uneasy look.

"I do not know," Mamurra replied, having received the order to join the general earlier in the day. It did not say whether others would be present. It had not occurred to him to wonder about it. "Why do you ask?"

Giacomo shook his head noncommittally. "Just curious."

WHEN THE LEGIONS MARCHED, Caesar liked to keep some distance between them, rather than maintaining one long, continuous line. He told his commanders this provided him with more flexibility in deploying for battle. It also made it harder for an enemy to launch a devastating surprise attack, because they would have to remain hidden over a considerable distance. This was exceedingly difficult for an opponent because Caesar was constantly probing and scouting with the cavalry units attached to each legion, on the lookout for lurking enemies. With five legions at his disposal, Caesar tended to keep the Tenth in the middle, with two in front and two behind. This would enable his most reliable troops to come to the aid of either the front spearhead or the rear guard, should either come under attack.

By the time Mamurra and his aide reached the camp of the Tenth Legion, the stockade was nearly complete. They made their way down the center lane to the group of khaki canvas command tents, passing a beehive of activity as more of the baggage carts were being unloaded with equipment for the night's stay. Cook fires were now blazing, with stews and chops of meat being made ready for the night's dinner. The aroma made Mamurra realize he had not eaten for hours, and his stomach growled in protest.

Happily, the engineering squad of the Tenth had already erected his tent and moved his gear into it. Most importantly, they had set up a large metal tub for his bath. Outside the tent, a kettle of water hung on a metal rod held by two forked sticks above a small fire.

Mamurra was still getting accustomed to the perquisites of his office, one of which included a handsome slave in his twenties, still carrying boyish good looks, who served as his personal valet. No one knew the man's nationality, for he had been taken captive as a small child and then bought and sold several times before ending up as property of an officer of the Tenth Legion, who had won him in a wager. This officer had given him the name Dominicus. The officer had subsequently been killed in a battle, and the legion kept the slave for labor as needed, before assigning him to the engineers. The lad had no memory of his parents, or of ever having been free. He was of medium height and well proportioned, with luxurious dark straight hair, black eyes, a broad nose, and a sensuous mouth. Some of the officers speculated that he was of Spanish descent.

Dominicus helped Mamurra out of his boots, removed his socks, and then waited as Mamurra stripped off his tunic and breeches. He went outside to fetch the heated water, then filled the tub. Mamurra sighed as he eased himself into the glorious bath.

His young slave stood by as Mamurra soaked, allowing the water to dissolve much of the day's grime as well as the tension pent up from the relentless stress of managing the march. When he felt the water had done its task, he stood in the tub and waited as Dominicus approached with a bottle of olive oil. The slave rubbed the oil all over his master's body.

He lingered at Mamurra's genitals. "Do you want release, master?" he asked.

Mamurra was confused. "What do you mean?"

Dominicus began fondling Mamurra's penis. Mamurra pulled away in horror.

The slave's face was passive. "You do not care for it?"

"No," Mamurra said, mightily embarrassed. "Where have you learned this?"

The slave smiled. "Many of my masters have required such service. And more, if you wish it."

"More?"

Dominicus stepped back from the tub and slipped his tunic off his shoulders, allowing the garment to fall to the floor. Mamurra took in his well-proportioned torso; he looked like he had been chiseled from marble.

"I have been used in all ways one might desire," the slave said matter-of-factly.

Mamurra turned his head and pointed to a nearby table. "Take up the strigil, boy, and get to work."

Dominicus, still showing no emotion, stepped over to the table and picked up the curved brass blade used to scrape the bathing oil from the body.

Before the slave could begin his task, Mamurra snapped, "And put your clothes back on! I can't have someone walk in here and wonder what is going on!"

Dominicus said nothing and donned his garment. There was no reason to tell his new master that certain veterans of the Tenth Legion would not be surprised by anything they saw.

X

SPIENNES

THE LARGE LIMESTONE BUILDING that housed the meeting hall also had many individual rooms. Boduognatus had established his personal quarters in the largest of these. There was a kitchen just off the great room so that meals might be easily prepared and served to a gathering. And in a smaller room, behind the kitchen and down a corridor from his sleeping chamber, Boduognatus's pleasure slaves were kept, half a dozen in all. These unfortunate women had been culled from the droves of captives taken each time Boduognatus had gone raiding into the territory of the Aedui. Several were very young, barely more than children. They had no choice but to submit to his carnal appetites or face a terrifying death from any one of Boduognatus's deranged means of torture. When any of these pleasure slaves became pregnant from his use of them, he would send the woman away, to be sold to anyone who might be a buyer, and he would pocket the money.

Boduognatus had just finished sating himself with the youngest of his prey when he was informed that Correus, the influential chieftain of the Bellovaci tribe, was en route to his quarters. With a dismissive flick of his wrist, Boduognatus dispatched the girl from his presence. He pulled on breeches and his boots, then selected a leather vest, open in the front so that his visitor could see his furry but muscled chest and stomach. He wanted Correus to understand how he had taken charge of the Nervii by besting the many faction leaders in deadly combat. Finally, he pulled a cord over his head that bore a heavy golden amulet in the shape of a bear, the symbol of the leadership of the tribe. He did not, however, arm himself with a sword—by prior agreement, the meeting was to be weapons-free.

This was a critical meeting. The Bellovaci were a large and prosperous clan. Their territory was strategic to the control of northern Gaul, and they could provide thousands of men for the front lines of the battle with the Romans. Like his own Nervii, they boasted Germanic ancestry, meaning they were savage and fearless fighters. An alliance with them could ensure success.

Moments later, Correus strode into the room, accompanied by a much younger man. Their resemblance to each other was striking—both had a high forehead with a receding hairline and fishlike eyes that bulged as though they might pop out of their sockets at any moment. The younger fellow, however, had a blotchy face, pitted by acne. Boduognatus thought it a good sign that Correus had brought the boy.

The two leaders clasped hands in greeting, and then Correus said, "I have brought with me my oldest son, Maccheor."

Boduognatus faced the younger man, who grinned and extended an arm in greeting. Maccheor's open mouth revealed a terrible mess of crooked and broken teeth.

Before Boduognatus could inquire, Correus proffered an explanation. "As a boy, Maccheor was kicked in the head by an angry cow who didn't like the way he was milking her." He laughed, and Boduognatus joined him.

"I do not expect you to bite the Romans to death," Boduognatus said in a jocular manner. "Your arm is what we will need, and it seems plenty strong to me!"

The boy did not respond, managing only a self-conscious smile.

A half-wit, Boduognatus thought derisively. He pointed to several large cushions. "Have a seat, and let us get down to our business."

The men eased themselves onto the cushions. Boduognatus clapped his hands loudly to indicate he was ready to be served.

Devorra entered the meeting room bearing a wooden tray containing three silver goblets, all filled with warmed mead. She hurried over to the men sitting on the floor and lowered the tray before Correus, necessarily affording him a panoramic view of her barely contained bosom. Correus lingered over his choice of a cup, as if he cared about the carving etched into the sides of it, but any fool could see what he was studying. After several long moments, he took one and handed it to Maccheor, then took another for himself.

Boduognatus, watching closely, could see the lad was impressed.

He gestured for Devorra to present the tray before him, which required her to bend over again, this time providing the guests with a generous glimpse of her well-proportioned backside. He too lingered for a moment, to give them their fill of her.

As she hurried from the room, Boduognatus held up his goblet. "To our common cause. May we send the Roman dogs back to Italy with their tails between their legs!"

Correus lifted his beverage, but said, "Whether we join you in this effort depends upon what we hear from you today."

Boduognatus took a sip of the pungent, grainy mead. "The Romans call this mead *milites*. I hope never to hear of the Romans again."

"This is a risky course you have set yourself on, Boduognatus," Correus said, also sipping, savoring the taste of the fermented honey. "Their general, Caesar, has proved himself a great leader on the battlefield. I thought no one could beat Ariovistus head to head, yet Caesar did."

Boduognatus spread his arms expressively. "What is the risk of not challenging Caesar? You have followed his actions since he arrived in Gaul—he has subjugated tribe after tribe, requiring them to pay tribute to Rome in exchange for a supposed alliance. How long before he gets around to the Bellovaci, Correus? And then what will you do? Fight him alone? Mighty as the Bellovaci are, you cannot beat a Roman army under Caesar without help. We must fight him together, and fight him now, before he gains any more professed allies."

While Correus was thinking on this, Boduognatus stole a glance at the son, who was clearly more interested in his mead than in the conversation. *Imbecile*, Boduognatus thought, his innate greed sensing an opportunity. *When the old man is gone, he will be easy to manipulate.*

"Perhaps paying taxes to Rome is better than fighting them and losing," Correus reflected. "We may not survive the battle."

"Better to die fighting than to live like a worm under the Roman boot," Boduognatus snarled. "And I have a plan for how to attack the Romans. It will work, I am certain."

At this, Maccheor perked up a bit. "Tell us about the plan," he said quickly.

"I only share the plan with those who pledge to join us," Boduognatus said. "We cannot have someone tip off the Romans in exchange for some treacherous deal."

Correus thought for a moment, then asked, "If we join you, and we prevail, what would be our arrangement afterward? We must each remain in control of our own territory, without interference from the other, and we must swear a solemn oath never to attack the other."

"That is the agreement we have made with the Remi, the Atrebates, and the Suessiones," Boduognatus replied. "That, and we will have a council of the tribes, with each tribe having a vote. The council will rule on any disputes that may arise, and we all pledge to accept the council's decision, even if it goes against any of us individually."

Correus stroked his beard pensively. "After all the years of fighting and raiding between the tribes, you are proposing an arrangement that relies on trust. A great deal of trust."

Boduognatus had been expecting this. "I am prepared to back my word with the hand of my own daughter. An alliance sealed by marriage."

Correus raised his eyebrows. "That would be a serious oath," he had to agree. His gaze turned to his son. This sudden talk of a marriage had the lad looking nervous. Guessing at what he was thinking, Correus said, "I cannot pledge to marry off my son without considering the match. I mean no offense to you, Boduognatus, but we would have to see the girl."

A broad smile spread across Boduognatus's face. They had fallen very neatly into his trap.

"But you have already seen her," he said, feigning innocence. "She just served your drinks."

At this, Maccheor sat upright and looked eagerly at his father.

Boduognatus knew he had them.

⸎

DEVORRA WAS WAITING in the dimly lit corridor between Boduognatus's meeting room and the kitchen, overcome with a sense of dread. *The boy is repulsive. I shall be unhappy all of my days!* She knew better than to seek comfort from Aloucca, who was cowering behind her.

After several long minutes of painful silence, Devorra heard the sounds of the meeting breaking up as the men approached the corridor.

Moments later, the trio came down the corridor. The boy gave Devorra a leer as he passed. In a heartbeat, Devorra knew her fate was sealed.

Before she could do anything, Boduognatus pushed the two Bellovaci past her and on down the hallway, leading them out to their waiting horses. But he turned for a moment, and said in his most threatening voice, "Wait for me in my chamber, both of you."

Devorra's heart sank even further. He might as well have sentenced her to death. Aloucca tugged her arm and led her to her father's quarters.

Boduognatus returned to the room with a look of ruthless determination. He took up his goblet and slowly drained it. Devorra seethed, knowing he did this simply to prolong the awful dread she was suffering.

"Daughter," he started, "the leader of the Bellovaci has just offered us a great alliance with the Nervii. We would bond the treaty by a marriage of our children."

Devorra had been staring at the stone floor, but now she lifted her chin and met his gaze head on. "And what was your answer, Father?"

He stepped closer, to tower above her. "I have accepted his offer."

Boduognatus waited, expecting her to wail and beg him to change his mind.

Devorra knew there was no alternative but to mollify him. "As you wish, Father," she said simply, showing no emotion. She glanced at Aloucca, determined to convince the disloyal slave that her advice had sunk in.

Boduognatus seemed practically giddy. "I am pleased, daughter."

"May I ask, when will we be wed?"

Boduognatus's smile turned to a scowl. "Correus has insisted that the wedding not occur until after we have beaten the Romans."

Devorra felt a sweet flood of relief. But she merely said, "Whatever suits you, Father."

"Good," he replied. He pointed toward the door, dismissing her. Both Devorra and Aloucca bowed slightly and hurried out.

Back in the hall, Aloucca hugged Devorra. "You're going to be a bride!"

Devorra knew whatever she said would be reported back to her father. "Not yet. It may be months before the Romans are conquered."

Aloucca waved that detail away. "Well, we still have much planning to do!"

Just then, a woman came scurrying down the corridor. "Aloucca! Aloucca! The wife of one of the warriors is in labor! You are needed now!"

Aloucca took off down the hall, but Devorra lingered for a moment, deep in thought.

There were indeed plans to be made, she thought, full of determination. *Just not the plans my father is expecting.*

ALONE AGAIN, Boduognatus plopped back onto the cushion and made himself comfortable. He felt quite pleased with himself. Recruiting the Bellovaci into his war with the Romans was a huge coup—it put victory very much within his reach.

True, the delay in the wedding was not what Boduognatus wanted, but Correus had been adamant. He had told Boduognatus that it was an ill omen to have their children marry on the eve of a fateful battle, fraught with risk for the outcome. Better to make sure the Roman threat was neutralized, Correus had insisted. Boduognatus did not believe him, of course; he suspected that Correus was hedging his bet. If the tribes failed to beat the Romans, it would be easier for Correus to break the alliance and make a separate peace with the invaders if the wedding had not yet occurred.

He allowed himself to daydream a bit. After beating the Romans, and with his daughter married to the son of Correus, there was an excellent chance that upon Correus's death, Boduognatus could declare himself King of all the Belgae tribes.

King of the Belgae! He could not repress a self-satisfied smile.

But something was gnawing at him. Devorra's reaction had been so unexpected, so submissive. It was totally out of character for her. Perhaps the old lady had done her job well and talked some sense into the girl. But what if his daughter merely wanted to lull him into thinking she was accepting his wishes? What if she was up to some other mischief?

The more he thought about it, the more he fretted. The stakes were too high, he finally decided.

"Pomorro!" he shouted abruptly, summoning the guard who was never far from his leader's presence.

A burly, heavily armed thug appeared in the doorway.

"I have something for you to do," Boduognatus said. "Something important."

XI

AT THE ROMAN CAMP

A S MAMURRA EXPECTED, Caesar was established in the largest tent in the camp. More surprisingly, the setup was remarkably comfortable, considering that the army was on the march near hostile territory, including a couch with tufted cushions, several tables on which intricate sculptures and busts were displayed, and a large desk covered with maps and scrolls. As Labienus had alerted him, the tent featured two flaps, giving its occupant a second way out if need be.

But most amazingly, the tent had been pitched over a wooden floor. Mamurra marveled at that—Roman army tents were merely pitched atop the grass. Some senior officers might have a canvas mat to keep their feet from the natural soil, but Mamurra had never seen a wooden floor in a tent. As always, his methodical mind considered the logistics—the floor must have been designed and built to incorporate interlocking panels, so it might be easily assembled at the end of each day and then disassembled the following morning and packed on a wagon for the day's journey.

This is how a consul of Rome gets to travel, Mamurra realized.

Caesar was seated at a table, chatting amiably with a portly, silver-headed man wearing a white tunic with a purple stripe running from the shoulder down to the hem—the garb of a Roman senator. And, of course, there was Curio, listening attentively as always.

"Ah, Mamurra," Caesar said lightly when the engineer came into sight. "Join us."

Caesar pointed to an empty stool across from the senator, and Mamurra took his place.

"This is my new prefect of engineers," Caesar said, introducing Mamurra to the senator.

A cut glass decanter of red wine stood on the table beside a large bowl filled with berries. Caesar and the other man each had a cannikin-type cup before them. Curio brought over another cup, placed it before Mamurra, and filled it from the decanter.

The senator took a swig of his wine.

"Catullus here has just arrived from Rome," Caesar said, tilting his head toward the civilian. "Apparently the noble senators want a report on our progress in Gaul."

Mamurra considered this information warily. *Why would the Senate be so inclined to send an envoy all this way for a look at what was going on? Had not Caesar sent them regular tidings of great victories, wagonloads of gold and silver plundered from the conquered tribes, and countless captives for sale on the blocks in the slave markets of Rome?*

Catullus greeted Mamurra with a sly smile. "Caesar, you have reached far into the ranks for such a young engineer, have you not?" Everything about this fellow seemed oily to Mamurra: his thinning hair was slicked back and plastered to the sides of his head in the manner of some common merchant, and his eyes, flecked with brown and green, shifted back and forth when he spoke, avoiding eye contact. The man had an unusual nose: it jutted out from just below his eyes and then dropped like a cliff. To Mamurra's practiced eye, it looked like a right angle, turned above a scruffy beard. All his instincts told Mamurra this was not a man to be trusted.

But Caesar seemed relaxed—he had fielded this question on more than one occasion. "It is true that Mamurra is not the most senior engineer on the staff by age," the general said placidly, "but he is quite gifted in his trade. I am entirely satisfied with his work."

Catullus's dancing eyes flicked at Curio, whose face was impassive, likely looking for a hint of rivalry between the two young officers, both obviously beneficiaries of Caesar's favor. But Curio was too experienced at this game and gave Catullus no indication of what he was thinking. And Mamurra was too naïve to even have a clue what Catullus had on his mind. The senator's shifty eyes flitted back to Caesar. "Perhaps you see in these young officers the son the gods have denied you?"

It was well known that Caesar's failure to produce a male heir grated on him. He was on his third wife, Calpurnia, whom he'd married when she was only sixteen. Over three wives, Caesar had produced only one child.

Caesar remained calm. "The gods have blessed me with my fair Julia. I am grateful for their bounty."

"Ah, yes, the lovely Julia," Catullus mused. "Speaking of whom, I have brought you a packet from her."

He reached into a knapsack he had carried with him from Rome and produced a bundle wrapped in linen.

Caesar, delighted, took it happily. "My thanks to you, Catullus, for bringing me this gift from my daughter. You saw her while visiting with my son-in-law, no doubt." Catullus was a well-known member of the Pompeian faction in the Senate.

"That was quite some feat you arranged, marrying your only daughter to Pompey the Great. How long has it been?"

"Two years now," Caesar replied, as if disinterested.

Mamurra knew better. Caesar had been locked in a titanic power struggle with Pompey and another powerful Roman, Marcus Licinius Crassus. Crassus was the richest man in Rome, having built a vast fortune by speculating in real estate. Pompey was commonly regarded as the greatest military commander alive, having won a string of victories in Africa and in the Middle East and having cleared the Mediterranean of the scourge of piracy. Both men had served as consul of Rome, the most important elected office. Caesar had joined with them to form a Triumvirate, operating together to work their will upon the Senate. Crassus's son, Publius, was a junior officer serving on Caesar's staff. The arrangement with Pompey included Caesar's election as consul of Rome and approval for Caesar's campaign in Gaul, by which Caesar wanted to establish his own military reputation. To bind the deal, Caesar had offered his only daughter to Pompey in marriage. Pulling off the marriage had been no mean feat—Pompey had to divorce his wife, herself the daughter of a prominent family, to clear the way for it.

"Pompey is so much older than your daughter—I believe there are thirty years between them?" Catullus asked, evidently desiring to tweak Caesar further.

"I understand they are very happy," Caesar said dismissively.

Catullus apparently had been hoping to get Caesar to say something negative about Pompey, but he took the hint and moved on. "And what of young Crassus? His father is most keen for news."

Caesar had his answer ready. "Crassus is not with us on this campaign."

Catullus's eyebrows jumped at this news. "But why not?"

"Tell his father that I have entrusted young Crassus with a most important mission," Caesar said in a conspiratorial tone. All these senators loved to receive sensitive information before the full Senate could be advised. "Prior to our departure on this campaign, I dispatched him as our emissary to the tribes of the northern coastal region of Gaul. He is offering them our standard ultimatum: Accept Roman governance and pay tribute—or be conquered."

Catullus silently ruminated on this development for a few moments, then remarked, "It seems like a sensitive mission for one so young. And dangerous, too."

Caesar waved off the comment. "He is accompanied by a full legion for protection. And he is not to engage any of the tribes if they refuse—we will deal with any recalcitrants after we have finished with the Belgae."

"And how is it going?" Catullus asked, still not sure.

"Very well, so far," Caesar said. "These particular tribes are quite mercantile. They prosper from an active trade with the people of Britannia, across the water from Gaul. They see that it is in their best interests to be at peace with Rome, notwithstanding the cost of the taxes. You may tell Crassus that his son has inherited his father's skill at bargaining. He can be very proud of that young man."

Catullus went silent again, visibly digesting this news. Clearly, Caesar had not wanted to expose young Crassus to the risk of combat against the Belgae and had come up with this diplomatic mission for the lad. Perhaps this was by some private arrangement between Caesar and Crassus—the heir to the greatest fortune in Rome was not to be unduly placed at risk.

The senator turned his attention to the newcomer. "So, Mamurra, how is the campaign progressing?"

Curio cast a warning glance at Mamurra.

Mamurra froze. He knew better than to speak to an outsider about military matters, especially in front of Caesar himself!

Caesar, seeing Mamurra's reticence, gestured with his hand toward his engineer. "Go ahead. He is a senator of Rome. You may speak freely."

Mamurra, unable to get over his innate distrust, said simply, "The campaign is proceeding in a most orderly manner. We have encountered a couple days of delay due to the spring rains, but overall the progress is good."

"No problems with your roads or bridges?" the senator quizzed.

"None, sir. The roads and bridges have been built in advance of the march, to our most strict army standards. I am aware of no problems to date."

As Mamurra spoke, Catullus cocked his head to the side and slowly ran his eyes from Mamurra's forehead down to his sandals. He studied the young fellow for so long that Mamurra looked away, embarrassed. When he dared to turn his eyes back to the senator, he noted that Catullus had moved his gaze to Caesar, whom he was now regarding with what Mamurra could only describe as amused suspicion.

Caesar was clearly irritated by whatever it was the senator was not saying. "What is it, man?" the general demanded.

Catullus put up his hands, the picture of smug innocence. "Oh, nothing, Caesar. Nothing at all." He smirked and threw one last glance at Mamurra before turning back to Caesar. "May I ask what your overall plan entails?"

"We have scouted an excellent location on a broad plateau above a river the locals call the Sabis, well into the territory of the Belgae. It is sufficiently large for a more formal encampment to house most of the army. Mamurra here already has one of our forward teams working on the construction. I plan to establish ourselves there."

Catullus stroked his scraggly chin thoughtfully. "And what do you expect to do when you get yourself established in this new base?"

Caesar took a sip of wine, letting the senator wait for his answer. Finally, he said, "What I always do with these barbarian tribesmen. I will seek to conclude a suitable treaty with them, by which they agree to become allies of Rome, in return for the annual payment of taxes to the Roman Treasury."

"And if they do not agree?"

Caesar's voice grew hard. "We will offer battle and annihilate them. The survivors will be slaves when they could have been allies."

Catullus gave the trio a satisfied look. This was the kind of imperialistic talk the Senate loved. But he had come for more than a mere military briefing. "Caesar, I desire a brief private conversation with you."

Mamurra saw Curio shoot a look of alarm at Caesar. But Caesar was a politician every bit as much as he was a general, and seeming unconcerned, he motioned for his colleagues to take their leave. The two nodded and stepped out.

"What's that about?" Mamurra asked when he and Curio were outside.

"I have no idea," Curio said. "But I'm sure it's nothing good."

He led Mamurra down a row of tents and across a lane, to his own quarters. Curio's tent was roughly the same size as Mamurra's, but more sparsely furnished, with only a cot, a desk, two camp stools, and his trunk. Each man took a seat, and Curio poured wine for them.

"So, Mamurra," Curio said, "how are you finding life as prefect of engineers?"

The wine, Mamurra's second cup of the evening, was beginning to work on him, and he felt relaxed. "I am unqualified for the position," he said, with complete honesty. "I would be lost without the staff, who are superb."

Curio swigged a bit of the wine. "Every man who works for Caesar is good at what he does. Or else he gets rid of them."

Mamurra said, "I understand you grew up with him."

Curio nodded. "My father was a simple farmer on his father's estate. Even though his station was higher than mine, he befriended me."

"How did that come about?"

Curio stifled a smile.

"I am most curious," Mamurra entreated.

Curio drew in a deep breath, then exhaled slowly. "What tasks did your father give you when you were a boy?"

Mamurra scowled. "My father was a shipping merchant. Whenever a ship arrived with goods, I had to go on board and help unload the cargo. It can be very hot in the hold of a sailing ship. I hated it!"

Curio leaned forward. "Well, my father was a farmer. It was my chore to muck out the stalls in the barn. I came to know the young Caesar because he would come in for his daily ride. I groomed his horse. We became friends. And he would often bring along his riding companion, Vatteus."

Mamurra thought for a moment, then asked, "The same Vatteus who is the army surgeon?"

"The same," Curio replied. "The three of us were rascals, always getting into trouble with our pranks."

Mamurra sensed there was more. "And?"

"I don't know you well, Mamurra, but I believe you are a man who can be trusted," Curio began. "Can you keep a confidence?"

Mamurra set his wine cup down and looked Curio straight in the eye. "On my honor as Caesar's engineer."

Curio was satisfied. "One day, Caesar brought in a flask of wine he had pilfered from his father's cellar, and we were slugging it down. It was a little too much, and Caesar accidentally kicked over a lamp in the barn. The hay ignited in an instant. In the blink of an eye, the flames were everywhere."

Mamurra was riveted. "What happened?"

"Caesar was paralyzed. He was transfixed by the flames." Curio took a long, slow swig from his cup, for dramatic effect. "Vatteus and I grabbed him and pulled him out of the barn. We saved his life." Curio tugged at the marred tissue of his cheek. "A burning timber collapsed on me as we were getting out."

Mamurra sat quietly, captivated by the story, recalling Labienus's reference to this event. "So this is why Caesar is so obsessed with always having a second exit."

"That's not all," Curio added, with a laugh. "They hauled the three of us before Caesar's father, to explain how we managed to burn down the barn. Vatteus and I took the blame for kicking over the lamp."

"Surely you jest!"

Curio shook his head. "His father was so angry at Vatteus and me, he was going to have us flogged. But Caesar pleaded with him to show mercy, especially since I was burned by the fire."

"And did he?"

"Yes, his father relented. The sentence was reduced to a month of bread and water. But Caesar stole food from the kitchen every night and brought it to us, so it was tolerable. And Vatteus was so interested in the poultices they were applying to my burn, he was drawn into his career as a doctor."

Curio turned to the trunk behind his desk and withdrew a board and a small ivory box. He set them before the engineer.

"What is that?" Mamurra asked.

Curio took polished stone pieces from the box and set them on the board. "It's a game called latrones. It's Caesar's favorite. Well, at least it was when we were young—he rarely has time for it anymore. I will teach you."

"I have to say," Mamurra remarked, "I am amazed that Caesar allowed you take the blame for setting the barn fire."

Curio kept at his task, merely shrugging at the suggestion that his commander might have behaved dishonorably.

LATER, CAESAR SUMMONED Curio back to him, and Curio left Mamurra alone with his thoughts. As he walked to Caesar's tent, Curio considered the new prefect of engineers. He liked the young man, who had a knack for his favorite game, but he had refrained from telling Mamurra the real secret of the barn fire: Caesar had kicked over the lamp because it was the first time he'd experienced one of those awful spells.

Stepping into Caesar's tent, Curio repeated Mamurra's question: "What was that about?"

Caesar rolled his eyes. "The rogue wants to take part in the slave trade—he's convinced we're going to be sending hordes of Nervii to the pens."

Curio, aghast, said, "Surely you told him that's impossible. We have too many hands out already, seeking a cut of the proceeds!"

Caesar gave him a cool look. "Catullus is Pompey's ass-licker. I told him if he wants a share of the spoils, he should ask his patron, not me."

Caesar took up the package Catullus had delivered and unwrapped it. Delighted, he held up a letter from his daughter and a handsomely tooled leather sheath containing a short but elegant dagger. Scanning the letter, Caesar said, "Ah, Julia has sent me a gift to bestow good fortune upon our campaign. What a loving daughter she is!"

He removed the dagger from the sheath. It was expertly balanced at the hilt, the weight of the blade equal to that of the handle. Inspecting the ivory in the handle, Caesar brought forth a satisfied snort. "See here, Curio, she has made them engrave the Roman eagle! I shall treasure this gift all my days."

"It is a great sign of her affection," Curio agreed, admiring the sharpness of the blade.

Caesar set it down. "Will you be joining us for dinner?"

Curio, convinced now that Mamurra could hold his own, decided to skip the dinner. Pleading that there were reams of orders to be issued for the next day's march, he demurred.

If Caesar was disappointed, he gave no sign of it. He called for his valet and asked that dinner be served. Curio took his leave and returned to his own tent to take up his night's work, sending Mamurra back to Caesar.

⁘

As they were waiting for the food, Caesar sat back and asked Mamurra, "So what do you make of this visit by Catullus?"

Mamurra, of course, had no idea. "Sir, I am a simple engineer. The politics of the Senate are far beyond me."

Caesar reached for the decanter and deliberately poured wine into two cups. Mamurra admired the glass container, which was etched with symbols Mamurra did not recognize.

"It is the best Egyptian glass, a gift from Crassus, who revels in such objects," Caesar explained. "I expect to visit Egypt someday."

Mamurra said nothing. He could not imagine a place so far away as Egypt. He tasted the wine. It was rich and full bodied, nothing like the swill provided to the common soldiers. He took another sip.

"I have opponents in the Senate," Caesar said abruptly. "They envy our success here in Gaul, where we are expanding Rome's power—and our own wealth. They fear that I will use this wealth to acquire more supporters. They think I have moved against the Belgae so I can obtain more for myself."

"But why send Catullus? Did he tell you this?" Mamurra asked.

Caesar said simply, "He didn't have to. Their motives are as plain as that awful nose on his face. Why else would they send someone all the way out here to see what I'm up to?"

Just then, the servers arrived with their meal, and Caesar fell silent as platters of roasted venison and assorted vegetables were set before them, as well as more wine.

"That scoundrel Catullus," Caesar said between sips. "He fancies himself a poet; did you know that?"

Mamurra could not conceal his confusion. "A poet?"

"Not a very good one at that," Caesar clucked. "His so-called poems are typically political attacks on his enemies. He publishes them as a way of influencing the handful of the electorate who can actually read."

"Do you have any of his works?" Mamurra asked, interested now.

Caesar scoffed. "I wouldn't use one of his poems to wipe my ass!"

Chastened, Mamurra said nothing. He selected a carrot and began to chew on it.

"Enough of this political intrigue," Caesar said as he placed a small portion of the venison onto a silver plate, then filled the rest of it with vegetables. "Tell me about how you are settling into your new position."

Mamurra, now on his third cup of wine for the evening, proceeded to tell Caesar about various aspects of the engineering staff and the ongoing projects. Caesar asked him highly detailed questions about a number of items. As the conversation progressed, Mamurra became more and more engaged, and he yet again marveled at the scope of Caesar's grasp of the most arcane aspects of the campaign. He found himself understanding more than ever how his general had compiled such a record of success.

A dessert of berries in cream was served. Mamurra found them delicious.

He was finishing a second helping when Caesar asked yet another question. "Are you pleased with your valet?" His penetrating hazel eyes bored a hole through the engineer.

Mamurra nearly choked on his berries. "Y-y-yes, sir," he stuttered, deeply embarrassed.

"I asked Gordianus to assign the boy to you," Caesar said, studying Mamurra for a reaction.

Mamurra felt as though the air had been sucked out of his lungs. Ever since that night when Dominicus had offered him sex, Mamurra had been torn over his urges. He felt himself attracted to men, it was true, but the topic had been taboo in his family upbringing. Night after night, with Dominicus so readily available, Mamurra had felt his resolve gradually giving way to desire, yet he was hardly going to say as much to Caesar.

"Make such use of him as you see fit," Caesar said without looking up, as if fascinated by the last morsel on his plate.

"Thank you, sir," was all Mamurra could manage.

"He has been assigned to me in the past," Caesar said in a completely noncommittal tone. "I found him to be very dedicated to his duties."

XII

SPIENNES

THE TEMPERAMENTAL SPRING WEATHER broke cold the next morning. As they were taking their breakfast of warm mashed oats and goat's milk, Devorra told Aloucca she had started her monthly bleeding and was experiencing painful cramps from it.

"I do not feel up to going to the market today," she told the slave. "You go by yourself. And try to find us suitable vegetables to make a good stew."

Aloucca wrapped a rough woolen shawl about her shoulders.

Devorra drew several pieces of silver from her purse and gave them to her handmaid. "Shop wisely," she instructed. "Father is never very generous with me."

Aloucca left on her mission. Devorra waited until she was safely out of sight, then pulled on a wrap of her own and left the cabin. She looked around to make sure no one was watching her, and then she headed into the woods on the path to the river. She prayed that Gabinier would be there today.

She hurried along, knowing Aloucca would be gone for only a couple of hours. But with each step, her resolve hardened, as she could not banish from her mind the image of that pimply-faced youth with the horrible teeth.

The gods smiled upon her. As she came into the familiar clearing alongside the river, she found Gabinier huddled beside a small fire, just a few feet away from his tent.

His face lit up as he saw her, and he jumped up to pull her into an embrace.

"I have ached to have you back in my arms," he purred in her ear. Then, pointing to the bracelet, he laughed. "See, I've never taken it off! Some of the fellows have asked me where it came from!"

71

Cradled in his strong arms, Devorra marveled at the taut muscles she felt through his rough linen tunic. "And what did you tell them?"

"I told them it was a gift from the most wonderful girl in the world," he whispered, and kissed her again.

"Have you heard about my father's parley with the leader of the Bellovaci?" she asked abruptly.

Gabinier's blank look was all the answer she needed. "I know only that they met yesterday," he replied. "They do not share details with mere warriors."

Devorra felt angry tears welling up as she spoke. "My father has pledged me in marriage to his son."

Gabinier was taken aback, evidently not having expected Boduognatus to bargain away his daughter so quickly. "This must mean that the Romans are approaching," he said. "Why else would your father hurry so?"

"I won't marry him," Devorra said. "I'll . . ." She drew a sharp breath, then blew it out slowly as she understood what she must do. "I'll just have to leave."

Gabinier pushed her pale hair back over her ears and then took her lovely face in his calloused hands. "I have thought of nothing but you, Devorra," he said, and then he kissed her again. "I will not let this happen."

"What power do you have over my father?" She feared what would happen to Gabinier if he were caught helping her escape.

Gabinier did not hesitate. "We will run away together. We can leave tonight."

She considered this. "No," she said after a few moments. "We must make a plan. Where will we go? I will need to procure money. And we must be able to get far enough away, quickly, before they realize we are gone, so they cannot catch us."

"When does he plan to stage this marriage?" Gabinier asked.

Devorra finally managed a small smile. "Well, we do have some time, at least. Father told me that Correus would not agree to a wedding until after the Romans are defeated."

Gabinier loosed a sigh of relief. "Very well, then. We can work on a plan. I will think of nothing else."

"Nor will I," Devorra said.

Their kiss was intensified by the shared mission they would carry secretly between them. As Gabinier pressed against her, she felt the urgency of his passion between his thighs, and his hand started to explore her breasts.

"No," she whispered. "Not here, not now."

Gabinier pulled back, obviously disappointed, but knowing she was right.

"I must get back before they find I am missing." She forced a smile for him. "I will not rest until we can escape together."

They kissed again, and she hurried away, too intent on her nascent plan to notice the rustling in the brush behind her.

CAREFULLY HIDDEN IN the dense undergrowth of the forest, Pomorro watched the winsome lass as she moved out of sight. It took all his self-control to stifle his urge to laugh at the lovesick Gabinier, who was left standing all alone at his humble campsite, looking forlorn at the girl's departure. *What a fool,* he thought. *Boduognatus would never allow a prize like his beautiful daughter to run off with a common dirt farmer. And once he hears the news, he will waste no time putting an end to this ill-fated match.*

XIII

IN THE ROMAN LINES

C AESAR, MOUNTED ATOP A FABULOUS STALLION whiter than the Alpine peaks, rode next to Curio's more modest mount, casting a critical eye upon the long line of moaning slaves trudging past. Each captive's wrist was locked into Nofio's chain coffles. The men had been stripped to their loincloths; the women were issued scratchy woolen shifts. All were bare-foot; deprived of footwear, they could not get far in an escape attempt. Grim-faced legionaries prodded the slackers along at spear-point to keep them moving to the rear of the army. The take of captives from the defeated Remi after the surrender of the cowardly garrison at Soissons had been substantial. An actual inventory was pending, but the estimated numbers seemed satisfactory, especially for a campaign still in its early stages.

Some of the specimens were quite favorable—strapping lads with strong backs who would bring a good price on the docks for service in the galleys or the mines, and a smattering of young maidens fair enough to command a premium, to be shepherded into brothels throughout Italia. None had any clue of the dreadful fate awaiting them. All together they would bring a respectable sum to the army's coffers, to be divided into shares and distributed to the men as Caesar alone might choose to award.

But Curio was dissatisfied with the lot as a whole. There were too many older prisoners, worthless unless they happened to have some particular skill that might be of interest to a buyer at the slave markets. Under the surrender terms, Caesar had agreed to take only half the people at Soissons.

Caesar apparently was thinking along the same lines. "Too many feeble slaves," he muttered. "I want the inventory completed tonight. In the morning, cut the rations in half for any captive over the age of twenty-five who cannot demonstrate a trade or skill. Give the other half to the prettiest girls. I want them looking healthy when they are stripped for the blocks."

Ever aware of logistics, Curio replied, "Sir, are you sure? The rations are barely enough to maintain their strength to continue on the march. If you cut their food, many of them will perish on their way to the slave dealers."

Caesar knew this, of course. "They are barbarians, not deserving of such consideration," he said crisply. "We'll take plenty more. Why waste food on the ones who won't bring a suitable price at the auctions? We are in this for profit, Curio."

As another coffled group was moving past, a voluptuous lass with long black tresses, unusual amongst the Belgae tribes, caught the general's attention. Even in that most unflattering garb and with her feet caked with dirt from the march, she radiated allure.

"Halt!" Caesar barked. The guard attending the coffle yanked hard on the chain, jerking the group to a sudden stop. Several of the slaves stumbled to the ground.

"Remove that one," he commanded, pointing to the girl.

The legionary stepped forward to obey. As he was unlocking her wrist cuff, a brawny fellow behind her cried out in anger and tried to lunge at the guard, as if to defend her. With his free hand, he attempted a swing at the soldier's helmet and barely missed. The guard brought up the butt of his spear and rammed it into the man's abdomen, knocking the wind completely out of him, crumpling the slave to his knees.

Caesar, amused by this little drama, said to Curio, "Have the girl cleaned up and brought to my tent. Be sure to have one of the interpreters explain what I expect of her."

Turning his attention to the fallen slave still gasping for breath, Caesar grew grim. "Flog this man tonight in full view of the captives," he commanded. "Show them what happens when a slave attacks a Roman soldier."

A sadistic grin spread across the legionary's face.

Caesar knew that look. "I said *flog*," he admonished the man, "not scourge. Don't kill him; just beat him until he's raw."

"Aye, sir," the guard said. He gave the hapless slave on the ground a hard kick.

"I'm going to check on the progress of the baggage train," Caesar said, turning back to Curio. "Have her ready when I return."

Curio gave Caesar a salute as the general wheeled about on his horse. He worked his jaw, weary of the skin's tightness, knowing what he needed to do with the woman. He had done it many times before.

THE GIRL, NAKED NOW and trembling with terror, huddled on the divan in Caesar's command tent. She had been thoroughly washed by Caesar's valet. Curio had arrived just as the army doctor was finishing an examination of her private parts.

"Well, Vatteus, what do you find?" he asked.

"Our old friend has not lost his eye for talent," Vatteus said with a grin. He was a burly man, quite unlike his fit boyhood friends, with a bushy head of hair and a well-kept black beard. "No disease, and a virgin, too."

Curio stepped back out of the tent and returned a moment later, accompanied by a Belgic interpreter, a smarmy little man drawn from the pool of such individuals the army employed. Curio had already developed a distaste for the fellow. The interpreter leered at the girl, obviously delighted to take in her buxom nudity.

"Your work is finished, thank you," Curio said with approval, and Vatteus, with a wistful last look at the tender morsel waiting on Caesar's couch, left the tent. Turning to the interpreter, Curio asked, "What is her name?"

As the question was relayed to her, she stared at Curio's burned cheek, as if she had never seen such a wound. Accustomed to this reaction as he was, at times it cut deeply into him. The scars on his psyche were far worse than the one on his face.

When the interpreter gave him her name, Curio said, "Tell her this: Molena, a very important and powerful man will be here soon. He will want to use your body. You must do whatever he asks of you. Your very life depends on your pleasing him in every way he might demand."

Molena had beautiful eyes, the shape of almonds, black as onyx. Curio saw innocence in them as the interpreter spoke to her. They grew large as she absorbed what the interpreter told her, and then filled with tears.

"Tell her she must be strong," Curio said kindly, inexplicably drawn to her vulnerability. "She must accept that she is a slave now. If she values her life, she must do her master's bidding without hesitation."

This message had no effect. The girl began to sob.

Curio had a flash of inspiration. "Ask her who that man was who tried to stop us from taking her away."

"Her brother," the interpreter reported. Something in this native's manner was increasingly offensive to Curio, as if he felt bothered providing a service to the Romans, notwithstanding that he was being well paid. Curio made a mental note to have this fellow discharged from the service.

"Ask her the name of her brother."

She replied, "Elliandro."

Curio made one last try. "Tell her that if she pleases the man who is coming to use her, he will free her and Elliandro."

This was a blatant lie, of course, but it did not matter. By the time she discovered it, there would be nothing she could do.

Curio sighed with relief as hope spread over the girl's features. Her naivete was refreshing, if tragic.

Satisfied that he had done all that he could, Curio took the interpreter by the arm and led him out of Caesar's tent, leaving Molena in the hands of the gods.

TIRED THOUGH HE WAS by the long day's duties, Curio could not sleep, fearful of how the encounter in Caesar's tent nearby might be proceeding. He was haunted by the girl's fragility, and her fear. How fickle the fates could be, blessing this lass with such beauty, and then delivering her to such a cruel future. He forced himself to dispatch yet another ream of documents and reports, until he heard footsteps approaching. He looked up from his small camp desk as a dour-looking centurion entered, the slave girl Molena trailing behind him, clad now in her ill-fitting dress, her hands and feet in irons.

"Caesar says he was disappointed by this woman. He said you would know what to do."

The girl seemed confused, almost mystified. She bore no apparent marks of physical abuse.

"Fetch the interpreter for me," he said to the soldier, who turned smartly on his heel and stomped out.

Curio could only sit and assess the girl while he waited. She had a long, oval face with perfectly clear skin. Apart from her striking natural beauty, she radiated a gentle sensitivity that somehow appealed to him. She could not meet his gaze—perhaps she thought him some kind of a freak, damaged as he was. But no matter what she thought of him, Curio regretted what awaited her.

Soon enough, the interpreter appeared, rubbing sleep from his eyes, his hair a tousled mess. He was obviously crabby, having been roused from a peaceful slumber.

"Wait outside," Curio ordered the soldier. When the man was gone, he said with a heavy sigh, "Ask her what happened."

Curio waited while the two conversed briefly, growing concerned when the interpreter started to laugh.

"She says that Caesar wanted to use her, but he could not become sufficiently aroused to enter her," the man said, almost incredulous. "She remains a virgin."

Curio put his head in his hands. *Not again! Oh, Jupiter, can't you put some lightning in his rod?*

He wondered if Caesar's impotence might be a symptom of his other recurring malady. If so, there might be a remedy for it. This would require a conversation with Vatteus. Meanwhile, he was uncertain what to do about the woman. If left alive, she no doubt would tell any Belgae with whom she came into contact about her experience with Caesar. Normally, he would have had her throat slit and been done with her. But those lovely eyes were haunting him. *What a waste to have her killed, just to keep her quiet.*

The interpreter wore a smirk, as if he couldn't wait to start telling others what he had learned. Curio knew he must take serious measures. He thought quickly.

"Tell the girl that she and her brother will die if she is ever to speak again about her encounter with Caesar," he told the interpreter.

The message was relayed, and the girl nodded in response.

Curio told the interpreter to take the girl outside and wait, then called for the centurion.

"The interpreter has insulted Caesar," he said briskly, though keeping his voice low so it would not carry through the canvas walls. "Bind and gag him, then take him to the edge of camp. Remove his head and bring it back to me so that I will know it was done."

The soldier was unperturbed by this order. It was just another command from an officer, and his duty was to obey. As the man turned to go, Curio told him to have another soldier report to the tent.

When the legionary arrived at the tent, Curio abruptly said, "Take this girl to the cooking staff. Tell them I said to teach her their trade. She'll fetch a handsome price if she has a skill in addition to her beauty."

The soldier waited for further orders.

"Dismissed," Curio said curtly, frustrated at how things had turned out.

When they were gone, Curio returned to his work. It occurred to him that interpreters were an unavoidable nuisance. He resolved that in the morning he would have one of them begin teaching him the Germanic tongue, so that he might converse with the Belgae without assistance. Caesar himself had already been practicing the language, after all.

Then his thoughts wandered to the unfortunate but alluring Molena. *How could Caesar not be aroused by her? Perhaps he will give up trying to bed these slave girls.*

And then Curio laughed aloud, for he knew full well that the general would never give up.

XIV

TERRITORY OF THE BELGAE

B ODUOGNATUS WAS NOT HAPPY.
The leader of the Nervii was huddled with the chiefs of several other tribes of the Belgae, most notably Correus and his son. They were seated about a small campfire, one of thousands flickering across the rolling landscape surrounding them, like stars in the night sky. The tribes were on the move, heading toward the Romans, but Correus had called a halt with a demand that the council hold a parley.

"What is the purpose of assembling the council?" Boduognatus asked irritably. It was incredibly difficult to get the thousands of tribesmen, many of whom were traveling with their families and their livestock, all moving in the same direction and then keep them trudging at a reasonable pace. Calling a halt meant the loss of momentum, and then that whole start-up process would have to be repeated. The delay could be fatal to his plan.

Correus was in no better mood and had come to have it out with Boduognatus.

"I am told that the Remi tribe launched an attack on the Romans five days ago," Correus said. Several of the chiefs shifted uncomfortably—the plan had been for the Remi to fall back when the Romans entered their territory, so they might lend their strength to the larger mass of unified clans waiting for the Romans deeper in the territory of the Belgae.

Boduognatus was outraged by this news. "That wasn't what we agreed upon!" He spit a gob of green phlegm into the fire. "What happened?"

Correus tilted his head sadly. "Apparently, the Romans are not marching in a continuous line—Caesar has separated his legions by some distance from one another. When the Remi encountered the Roman vanguard, they thought it was the entire force, and since it was only a single legion, they attacked it."

Boduognatus put his head in his hands, dreading what he knew was coming. "And . . . ?"

"The first legion held its ground until the legion behind came up, and then their additional strength turned it into a rout."

"The leader of the Remi is a fool," Boduognatus snarled. He had never liked the man. "What possessed him to think he could attack alone?"

"We'll never know," Correus said with contempt. "He did not survive."

"And his people?" Boduognatus asked, already knowing the answer.

"All taken as slaves. Marched away in chains."

The chiefs were stone-faced. This brought home the seriousness of the course they were set upon.

Boduognatus, fearing that his coalition might unravel, said with a sneer, "Well, let this be a lesson to us all—we must stand united or the Romans will enslave us, one by one."

"I'm afraid that isn't all," Correus added. "After the Remi were wiped out, the Romans moved quickly into the territory of the Suessiones, and formed up before the town of Noviodunum, which some people call Soissons."

Boduognatus felt a rush of dread course through his veins.

"When the Romans brought up their siege engines and artillery," Correus continued, "the mere sight of these devices terrorized the garrison. They surrendered without a struggle."

This was devastating news. "They simply surrendered? What cowards!" Boduognatus snarled in disgust.

"Caesar offered them a deal—he only took half of the Suessiones as slaves, chosen by lot. The rest he made swear allegiance to Rome, but then left them in their homes."

Boduognatus tugged at his beard. He had been counting on a siege of the town to slow the Roman advance and bleed their forces. Now the Romans would only be emboldened. He cast a cagey eye on the doubtful chieftains around him.

"Where are they now?" he asked.

"They have entered my territory," Correus said quietly, his eyes narrowing. "They are laying waste to the Bellovaci lands."

"Stay strong," Boduognatus said. "I believe I know their plan."

Correus cocked his head. "Oh?"

"The Romans are laying out a very large camp along the Sabis River. I believe Caesar intends to make it his base camp for his war against us."

"And what is your plan?" Correus asked, not for the first time.

"There will be several legions working at once. They will bring up their baggage train. They will be strung out and not in formation. We will pour out of the forest from three sides and catch them without warning."

Several of the chiefs mumbled their approval.

Correus was dubious. "If you attack before the entire Roman army is assembled, then the trailing elements will come up and counterattack against us, just as they did against the Remi."

Boduognatus was ready. "That is why I will send a fourth group through the forest. They will attack the rear-guard forces and hold them in place while the main attack is launched against the men working at the camp."

Correus remained skeptical. "Who do you propose will lead it?"

Boduognatus faced them head on. "The Nervii will take that duty, as well as leading the main attack at the camp. I have already identified the warrior who will be the first man out of the forest against the rear guard."

It was surely not lost on any of the men listening that Boduognatus did not intend to lead that attack himself.

AFTER A LONG AFTERNOON of conversations among the tribal leaders, the battle plan was set. The assault on the Romans engaged in building their camp would come from three main groups of tribes. The Nervii, with the greatest numbers by far, would take the center, flanked by the Bellovaci on the right. On the left, two smaller tribes, the Atrebates and the Viromandui, would join forces. Because he controlled the largest numbers and was taking the middle position, Boduognatus would be in command of the entire operation, and all chiefs agreed to follow his orders, given through a courier system. In addition to taking the center position in the main assault, Boduognatus agreed to dedicate a substantial portion of his forces against the Roman rear guard. A fifth tribe, the Atuatuci, had been making very slow progress on the march and probably would not be in position to join in the coordinated offensive. Their leader agreed to redouble his efforts and try to reach the battlefield in time, but they would be brought up behind the Nervii in the center to serve as a reserve—if they got there at all.

A series of flaming arrows flung into the sky would serve as the signal that Boduognatus had launched his men at the Romans. Upon seeing the signal, the other commanders would initiate their own attacks. All involved understood that success would depend on getting all four major offensives underway simultaneously.

This grand strategizing, however, belied the underlying reality. The simple fact was that the tribes were loosely assembled ragtag groups of common hunters, farmers, and tradesmen—mostly groups of relatives, each with their own personalities and petty squabbles. They lacked any formal organizational structure and had no central supply operation. Poorly and randomly equipped, they certainly had no unit cohesion or joint operating experience. Simply keeping this motley collection together and fed, watered, and working toward a common goal was a staggering task every single day. And pitting this free-wheeling congregation against the battle-hardened, brilliantly organized, and highly disciplined legionaries was fraught with danger. Often, masses of men would turn and run at the mere sight of the gleaming steel and precision operation of the Roman legions.

Boduognatus was no dreamer—he saw the situation with clear-eyed ambition. He was relying on the benefit of surprise and the sheer weight of his superior numbers. He estimated that the Romans, with perhaps twenty-five thousand men in five legions, could not withstand the mass of humanity he would hurl at them. He put his numbers at over one hundred thousand screaming tribesmen. And even if his fighters were not formally trained, many of them were vicious, fearless, and brutal. They would hack their way through to victory.

He had one other clear advantage: he did not care about any of them. Casualties were of no concern.

During the day, Boduognatus had instructed his immediate circle of commanders to summon the individual Nervii clan leaders and other officers for a meeting at sunset at his headquarters. This had been accomplished, and he kept them waiting outside his main command tent while he treated himself to a meal of cold porridge, salted pork, and bread so hard he had to soak it in the dense red wine in his cup.

Thus fortified, he donned the bear amulet, proof of his position as leader of the tribe, which had always brought him luck. He strapped on his sword and lifted his battle-ax. He took a few swipes at the air, enjoying the heft of it, imagining he was killing Romans with each swing.

The waiting men cheered and hoisted their swords and pikes when their leader emerged from his tent, brandishing the battle-ax. Boduognatus strode to a cart that had been positioned at the front of the group and jumped onto it, so all could see and hear him. He basked in the adulation of his troops for a few moments, then held up his hands for silence.

"Men of the Nervii, hear me well," he shouted. "Only a short distance from here, the Roman invaders expect to build their camp. From that camp, they will wage their campaign to turn all of us into slaves! Will we allow our women and children to be sold naked on the blocks, to serve lazy, fat Romans sunning themselves in Italy?"

This brought the desired roar of objection.

He waited for the umbrage to die down. "This Caesar of theirs has already swept away most of the tribes of Gaul. Some of them have taken the bait of the Roman trap: they pretend to offer an alliance, assuring the tribes of Roman protection in exchange for accepting a Roman governor, Roman law, and Roman taxes! Will we take such a fool's bargain?"

Another cry to the negative ensued.

"I say we fight!"

More cheers.

"The Nervii will carry out two attacks. I will lead you in the main attack on the Roman camp while they are busy building it. They will be spread out, carrying on their work, separated from their weapons, and not expecting what we will hit them with. We shall destroy them!"

Oddly, this remark did not draw much response, perhaps because the audience was pondering the actual task before them. *How were they going to pull off a surprise attack?*

Boduognatus provided some details. "All the women and children remain here. No more campfires, on pain of death. We must use stealth. We will approach the Roman position on foot through the forest. No animals will be brought forward. Voices must be kept low; every leader must enforce the strictest quiet in the movement through the trees. You must be alert for Roman scouts, and any you encounter must be captured or killed. Caesar must not learn of the threat we are mounting in the forest!"

Many of the men murmured their assent.

Turning to the other prong, Boduognatus announced, "A second force of the Nervii will move farther west through the forest. When the signal is given that the assault on the Roman camp has begun, these men will emerge and attack the Roman rear guard, coming up behind the main force working on the camp."

Nods of approval rippled through the crowd.

"This mission is vital. The Romans must not be allowed to bring more legions onto the field to relieve their men under pressure from our assault at the camp. We must have our bravest man, our best fighter, to lead this onslaught against them."

Crafty as he was, Boduognatus could see many faces in the crowd light up at this pronouncement, each man anticipating that surely he would be the most deserving candidate to be designated this great honor of leading the attack.

"In recent days, one of our best young warriors has impressed me with his cunning and his boundless courage in scouting the Romans and learning their dispositions. He will be the first man out of the forest to terrify the Roman invaders. He is the man who will lead you to victory over their rear guard."

The men in the crowd waited to hear who this new champion might be.

"Gabinier, come forward!" Boduognatus shouted.

The men had blank looks on their faces. *Who?*

Gabinier himself, standing near the back of the knot of men, could not comprehend this turn of events.

And then men around him began slapping him on the back, pushing him forward, past others he felt were far more qualified than himself, finally up to the cart. Gabinier was in disbelief.

Boduognatus reached down, motioned for Gabinier's hand, and pulled him up onto the makeshift pedestal. Still clutching the younger man's hand, he thrust it high into the air, and shouted, "To victory! To victory! To victory!"

The men picked up the chant.

Boduognatus let this go on for a bit, and then shouted, "Enough of this! Everyone to work!"

As the meeting broke up, Boduognatus pointed Gabinier to Pomorro, standing with a group of men who, in a more formal organization, would have been considered staff officers. "Meet with them," he said to Gabinier. "They will show you what you need to do."

Gabinier, still unclear about the role imposed upon him, babbled out, "I will not let you down."

Boduognatus stood by, watching as Gabinier was led away to assume his new duties.

Looking skeptical, Pomorro stepped up alongside his leader. "First man out of the forest?" he asked quietly. "The Romans will cut him down with their pila spears before he makes it a hundred yards."

Boduognatus shot him a wicked look. "That's what I'm counting on."

"There's only one small problem," Pomorro observed.

Boduognatus turned to the churlish man beside him. "Which is?"

Pomorro scuffed at the dirt with his boot, wishing to avoid eye contact. "If he gets cut down in the first wave, the whole attack may fail. And if that happens, the Romans might get to their camp in time to save the day."

Boduognatus reflected on this. "You're right. When it comes down to it, don't put him at the head of the attack."

Pomorro acknowledged the command, but pointed out, "That raises a different problem. What if he prevails?"

His patience at an end, Boduognatus put his hand on Pomorro's shoulder. "That's why I'm appointing you second-in-command. I'm sure you can make certain he does not survive the battle."

XV

AT THE BELGAE CAMP

T HE WESTERLY TREK of tens of thousands of Nervii toward their fateful meeting with the Romans had been one long, unremitting nightmare for Devorra and Aloucca.

The conditions had been hideous: little more than salted pork and stale bread for food, water fetched in buckets from whatever source they might find, only the warmth of a campfire at night, sheltered in a small tent on the hard ground, an open trench for bodily functions on full display to all, manure from the livestock and pack animals everywhere. It was a horrible daily ordeal.

Her father provided a modest canvas-covered wagon, drawn by oxen, for her. The teamster for the wagon was another slave, a toothless old man named Bohannus, who smelled so bad that Devorra had sent him to the river for a bath on their first day together. There was a narrow plank of unfinished wood that served as a highly uncomfortable bench seat at the front of the wagon. Fortunately, Bohannus was sufficiently diminutive that Devorra could fit on the seat next to him, enabling her to ride, albeit jostled about constantly on the beaten path. Aloucca was compelled to trudge alongside every step of the way. After a couple of days on the trail, the poor woman's sandals were completely worn out. Devorra quickly obtained a pair of good boots for her.

But far worse for Devorra than these conditions was the impossibility of any contact with Gabinier. Groups of warriors and scouts were constantly riding about as the throng moved inexorably to the west. Devorra kept her eyes peeled on each group that happened by, fervently praying to the gods that he might be among them, only to have her hopes dashed over and over. And even if she were to come across her handsome warrior, Aloucca was her constant companion, ready to report any meeting to her father. She was in despair, exhausted from constant worry for Gabinier's safety.

Her anxiety had been heightened throughout the day by signs that a battle might be imminent. Grim groups of warriors were riding about, while others were sharpening weapons and preparing shields and other implements for action, painting themselves with various colored dyes to make themselves even more frightful looking.

Devorra and Aloucca huddled by a small campfire, sharing the meager warmth with a mother who was trying to satisfy her brood of children with their small ration of food. The woman's husband was in the front lines with the other men, leaving her to fend for the family. Devorra could tell from the doleful look on the children's faces that they were still hungry.

The mother's plight touched Devorra's heart. She went to the wagon and returned carrying a cloth bag, which she placed before the children.

Aloucca gasped. "Your grapes?"

Devorra had been hoarding the fruit, hoping to share it with Gabinier if she had the chance to see him. "They need it more than we do," she said simply. The delight in the children's faces, and the evident relief of their mother, was the first bit of pleasure Devorra had experienced in days.

"Come, Aloucca," she said to her dismayed companion. "Let us sleep. It will be a long day tomorrow."

They crawled into their tent and pulled the flap down to keep out insects and the cold night air. Devorra was just nestling under a thick blanket when she heard Bohannus's creaky voice outside the tent.

"Mistress, one of the women in the camp is in labor. They are calling for help. They say they need Aloucca."

The slave woman grunted irritably—she was already nearly asleep, worn out from the long day's hike.

But Devorra nudged her in the ribs. "They need you. You must go!"

With a weary sigh, Aloucca sat up. "Why can these babies never come during the day?" she mumbled while pulling on her new boots. She drew back the flap. There was a young boy standing beside Bohannus. "This is the boy who came looking for you. He will lead you to the tent."

Devorra was concerned for Aloucca's safety in the rough-and-tumble camp of the Nervii. "Go with her," she told Bohannus.

Devorra had barely settled back under the blanket when the flap opened again.

In an instant, a large man slipped into the tent and pulled the flap back into place. He clapped his hand over her mouth.

Devorra was petrified. In the dim light of the tent, it took her a few seconds to realize what was happening. And then happiness surged through her, and the man lifted his hand.

"Gabinier!" she exclaimed. But he put his finger on her lips.

"Speak softly, my love," he whispered. And then he kissed her.

She clutched him closer. "What are you doing here? This is madness! It's so dangerous!"

"Not nearly so dangerous as what is close at hand," Gabinier said, running his fingers through her hair. "The Romans are approaching. We attack tomorrow. The warriors were told a little while ago."

Devorra shuddered. A battle with the Romans could be the end of them all.

"I have important news," Gabinier said, barely able to contain his excitement. "Your father has chosen me to lead an attack on the Roman rear guard. This will be my opportunity to impress him. We will drive away the Romans, and your father will reward me. He can hardly deny our union after that."

But Devorra knew it could not be so simple. *How does my father even know who Gabinier is? Has he somehow learned about our relationship?*

"Gabinier, you have never led men in battle," she whispered. "How will you know what to do?"

He made a brushing movement with his hand, as if to wipe away her concerns. "Your father has made Pomorro my second-in-command. He's already told me what we must do!"

"Pomorro?" she asked with a shudder. "I don't trust that man. Please, Gabinier, don't do anything foolish. Let someone else kill all the Romans."

"Don't you see?" he pleaded with her. "This is the only way for us to be together!"

She could not let him see her fear, could not do anything that might make him weak. Instead of protesting, she leaned into a kiss, and they lay side by side, stroking each other with increasing urgency.

He grew bolder with his hands, moving them over her body.

Devorra felt the temptation of her own stirring desire. This might be their last time together. For a moment, the thought terrified her.

"Be with me," he breathed.

"I dare not," she said, fighting to control her own wishes. "Not now."

"We must hurry," he said, pressing himself against her. "Aloucca may be back at any moment."

"But she's delivering a baby. It could take hours."

89

Gabinier flashed her a dazzling smile, that same one that had nearly stopped her heart in the marketplace many weeks before. "Your handmaid is on a bit of a fool's errand," he said with a laugh. "When the boy gets her to the far side of the camp, he will take off running."

Despite everything, Devorra began to laugh. Poor Aloucca, wandering about the camp looking for a baby to deliver, so that Gabinier might steal a few minutes alone with her!

Gabinier kissed her again.

"You must go now," she said. As much as she wanted him, she could not overcome her fear for what the next day might bring. "But you must come back to me, Gabinier. You must come back!"

He clutched her again, and then got to his knees to crawl out of the tent.

"I love you, Gabinier," she whispered, reaching for him.

"And I love you. The next time you see me, I will be at your father's side with a garland of honor on my head," he said with iron conviction. "And then I will be with you forever."

With that, he was gone.

Devorra fretted, alone with her thoughts, until she heard footsteps approach the tent. She rolled over and pretended to be asleep.

She heard Aloucca complaining to Bohannus about how someone had played a nasty trick on them, and how swiftly the boy had disappeared into the mass of tents under the night sky.

Devorra stifled a laugh. Then exhaustion overtook her, and she tumbled into a fitful sleep.

XVI

AT THE SABIS RIVER, BELGAE TERRITORY

BUILDING SO MASSIVE A FORT amid enemy territory was a serious challenge. The Roman deployment called for two legions, the Seventh and the Twenty-Fourth, to cross the Sabis River and set up a defensive perimeter. The baggage train, with many of the materials and tools needed for the construction, would then cross, accompanied by the escorting Twelfth. The redoubtable Tenth Legion would trail behind, able to either protect the front or to help the Ninth Legion, bringing up the rear of the army, as might be necessary.

The gods favored the Roman cause with fair weather—the early morning sun rose gently into a cloudless azure sky, with the temperature starting out cool but rising to a comfortable warmth as the sun went higher. The conditions were perfect for the long day of construction that lay before them.

Just before the cavalry units leading the Roman march reached the Sabis, Mamurra and his team moved forward to join them as they crossed the waterway. He wanted to arrive at the site of the huge new camp and check on the progress before Caesar came up with the first trailing legion, the Twenty-Fourth, to make sure that all was in order.

The advance party had done its work effectively. They had chosen a large area at the crown of a vast hill overlooking the Sabis, perfectly situated to take advantage of the river as a defensive barrier. Stakes had been precisely driven to lay out the lines of the camp, including the outer trench, the stockade walls, the long rows of streets, and planned tent placements. Latrines had been dug, with connections to the downstream portion of the river, and the outlines of what would become the defensive trench were in place.

Pleased with his review of the work, Mamurra noticed that most of the cavalry force had ridden off, heading to the north, leaving only a squadron behind to guard the work site.

"Giacomo, where is the cavalry?" he asked his aide, fretful that the bulk of their defensive screen had disappeared.

"They must have spotted some of the enemy and given chase," Giacomo said, squinting out at the verdant plain below the fort. "Should I send a messenger to the remaining squadron for an explanation?"

Despite his irritation, Mamurra did not want to interfere with the judgment of the cavalry commander. "No," he said, "there's plenty for us to attend to here."

PERCHED ATOP A TALL ELM TREE just inside the edge of the forest, Boduognatus watched with delight as the Roman cavalry wheeled and gave chase to the Belgae horsemen he had dispatched earlier in the morning. *They've taken the bait!* he thought. He wanted to draw off the Roman cavalry and keep them from scouting into the forest, where thousands of his warriors were lurking, weapons ready, waiting for the signal to attack. The mounted Belgae were instructed to lead the Romans as far as they could from the campsite, and then turn to attack. The outcome of this engagement was irrelevant to the larger battle—Boduognatus merely wanted the Roman cavalry sufficiently preoccupied to prevent them from discovering what was about to happen.

He was especially pleased that several Roman scouts had been captured in the forest itself. These men would not be able to report back to Caesar to sound the alarm, which would give the Belgae the advantage of complete surprise. His efforts to interrogate these unfortunate men had proved futile—every man died under torture without giving up any useful information about the Roman intentions.

From his elevated position, Boduognatus watched as the first legion emerged from the forest opposite the river and began crossing over to the campsite. He noted the flapping white battle standard at the head of the legion and recognized it at once. Caesar himself was on the field.

ACCOMPANIED BY LABIENUS and a sizeable cordon of staff officers, Caesar, clad as an ordinary legionary, albeit mounted on his marvelous snow-white stallion, splashed across the river at the scouted fording point. His group then pulled aside and watched as the troops of the Twenty-Fourth Legion slogged through the mild current of the Sabis.

As the men came across, engineers were waiting to lead the cohorts to their respective tasks. Given the scale of this major fortification, they would break from the normal routine of pitching a camp. As they reached their respective assignments, the men dropped their shields and armor and kept only their swords close at hand.

Caesar rode up the hill to join Mamurra and asked, "Where is the cavalry?"

Mamurra offered up Giacomo's earlier hypothesis and faced an icy stare from his commander.

"Their task was to protect the crossing, not go off chasing a group of barbarians," he snapped. "Labienus!"

The second-in-command prodded his horse to come alongside Caesar.

"Have we heard anything from those missing scouts?" the general asked.

The grim look on Labienus's face was all the answer Caesar needed. He motioned for Curio to come forward.

"The cavalry has gone off on a frolic, and several of our scouts have not been heard from. This is not a good sign," he said. Caesar pointed to the portion of the fortifications at which the men of Twenty-Fourth were taking up their shovels. "Ride down there and find the tribune Metellus. Tell him to have two cohorts stop their work and take up a defensive position." He pointed to the tree line. "Move them over there, where the forest is closest to the base of the hill."

Mamurra could see the wisdom of this move. If anyone was going to attack from the forest, surely they would choose to make their strike across the shortest distance to the Romans. But he dismissed the effort as a mere precaution. Other than the rabble that had shown themselves to the cavalry, there had been no indication that any menace was lurking.

BODUOGNATUS FELT HIS BLOOD run cold as he saw two cohorts of Roman soldiers, a thousand men in all, put down their tools, retrieve their shields and armor, and march directly toward him. At first, he thought they were going to come all the way to the forest, a terrifying prospect. He briefly considered giving the signal to launch the attack, but he held off. There was only one legion splayed out and working on the camp, and the Belgae plan called for the attack to be launched when at least half of the enemy army had arrived. He held out for just a few minutes, wanting to see what this detachment was up to.

He started breathing again when the Roman contingent pulled up about midway between the fort and the edge of the forest and organized themselves in a long line of crimson stretching over the plain, with the sun reflecting garishly off the polished metal of their helmets and shields.

Boduognatus relaxed a bit. With the vast horde he intended to send across the plain, this feeble group would be overrun in no time at all.

THE HEIGHT OF THE SUN indicated that it was about noon, and Mamurra contemplated calling for a break in the work to rest and nourish the laboring troops. The remaining eight cohorts of the Twenty-Fourth Legion were hard at their task, joined by the men of the Seventh Legion, who'd crossed the river at midmorning. But the leading elements of the Twelfth Legion, with the baggage train in tow, had made their way out of the forest and were just about midstream. He decided to wait until the baggage train was safely across and established behind the two legions already toiling on the fortifications.

Mamurra now understood why Caesar had dressed himself as a common legionary for the day. The general had spent the morning touring the work sites, stopping at each one to dismount and take up a shovel or an ax himself. This had a most salutary effect on the morale of the men, for they could see that their commander shared in their burdens and was not above dirtying his own hands.

The wagons and mules of the baggage train were beginning to accumulate on the fort side of the river now. Wanting to speed up the distribution of the supplies throughout the project, Mamurra motioned to Giacomo to bring up the horses. While this was being done, Mamurra saw that Caesar had remounted and his retinue was headed for the engineering command post.

"What could he want?" Mamurra asked Giacomo.

"Hard to say," Giacomo said with a grimace, "but he usually doesn't come up here if all he wants is to tell you he's happy."

BODUOGNATUS WAS PULLING on his beard with anxiety. Seeing the baggage train come into view so soon was a setback—he had been expecting it to be one of the last elements of the Roman army to arrive, at a time when nearly all the legionaries would be strung out and digging. Clearly, Caesar had decided to bring it up much sooner. He could see only three legion standards, meaning that nearly half the army was still well behind them, and had yet to cross the river. But the force assembled before him was making startling progress with the fortifications, and now that the baggage train was up, things would go even faster.

His whole plan was in jeopardy. If he waited for more of the enemy to become exposed, their defenses might become insurmountable to his planned assault. But if he attacked now, everything would turn on the ability of Gabinier and Pomorro to engage the back half of the Roman army and keep them from linking up with the forces in front of him.

He was mightily upset that the laggard Atuatuci reinforcements still had not made it to the scene. He would much rather have those warriors at his disposal, but if he waited any longer for them to arrive, it might all be for naught, because the Roman cavalry might return, or even worse, some Roman scouting party might spot the huge force of Belgae hiding in the woods. They had enjoyed phenomenal good fortune in keeping out of the Romans' sight thus far—but how long could that last?

Boduognatus had not clawed his way to the top of the Nervii tribe by being conservative or indecisive.

A group of archers was assembled in a small clearing cut near the base of his tree. They were all watching him.

He raised his arm and clenched his fist, then dropped it as if striking a blow.

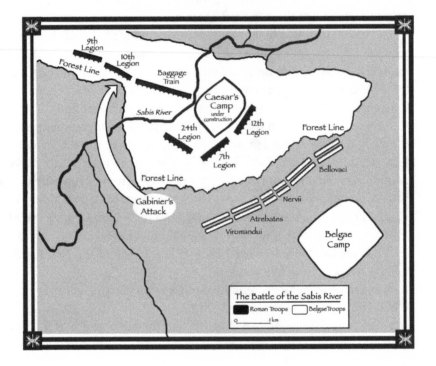

9th
Legion
Forest Line
10th
Legion
Baggage
Train
Caesar's
Camp
under
construction
Sabis River
24th
Legion
12th
Legion
Forest Line
7th
Legion
Bellovaci
Forest Line
Nervii
Gabinier's
Attack
Atrebates
Viromandui
Belgae
Camp

The Battle of the Sabis River
Roman Troops   Belgae Troops
0   1 km

GIACOMO'S INSTINCTS had been proven right: Caesar had come calling with a complaint.

"The men are thirsty," he barked at Mamurra. "We must improve the watering operation."

Mamurra looked out over the work site. Each cohort was accompanied by two water wagons. These were rotated: one would be kept near the men to provide refreshment, while the other made a run to the river to be refilled. But under the intense working conditions on a warm day like this, the men were draining the wagons faster than the wagoners could keep up, especially given the varying distances some of the wagons had to traverse to get to the river.

Mamurra considered the problem for a minute. Strictly speaking, this was a legion-level logistics issue, not an engineering matter. But Mamurra understood all too well that an unhappy Caesar was not a good Caesar, and it wouldn't be wise to try to blame someone else.

"Sir," he suggested, "we have additional water wagons with the baggage train. What if we station them between the men and the river? That way, each leg of the wagons' journey will be shorter, and we can replenish them faster."

Before Caesar could reply, one of the officers in his command group cried out, "Look! What is that?"

They all turned to stare into the sky, where the man was pointing.

A series of flaming arrows arced across the forest.

Before anyone could say anything, Caesar shouted, "We're under attack! Trumpeter! Sound the alarm! Ride up and down the ranks while you blow! And hurry!"

Before the trumpeter could lift his instrument to his lips, the air was pierced by the screaming howls of thousands of warriors charging out of the forest and toward the Romans. Mamurra blanched as the horde grew, shouting and running at top speed despite their burden of spears, swords, battle-axes, and maces. They poured out of the woods, seemingly without end. Against this backdrop of nightmarish noise, the trumpeter began wailing the notes of the alarm.

Terrified, Mamurra looked to the animated Caesar, who was furiously shouting orders to his staff.

"Labienus, go over to the Twelfth. Get them organized and make sure they hold the left flank." He pointed at Curio. "Curio, go to the Seventh in the center, and try to move them over toward the Twenty-Fourth. We need some kind of formation."

Mamurra could only watch helplessly as the legionaries reacted to the alarm. They dropped their tools and scrambled back to their arms, trying to at least get into helmets and pick up their shields as the roaring mass of maniacal barbarians drew closer and closer. The legion officers were desperately trying to get their units into fighting order, and most important of all, keep panic from setting in. In such circumstances, panic was a deadlier threat than the enemy warriors: if the soldiers lost their nerve and turned to run, all would be wiped out.

By now, the surging mass of warriors had smashed into the picket line formed by the two cohorts of the Twenty-Fourth Legion previously dispatched by Caesar. These men gamely held their ground, and in fact launched two volleys of their pila spears into the oncoming mob, cutting down hundreds of them.

It did not matter—the sheer mass of the unexpected onslaught was too much, and within moments the cohort commanders shouted orders to form squares because they were about to be enveloped by the far greater numbers of the Nervii.

Seeing the plight of his brave men who had failed to stem the tide of humanity now storming up the hill toward the still-jumbled Roman ranks, Caesar turned to yet another staff officer and said with unmistakable urgency, "Find Gordianus. He must bring up the Tenth with all the speed he can muster. Tell him if he does not hurry, he may not find an army left to rescue."

XVII

SEVERAL MILES BEHIND THE SABIS RIVER

THE INSECTS WERE MADDENING!

Gabinier, with Pomorro at his side, gritted his teeth and tried to ignore the vicious bites of the mosquitoes. The men of the Nervii had positioned themselves many yards distant from the Roman plank road, hiding in the dense woods and watching as the Romans marched past them en route to the main camp under construction. It was nerve-racking, but their orders were to hold their attack until they saw the flaming arrows.

It had been especially difficult to stand their ground when the long and slow-moving baggage train moved past. A veritable cornucopia of riches had passed by them—food, weapons, camp furnishings. Gabinier marveled at the vast array of materials the Romans brought with them on the campaign.

Gabinier was trying to concentrate on the mission at hand, but his mind would drift to Devorra. How he wished they'd had more time in the tent! He remembered how she felt against him, her scent, her lovely golden hair, and those emerald eyes, full of life and conviction that they would be together. He grasped his sword tightly, vowing yet again to win glory in this imminent battle and claim her as his reward.

Another legion was moving past them now. Pomorro nudged him and pointed at the standard at the head of troops. "It's the Tenth Legion," he whispered. "Caesar's favorite."

Gabinier did not care. Romans were Romans. He was ready to kill all of them.

A considerable portion of the legion was already past their hiding place when a cry arose from the front ranks and the marching Romans turned their heads skyward.

They saw two streaks of flame pass over them. But what did it mean?

"That's it!" Gabinier shouted, jumping from his crouch. "Attack! Attack!"

He started to move forward, but Pomorro grabbed his arm with a grip like an iron vise and held him back. "No!" he shouted. "You are in command! You must stay back to direct the men where they are most needed!"

Gabinier, totally inexperienced in such matters, reluctantly acquiesced, and stood by as the other warriors streamed past him, heading for the front.

Howling and shrieking their fierce battle cries, swarms of Nervii pushed through the thickets and brambles, wrangling the undergrowth, some tripping and falling, becoming entangled with each other, frantically trying to reach the cleared area on either side of the plank road. There was no thought of formation or order, just a bloodthirsty all-out rush to engage the hated Roman soldiers.

The long minutes spent in this struggle against nature's barrier were crucial, however. The experienced Roman officers began shouting orders. The troops marched in rows of eight across. They were trained in such a situation to divide down the middle and wheel about, four men on each side, facing the respective sides of the forest. Each marching legionary carried his armor and his weapons on a T-shaped bracket, and by the time the first of the Nervii emerged, most of the Romans were ready for them.

Still, the Nervii were brave and savage fighters. They made a furious charge into the outermost Roman line, straight into their shield wall, which was still somewhat ragged and not fully formed. The line, propped up by the rank immediately behind it, held fast, and the Romans made deadly work of cutting up the attackers with their short gladius swords. Worse, the two ranks behind the front line were able to toss their pila over the top of the engaged fighters with lethal effect. The ground grew slippery from the flowing blood of the injured men as the carnage raged on. The noise was nearly as terrible as the killing—men everywhere shouting to make themselves heard over the cries of the wounded and dying.

POMORRO, FAR MORE EXPERIENCED in combat than Gabinier, could see that things were not going well for the Nervii. He pointed to an area where the Romans had begun to force his warriors back. "Over there, Gabinier, our men are faltering. Go out and rally them!"

Needing no further encouragement, Gabinier ran toward the melee. He pointed his sword at several men who had turned their backs on the Romans to run away and shouted, "Face me, or face the Romans!" He managed to get them turned around and back into the fight.

He repeated this again and again, pressing his men to break down the Roman lines. He gathered other men who were lingering behind the front line of engagement and fed them into the gaps that were forming in the Nervii's own line.

Pomorro, watching all this, realized why the Tenth was Caesar's favorite. They matched the ferocity of the Nervii with an intensity of their own, and they had the advantage of better equipment and training. The battle had become a meat grinder, and the Romans seemed to be winning. But it did not matter. The main battle, he knew, was being fought elsewhere, by Boduognatus and the allied tribes. All they had to do here was keep the Romans bogged down, to prevent them from going to Caesar's aid at the fort.

And, he had to admit, Gabinier was proving himself to be an effective battlefield leader as well as a fearless fighter. The young man seemed to be everywhere, exhorting his men to keep pushing, keep fighting. Pomorro began to think that behind this fellow, the Nervii might just carry the day.

Unfortunately, Pomorro was not the only observer of Gabinier's heroics. The Roman officers were well schooled in the importance of identifying an enemy's leaders on the battlefield and trying to knock them out of the fight. One centurion had taken note of Gabinier's success in halting yet another group of Nervii about to flee the awful stabbing action of the Roman gladii and pushing them back into the engagement. The centurion picked up a pilum, took aim, and launched it.

Gabinier never saw the missile coming. It caught him in his upper body, plunging deep into his shoulder. Staggered by the blow, his face contorted in pain, he looked down at the spear in disbelief at the spurting blood. He staggered a few steps backward, then collapsed in a heap.

Some of the Nervii who saw him fall wailed over his loss. As awareness spread that their leader was down, more and more of the warriors disengaged and turned to run. Sensing that the tide had turned, the Romans released small groups of soldiers to give pursuit, refilling the gaps in the line from the back ranks. The fleeing men were cut down with merciless efficiency.

From the safety of his perch farther back in the woods, Pomorro could see that the battle was lost, but it still was not a rout. Many of the Nervii had not given up, and the Romans had taken significant casualties. He estimated that it might take some time for the Romans to finish mopping up the pockets of resistance still being mounted against them. He figured it should be sufficient to keep the Tenth from reaching the Sabis for hours.

It was time to report to Boduognatus. Pomorro knew his leader would be pleased, and not just because the Tenth Legion was out of the reckoning.

Pomorro could also report that Gabinier was dead.

XVIII

AT THE SABIS RIVER

U TTER CHAOS RAGED ACROSS THE BATTLEFIELD.
Most of the Roman soldiers barely managed to get to their
weapons and don their helmets, let alone attach the plumes or remove the
leather covers from their shields. Even worse, being out of formation, they
had not been able to launch the customary concentrated barrage of pila that
normally had the effect of disheartening an attacking force. Scores of Nervii
warriors pulsed up the hill and tore into the hastily formed Roman lines,
and many broke through, requiring attention from the disorganized members of the second rank.

From high upon the hill, Caesar and his team of officers, including
Mamurra, could see that the natives somehow had mounted an all-out
simultaneous attack from three different sides. The attacking swarm
carried no flags or stanchions, so it was impossible to tell which tribe was
which . . . not that it would have mattered, given the free-for-all raging
below them.

Mamurra felt overwhelmed by the sheer carnage—dying and wounded
men from both sides shrieking for help, the field cluttered with debris and
weapons, the cacophonous noise from shouts and cries and trumpets and
the clash of metal on metal . . . it was all too much.

Caesar shouted over the din, "The Twelfth is hard-pressed!" In a glance,
Mamurra saw that the men guarding the baggage train were crowded back
toward their standards, packed so tightly that their fighting ability was
hampered. Hortensius and Lentulus, the two officers Caesar had castigated
so crossly back at Vesontio, scrambled courageously, trying to get their
men into better order. Labienus, having been dispatched by Caesar to assist
them, had stiffened the men's resolve, but the enemy was breaking through.
Those warriors who did were already beginning to ravage the baggage train,

103

panicking the wagoners, who fled for their lives. Attacked from all sides, the soldiers' resolve was quickly beginning to crumble. Mamurra could see they needed help.

But alas, no reserve was available to feed into the fray.

With a wave, Caesar motioned for his retinue to follow him down the hill, toward the endangered Twelfth. Mamurra, a novice at combat, felt obliged to ride along, but his heart was pounding in his chest. Giacomo, still at his side, somehow produced Mamurra's battle helmet, with its white horsehair plume, and helped him to strap it on. He was not accustomed to the weight, and it strained his neck to keep his chin elevated.

As they rode down the hill, Giacomo shouted to Mamurra, "Keep your head up—the air is full of rocks and spears."

Merely seeing their general headed in their direction, the men gave a great shout and enlivened their resistance. As he neared their ranks, Caesar began calling out orders, sending one group of men toward a breakthrough, another group to restore order to the savages marauding through the baggage train, and yet others to bolster the front line.

But the situation remained grim. The enemy warriors continued to storm out of the woods and make their way across the plain toward the Roman lines, which hardly maintained any semblance of cohesion under the brunt of the assault. Slowly, steadily, the men of the Twelfth were being pushed back and were breaking into smaller pockets of scattered fighters. This meant doom in a situation where they were outnumbered.

Caesar instructed his staff officers to round up the stragglers and walking wounded lingering in the rear of the Roman lines and push them back into the clash. He jumped off his stallion and approached one of these men.

"Give me your sword and your shield," Caesar shouted at the hapless fellow. "If you will not fight for your life, I will!"

He ripped away the man's heavy wooden shield, painted in the imperial Roman red with a pattern of golden arrows emblazoned across the front. Drawing his own sword, Caesar shouted to the throng surrounding him, "Are you with me?" and headed into the heat of the combat.

Not knowing what else to do, Mamurra dismounted, picked up a sword, and waded in behind Caesar.

It was complete bedlam.

Caesar pushed men aside, determined to get to the front line. As he did so, some of the men blocked his path, pleading with him to return to the rear, but Caesar kept shouting, "These barbarians will not beat us. I will not allow it!"

At that moment, several of the Belgae broke through the Roman shield wall and started hacking their way toward Caesar's group, fighting with incredible determination. In moments, Caesar himself engaged one of the barbarians, a huge brute of a man, shaggy haired, made even more fearsome by having painted himself blue with dye distilled from wood, streaked from the sweat of his exertion. The swordplay was intense for a few moments, until Mamurra jumped to Caesar's aid and slew the man. Amazed by his own bold action, he stood there, dumbfounded, staring at the gore on his sword, blood dripping onto the ground. He had never killed anyone before.

Mamurra's sudden loss of concentration might have been fatal. A bare-chested warrior came up behind him, aiming to smash the engineer's head with a mace. Just as the man raised his arm for the blow, another Roman struck with his sword, amputating the man's arm in one swift cut. Blood spurted from the severed limb and drenched Mamurra, who whirled in blood-soaked disorientation. In a glance, he realized it was Curio who had saved him.

The other officers succeeded in pushing Caesar back from the fight, insisting that he must not expose himself or the whole cause would be lost.

Fortunately, Caesar's valiant charge had its desired effect: the legionaries, seeing their own general fighting in their ranks, were fortified in their courage and redoubled their efforts, stabilizing the line and holding out doggedly against the fierce Belgae.

THE EXTREME PHYSICAL EXERTION took a toll on Caesar. He staggered a bit, and slumped onto his knees and began to wobble, as if he were fighting for consciousness. Curio, only a short distance away, was ever alert for this potential catastrophe. His horse was nearby. He dashed to it, opened his saddlebag, and withdrew a vial of the precious elixir. Running to Caesar's side, he poured the fluid down the general's throat. Then, seeing all the flying projectiles in the air, Curio hoisted a shield lying nearby and stood over Caesar to protect him. Curio prayed with all his might for the medicine to take effect.

Labienus, seeing Caesar on the ground, hurried over. "Is he wounded?" he shouted over the din, knowing that if the ranks found out their general was down, their tenuous grasp on the men's discipline would collapse.

"No," Curio shouted back, "He was hit in the helmet by a rock. He's just stunned."

Labienus also picked up a discarded shield and took up a stance opposite Curio, forming a dome to protect their leader.

Finally, Caesar perked up and regained his senses. "What happened?" he gasped.

Curio repeated the "hit by a rock" story as the general pulled himself back to his feet and took stock of the situation, which was little changed in the minutes he had been out of commission.

A soldier had fetched Caesar's horse, and Curio helped him remount. Caesar's attention was now needed in the center, as the Seventh was beginning to falter and might be on the verge of panic. If the center collapsed, it would be the end of all of them. He kicked the stallion in the ribs and galloped toward the weakening line.

❧

MAMURRA, MEANWHILE, his life saved by Curio, had wiped off the blood from the slain Nervii warrior and remounted his horse, intending to rejoin the command group.

By the time Mamurra made it to the Seventh, Caesar had succeeded in halting the flow of men who had begun to fall back from the onslaught and was getting them back into line. Better yet, Caesar had extended the line toward the Twelfth on the left, so that the Romans might hold a continuous front against the enemy.

Mamurra found Caesar pointing at him, shouting, "Go to the Twenty-Fourth, on the right, and tell them I want them to wheel back toward us and form a square, so that we can fight back to back!"

Mamurra was relieved to be relaying orders rather than facing another plunge into the actual combat, which raged hotter than ever. The legionaries, for all their discipline and training, were growing fatigued, and no matter how many of the barbarians they chopped down, more replacements came forward.

The officers of the Twenty-Fourth, holding the right side of the Roman position, were easy to locate, having established themselves with their standards and their flags in a central location behind their line. And they had found the time to attach their bristled horsehair crests to their helmets.

Mamurra pulled up his horse before the tribune Metellus and offered the customary salute, striking his breast with his fist.

"Greetings, Mamurra!" Metellus shouted with a grin. "This is quite the kettle of fish, isn't it?"

Mamurra was shocked that the commander of the Twenty-Fourth could be so cheerful while facing such danger. "We are hard-pressed on all sides," Mamurra shouted back, wheezing a bit from the dust in the air. "Caesar wants you to wheel back toward the Seventh and form a square. He says we must fight back to back!"

Metellus rolled his eyes under the white plume of his brass helmet. "Has he lost his mind?"

Mamurra was confused. "What do you mean?"

The tribune pointed at the conflict raging all about them. "How does he expect us to disengage sufficiently to execute a maneuver like that?"

Mamurra, in the army long enough to develop his own skill at sharp retorts, said, "I'll go back and tell him you won't do what he wants." And he made a show of hitching up the reins to turn his animal.

Metellus blanched. "No, no!" he yelled. "We shall follow orders."

While keeping an eye posted for any stones or javelins that might be thrown at him, Mamurra watched as the tribune sent out his staff officers to the different units. When Metellus was satisfied that the order to wheel had been sufficiently conveyed to the ranks, he fished a long whistle out of his tunic and held it to his lips.

The shrill blast from the whistle was loud enough to be heard by all the men, who followed their training and began to ease backward, leaving piles of enemies, and too many Romans as well, dead in their wake. At a second blast of the whistle, the line formed a long arc, rotating back toward the center of the Roman front and then falling in behind the Seventh, leaving the two legions standing back-to-back.

This maneuver would have been impressive enough on a practice field, but its execution in the heat of combat, with the enemy pressing against the line, was a thing of beauty, Mamurra thought. And then an awful realization struck him: forming squares was usually the last resort of a Roman commander—they would win or die from this formation.

The Belgae, though reeling from the heavy losses they had suffered, sensed the significance of this desperate new formation and pulled back to organize themselves for a fresh assault on the new Roman position.

During this lull in the fighting, the Roman officers scurried about, dressing their lines, gathering up as many of the deadly pila as they could find and distributing them to the troops. On Caesar's own order, an effort was made to distribute water to refresh the men. Throughout all of this, Caesar roamed among the legions, exhorting his soldiers to brace for the next assault.

It was not long in coming. Having gotten their own scattered forces into some semblance of order, the tribal leaders gave a great shout and stormed back toward the Roman lines. This time, however, they were met with a blizzard of the long, narrow pila, with their deadly sharp points, thrown by the legionaries to bring down hundreds of the Belgae before they could get within striking distance of the Roman shields.

On they came, stepping in blood over their dying comrades, determined to break the Roman shield wall once and for all.

"Their courage is remarkable," Caesar muttered begrudgingly to Curio.

The adjutant was fatalistic. "You have done all that you can," he said to Caesar. "It's in the hands of the gods."

Caesar, who had been scanning the distant horizon, became animated. "Look there!" he exclaimed, pointing across the river. "The gods have given us their answer. It's the Tenth!"

And there they were, coming up double-time, dashing out of the woods and splashing across the river, trumpets blaring, ramming into what was now the rear of the Belgae forces.

Thousands of Roman soldiers, although winded from their urgent dash to the Sabis, continued to stream onto the battlefield. Caesar and Mamurra watched with elation as Gordianus—good old dependable Gordianus—skillfully fed them into the battle, hacking at the backsides of the Belgae warriors.

This steady stream of Romans could not be the Tenth Legion alone. At the appearance of a new set of standards, Caesar became exultant. "Curio! It's the Ninth!"

Somehow, Gordianus had gotten the Ninth Legion to catch up with the Tenth so that now *two* Roman legions had joined the fight.

Within minutes, panic set in among the Belgae, and they began to flee. The pursuing Romans relentlessly cut them down, like a scythe slicing through wheat.

And against all odds, Caesar had once again turned an imminent disaster into a ruthless slaughter.

XIX

At the Sabis River

HORRIFIED, BODUOGNATUS WATCHED HELPLESSLY from the treetop as his men fell like rain on the grassy plain before him. The Belgae warriors were being methodically exterminated.

"Stop running!" he screamed, as if it might make a difference. "Turn around and fight them!"

It was futile. The panicked Belgae were running for their lives, which, of course, was the worst thing they could possibly do.

Damn the Atuatuci! If only they had gotten here! A counterattack now would turn the tide.

Boduognatus clambered down the tree, skinning himself on the rough bark in his haste. Upon reaching the forest floor, he began to make for the battlefield, but was restrained by his bodyguards, who saw the folly of trying to intervene in the lost cause.

"It's a rout," one of them said. "To go out there now is death."

He sagged against them. "All is lost," he wailed. "Let me die with honor."

But the guards would not relent. "We must go back to the camp and organize a defense," one of them said. "If we must die, let us do it defending our families."

They heard a thrashing in the woods behind them. Fearful that the Romans had somehow gotten behind them, they all drew their swords, only to heave a sigh of relief when Pomorro came into view.

Seeing the despair on their faces, Pomorro knew things had gone badly.

Boduognatus, enraged, charged at Pomorro, screaming, "Why didn't you keep the rear guard off the field?"

But Pomorro was a veteran fighter himself, and he easily parried his leader's thrust. Before things could escalate, bodyguards separated the two men.

"We need every man available to defend the camp!" one of them shouted at the two antagonists. "We must not fight among ourselves!"

"What has happened?" Pomorro demanded.

"We were on the verge of victory," Boduognatus snarled. "We had them! The Romans had formed a square to fight to the death, but the Tenth Legion arrived on the field, and our men panicked. All is lost."

Pomorro stared in disbelief. "It cannot be! We attacked the Roman column when we saw the arrows. We caught them completely unawares. They lost many men! When I left to bring you a report, we had them fighting for their lives."

"Perhaps they grew wings and flew here," Boduognatus spat. "You failed in your mission."

Stung by this criticism, Pomorro lunged at Boduognatus, but was thwarted again by the other men.

"It was not a complete failure," he snarled under his breath. "Gabinier is dead."

Boduognatus reflected on this news. "It matters not. The Romans will never allow the Nervii alliance with the Bellovaci to stand."

Before Pomorro could respond, yet another bodyguard interjected, "If we don't get back to the camp, there won't be any Nervii left to make an alliance!"

The man was right. Without another word, Boduognatus turned away and headed toward the Nervii encampment.

CURIO FOLLOWED CAESAR to the top of hill where the Roman camp was being built, to get a better view of the field. The battered Twelfth, Twenty-Fourth, and Seventh Legions had not been released to take up the chase of the fleeing Belgae, even though the enemy warriors who had come so close to victory had now turned tail and fled. Caesar wanted the bloodied legions consolidated into a single fighting force and retrenched into an impregnable defensive position in case things should turn against the Romans again.

As they reached the crest of the hill, it became obvious that this precaution was needless. The carnage of Belgae warriors strewn about the landscape was stunning.

The fleeing survivors reached the edges of the forest and plunged into the vast wilderness, frantically seeking cover and escape. Caesar quickly realized, and Curio concurred, that it was dangerous to give pursuit in that labyrinthine chaparral. Unit cohesion could not be maintained, and there was no way of knowing how many more Belgae might be lurking behind the glade. Worse, the sun was past its high point in the sky, and daylight would begin to dwindle soon.

"Sound the recall," he said to the trumpeter. "No need to chase those heathens like rabbits through the woods. We will finish the fort before they can get organized for another attack."

Caesar then turned to Curio. "Find the cavalry commander and have him report to me," he said grimly. "I should like an explanation of why he left us alone on the field when there was such a significant force hidden in the forest waiting to strike."

◦◦◦

AS THE AFTERNOON wore on at the Nervii encampment, wailing and cries of denial rent the air as word of the disaster at the Sabis permeated the vast makeshift settlement. Even worse, with the onset of darkness, the scale of destruction of the Nervii force became apparent as the stream of stragglers from the battlefield slowed to a trickle. Many thousands of warriors had left the camp that morning; only a fraction returned.

Boduognatus sat dazed before a fire, unable to absorb the magnitude of the catastrophe. It fell to Pomorro to take charge and try to mount a defense. He roused the exhausted returned fighters from their stupor and organized a line around the camp facing the only directions from which the Romans might approach. With the most brutal of the surviving warriors, he pressed every able-bodied person he could find, women and children included, into digging a deep perimeter ditch. Saplings were cut and formed into sharpened spikes that were then planted into the floor of the ditch. Pomorro lied to weeping relatives throughout the camp about the chances that their loved ones might have survived. He needed their labor.

As he went about the ugly business of pressing camp residents into service, he came upon the tent in which Devorra and Aloucca were lodged.

When she caught sight of Pomorro, Devorra ran to him, pleading, "Oh, Pomorro, where is Gabinier?"

Pomorro's stony face told her all she needed to know. She fell to the ground, wailing and pounding the grass. "No! No! No! Not Gabinier!"

It was a pitiful scene. Aloucca gave Pomorro a hateful glare but did not dare speak. She dropped to her knees and tried to console her mistress.

111

Pomorro reached down, grabbed Aloucca by the arm, and jerked her to her feet.

"Every able-bodied person is needed at the barrier," he growled. "Especially slaves."

Aloucca shrieked as Pomorro pushed her frail body toward the men assisting him. Devorra, prostrate on the ground, tried to get to her feet. "I must go with you," she said dully, clearly in shock.

"You are the daughter of Boduognatus," Pomorro snapped. "You will remain here."

He turned to one of the thugs in his entourage. "Stay here with her. Do not let her out of your sight."

With that, prodding along a throng of Nervii civilians at the point of his sword, Pomorro returned to the line, determined to keep the work going all night in the hope that his fortifications might be ready before the Romans showed up.

BUT THE ROMANS were not coming, at least not this night.

The huge construction site was a frenzy of torchlit activity. Caesar, with Mamurra at his side, seemed to be everywhere, exhorting the men to finish their encampment before the natives could come charging out of the woods again. The daunting task was made more difficult by the need to deal with the wounded and dead soldiers from the battle itself. Casualties in the Twenty-Fourth Legion, which included the total loss of the two cohorts dispatched to provide a screen for the workers, were so severe that Caesar was forced to disband what was left of the Twenty-Fourth and assign the survivors to replace the losses in the Twelfth and the Seventh Legions. The standards and flags of the Twenty-Fourth were recovered and safely stored, with an eye to a new recruiting effort once the current campaign was concluded.

The unfortunate commander of the Roman cavalry, a lanky, sandy-haired fellow named Flavius, returned to the campsite expecting to be commended for routing the Belgae cavalry. Instead, he was forced to endure a tongue- lashing by an angry Caesar, who was furious for being left in the dark while the enemy assembled an enormous attack force right under his nose, without detection. Things might have gone badly for poor Flavius, but the general was not going to make a change under these conditions.

Deep into the night, they received encouraging reports from freshly dispatched scouting teams. The Belgae, badly mauled, had disintegrated into small bands roaming about, foraging for food and water. The scouting teams were picking them off, group by group. There was no chance that this rabble could mount an organized attack anytime soon.

Thus reassured, Caesar allowed Mamurra to call a halt to the work. The exhausted legionaries fell to the ground where they stood and lapsed into a deep slumber, happy to have survived the battle, knowing it had been a very close thing indeed.

⟊⟊⟊

STARING INTO THE FADING orange embers of the campfire, all Boduognatus could see were ashes—ashes of his shattered dream for a union of the Belgae tribes under his leadership, ashes of the Nervii tribe decimated by the hated Romans, ashes of all the families facing starvation and ruin without their men to provide for them. He had gambled it all on the attack against Caesar's army . . . and lost. Now they faced nothing but slavery or death. He preferred the latter.

Over and over, Boduognatus cursed the Atuatuci tribe. He would have had a reserve to feed into the battle, to stem the panic, to halt the rout. He could have counterattacked, just as the Roman rear guard had counterattacked. The outcome would have been completely different! *If only, if only, if only . . .*

He was vaguely aware that he had been sitting there for hours, only because of the growls rumbling from his empty stomach. And then, sensing that someone was watching him, he looked up and scowled, seeing that it was his daughter.

Her demeanor was calm, her skin pallid. Those jade eyes, normally buoyant with the joy of life, were dull and listless, puffy from hours of weeping. Devorra seemed lethargic, as if the mere act of walking to his headquarters had exhausted her.

"What do you want?" he asked irritably, her mere presence a bother.

Devorra steeled herself with a deep breath. "Gabinier is dead, isn't he?"

Boduognatus looked at her with disgust. "Many of the Nervii are dead."

"You sent him to his death," she said flatly.

Normally, Boduognatus would have erupted in rage at such a brazen accusation, but he sighed and returned his sight to the barely kindled fire. There was no point to engaging her in this talk.

"You knew that I cared for him, and you gave him a most dangerous assignment, expecting that he would not survive."

Boduognatus felt the burning sensation of bile rising inside him as his anger overcame the shock over the day's events that had rendered him so listless. Then he realized something: *The slave must have told her she was my spy. How else could she know that I knew about Gabinier? That nettlesome old woman will die in the morning . . . slowly.*

He shrugged. "Go away," he warned her. "Do not suppose that you can insult me like this just because you are my daughter."

But she did not move. "Do you know whether Maccheor survived the battle?"

Boduognatus could not repress a small laugh. "I have no idea what became of the Bellovaci," he snorted. "But if he did, I will see you married to him, just as you promised."

For the first time in the conversation, color rose in Devorra's cheeks. "I renounce you as my father," she said defiantly. "I will never marry that disgusting boy."

With the lithe quickness of a cat, Boduognatus leaped to his feet and pounced on her, striking her a vicious blow that knocked her onto the ground. In an instant, he was atop her, his hands around her neck, squeezing the life out of her.

Devorra fought for air and clawed at her father with her nails, but he was far too strong. Terrified by the sensation of suffocation, she felt herself about to lose consciousness, knowing that if she did, she would never awaken.

In the fog of her dulled awareness, she heard someone call out sharply, "Boduognatus, stop!"

A second later, she felt the vise around her neck release. Coughing and gasping, she tried to focus on her rescuer.

Pomorro had pulled her father away from her and shoved him to the other side of the fire.

"I should have killed you in the forest," Boduognatus roared, lunging for his sword.

"Stop, you fool," Pomorro cried. "The Atuatuci have finally arrived!"

In an instant, Boduognatus forgot about Devorra, who was rolling about and trying to catch her breath, her neck badly bruised from her father's vicious assault. "What?" he bellowed.

"Yes," Pomorro replied. "They finally arrived. The leading elements of their tribe are at the trench. They are asking for you."

Boduognatus struggled to calm himself. "Well, perhaps there is hope for our cause after all." He sneered wickedly, turning to follow Pomorro to the front lines. But he stopped and grabbed Pomorro by the arm. "Have someone tie her to a tree. Release her for nothing. She can piss and shit herself where she stands, for all I care."

And then he addressed his daughter in a frightful tone: "I'll deal with you later. After I've boiled your slave woman."

XX

AT THE ROMAN CAMP

T HOROUGHLY EXHAUSTED, Caesar lay sprawled on the cot in his command tent, the first one erected as the fort was being constructed. He had been too tired to even remove his own boots, that task falling to his faithful valet. The valet had also peeled off Caesar's sweat-soaked common tunic and wrapped his owner in a linen robe.

Curio watched attentively as the slave applied cool, damp compresses to Caesar's forehead. Only Curio knew what had really transpired on the battlefield. It was an ominous sign—Caesar had never experienced a spell while a battle was raging. Curio knew they were incredibly fortunate that no one had noticed, and he had been able to spread the story that Caesar had merely been stunned by a blow to the head and was fully recovered. Had not the men seen the general bring them through to victory with their own eyes? Curio alone knew how close they had come to total disaster, and he worried that Caesar's reserves had been depleted in recovering from the seizure.

Curio agonized over how much longer the potion could keep working. Vatteus had told him of the warning from the old apothecary who had brewed it for him. "Use it sparingly," the ancient fellow had brayed. "Potent elixirs should not be casually dispensed. The body will become accustomed to it, and its effectiveness will wane."

What will I do if the serum fails us? What if he is overcome when I am not there?

Caesar let out a low moan, interrupting Curio's reverie.

Curio dismissed the slave and drew near Caesar's cot. "Is there anything I can get for you?" he asked gently.

With the last bits of his strength, Caesar asked with closed eyes, "I had a seizure during the battle, didn't I?"

Curio knew there was no point in lying. "Yes, but no one noticed; I can assure you of that. I was able to convince them that I saw a rock hit your helmet."

The faintest hint of a smile passed over Caesar's lips. "Poor Rio," he whispered. "Still covering for me, after all these years."

"You weren't out for long. It had no impact on the battle."

But Caesar had already lapsed into heavy slumber.

Curio placed a blanket over his commander and left for his own tent, wanting to put down on parchment a detailed account of the battle. Despite his own near-exhaustion, he needed to create the record while it was still fresh in his mind. This would facilitate his treatment of the episode in the next chapter of Caesar's book about the campaign. He knew, however, that there could never be a mention of what might have happened that day had the potion failed to revive the putative author.

BY NOON ON THE DAY following the battle, the Roman camp was completely enclosed by the stockade wall and protected by the deep defensive trench and its accompanying earthen barrier. The army turned its attention to the setup within the walls, pitching their tents and establishing the necessities of daily life.

Caesar, recovered and in full throat, invited Mamurra to join him and Curio in his command tent, by now fully outfitted with his prized possessions.

"Your engineers have outdone themselves," Caesar said, relaxing on the ornate couch that somehow had survived the rampage of the enemy through the baggage train. He poured himself a cup of deep burgundy wine and offered the porcelain jug to Curio. "Who could have imagined that such a fortress as this could be built in only two days? And with an all-out battle interrupting the construction? Amazing!"

Mamurra remained silent as Curio filled his cup. Then, seeking to be modest, he said, "All credit belongs to the staff."

"Nonsense," Caesar said lightly. "There will be times when you must take the blame for the failure of others. Do not deny yourself the opportunity to take credit on those rare occasions when you have the chance to do so."

Mamurra smiled at this insight, then replied, "The key to it all is organization and preparation." After reflecting a bit further, he added, "The actual time spent in construction can be greatly reduced if we are given enough men and have a well-organized advance plan."

Caesar seemed lost in thought. Mamurra and Curio waited patiently.

Finally, Caesar said, "Do you suppose such principles of rapid construction could be applied to a very large and daunting engineering challenge?"

Mamurra felt a deep sense of foreboding. He glanced at Curio, but if the adjutant had any clue what Caesar was thinking, he gave no sign of it. Mamurra's desire for Caesar's approval was overpowering. "Yes, of course. Given enough time to prepare."

Caesar swirled the wine in his cup and took another drink. "Perhaps when we are done with this campaign, we will explore an idea I have."

Curio, dreading where this might be going, asked, "Why not tell us now?"

Caesar did not smile. "I do not want your attention distracted from the campaign at hand." Then, turning to Curio while setting his cup on an end table of carved ivory, he asked, "Is there any news from the scouts?"

"We have a report from one scouting team, sir. They believe they have located the main camp of the Nervii. It's less than a day's march away."

Caesar sat up, his interest piqued. "They must be making haste for a withdrawal into their wilderness."

"Not so, sir. While the ranks of the Nervii themselves were badly depleted yesterday, they seem to have been reinforced overnight by a sizeable tribe arriving from the east."

Greatly agitated, Caesar pounded his fist on the table. "Curse these barbarians!" he exclaimed. "Will we ever run through all their tribes?"

"One of our local guides told us that the tribe is the Atuatuci," Curio added. "They are still coming up—apparently they are such a horde that they cannot move quickly."

Caesar rubbed his tired eyes. "Do the scouts think they are preparing to move against us?"

"Rather the opposite, sir. They are entrenching their position. They are alongside a stream, so they have plentiful water, and the Atuatuci are said to have substantial provisions with them."

Caesar studied a spot on the tent ceiling for a number of long moments, then said, "Thank you for this most interesting news. Dispatch more scouts, try to get an estimate of their numbers, and"—he glanced at Mamurra—"take along a staff engineer. I want an assessment of their fortifications."

He reflected for a moment, then asked, "Have we a count of the captives?"

The corners of Curio's mouth turned down. "Not what we might have hoped. The Tenth's blood was up when they counterattacked. They killed more Nervii than they took as prisoners."

Caesar sighed. "And all men, too. No women for the blocks unless we get into their camp."

Curio saluted and rose to leave.

"One other thing," Caesar said. "Tell Flavius to position the cavalry between their camp and ourselves. And this time, he must not be drawn off by a lure."

The adjutant saluted again and left.

Mamurra waited silently while Caesar contemplated this intelligence. "Well, Mamurra," he said finally, "What do you recommend?"

Mamurra hated being put on the spot about non-engineering matters, but there was no escaping the question. He reflected for a few moments, then said deliberately, "Sir, the army suffered significant casualties yesterday, notwithstanding your courageous leadership on the field. Many of the men have minor wounds, and they are exhausted by their efforts over the last two days. The Tenth, especially, needs rest after that mad dash they made to reach the battlefield at the critical moment. The newly reconstituted legions need time to train and integrate their new members."

Caesar listened patiently to this recital. "So, you would negotiate, and stall for time?" he asked.

"You told me when you hired me that I should always be honest with you," Mamurra said, with the smallest of grins. "Yes, we need time to recuperate and regroup."

Caesar sat back onto the cushions again and took up his cup. "Then that," he said between sips, "is what we shall do."

HAVING DISPATCHED THE TASKS given him by Caesar, Curio settled into his own tent. He stretched out on the cot and allowed the waves of fatigue from the frenetic events of the past two days to wash over him. He had kept all the anxiety, all the fear, all the stress tightly pushed into the back of his mind throughout the ordeal. Now, with a bit of quiet, he only could think about how narrowly they had escaped with their skins, and how, yet again, the Tenth had saved them all. *The goddess Fortuna favors Caesar!* Curio thought. *He has more lives than two cats!*

There was a rustling at the flap to his tent, and dread bolted through his weary mind, expecting word that yet some new assignment had been issued by the general.

Instead, a slave girl entered, carrying a platter with food. In a flash, he recognized her.

"Molena," he said softly, turning his head slightly to block her view of his cheek, as was his habit.

The woman did not meet his eyes. She placed the platter on Curio's desk and turned to go.

"Stop." It was one of the first Germanic words he had learned.

She turned to face him, trembling once again.

"Will I ever see you when you are not afraid?" he asked. It was a rhetorical question; his mastery of the Germanic tongue was not sufficiently advanced. She in turn could not comprehend his Latin.

He motioned with his hand for her to take a seat on the stool before his desk.

Fear mounted in her smoldering black eyes as she obeyed. He sat up on the cot and stared at the camp fare she had brought him. A pottery bowl of spelt mush, a thin slab of roasted beef, a crust of stale bread, and a pile of green grapes, still on the vine.

Dreadful, he thought, contemplating the food. A faint odor of rosemary from the spelt wafted across the tent, as if the herb might salvage the dish. He cast his gaze upon Molena. She was even more beautiful than he'd remembered. It occurred to him that Caesar had spotted her, chained in the coffle, surrounded by so many other slaves. *Caesar certainly has a keen eye for beauty.*

He pulled several grapes from their stem and offered them to her. The girl turned her head, overcome by fear.

"Well, I can see we will need to be better acquainted before you can relax," he said. She continued to look away.

It occurred to him that if he was going to keep her around, there was a risk that Caesar might remember her and demand to know why Curio had not dispatched the girl, as he had been ordered to do, and as he had done with others who had failed to arouse the general.

"Tomorrow," he said with a smile, "we will have you visit the barber. We shall see what you look like with red hair."

She gave no sign that she had any idea what he was talking about.

He searched his limited vocabulary for something he could say in her own tongue. He only had one word that might fit the situation.

"Go."

He felt a tinge of regret as relief passed over her face, and she scrambled to get out of the tent before he could change his mind.

Disappointed, he resolved to have his Germanic tutor step up the pace of his instruction in the language. And then he had another idea. He took up a stylus and began to write an order.

XXI

AT THE CAMP OF THE NERVII AND THE ATUATUCI

DEVORRA HAD SUFFERED through a miserable night, tightly bound to a large walnut tree some distance from Boduognatus's tent. Her neck was throbbing from the near strangulation. The insects had feasted on her, adding to her torment and leaving her covered in red bites. As her father had predicted, she had been unable to hold her own bodily functions through the chilly night. She had urinated in place, the warm stream running down her legs and soaking her undergarments, adding to her mortification. Even worse, the rough rope pressing her against the tree cut into her circulation, and she strained to fight the numbness that crept in. Throughout the night, tears gushed like rivulets of rain down her cheeks. She began to wish Pomorro had not prevented her father from killing her.

Oddly enough, the callous brute who'd tied her so effectively decided that his work was so well done that he need not remain to stand guard. He slipped away and had not been back.

Just before dawn, Devorra heard footsteps behind her. She braced herself, expecting that either the guard was returning or, even worse, it was her father. Squeezing her eyes shut, she asked the gods to deliver her.

"Devorra, my mistress, what have they done to you?"

She opened her eyes and was overjoyed to see Aloucca, caked with dirt and sweat from her hours of labor on the defenses. She was carrying a jug of water and some hard bread.

Aloucca herself began to cry, but Devorra shushed her, saying, "You must be quiet, Aloucca. They will hear you!"

The slave woman lifted the clay jug to Devorra's parched lips and tipped it gently, not allowing the water to choke the girl as she drank greedily. And then she tore off bits of the bread and fed them to Devorra, not unlike the way she had fed her as a young child.

"Why have they done this?" Aloucca whispered. "I heard that your own father ordered it."

The mention of her father struck a new fear into Devorra's breast. "You must hide," Devorra said urgently. "My father has threatened to kill you."

Terror spread across the old woman's face. "But why?"

"I told him I wouldn't marry Maccheor," she said. Not wanting her maid to know everything, she did not delve into the spying revelation. She merely added, "I think he blames you for some reason."

Aloucca's expression told Devorra she had judged it correctly. "Go and hide among your friends," she said. "Don't let them find you."

Aloucca did not need to be told. "Shall I untie you?"

Devorra desperately wanted out of this situation, but she was fearful what might happen when her father heard she had escaped. He would undoubtedly mount an intensive search for Aloucca and her, and it would go very badly if they were found out. She reckoned that despite his threats, he would not hurt her while there was still a chance he could marry her off.

"Not now," she decided. "You must hide. If I'm still here tomorrow night, sneak back and see me again, if there is no guard."

Aloucca stroked Devorra's cheek with her cracked, leathery hand, then stole away into the night.

As she watched Aloucca disappear into the trees, Devorra was saddened by the thought that her lifelong companion, this woman who had raised her, with whom she had shared everything, and who had now tried to bring her comfort in her suffering, was also the person who had betrayed her to her father. *How can I ever trust her again?*

BODUOGNATUS SPENT THE NIGHT in a very different manner, meeting with the various chieftains of the Atuatuci. They had already heard about the disastrous battle, and many were dubious about staying with the Belgae cause. They made it clear: if the Romans offered to talk, they would listen to the proposition. Boduognatus had no choice but to agree.

Boduognatus started back to his own tent, but he decided to visit his daughter first, with Pomorro at his side.

Seeing the two men approach, Devorra's fear gripped her tighter than the awful bonds fixing her to the tree.

"Well, pretty one," Boduognatus said with a smirk, "have you learned your lesson?"

"How can you do this to me?" Devorra cried. "I am your daughter!"

Boduognatus was stern. "You are my disobedient daughter. Do you want another night like that, under the stars?"

Devorra summoned up her last reserves of courage. "No, please, I beg you. Don't do this."

Her father laughed. "Maybe tonight I'll have them strip you naked and smear you with honey, to make you even more attractive to the bugs. The fellows would enjoy doing that, don't you think?"

This was too much. "No, please, I'll obey. I'll do anything you want. Please let me go, Father."

"Will you marry Maccheor, and spread your legs for him whenever he desires?"

Devorra's stomach lurched. If she could not have Gabinier, did it matter what happened to her? Perhaps not, but if she harbored any real chance at escape, it would certainly not come to fruition if she remained tied to this tree. She would need resources, and she would need strength. She had only one choice. She stood up straight and steeled her resolve, looking straight into her father's eyes. "Yes, Father. I'll do anything. Please don't leave me out here again."

Boduognatus came closer to her. He could see that her neck still bore marks from their previous encounter. He pulled out a dagger and pressed the tip against the edge of her bodice. He traced a line across her firm breast. "Cross me again and I'll cut them off. Do you understand me?"

"Yes, father," Devorra whispered. "I'll do whatever you say."

Boduognatus moved the dagger to cut her bonds.

Later that afternoon, the Nervii leader was conferring again with several Atuatuci when word arrived that an emissary of the Romans had approached under a white flag. The emissary turned out to be a captured Bellovaci named Garos, sent by Caesar with a proposition. Pomorro escorted him to Boduognatus's tent.

"Did you see Caesar himself?" Boduognatus asked the man, who clearly was relieved to be out of Roman custody and back among his allies.

Garos nodded. "Caesar told me he wishes to celebrate his great victory with a show of mercy."

This brought a loud murmur of skepticism from the gathered men in Boduognatus's tent.

"And how does mighty Caesar propose to do that?" Boduognatus asked.

"He will send a Roman officer to deliver his offer, but Boduognatus must first send over a child of his to serve as hostage for the safety of the Roman messenger. If you harm the messenger, the hostage will be killed."

Several of the men shifted uncomfortably. This was serious business.

"How do we know he will release the hostage unharmed if we do not accept his offer?" one of the Atuatuci asked.

Pomorro spoke up. "It is well known that Caesar has never harmed a hostage unless provoked by the betrayal or perfidy of the other side."

Several of the Atuatuci erupted in conversation about what to do, but Boduognatus held up his hand for silence.

"I have a daughter," he said to the group. "To show my good faith to all of you, I will send her to Caesar to be his hostage."

"This is a great sacrifice," said another of the Atuatuci.

"Peace requires great sacrifices," Boduognatus said, with all the pomposity he could muster.

Pomorro, witnessing this little charade, struggled to keep a straight face.

❦

SEVERAL HOURS LATER, freshly bathed and clad in a gown carefully draped to cover her bites and bruises, Devorra found herself in a wagon with Aloucca at her side, traveling toward the Roman lines. Her mind was still reeling at the swiftness with which her circumstances had changed so dramatically. The instructions she received from her father were fresh in her mind.

"If they ask you anything, pretend you don't understand. And if they keep pressing, tell them nothing that can help them," he'd ordered her.

"The Romans killed Gabinier," she replied to her father. "I hate them as much as you do."

Boduognatus was so pleased with this turn of events that he even granted Devorra's plea that Aloucca be allowed to travel with her.

After they'd traveled a short distance from the camp, the wagon was intercepted by the Roman cavalry. Devorra was accustomed to seeing motley groups of mounted warriors, each with their own gear and whatever clothing they might have on. The Romans looked completely different. See-ing these metal-helmeted men in matching scarlet tunics covered by chain-mail armor and all equipped with the same fearsome swords and spears, Devorra immediately recognized the superior organization of the Nervii's adversary—and the true danger of her precarious situation.

A long, lean rider came riding up. Judging from the ornamentation of his gleaming helmet and body armor, he was an officer. At his side was an interpreter.

"The tribune Flavius, on behalf of his commander, the pro-consul Gaius Julius Caesar, offers his greetings to you, madam," said the interpreter, bowing slightly from the waist. "Please be at ease, as you are a guest of the Roman army, and no harm will befall you, barring any treachery by your side."

She signaled her assent, and with Flavius in the lead, the wagon began rolling again.

Still exhausted from her ordeal at the hands of her father, Devorra dipped in and out of sleep as the wagon bumped along, flanked front and back by the squadron of Roman cavalry. The hours passed, and she grew strangely calm as they passed through several Roman checkpoints.

Her heart ached for her lost Gabinier—every time she thought of him, and that night in his arms in the tent, her emotions threatened to overcome her. *I cannot let them think I am weak*, she told herself over and over. She continually squeezed Aloucca's hand for reassurance.

As they got closer to the Roman camp, she noticed huge plumes of smoke rising into the sky in the distance. *What could that be?* she wondered.

Late in the afternoon, the wagon made a slow ascent up a steep hill. Upon rolling over the pinnacle, Devorra took in the stunning view of the valley below, and the even bigger hill on the other side. With a gasp, she realized the source of the mysterious columns of smoke: they were pyres, on which the Romans were throwing bodies of slain Nervii warriors. The stacks of them all across the open plain sickened her.

And then something else caught her attention, and she gasped again. On that high, distant hill, backlit by the setting sun, sat the most gigantic structure Devorra had ever seen. It took her several seconds to realize that it was the Roman camp, bristling with armed men in towers erected at intervals all along the stockade wall. Trails of smoke rose from multiple sources within—probably cooking fires. Numerous flags and banners flut-tered in the evening breeze. She sat agape with wonder at this temporary city's scale and complexity. *What manner of people are these Romans, capable of such a feat? And how can our devastated people, with their rustic ways and simple society, hope to resist them?*

Her sense of calm degenerated into despair as the wagon descended toward the valley.

⁂

FLANKED BY FLAVIUS and the interpreter, Devorra was escorted to a couch in what the interpreter told her was Caesar's own command tent. She was seated as the two men stood quietly beside her. She fought to control her trembling, not wanting to betray her nerves before the all-powerful Roman commander, who had not yet arrived.

In the long minutes of silence, Devorra could not help but gawk at the richness of the furnishings in the tent. One side of the couch's frame bore an ornate lion's head; she was awed by the sophisticated carving, down to the sharpness of the great beast's teeth. Opposite the lion, an equally fierce bear looked like he could snag her in his claws. Behind the couch stood a large candelabra, formed from solid gold—more gold than she had ever seen. And the cushions! She had never experienced such supple material or plush padding. *What a world these Romans live in!*

There was a rustle at the entrance and an older man strode in, dressed in an elegant white tunic with a purple stripe at the right shoulder, trailed by a younger soldier carrying an armful of scrolls. The cavalryman struck his breast in a salute, but by his demeanor alone, she knew the senior fellow must be Caesar. He was taller than she had expected, with a receding hairline partially masked by strands of thinning hair combed forward. He was tanned and remarkably fit-looking. His square, imposing jaw and prominent chin lent him an air of power. And because the only powerful man she'd ever known had been her father, she felt unsure of herself when Caesar gave her a warm smile.

"Rome welcomes you to our camp," he said lightly, in the Germanic tongue.

She was astounded that the Roman could speak her language.

Seeing her disbelief, Caesar chuckled proudly. "I have been in such close proximity to Germania for so long, I have picked up the language. Are you able to understand me?"

"Yes," she replied.

"I have mastered the dialect, I suppose. Would you like something to drink?" he asked her.

She was wary, but thirsty. "Yes, please. You are most gracious."

Caesar motioned with his finger, and the man holding the scrolls put them on a large table, which she decided must be Caesar's desk. It, too, was a masterpiece of carved wood. The man brought over an intricately tooled golden cup, encrusted with rubies. But her eyes locked on the man holding the cup, frozen on the horrible damage to his face.

Caesar pulled her attention back to him. "I am told the Nervii do not allow themselves to drink wine, thinking it will corrupt them," Caesar said, noting her fascination with the goblet. "Would you prefer water?"

"You are well informed," she replied modestly. "Yes, water. Thank you."

At a nod from Caesar, another young fellow brought a silver flask and poured water into her cup.

"Mamurra is our chief engineer," Caesar said, introducing the man holding the flask. "He is responsible for building this modest camp you have joined."

Devorra was amused. "Modest? I have never seen anything like it!"

Caesar gave a short laugh. "Well, perhaps someday you might visit Rome. Now, *there* are some sights worth seeing."

Devorra could not imagine ever being in Rome—the other end of the earth from her little village in the land of the Nervii.

Caesar changed the subject. "So, you are the daughter of Boduognatus?"

This did not seem like anything that could help the Romans, so she answered simply, "Yes."

"He is a worthy adversary," Caesar said. "The attack he launched, from three fronts with a simultaneous attack on our rear guard, was quite well done."

His mention of the rear-guard attack made her think of her lost love, and she caught her breath.

Caesar noted her reaction, but he did not probe. "The Nervii fought us with great courage. We were hard-pressed to prevail. Your people have earned my respect. I intend to send an honorable offer of peace to your father."

Devorra said nothing. She certainly could not tell Caesar that her father hardly deserved anyone's honor. Since her experience among the Romans would undoubtedly be shaped by her demeanor toward this man, she offered what she hoped was a demure smile of gratitude.

CURIO WATCHED AS CAESAR studied the yellow-haired girl for a moment. She was very pretty, in a simple way. Even her common linen dress could not disguise her appealing curves. Indeed, Curio was alarmed by the sparkle of intense lust in Caesar's eyes—something he had rarely seen in recent years. This would not end well. The girl was a hostage, the daughter of a powerful tribal chief—the situation was fraught with complexities. Unfortunately, Curio knew all too well that the challenge itself would only add to Caesar's arousal. Since he could not simply take her as he might a helpless slave girl, he would have to seduce her. Oh, Curio could see the wheels beginning to turn in the general's calculating mind.

Seeking to derail Caesar's imagination, Curio interjected, "We will make you comfortable during your stay with us."

Caesar recovered his composure and said, "You need not be afraid. No harm will befall you unless your father engages in some act of treachery against us, about which he has been sufficiently warned."

Worry flickered in her eyes, and Curio wondered whether she feared her father perfectly capable of doing something dastardly.

"All will be well," Caesar reassured her. "Even as we speak, our peace offer is being laid before your father. Your stay with us may be short."

Devorra released a quick, sharp laugh. "I am in no hurry to return to my father."

Caesar and Curio exchanged a glance. This was an interesting piece of intelligence, one that dismayed Curio but surely pleased Caesar. If the Nervii accepted the Roman peace plan, they would be required to deliver permanent hostages to be held by the Romans as collateral for their continued faithful performance of the treaty. Curio feared that he might be handling this unwitting siren for some time to come.

"Well, let us see how things go," Caesar said. "One step at a time."

And with that, the audience was ended. As Devorra rose and exited the tent, the fullness of her body was on display. Curio cringed to see Caesar's open admiration, blanching at the complications such a tryst would surely entail. *No, Jupiter,* he thought desperately, *this was not the lightning I wanted for his rod!*

XXII

On the Road to Vesontio

TWO ROMANS ON HORSEBACK approached the long line of wretched slaves, trudging in misery toward Vesontio. The march had been made considerably more difficult by the general's order to cut the rations of the older, unskilled slaves. These forsaken souls, mostly older women who lacked any marketable abilities, were collapsing from weakness on the route. Each collapse halted the coffle long enough for the afflicted individual to be released from the wrist cuff. In each case they cut the throat of the unfortunate laggard, kicked the body into the weeds, and then resumed the trek. Often, the executed slave would have relatives in the coffle, and the whole episode would provoke an outburst of weeping and lamentations. Application of the lash was usually required to get them moving again.

"What could these fellows possibly want?" the centurion in charge asked his standard bearer upon spotting the riders. Without waiting for an answer, he had the man wave the banner he was carrying, to catch their attention.

"Greetings, centurion," one of the riders announced when they pulled up before the Roman officer. "We bring you an order from Caesar's camp."

The order was terse:

> Four days ago, Caesar ordered that a slave be flogged for assaulting a Roman soldier. Find the man and release him to the custody of these two officers.
>
> Curio, Adjutant to Caesar

It was peculiar, but the centurion wasn't about to make waves.

"The request is easily granted," he told the riders. He motioned for them to follow him. They covered a short distance to a low, flat cart drawn by two mangy-looking oxen. The animals assigned to this despicable duty were bottom of the barrel. "Here is what you seek," the centurion told them, pointing to a naked male lying face down in the back of the cart. His wrists and ankles were in fetters, his entire body covered in bulging welts, many of them crusty with dried blood. The centurion jabbed at the unfortunate man with the butt of his sword, prodding him to turn over. With a low moan, exerting what seemed to be every bit of energy he had left, he managed to get onto his back. His face was wracked with agony. The riders could see that his front side was as thoroughly marked as the back. They recoiled at the awful sight of the flayed man.

"Caesar said to beat him until he was raw, but not to kill him," the centurion explained. "You can tell him we obeyed his order."

One rider called out to the man in the cart, "Is your name Elliandro?"

A moan was all the prisoner could muster.

Turning back to the centurion, the officer said, "We will be relieving you of this cart and its contents."

Just then, there was a commotion down the line of the trudging slaves.

"Yet another collapsed slave," the centurion said wearily. "Pardon me, gentlemen, but I have a throat to cut."

⁂

CURIO STRODE TO THE AREA of camp set aside for the hospital tents, where the wounded soldiers lucky enough to survive the battle were being treated under Vatteus's watchful eye.

"Come with me," Curio said to the doctor. "We have a patient who will sorely test your recuperative talents."

Both men flinched when they saw the slab of raw meat that had been brought to the camp. Curio motioned for the guards to unshackle him.

"Your name is Elliandro?" Curio asked the pathetic creature, who could only grunt softly in reply.

"What did this fellow do to deserve such a beating?" Vatteus inquired.

"He assaulted one of our men," Curio replied. "Caesar himself ordered this punishment."

Vatteus drew closer to the suffering man and inspected the wounds. "Nothing necessarily fatal, but he may not survive, particularly if an infection develops."

Curio slapped his lifelong friend on the back. "I'm confident you can save him."

The doctor was dubious. "I shall have one of the orderlies bathe him, and then I will have him rubbed with ointment to promote the healing."

"That will do," Curio said. Then, in a conspiratorial tone, he added, "One other thing. Keep this man isolated. Do not let him mingle with others, and make no record of his presence here."

It was an odd request. But Curio knew that Vatteus had been through enough escapades with Curio and Caesar to not bother questioning it.

"Now," Curio added, "take me to the apothecary's tent. Our friend has a new problem."

"What now?" Vatteus asked. "Has the potion to deal with his seizures lost its effectiveness?"

"No, thank the gods," Curio said. "It has been working. But it seems to have affected his performance with women. We need something to restore his . . . vitality."

"I warned you about that," Vatteus said. "The old man who gave me the potion was very clear this could happen."

Vatteus led the adjutant over to a nondescript tent, wherein they found the man who mixed all the compounds used by the doctors in their treatment of wounded or sick soldiers.

The apothecary, unlike most people who met Curio, managed not to gawk at the burn. He had seen far too many ailments to be surprised by anything.

"You are young to be in this trade," Curio remarked to the fellow. "I always think of apothecaries as shriveled-up prunes."

"That would be my father," the fellow replied, taking no offense at the remark. "He is out in the forest, looking for what we need to replenish our stores, which have been badly depleted by the battle. What brings you to our tent today?"

Vatteus said with a grin, "Our friend here has a limp pecker. What can you give him to cure it?"

Curio gave Vatteus a sidelong look, though he knew the doctor was right. They could hardly tell the apothecary whom the real patient was.

The apothecary was indifferent to the issue, and quickly retrieved a purple vial from a shelf filled with colorful potions. "It is a common occurrence among men of high station, adjutant. The stress of helping to manage the complex affairs of our army would make any man suffer from *impotencia*. This will help to stiffen your member," he said, handing the elixir to Curio. "Swallow a few drops perhaps an hour before you think you will need to perform. You will be pleased with the results."

Vatteus had the man explain to Curio what was in the potion. Curio gave the apothecary a coin to pay for the substance.

"Only a few drops," the man cautioned him, with a smile. "Anything more and you will kill the poor girl."

"Good," Curio said. *A sated Caesar will be much easier to handle.*

UPON ARRIVING AT HIS TENT, Curio found that Caesar had returned the draft of the chapter dealing with the Sabis River battle, marked with Caesar's own edits. Curio by now had gotten the hang of what Caesar wanted in these accounts—Caesar's battlefield acumen, Caesar's resolute determination in the face of catastrophic setbacks, Caesar's ability to snatch victory from the jaws of defeat, and, most important of all, very few references to anybody who was not Caesar, regardless of what they'd contributed to the outcome. But in this version, even Caesar himself had not downplayed the critical role played by the Tenth's timely appearance on the field, to the salvation of them all.

With a weary sigh, Curio set about reworking the manuscript to incorporate the general's changes. As he toiled over the incredible story, he found himself wondering, not for the first time, *Who is ever going to believe this could have happened?*

XXIII

AT THE ROMAN CAMP

A S THINGS TURNED OUT, Devorra knew her father perfectly well. He haggled for weeks.

Under the Roman proposal, the Nervii would retain possession of all their lands, but formal ownership would be vested in the Senate and the people of Rome. The Senate would parcel out large tracts to Roman citizens, including officers and soldiers of the army. As a practical matter, this meant that henceforth, the Nervii would pay rent to their landlords, who would retain a portion for their own pockets, and transmit the rest to Rome. In return, the Nervii would be protected as an ally of Rome, but would be subject to a Roman governor, who would rule only regarding payment of taxes, relations among the tribes of the Belgae, and certain other matters of interest to Rome. Matters involving the internal customs and issues among the Nervii themselves would continue to be subject to tribal rule. If the clans could not agree on a ruler, the Roman governor would select one.

There were a great many details to be worked out, of course. When would the rent be due? How would it be paid? If paid in agricultural produce, how would the value be determined? What would be the penalty for failure to pay? So forth and so on, *ad infinitum.*

Most importantly, all persons captured by the Romans during the campaign were to be kept as slaves, property of the Roman army, and available for sale on such terms as the army might accept from any bidder. This term, perhaps not surprisingly, was barely even discussed during the negotiations.

Fortunately, Caesar had been through all this before in settling with the other tribes of Gaul, so knew all the tricks to finalizing a deal. He also made certain that Curio sent word back to Rome and Vesontio that he'd won a great victory over the Nervii, but that heavy casualties required the recruitment and outfitting of a new Twenty-Fourth Legion, which was undertaken immediately.

Curio was keeping a close eye on Caesar's growing interest in the attractive young lady he was holding as his hostage. Caesar invited Devorra to dine with him regularly, and at several of these affairs, made gifts to her of jewelry or objets d'art. He took great care in the selection of the menu and settings for these evenings, demanding that Curio help him procure unheard-of delicacies.

Curio had deep reservations about Caesar's clearly obvious pursuit of the Nervii captive. It was not even the fact that she was a hostage and the daughter of a powerful tribal leader; he could see the poor woman was, for some reason, distraught about the prospect of returning to her father. Moreover, she seemed to be carrying a deep and mournful sense of loss. She had told Caesar that her mother died giving birth to her, but Curio doubted she could be so sad about something that had happened so many years ago. *Perhaps,* he mused, *she had been rejected by a lover?* In any event, he felt Caesar was ruthlessly toying with her emotions. This would lead to nothing but aggravation. But Caesar was Caesar, and he usually attained whatever he desired.

Soon enough, another detachment of wagons arrived from Vesontio for Caesar, one of which carried a supply of Roman-quality dresses, shoes, jewelry, and other finery intended to impress his guest.

During this interlude while the negotiations were dragging on, Curio instructed the cooking staff to have the slave woman Molena continue to provide food to his tent nightly. Under no circumstances, he told them sternly, was she ever to go near Caesar's tent. And her body was strictly off limits to the cooks.

On her next visit, he barely recognized her. The barber had cut her hair very short, and then applied a dye made from the root of the rose madder plant, turning what was left to a fiery red. He was confident that even if Caesar caught a glimpse of her, he would not realize who she was.

As the days passed, Curio's instruction in her language progressed quickly. He practiced by trying to engage her in simple conversation. She gradually relaxed, but mostly limited her involvement to single-word answers to his questions. Finally, one morning he had the tutor teach him a few new lines, which he tried out that evening.

Now that the camp was well established and functioning normally, the quality of the meals Molena brought him had improved. Tonight's offering included an onion soup, seasoned venison, and roasted vegetables. Even the bread was better now that the army masons had erected a brick oven for the chefs.

Curio waited until she arranged the food on his desk and then took her customary place on the camp stool.

"I am not going to hurt you," he said to her.

Molena perked up upon hearing his improved language. Then, as she absorbed what he was saying, a flash of hope brightened her face. It faded as quickly as it arose. She was not convinced.

Undeterred, he tried a different tack. "I know where your brother is," he said.

Her eyes lit up with excitement. "Where is he? Is he safe?"

Curio tore off a piece of the bread and dipped it in the juice of the venison. It was delicious. "He was whipped very severely for assaulting the guard that day we removed you from the group," Curio told her. He waited as this sank in. The joy in her face turned to dread. "But he is in a safe place," Curio assured her. "And he is recovering steadily from his wounds, though it will take many weeks."

"May I see him?" she asked.

"In time," Curio replied. "For now, you must concentrate on being the best serving girl you can be. Do nothing to draw attention to yourself."

She fell silent.

"You may go."

She looked up, surprised. "You are not going to use me?"

"Not now, and not like this," he said softly. "In time, perhaps. But only if it is what you want. I said I would not hurt you."

Molena looked bewildered, as if simple decency were something she had forgotten existed.

"Go now. You may return to the cooks," Curio said with a smile. "We will continue this discussion another time."

But instead of leaving the tent, she stepped toward him. She reached out and boldly put her hand on his scarred cheek. He knew too well how it felt: grainy, almost like poorly tanned hide. But she did not recoil at the sensation.

Mortified, Curio turned away.

"Does it hurt?" she asked innocently.

Only on the inside, he thought ruefully. Curio had spent every day since that terrible fire living not just with the pain, but from the burden of feeling ashamed of his disfigurement. *No woman will ever want me*, he'd told himself time and again. *Could this slave girl be different?* He shook his head.

Molena flashed him a smile. "I'm glad it does not hurt. You do not deserve to suffer." Then she turned and left.

He watched her go with a twinge of regret. It wasn't just the woman's delicate features that drew him to her. She had a quiet dignity about her that impressed him. Despite her lack of status and grim prospects, she carried herself with pride and an optimism that somehow, things would work out for her. It was naive of her, perhaps, but he admired her spirit. And he, of course, was in a position to do something about it.

With a sigh, he took up the latrones board and ivory box and left his tent. *Well, Mamurra,* he thought, *let's see if you're getting any better at this game.*

⁓

DEVORRA HAD RECOGNIZED quickly enough that Caesar was wooing her, and it had not been difficult to resist his ministrations. Despite her comfortable circumstances here, she felt she must retain her hatred for the Romans, constantly reminding herself that they were conquerors and enslavers, plundering bandits, and worst of all, they had killed Gabinier, the love of her life.

But Caesar was persistent, and the more she remained aloof, the harder he tried. And at night, alone in her bed, she shuddered at the thought of returning to the Nervii, to her monstrous father. The idea of being married off to the ugly and loutish Maccheor made her feel ill. She had not dared to tell Caesar about this arrangement, thinking that he might lose interest in her and return her to a life of hardship. She would accept his gifts and attention and bide her time. *Best to return his flirtations,* she reasoned, *and hope for the best.*

All was well until one day, while Devorra was sitting with Aloucca in their quarters making alterations to one of the gowns Caesar had provided, a soldier called her name from outside the tent. Caesar wished to see her at once, the soldier said. He waited while she gathered a shawl about herself and then escorted her to Caesar's headquarters, which had been established in a newly built log structure much too big to be called a cabin.

Caesar was in the company of several satisfied-looking officers. She recognized some of them: Labienus, who she had learned was the second-in-command and held considerable influence with Caesar; the very handsome Mamurra, head of the engineers; the cavalry officer Flavius, who had escorted her to the camp; and, of course, the ever-present Curio.

Caesar greeted her warmly. He led her to a comfortable chair but did not sit himself.

"We have concluded our treaty with the Nervii," Caesar told her.

Devorra projected a calm demeanor, though her stomach was churning.

"The final sticking point was your father's demand that Rome instruct the other tribes that the Nervii are to be left alone. He is fearful that in their weakened state, the Nervii will be easy pickings for the other plundering clans," Caesar explained. He studied her intently, trying to gauge her reaction. "Rome has given that assurance, by my authority as proconsul."

Devorra's heart was racing. "What does this mean for the treaties the Nervii has made with the other tribes?"

"They will be honored," Caesar replied.

So her father intended to carry out his deal with Correus and the Bellovaci. A lifetime of misery beckoned like a vast chasm. She took a deep breath. "And what is to become of me?"

Caesar considered her before speaking. "As I have explained before, we have required that the Nervii provide us with hostages as security for their faithful performance of the treaty. These hostages will remain in the custody of the Roman army for the duration of the war, unless replacements are arranged. Upon any breach of the treaty, their lives will be forfeited, and the penalty is death by crucifixion."

She shuddered, having seen her father punish his enemies with the awful pain of this excruciating public death.

"To assure their sincerity," Caesar continued, "each clan is required to give us a favorite son or daughter. Boduognatus, however, balked at this requirement."

Devorra's blood ran cold. "What hostage did my father propose?"

Caesar was matter-of-fact. "He wants you back. He says he has big plans for you. He told us he has many bastard children by various slave girls, and we could have as many of them as we wish."

Her eyes narrowed as she digested this, and she was somewhat surprised to see the hint of a smile tickling the corners of Caesar's lips. Could it be that he wanted her to stay?

She relaxed her expression, hoping to make herself look pleasant and calm. "And what was mighty Caesar's response?" She knew he loved this nickname, and he rewarded her with a full grin.

"We have told him that only the legitimate daughter of Boduognatus would be acceptable to mighty Caesar. He is continuing to protest this position, but I see no reason to relent."

She felt tears of relief flooding her eyes.

"You should begin your preparations to join us on the march," Caesar told her. Seeing her puzzlement, he added, "Our business with the Belgae is concluded. We will return to our main camp at Vesontio."

They waited until Devorra was gone, then Caesar, reverting to Latin, said to Mamurra, "Make arrangements to burn the camp when we leave it. It cannot be allowed to fall into the hands of these barbarians."

The engineer stifled a groan. *So much work to build this camp, and now we will burn it?*

Caesar was already moving on to other business. "Excuse me, gentlemen. I must attend to my correspondence. Rome has inquiries about my most recent report."

Several of the men looked apprehensive, and Caesar said reassuringly, "Fear not, fellows. None of their questions involve my recommendations for your rewards from the campaign against the Belgae. Not even yours, Mamurra."

Mamurra gave his amused commander a blank stare. *Reward?*

Caesar explained. "I have asked the Senate to approve an allotment of ten thousand acres of Belgae territory to our prefect of engineers. This is in recognition of his valor at the Sabis River in slaying the barbarian who would have taken my life."

The men, who might otherwise have felt envy at such a huge allotment of land for one of their peers, signaled their approval. They understood full well that had Caesar fallen in the battle, none of them would have survived. If Caesar wished to reward the man who saved his life, they had no objection.

But to ensure there was no lingering resentment, Caesar pointed at Gordianus. "And lest anyone think I have forgotten our dear colleague Gordianus, whose timely arrival on the field with the Tenth Legion turned the tide, he has received double the allotment of Mamurra. For Labienus, the same."

Gordianus beamed with satisfaction, but Mamurra was totally nonplussed. His family's compound in Formiae, which his older brother was to inherit, was about one hundred acres—this reward would make Mamurra one hundred times richer than his older brother!

Caesar put his hand on the young man's shoulder. "I see that you are rendered speechless by my recommendation. You have earned it."

His mind still reeling, Mamurra mumbled, "Thank you, sir."

Turning his attention to Flavius, Caesar grew somber. "Flavius, your bad judgment in letting yourself be drawn from the field by the barbarians' clever antics nearly cost all of us our skins. For you, only two thousand acres."

Flavius kept his eyes straight ahead, but then Caesar showed why he was a master at motivating men. "However," he added, "if you acquit yourself substantially during our next engagement, I shall restore you to the same level as Mamurra."

Flavius's countenance brightened considerably.

Caesar turned to Curio. "As always, I will provide for grants of land for the members of my staff out of my own allotment. Curio, for his services as my adjutant, will have ten thousand acres, the same as Mamurra." This was met with another murmur of approval—so long as Caesar was paying his staff out of his own winnings, no one cared.

"I hope to hear from the Senate very soon that my recommendations have been approved," he said. And then Caesar turned back to Mamurra and said in the joshing manner the men knew so well, "I reserve the right to revoke your grant if you cannot finish the bridge back at Vesontio before the end of the summer!"

This brought a laugh from the group, and Caesar gestured toward the door, indicating that he wanted to be alone.

As the officers filed out, Curio lingered.

When the others were gone, Curio said quietly, "Caesar, I feel I must advise you: your interest in the hostage Devorra poses a number of risks for you."

Caesar's face became a mask and Curio could not gauge the general's reaction. He knew he was on thin ice. Still, he persevered. "We are honor bound not to harm any hostage."

"How is it harming a hostage to have dinner and give her small gifts?" Caesar asked, his tone neutral.

Curio knew that Caesar's designs were not limited to having a dinner companion. "I am only advising you to proceed cautiously. If she makes accusations, however unjustified, the implications could be serious."

"Duly noted, Rio," Caesar said. The topic was closed.

Curio was about to take his leave when Caesar added, "Please notify the Lady Devorra that I would like her to join me for dinner tonight."

The adjutant swallowed hard.

"And ask her to wear one of those nice dresses from Rome."

XXIV

ROME

THE SUMMER AIR OUTSIDE ROME was unusually pleasant, and Pompey had chosen to take dinner with his lovely young wife and their guest on the veranda of their villa. From their vantage point, nestled into a high hill with a sweeping westerly view over the seaport at Ostia and the endless ocean, the setting sun cast a dazzling arcade of hues across the sky. The crash of the waves provided a subtle rhythm to the quiet conversation of the dinner party.

Despite the political circumstances that had brought about their union, Pompey found himself caring more and more for his pretty, petite bride. He thought she might like to hear firsthand the latest news from her father, as transmitted by Catullus, the senator charged with overseeing Caesar's expedition in Gaul. Pompey, of course, regarded Catullus as loathsome, typical of the conniving reprobates who had come to populate the once-great Roman Senate, but he'd thought he might better tolerate the vile man if he received him in the company of the fair Julia.

Catullus was sampling an array of delicacies spread on the table before him, but was more interested in the furniture itself. "A remarkable piece," he commented to his host, gesturing toward the ornately carved table. It was made with a light-colored wood, almost yellow, rarely seen around Rome.

"The rarest cedar from the forests of Lebanon," Pompey said casually, as if owning such a fabulous item was humdrum for him. "I brought it back after I hoisted the Roman flag over their territory."

Catullus studied the side panels of the table. They were carved to depict scenes from *The Iliad*: Paris awarding the golden apple to Aphrodite over Hera and Athena, Achilles seated by his beloved Patroclus, Achilles fighting Hector, and, of course, the great wooden horse. "The workmanship is outstanding," he marveled, no doubt trying to imagine what such a work might bring at sale.

Pompey was in no mood to discuss household furnishings. "So, Catullus," he said with all the amiability he could affect, "tell us the latest news from Caesar." He tore a piece of roasted squab from the plate before him, wrapped it around a slice of cool melon, and popped it into his wide mouth. Everything about Pompey was wide, befitting the title bestowed upon him by the dictator Sulla himself: Pompeius Magnus, or Pompey the Great. He was of medium height, but broad of beam, with muscular arms and legs, and thick shoulders that rose like Vesuvius into a densely muscled neck. Such a neck was a necessity, for Pompey's head looked like it already had been made into a classic Roman bust, solid and stout, with thinning silver hair cut in the classic Roman flat style.

Catullus turned to Julia. "Your father reports that he has won a great victory over the Belgae." He took a sip of the deep-red wine from the cup before him and swished it about his mouth as if to cleanse his teeth before swallowing it in a gulp.

"Another victory!" Julia exclaimed. "How long before those horrible barbarians in Gaul give up and accept Rome as their rightful ruler?"

"Subduing those barbarians is no easy work, I can say from experience," Pompey stated. He had, in fact, conquered the tribes in the southern part of Gaul.

"Caesar relates that the barbarians united four tribes against him and mounted a frightful surprise attack while he was making a new camp at the Sabis River," Catullus said, turning his attention to a delicate honey cake on a dish of sweets and fruits. "Tasty," he said, chomping into the delicacy.

Pompey was taken aback. It was not like Caesar to let himself be surprised. "How many casualties?" he asked pointedly.

"It was a fearsome struggle. The losses were so great in the Twenty-Fourth Legion that Caesar disbanded it and reassigned the survivors to the Seventh and the Twelfth, which also had significant casualties. He is returning to Vesontio and has asked the Senate for authorization to recruit a new Twenty-Fourth Legion." Catullus helped himself to another honey cake.

Pompey stroked his chin. It was a customary practice to reconstitute units in the field under such circumstances. No basis for criticism there. Then he ventured, "Let me guess. In Caesar's account, he was teetering on the brink of disaster, and the Tenth showed up just in time to save his hide?"

Catullus looked taken aback—where might Pompey have acquired such information?

Pompey, seeing the wheels turning in the politician's wily mind, gave him an answer. "The men of the Tenth are Caesar's best, most-dedicated troops. If his neck were in a Belgic noose, they would be the ones to chop the rope."

Catullus picked up his wine and offered a toast to Pompey, but said to Julia, "Your husband is astute, as always."

Julia, long inured to the patronizing remarks politicians were so apt at feeding her, merely responded with one of her sweet smiles. Pompey admired how adept his wife was at smoothing over a bump in the road of any conversation.

Pompey abhorred sycophancy, and so ignored Catullus's ingratiating comment. "What of young Crassus? I trust he was not injured in the battle?"

Catullus gave a short laugh. "He was not even with the army! Caesar has him off on a separate diplomatic mission in the north of Gaul, offering treaties to the tribes along the ocean."

This was not surprising. Caesar would have been interested in keeping Crassus's son out of harm's way, and if the mission succeeded, young Crassus could be given credit for having scored a great achievement for Rome. "And now that it's done, has Caesar made his customary treaty with the Belgae?"

Catullus, between bites, said, "Yes, indeed, the entire territory of the Nervii has been placed under a Roman governor; the other defeated tribes are to pay tribute annually."

"And I assume," Pompey said, feigning a carefree attitude, "that Caesar has requested the Senate to settle major estates upon himself and his senior officers?"

In fact, this matter was of great importance. The rewards of the campaign, doled out to Caesar's loyalists, were the base on which Caesar was building his own political organization.

At the mention of rewards, Catullus shifted, trying to keep his face placid. In fact, he was still furious over Caesar's refusal to cut him in for a share of the take from the sale of slaves taken in Gaul. The constant stream of new captives was making Caesar and his supporters richer by the day. And with that money, they could buy more influence in the Senate. Catullus assumed this was as unsettling to Pompey as it was to him.

"Yes," he said, not letting his disgruntlement show before Caesar's daughter. "Rewards as expected, to the usual recipients—save one."

"Oh?" Pompey said.

"His prefect of engineers, a rising star named Mamurra, from the town of Formiae," Catullus continued, gauging Pompey's reaction. "Caesar states that he himself had been forced to engage in hand-to-hand combat to turn the tide of the battle, and in that melee, Mamurra actually saved his life."

Julia looked alarmed, but Pompey snorted. "I have never heard of this fellow. And Caesar promoted him to be prefect of engineers in his army?"

"He did indeed. I met this Mamurra when I visited Caesar shortly after he left Vesontio. By all reports, the young man is something of an engineering prodigy . . ."

"And?" Pompey pressed.

Catullus gave him a sly smile. "He is a very *handsome* young man."

Pompey smirked at this, but a quick glance at Julia showed her to be oblivious to the long-swirling rumors about her father's varied tastes.

Pompey's mind returned to toying with a different concern. "You said that Caesar is going to recruit a new Twenty-Fourth Legion?"

"Correct."

Pompey gave the senator a little wink. "I believe I might know an engineer who'd be very well suited to a post in the Twenty-Fourth."

Catullus did not quite follow, and in truth, did not care. He was more preoccupied with the doling out of the spoils. "The Senate has sent a request to Caesar asking him to clarify the need for such generous land grants to his officers," he said. "We are awaiting his answer."

"I am pleased that Caesar has found a capable engineer," Pompey said. "At the next session of the Senate, tell them that Pompeius Magnus supports Caesar's recommendations, in all respects."

"As you wish," Catullus replied. Like many in the Senate, Catullus felt that the aging Pompey had seen his better days, and was prone to manipulation by the younger, and still ambitious, Caesar. And he knew that Pompey would not be willing to provoke a dispute with Caesar over something so trivial as wealth. These generals took money for granted—it was power they were after.

Catullus turned again to Julia. Oh, she was spawned by Caesar, no question about it—flowing auburn locks, a high forehead befitting her noble birth, always the hint of a smile about to burst forth, and that prominent square jaw, undeniably inherited from her father. Julia was like a prize filly married off to a plodding draft horse. How could Caesar have given such a pretty girl to a slogger like Pompey? Were there no limits to the man's ambitions?

"Have you seen my latest poem?" Catullus asked her, moving the conversation away from war.

"I'm afraid not," she said politely. "We get very little material sent to us here, other than all the official dispatches, of which there are many."

"I will send you a copy for your enjoyment," Catullus replied. "You will approve; it mocks that blowhard Cicero, who fancies himself the greatest orator ever to grace the Senate floor."

"Ah, Cicero," Julia said with a frown. "He is no friend to my father, or my husband."

Pompey gave Catullus just the slightest frown. Typically, Catullus did not publish criticism of Roman politicians without Pompey's prior consent, but he had gone renegade on the Cicero piece, and in truth, he did not regret it.

"Thank you for coming all the way out here to see me," Pompey said, dismissing the senator with a yawn. "Come, Julia. The hour grows late."

Catullus watched as the bulky man and his diminutive bride bade him farewell and entered their fabulous villa.

Poor girl, he thought lasciviously. *So slender for such a bull of a man! Pompey will make her pay tonight for his generosity to her father.*

XXV

VESONTIO

ESTABLISHED IN A MODEST SUITE OF ROOMS on an upper floor of the fortress building in which Caesar's headquarters were established, Devorra was considering the most important issue she had to face for the day: which dress to don for her dinner with Caesar.

Laid out on a long divan before her were two dazzling gowns, just in from Rome. Caesar had forwarded her measurements to his favorite tailor in the same packet with his report to Catullus, so not only were the dresses sure to fit, they also reflected Caesar's personal taste in women's attire.

She ran her fingers across the material. It was like nothing she had ever felt before—flawlessly smooth and delicate to the touch. In the soft light of the oil lamps, the fabric almost glowed. *What could it be?* And the colors: one was a light green, almost a perfect match to her eyes; the other was a lovely shade of yellow, which would complement her wheat-colored hair.

She noted that the neckline of each dress was provocatively low. But the green dress was too revealing, with a slit cut so high it seriously challenged the bounds of decency. Clearly, Caesar was inviting her to put herself on display. She decided to go with the yellow, which was more modestly hemmed while providing an alluring glimpse of the sides of her torso.

Even more amazing were the gemstone necklaces Caesar had provided to accent the dresses: a fabulous triangular piece of polished beryl on a simple golden chain, and, as an alternative, a dazzling oval pendant of citrine on a more elaborate chain.

Aloucca, as always, was critical of Devorra's ongoing relationship with the Roman general. "You cannot let yourself be attracted to this man," she hissed. "He is the oppressor of our people!"

Devorra gave Aloucca a withering look. "I am not attracted to him at all. I am doing what I have to do to stay away from my father. Caesar keeps reminding me that Boduognatus has not stopped asking for my return. Perhaps I should suggest that Caesar instead send you back to him, so he can boil you in that big pot?"

Aloucca's face was frozen in terror, and while she hadn't meant to scare the poor woman, Devorra at least felt justified in her plan of action.

She reached for the hem of her everyday shift and pulled the garment over her head. She removed her undergarments and studied herself in the full-length mirror—itself another wonder provided by Caesar, far more reflective than anything the Nervii could have produced. It was set in an ornate bronze frame beneath a likeness of one of the Roman goddesses— she knew not which one—who smiled down at whoever might be posing before the mirror. She was pleased to see that the extravagant food and luxurious living provided by her host had not impacted her figure—her bosom was as firm as ever, her belly was taut, and her long legs remained toned. Even in the more demure yellow dress, they would be sufficiently on display.

CURIO WAS IN CAESAR'S OFFICE, going through yet another day's worth of routine matters, when the dispatch package arrived. There were two messages of note. The first was a formal notification, signed by the senator Catullus, advising Caesar that all the land grants he had recommended for his soldiers out of the Belgae spoils were approved. The second was a letter from his daughter, which he read aloud to Curio.

> *Dearest Father:*
>
> *I received with joy the glad tidings of your victory over the Belgae tribe. All of Rome is agog with your great achievements in Gaul. That knave Catullus, about whom you warned me, was a recent visitor and told us the news. With my own ears, I heard my dear husband Pompeius Magnus instruct him to tell the Senate to approve your proposed rewards to your men. You may be assured that your alliance with Pompeius is sound, and he is fulfilling his promises in all respects.*
>
> *I promise you that I too am doing my part to keep your partnership sound. I make every effort to give him no cause for*

complaint. I dream of giving you a grandchild and have visited the Temple of Juno to make offerings for a pregnancy. I have also called upon the Temple of Venus and prayed that the child be male. If we are so blessed, we shall name him Caesar Pompeius (although the father may insist on Pompeius Caesar!), and the joinder of the two greatest families of Rome will be complete.

Be careful always, and hurry home to see me. I pray for you daily.

Come home to us safely,

Julia

Caesar dropped the scroll and made a loud clap of his hands, startling Curio, who was scouring a table of figures, trying to figure out where the quartermaster might be hiding supplies. He gave the general a quizzical look.

"You hear that, Rio? Perhaps I am to be a grandfather!" Caesar exclaimed. "Assuming the old goat still has some seed left in him."

"I will join Julia in praying for that result, Caesar," Curio replied, working his jaw and mouth in his habitual effort to stretch the puckered skin. He had been waiting for an opportune moment, and nothing could be better for what he had in mind. "I have something for you, sir. Consider it a gift in celebration of your good news today."

One of those famous eyebrows shot skyward. "Oh?"

Curio reached down and took up a leather pouch he had stashed behind his desk. He withdrew a ceramic vial with a cork stopper. He placed it on the desk before Caesar. "Vatteus has enlisted our trusty apothecary to come up with an offering to help you with your . . . uh . . . stamina."

"My issues in that area arose—or should I say, *failed* to arise—when you gave me the elixir for my seizures. If this potion solves that issue, what new problem will *it* cause?"

Curio looked his general straight in the eye. "I do not know. All I know is that the apothecary says it has worked for others."

Caesar pulled out the stopper and sniffed the spout. "Ugh. What's in it?"

"Ground-up bone for calcium, a touch of manganese, salt to provide sodium, dried liver from a stallion, and oleander, which has powerful medicinal effects."

Caesar wrinkled his nose. He put his index finger on the spout, tilted the vial, and examined the cobalt blue fluid on his fingertip. "I suppose it can't hurt to try it," he said, still dubious.

"The apothecary said to use it sparingly—the effect is powerful. Take a few drops an hour or two before you think you will need it."

Caesar replaced the cork stopper. "I will keep it nearby," he said with a grin. "One never knows when the opportunity may strike."

Curio debated in his mind whether to express again his misgivings about Caesar's pursuit of the hostage woman. But Caesar was in good spirits over the news from Rome, and Curio did not want to disturb him.

DEVORRA DESCENDED a curving stone stairway lit by small oil lamps to Caesar's suite, her handsomely tooled leather sandals—another gift—making a flapping sound on the smooth flagstone steps. She could not help but marvel at her own feet: at Caesar's insistence, a skilled attendant had labored over her toenails, first trimming and shaping them, and then applying a dye of scarlet red, of course, the imperial Roman color. Initially aghast at this attention to something so common as her feet, Devorra had been mystified at Caesar's interest in this aspect of her grooming.

She found Caesar seated at the far end of a long dining table in an oversized room, presumably intended for larger gatherings of warriors or tribal leaders. There was no choice about where she would sit—there was only one empty chair, and it was adjacent to Caesar's at the head of the table. She took care to let the slit in her dress reveal as little as possible as she glided over the masonry floor.

Caesar rose to greet her. She noted that he had dispensed with his usual military tunic and was wrapped in a pure white toga, the only marking being a purple stripe running down the side, which she had learned was the symbol of a senator of Rome. He gave her a little kiss on the cheek, a greeting she had come to recognize as common.

"I see that the tailor has done his work well," Caesar said approvingly. "The dress is to your liking?"

"Oh, yes. But the material—what is it? It feels so unusual."

The general ran his own hand over it. "It is called silk. It comes from an island near Greece, called Cos. It is extracted from the cocoons of moths, of all things."

She shuddered for a moment. "Moths?"

"Yes, but do not be afraid; many hands have worked on this material before it made its way to your delicate skin."

Devorra was careful not to expose her leg through the slit. "I suppose the more important question is, does the dress meet with the approval of mighty Caesar?"

Caesar's eyes roved the length of her body. "It flatters you, I would say."

She fingered the pale yellow gem lying flat just above her cleavage. "The necklace is lovely."

"It pleases you?"

"Very much so." She wiggled her toes. "And these?"

"Quite civilized," he murmured approvingly. "And I see you have mastered the cosmetics as well."

It was true—at prior dinners, Caesar had commented on her rouge and her eye makeup, finicky about the shade and the quantity of application, until now, apparently, when she had gotten it precisely to his liking.

"What about my hair?" Devorra and Aloucca had spent hours that afternoon, washing and then brushing her hair endlessly so that it flowed luxuriantly down the sides of her face and over her shoulders.

"It is satisfactory," he said, feigning indifference. Then, at her crestfallen pout, he hurried to add, "I only jest—your hair would be the envy of Venus herself."

"Venus?" she asked.

"She is the Roman goddess of love and beauty," Caesar replied. "It is she who sits atop the mirror I had installed in your chambers."

Devorra could not help being flattered by this comparison. She gave him her sweetest smile, happy that he was pleased. She might even go so far as to say that he seemed truly taken with her. He might fancy himself a master of self-discipline, but Devorra knew all too well the lustful eyes of men—and what was Caesar but a man?

He guided her to the lavishly upholstered chair, embroidered with a rendering of a deer surrounded by leaves. She settled herself demurely over the deer's antlers, modestly trying not to let too much leg show. Still, his eyes grazed the length of the slit as if willing the rich fabric to stand aside.

At a loud clap of his hands, servants hurried into the room carrying platters of vegetables, mutton, venison, pork, and various breads and sauces. It was enough food for ten. Devorra was accustomed to such excess by now—Caesar did not consider it a fit meal unless a huge amount of food went uneaten.

150

"You are as lovely as any of the highest ladies in Rome tonight," Caesar said, as the food was being delivered.

"You are most gracious," she replied.

They made small talk as the food was distributed to their silver platters and they began to eat. Caesar asked whether she was comfortable in her new quarters, and, of course, she replied she was. She asked him about the bridge over the Doubs River, on which work had resumed following a suspension during the army's foray north. He reported that the work was coming along nicely, then asked if she would like Mamurra to give her a tour of the project and explain the intricacies of its engineering. She happily agreed, noting, "Your engineer Mamurra seems quite capable."

"Oh? Why do you think that?"

"Well, I have been watching them work on the bridge every day—it is an amazing structure. He must be very bright to manage such a task."

Caesar laughed. "That is elementary engineering, my dear. There are hundreds of bridges like that in Rome."

Devorra's eyes widened.

He laughed again. "The bridges are the least of it. In Rome, vast quantities of water are distributed throughout the city by an elaborate stone structure we call the aqueduct." He proceeded to describe how it all worked. She was awed once again by the amazing things these Romans could do.

Just then, a serving slave came alongside Devorra and offered her a platter bearing slices of several varieties of cheese. As she made her selection, she saw out of the corner of her eye Caesar reaching into his pocket and withdrawing a small container, which he emptied into his mouth. When she looked up from the platter, he hurriedly tucked the purple vial back into his pocket. Although she was curious, she knew better than to question him. Instead, as she sampled the strong-tasting cheese, she said, "Tell me about your house."

"I live in a public house, called the Domus Publica, because I hold the office of Pontifex Maximus, which is in theory the highest office of the priests."

This was a revelation. "You are a *priest?*" she exclaimed. In her limited experience, the Roman priests accompanying the army were austere, humorless men who pompously regarded their white robes as an entitlement to respect, whether they deserved it or not. "A great general such as yourself can also be a priest?"

"Well, the title is mostly honorary," he explained, "and the duties are very light. But the position does carry with it the right to occupy a modest house near the Forum complex, where the Senate meets. I continue to live in it to avoid an ostentatious show of wealth."

This was surprising. "Why?"

Caesar sighed. "The politics of Rome are complex, madam. I have rigorously cultivated the lower classes of the citizenry, the plebs, tilling for their votes much like a farmer works his fields. To keep their support, it behooves me to show that I live simply, as they do."

"But if they are of the lower classes, why do you want them?" she asked.

"Because there are so many *more* of them. He who controls the plebs will control all of Rome."

Later, as they were picking over a dessert of fresh fruits, she finally worked up the courage to tell him what had long been on her mind.

"Rome must be such an incredible place," she began.

Caesar offered her a slice of a golden yellow fruit he had selected.

"What is it?" she asked.

"It is a quince," he replied. "Very similar to a pear."

She tried it and found it not at all as sweet as a pear.

"Do they have quinces in Rome?" she asked, trying again to redirect their conversation.

"In Rome, one can find anything you want . . . or can imagine," he said, chewing slowly.

"I would love to see it myself someday," she said, giving him her most enticing smile. This was bold, she knew, as she had learned from a serving girl that Caesar had a wife, Calpurnia, in Rome. But she had a feeling that the risk inherent in such a suggestion might be exciting to the general.

"You would, would you?" he asked flirtatiously.

Devorra did not hesitate. "Oh, yes, of course! I've heard so much about it from you and the other soldiers.."

"Well, well," he demurred, an amused smile creeping across his face. "Perhaps when our work in Gaul is complete."

She was encouraged by this, but cautious. Was he bargaining with her? Knowing what he would want in trade, and not wanting to invite further bartering, she decided to change the subject.

"I understand you have a daughter," she said, now taking a sip of wine, savoring the full-bodied taste. She forced herself to restrain a giggle. *Imagine what the Nervii would say about one of their own, breaking the tribe's strict tradition of avoiding spirits in order to remain strong in character!*

"Oh, yes," he agreed. "She is the light of my life." He went on at length about Julia, extolling her charm and intelligence, her strength of character, her lovely appearance, and most important to a prominent man of Rome, her willing obedience when he offered her hand in marriage to the much older, and arguably more resourceful, Pompey the Great.

Devorra was hushed by the realization that Caesar's daughter willingly had done what she herself had resisted—marrying a man selected by her father to advance his own career, rather than her happiness. *All these men are the same, regarding us as mere possessions to be traded whenever it suits their fancy . . .*

She quickly thrust this thought from her mind. It was absurd to compare Caesar to her father. Caesar was worldly, brilliant, generous, and gracious—none of which could be said of Boduognatus. And more importantly, the general had rescued her from the awful fate her father had tried to arrange for her.

"Only one daughter?" she asked. "No sons?" She knew the answer to this question; she had also learned from the serving girl that Calpurnia was his third wife, and still no son to show for his efforts.

He tensed; she had wandered onto swampy ground. "No sons," he said simply, his tone making it plain that he wanted no further discussion on this topic. The smile he gave her did not include his eyes. Had she gone too far?

"I thank you for the pleasure of your company tonight." He rose, indicating the dinner was ended.

Devorra's heart pounded as if it might leap out of her décolletage. She feared she had damaged her relationship with her patron. If he tired of her company, she knew what fate awaited her. The prospect of a lifetime with Maccheor terrified her.

She stood and Caesar approached, poised to give her one of his typical small kisses.

As he bent a bit to put his lips to her cheek, he brushed his hand on the bare leg that was displayed. Desperate to stay in his good graces, Devorra took his hand in hers, not to push it away, but to hold it there. She was way out on a limb, she knew, but she felt she was out of options.

And at that, he did in fact kiss her, but on her full, ripe lips rather than a peck on her cheek. She allowed him to put his free hand at the small of her back and draw her close. They kissed again, deeper this time, and longer.

And then again. Almost against her will, Devorra felt herself warming to his touch.

But as they kissed, Caesar made no attempt to move his hand, which remained locked in her clasp.

Devorra felt her fear giving way to arousal, almost like that night in the tent with Gabinier. The sudden thought of her love for Gabinier cut into her heart for a moment like a dagger. *Oh, Gabinier, if only you had come back to me!* But she forced herself to put it out of her mind. Gabinier was dead, and she could not go back to her father. She had no choice but to fend for herself.

She gave Caesar's lip a playful bite, then whispered throatily, "Mighty Caesar does not usually hesitate to take new territory." She pressed upward on his hand ever so slightly, inviting him to reach under the slit in her skirt.

He pushed her backward onto a cleared area of the table and lifted his toga. She could see he was fully aroused.

And as he entered that new territory, she heard him whisper, "*Veni, vidi, vici.*"

XXVI

VESONTIO

AS THE DAYS STRETCHED LAZILY INTO SUMMER, **Mamurra** eased back into the routine at the Roman base happily enough. The bridge over the Doubs was coming along nicely, the recruiting of a new Twenty-Fourth Legion was proceeding apace, and planning was already underway for Caesar's next foray. Young Crassus, for the most part, had succeeded in making the several tribes in the northern coastal area see the wisdom of an alliance with the Romans. But there was a holdout, and so the last major area of Gaul not under the Roman thumb was in the western half of the coast, in a region known as Brittany. It was controlled by a seafaring tribe, the Veneti. Caesar had them squarely in his sights.

The prefect was at his desk, engrossed in studying the plans for a new set of fortifications on the river side of the Vesontio camp. Giacomo stood before him, accompanied by a stubby fellow. He put the drawing down. "Yes?"

Giacomo tilted his head toward the newcomer. "This is Garibus. He has been sent to us from Rome in response to your request for an experienced engineer for the Twenty-Fourth."

Mamurra took stock of this new member of his team. He was short and blocky, with his head shaved in customary legion manner. His only notable feature was that he was missing the bottom half of his left ear. Mamurra tapped the bottom of his own ear and asked, "What happened to you?"

"I lost it in the battle against the Cilician pirates."

Mamurra sat back in his chair. "Oh? You served with Pompey?"

"Aye, sir," Garibus replied. "Over ten years with his command group."

Mamurra shot a glance at Giacomo. He was fully aware of the tension between Pompey and Caesar over politics in Rome. "How did this come about?"

Giacomo shrugged. "Who knows how they make these decisions back in Rome?"

Garibus remained silent. Mamurra stroked his chin, then proceeded to ask the man about his experience and his knowledge of various engineering issues. The answers were entirely satisfactory—the fellow was clearly qualified.

"Very well," Mamurra said. "I'm seeing Caesar this afternoon. I'll tell him we have a candidate to head the Twenty-Fourth's engineering crew. Giacomo, take him over to the camp where they are assembling the new legion, and get him settled."

As they headed away, Garibus gave a little sigh, sounding almost relieved. With credentials such as his, why would this seasoned veteran have been anxious about Mamurra's approval? Mamurra looked after him, unable to shake the faintest feeling that something was off about this new recruit.

<hr />

HIS MASTERY OF the Germanic tongue having improved markedly, Curio had come to enjoy the occasional opportunities he had to take a meal in his private quarters, always served by Molena.

He cast his discerning eye over the lass as he picked at his lunch. The cooks, reinstalled in their well-stocked kitchens in the Vesontio fortress, had brought forth a hearty stew of mutton, pheasant, pork shoulder, and vegetables, including green beans, chickpeas, and lentils, lightly spiced with paprika and thyme. He found it delicious.

"Did you try the stew?" he asked her.

"Not yet," she said, shaking her head. Her hair had grown out since he had first sent her to the army barbers, but he still had them dying it red. It flowed over her shoulders, making her face even more lovely, providing stark contrast to her molten black eyes. "Slaves are not fed until all the soldiers have been satisfied."

Curio was not surprised by this. He noticed her hands were red and cracked. "Why are your hands so raw?"

Molena became downcast and went silent.

"You must tell me how they are treating you," Curio said sharply. "I cannot help you if I do not know what is happening."

"I scrub the pots and pans, and all the dishes," she said.

He supposed she was reluctant to complain; surely she knew there were far less pleasant duties to which she could be assigned. Yet he was immensely annoyed. He had asked the cooks to train her in their craft, so that her value to potential owners might be enhanced if ever it became necessary to sell her. Not that he wanted to do that. "Are they not teaching you anything?"

"No."

Curio fished a chunk of mutton out of the stew, but before he put it in his mouth, he said, "I will speak to the chief cook. Enough of this dishwashing detail."

She smiled. "May I ask you a question, sir?"

Curio replied gently, "You do not need my permission to ask a question. Just go ahead and ask."

She flashed him another smile, then steadied her resolve. "I know you have told me that my brother is recovering from his wounds. May I see him?"

Curio put down his spoon. He'd known for some time this question would be coming. "Tell me about your brother."

Molena hesitated. He had done all he could to show her that he would not hurt her, but she was still a slave. She knew her body was his to use any time he wanted; of course she would fear him. But he had been nothing but respectful to her, had not even touched her, and he held out hope that it would lead her to see him in a different light.

"Go ahead," Curio encouraged her. "I will not do anything to hurt him because of what you may tell me."

She studied his eyes and at last seemed to find him worthy of her trust. "Elliandro is older than me, by eight years," she said hesitantly. "Our parents were killed in a raid by the Nervii when I was only six years old. But my brother and I were in the woods when the raiders came, so we escaped."

Curio nodded sympathetically. The tribes of Gaul were continually raiding each other—it was a common occurrence. "How long ago was that?"

Molena had to think for a second. "It was thirteen years ago."

"Who raised you, during those thirteen years?"

"Elliandro. For some reason, the raiders did not burn our hut. My brother kept working our little farm. We lived there until your army came and made slaves of us."

Curio considered the girl's request. Her brother was considerably improved, but it was too risky to bring him here, to his quarters, to meet with Molena. There was an easier solution.

"Soon your brother will be able to move about without assistance," he told her. "We shall assign him to service with the hospital crew. You can be reunited with him then."

Molena's face glowed with joy. "Thank you, sir, thank you!"

"It gives me pleasure to make you happy," Curio said softly.

The girl flushed, too timid to meet his eyes with hers.

"You may return to the kitchens," he said.

He watched as she gathered up the dishes and turned to leave with the heavy tray. It was a risky game he was playing. But he was drawn to the girl, like a moth to the flame.

A flame, he thought with irony. *Perhaps it is not Caesar who will be done in by fire . . .*

THE AFTERNOON MEETING had been scheduled as a review of the overall plan for the upcoming campaign against the Veneti. All the senior officers were present: Labienus, the legion commanders, Curio, Mamurra and Giacomo, and the officers responsible for management of the baggage train. Young Crassus was there, too, as a paean to his service in bringing all the other tribes to heel.

They were all seated on stools facing a huge sheet of vellum mounted to the wall, on which was drawn a map of northern Gaul, showing the coastline and the two great peninsulas jutting out into the sea. The locals referred to the area as Brittany, perhaps in recognition of the proximity of Britannia, not far across the water, which was also marked on the map.

There was a rustle at the door, and they all stood as Caesar strode in. Trailing behind him was a new face, a fellow old enough to be a contemporary of Caesar, with a bearing and manner that suggested he too was accustomed to the mantle of command. And then Mamurra noticed that the newcomer was wearing a military tunic adorned with the same gold piping as Caesar: the man was a very high-ranking official himself. In contrast to the balding and clean-shaven Caesar, this stout fellow had a thick head of wavy hair, matched by a manicured beard, both streaked with gray throughout.

With a wave of his hand, Caesar indicated for them to be seated. When he was satisfied that the staff was settled, he gestured to the new man and said, "Gentlemen, allow me to introduce Admiral Decimus Brutus. He is in fact my cousin. We have the greatest respect for him, even if he has made the serious career blunder of choosing the navy over the army."

This brought a laugh from the men, but Caesar could see that they were mystified. Why had Caesar brought an admiral to the meeting?

Seeing their confusion, Caesar pointed to the map and said, "Young Crassus, perhaps you can tell us about the strongholds of the Veneti along the coast."

Crassus, perhaps befitting someone who knew he would someday be the richest man in Rome, rose and approached the map with a self-assured air. He pointed to a series of communities identified on the map all along the shoreline across Brittany. "Each of these towns," he said, ticking off the names, "is fortified on the land side, but the fortifications are modest, and certainly no challenge for the engineering skill of our army."

Mamurra wanted to feel flattered, but he sensed something else was coming.

"When I was on my mission to persuade the tribes to accept our dominion over them, I was given permission by Caesar to test the defenses of one of these towns," Crassus continued. "We enveloped it on the land side easily enough, and began our excavations of the foundations of their walls in the customary manner. The Veneti resorted to the expected defenses—they rained down arrows and rocks and boiling oil—but our shields protected the slaves we pressed into doing the digging, and the progress was most satisfactory. Until, that is, we were on the verge of breaking down their walls."

Caesar encouraged the junior officer. "Go ahead, tell them what happened to your well-planned siege."

Crassus gave them a toothy grin. *He is handsome in the Roman manner,* Mamurra observed. *Born rich, and good-looking to boot . . . how much favor can the gods bestow upon one man?* he mused, stifling a smirk.

"On the day before we were going to launch the final assault," Crassus began, "the people of the town were loaded onto the Veneti sailing ships, and the entire population was evacuated with their most precious valuables. We stormed the place, and there was no one to be found. And no booty, either, save for some scrawny animals and broken-down slaves."

Mamurra quickly saw the implications of this tactic. There were many of these towns along the coast, far too many to garrison each of them with a Roman force. Even if the Romans burned each of the towns to the ground, the Veneti would merely wait until the Romans left and then return to rebuild. There was only one way to subdue them.

Nods bobbed throughout the group. "We must mount a dual action against the Veneti," Caesar declared. "While the army attacks from the land side, Brutus here will seal off their retreat with an attacking force from the sea. There is only one problem with the plan. Mamurra?"

Mamurra squirmed on his stool. *Damn it, Caesar! Always putting me on the spot with these military questions. I am an engineer, not a general!*

"Go ahead," Caesar goaded him. "Do not be modest."

"The flaw is evident," Mamurra said, remembering Caesar's line about the siege tower from the day he was being interviewed. "We have no ships."

This brought another laugh from the assembled group.

Caesar let his men enjoy a moment of levity. When they had quieted down, he said with a tone that left no room for doubt, "By the spring, we will have a fleet ready for the admiral."

Mamurra felt an intense sense of dread in the bottom of his stomach.

Labienus spoke up. "Caesar, may I ask, sir, just how you propose to do that?"

Caesar fixed his clear-eyed gaze firmly on his prefect of engineers. "You already know the answer to that, don't you, Mamurra?"

Mamurra pursed his lips together, then said with a weary sigh, "I will build them for you, sir."

"And?"

"They will be ready when you want them."

The meeting went on for several hours as they picked over the myriad details of scheduling, order of march, logistics, and the like. Midway through the meeting, Caesar announced yet another mission for Crassus. While the main body of the army was engaged against the Veneti, Crassus would proceed to the southwest region of Gaul, known generally as Aquitania. His mission was to keep the natives there occupied and thereby unable to move north to come to the aid of the Veneti. Caesar presented this as something of a reward for the good work Crassus had performed previously, and the young man was beaming with pride at this high praise from the army's commander. Finally, when every officer knew what his orders were and what was expected of his men, they adjourned.

"Mamurra, a word with you," Caesar said. "Curio, you as well."

Moments later, when the three men were alone, Caesar motioned for Mamurra to sit again, while he walked over to his desk and returned with yet another map.

Mamurra recognized it without effort. It was eastern Gaul, centered on Vesontio.

"As you are well aware," Caesar said, "the Doubs River is but a tributary of the Rhine. We are only a few miles away from it."

Mamurra, feeling nervous, looked to Curio for a clue, but the adjutant's face gave nothing away.

"When we have finished with the Veneti," Caesar said deliberately, keenly studying his engineer, "I want to turn our attention to the Germanic tribes."

Mamurra was rendered speechless. Ever since joining the army in Gaul, all he had heard about was the ferocity and viciousness of the Germanic warriors. *And Caesar is contemplating taking them on?* But there was only one response he could give: "As you wish, sir; always."

"You will be leaving very soon for the north coast, to begin work on the fleet," Caesar said. "Before you leave, I want you to assemble a team that will remain behind. While we are gone, this team will develop a plan for how we will transport the army to Germania."

Mamurra was not sure what Caesar meant. "The Rhine is a river, sir. Much wider than most, and with a fast current. But it is a mere exercise in transport, not engineering. With enough boats, we can ferry the army across it in good order. If you like, we can begin work building them."

"No," Caesar replied.

Mamurra did not understand. "Sir?"

"No boats," Caesar said. "I want a bridge."

It took all Mamurra's self-possession to keep from falling out of his chair. Curio gave him a wicked grin.

"A bridge? Over the Rhine River? Big enough to carry the entire army?" Mamurra spluttered. *It would take years! There are not enough masons in all of Italy to build the foundations! And the Germanic tribes would certainly attack it constantly.* It was all he could do to keep from saying, *Have you lost your senses?* But instead, he asked, "But why, sir? Such an effort! It would be so much easier to ferry the men across."

Caesar flicked his eyes at Curio, then said to Mamurra with determination, "This is the greatest army in the history of the world. I want to show our adversaries what we are capable of."

By now Mamurra was astute enough about Roman politics to wonder, *Our adversaries in Germania, or his adversaries in Rome?*

Caesar took up a clean sheet of parchment and a quill. He dipped the nib into a nearby ink bottle and began sketching. "I have been giving this some thought over many months," he said. "We can drive wooden piles into the river like this, at an angle, and then place planks over the piles to provide a deck."

It was such folly, Mamurra did not know where to start. "Sir, the current is swift, the force is tremendous. You must have stone foundations to hold the deck, not wood, and they must be dug deep into the river bottom. It would take a lifetime to build such a structure."

Caesar put the stylus down and gave Mamurra a cold look, one that had broken far braver men. "Really, Mamurra, you must free your mind from the shackles of small thinking. You are conceiving this like a bridge we would want over the Tiber in Rome."

Mamurra was bewildered. "Sir, the forces of nature cannot be denied. A wooden bridge such as you are describing cannot endure the harshness of the seasons or the spring floods."

Curio spoke up. "Sir, perhaps your engineer does not grasp the reason you want the bridge."

Caesar slammed his fist onto the table, startling both men. "I do not need it to endure for all time," Caesar snapped. "I need only for it to last for a season of campaigning."

It was like someone had thrown cold water into Mamurra's face. Now this was something different. Caesar was talking about a *temporary* bridge! *Perhaps corners could be cut . . .* Mamurra's mind raced through the possibilities.

"Put someone good on it," Caesar admonished him. He handed the papers with his sketches to Mamurra. "Who might you recommend?"

"We just obtained an engineer for the new Twenty-Fourth," Mamurra suggested. "He was sent to us from Rome."

Instantly, Caesar was on alert. His eyes darted to Curio, who gave him a knowing glance in return. "From Rome?"

Mamurra said defensively, "He served on the staff of Pompey himself for over ten years."

"They have sent me one of Pompey's engineers?" Caesar looked again to Curio. "It's so transparent as to be laughable." He stewed for a few moments, then snorted. "No, it's actually an insult to my intelligence; do they think I cannot realize they've planted a spy in my camp? May the gods grant me vengeance against them!"

Mamurra went silent.

"Take this new man with you to the coast," Caesar said firmly, leaving no room for further discussion. "And don't let him hear a word about the bridge project. The last thing I need is for Pompey and Crassus to get wind of what I plan to do."

Crassus in league with Pompey against Caesar? This was a revelation to Mamurra. *No wonder Caesar kept sending the young Crassus away to deal with the remote tribes while he campaigned elsewhere. He had deftly removed another spy from his ranks.*

❦

WHEN MAMURRA WAS GONE, Caesar sat, staring at Curio for long moments.

"Well, Rio, their games against me have no end," he said finally.

Curio took down the large map the group had been discussing. "At least this was obvious," he said, folding the drawing. "It's the scheming we haven't detected that worries me."

"Oh, I'm sure there's plenty of that," Caesar agreed, "but most of it occurs in Rome, and thankfully, I have many friends there to look out for me." He plucked an apple from a tray, took the dagger his daughter had given him from a pocket in his tunic, unsheathed the dagger, and began deftly peeling the apple, keeping its skin continuous in one long, curling rind.

"Perhaps," Caesar said, intent upon not breaking the spiraling peel, "I should give up this military life and retire, get myself a nice villa on the ocean, like Pompey. Banish all talk of politics from my life. Can you even imagine a day not filled with all these orders and requisitions and reports?"

Curio knew better. "You wouldn't last a fortnight. After terrorizing your gardener and your household staff, you'd be hopelessly bored." It was a joke, but Caesar didn't laugh.

"Surely by now you see the reality of command," Caesar said, still peeling. The long apple skin was dangling nearly to the floor. "The responsibility is unrelenting, and worst of all, one can never let the men see that you are fearful or unsure what to do. Such doubts must be confined to one's pillow during the night."

Curio by now had begun reviewing notes from the meeting. He was well-accustomed to his role as sympathetic ear for Caesar's occasional bouts with self-doubt. The great man would confide such highly personal thoughts only to him, and no word of it would ever pass his lips to an outsider.

"The rascals in Rome are no match for you," Curio said with a smile. "They will fall before you like the tribes of Gaul."

Caesar gave a slight smile. He set the apple peel on the tray from whence it came and with great concentration assembled it back into its round shape, as though the apple were still within. Finished, he looked satisfied with himself, for even in this meaningless task, he had achieved something significant—the apple itself was irrelevant. He wiped the dagger clean, sheathed it, and tucked it back into his tunic.

Since Caesar was in a reflective mood, Curio saw an opportunity to bring up what had been troubling him. "If I may say so, your continuing dalliance with the Lady Devorra could cause problems in the days to come."

Caesar was turning the apple skin, admiring the evenness of his work. "How so?"

Curio took a deep breath. "You are obviously taken with her. And I am glad that the apothecary's mixture has revived your libido. But she may be taking the relationship much too seriously. No good can come of this."

"Why does it matter?" Caesar sneered. "When I am done with her, we will send her away."

"We will not be able to dispatch her the way we have your slave girls when you tire of them," Curio asserted. "She is a hostage, protected by our treaty."

Caesar was unmoved. "I am sure, adjutant of mine," he said cynically, "that you will solve the dilemma when it presents itself."

Curio sighed. There was no point in continuing this line of discussion. "Well, there is one other problem with the idyllic life of leisurely retirement you envision," he said, with a touch of irony in his voice.

Caesar waited.

"You would have Calpurnia nipping at your heels, constantly."

Caesar reached out and crumpled the apple skin in a sudden gesture.

"Regrettably," he said, tossing it into a pile of refuse from the day's meeting, "you are correct."

MAMURRA SPENT THE BALANCE of the day putting in place the logistics required to move the engineering staff to the location chosen to serve as the new base for the northern campaign. During his travels, Crassus had established a small fortified base at the town of Corbilo, on the ocean at the estuary with the Liger River, called the Loire by some locals. The venue was particularly attractive because it boasted an expansive natural harbor, and on the land side to the north it was protected by a huge swampy area through which no attacking army could march. The command group decided to vastly enlarge this base and make it the primary site for building the fleet. The thick forests of the Brittany region would provide ample raw materials for the effort.

The transport plan called for the engineering team, with a full legion in support, to march northwest from Vesontio to the town of Cenabum, inhabited by the Carnutes tribe. Cenabum was a major trading center on the Liger, and the tribe had wisely concluded an alliance with Caesar early in his program of conquest. The engineers and their supporting legion would board boats there and sail downriver to Corbilo.

The engineering staff quarters were equipped with texts on a variety of topics, and fortunately, Mamurra found a treatise on naval architecture. It wasn't much, but at least he could read up on the subject and hopefully have a sense of what would be needed by the time he arrived at the Liger base. The scale of the task was daunting: Brutus wanted fifty warships.

Having settled the details of the movement north and west to build Decimus's fleet, Mamurra turned his attention to the much more delicate question of the bridge over the Rhine. He readily concluded there was only one man he could trust with the sensitive job. As much as he wanted to have Giacomo with him at Corbilo to help build the fleet, Mamurra knew that he had to give him the bridge project.

Mamurra asked Giacomo to step outside the building for a brief conversation, so that no one might overhear them. He took along Caesar's sketch.

Giacomo reacted calmly when Mamurra laid out what Caesar wanted to do, and why. He studied the scratchings of Caesar's pen. "It seems feasible," Giacomo said, without betraying any emotion. "Why does he propose to have the wooden piles driven into the river bottom at an angle, rather than vertically?"

"He believes the angled piles will better withstand the current for the short duration he expects the bridge to survive," Mamurra explained. "You will need to send a crew to the river to drive a number of test piles, at different angles, to determine the best attitude for them. The crew should also take soundings to determine the river's depth along the proposed path so that the piles can be prepared to the proper lengths."

Giacomo was making notes. "I will dispatch that crew at the same time I send over the surveying team to find the best spot for the crossing."

"Be sure to send them along with at least a cohort of the garrison remaining here at Vesontio," Mamurra cautioned. "Ariovistus will no doubt get wind that something is going on, and he could decide to try for an attack."

Giacomo now looked worried. "And if he does?"

"Do not engage them," Mamurra said with certainty. "Withdraw your group at the first sign of the natives. This is merely an exploratory operation."

Giacomo stood quietly for a long moment, studying the sketches. "Does he understand the scope of this undertaking? It will take years to plan and build."

"He understands it fully," Mamurra said, gritting his teeth. "But he will want it built in weeks, not years."

Now Giacomo was incredulous. "Has he gone mad?"

"That's what I thought, but didn't dare to ask!" Mamurra laughed. "No, I am afraid he's quite serious."

Giacomo shook his head in disbelief.

Mamurra hastened to add, "We must finish the plan before he returns from Brittany. When you send me the plan for approval, start as many men as you can spare on preparing the pilings and the planks for the bridge deck. Lay out a roadway between Vesontio and the proposed site of the bridge. And identify all the boats you will need for the river work. Do everything you can to have all the components of the bridge fabricated and ready."

Giacomo stood bewildered.

"One last thing," Mamurra added, "and this is more important than anything else: Not a word of this activity is to reach Rome. Caesar will crucify any man who discloses it."

This brought a grin to Giacomo's face. "Does this mean you'll be taking Garibus to help you build ships?"

Mamurra returned the smile. "Well, he did help Pompey fight the pirates!"

❧❦❧

WEARY FROM HIS long day of work, Mamurra retired to his private quarters well after sundown. He found a meal of porridge and fruit waiting for him, with a thick cut of butchered ox roasting over a fire in the hearth, tended by Dominicus. Mamurra eased onto a stool at the small table and watched as the slave, clad in a relatively short tunic, applied a sauce to the cooking meat. The succulent aroma drifted across the room as Mamurra sorted through the bowl of fruit. He selected a pomegranate and broke it open.

While separating the seeds from the pith, Mamurra studied Dominicus as he bent over the fire, his firm leg muscles flexing, the hint of his buttocks pressing against the brown tunic. The slave had removed his sandals and was cooking barefoot. *Even his feet are nicely shaped,* Mamurra thought.

When the meat was ready, Dominicus put it onto a platter and brought it to his master. Mamurra poured the pink seeds into the porridge and stirred the mix as Dominicus sliced the meat and then stepped back. Mamurra took several spoonfuls of porridge. Its bitter taste was made more tolerable by the tartness of the pomegranate.

"Does master require anything further?" Dominicus asked.

Mamurra poured some wine into a goblet and drank deeply. Then he said, "Remove your tunic."

For only a moment, Dominicus looked surprised. Then he gave his master a slight smile and complied. The lad had a chiseled physique.

Mamurra took a bite of the ox. It was not unduly tough. "You seasoned the meat nicely."

"I am happy that you are pleased," Dominicus replied.

"You are a capable cook," Mamurra remarked. He took another swig of the wine. It was a bit dry to his palate, but perhaps the dryness in his mouth was due to his anxiety. He had been agonizing ever since that first night in the bathtub, again and again debating whether to give in to his yearning and exploit the availability of his manservant, who so clearly was willing to do anything Mamurra might request. With a quick motion, he slugged down the rest of the wine.

Perhaps it was the wine. It might have been the cumulative effect of the daily stress of trying to please such a demanding commander. Or possibly it was just his own long-suppressed desire finally getting the better of him. Whatever the reason, he said quietly, "Show me more of your skills."

Dominicus moved past his master, fetched a thick towel, and returned to place it on the floor before Mamurra. He sank to his knees on the towel and began gently massaging Mamurra's thighs. He gradually increased the pressure, all the while working his hands ever higher.

Mamurra closed his eyes and gave way to the passion coursing through him. He felt Dominicus come closer, and then felt the wetness and warmth of a new sensation. With a gentle sigh, Mamurra accepted that his life would never be quite the same again.

XXVII

VESONTIO

WELL, HAS IT STARTED?"

Devorra, awakened from a restless slumber by Aloucca's sharp tone, rubbed the sleep from her eyes and tried to focus on the animated old woman standing before her. As she regained awareness, she realized what the woman was asking, and she reached between her legs.

"Nothing," she said.

Aloucca let out a long, low groan and put her head in her hands. "I knew it, I knew it," she moaned. "You know what this means!"

Devorra sat up and swung her bare legs over the edge of the bed, her feet not quite reaching the floor. She sat there for a few moments, trying to sort out her feelings. She had not sensed anything stirring in her womb, but there was little doubt in her mind. Ever since she had started the dreaded bleeding as a girl, she had been flawlessly regular, every twenty-eight days, without fail. Now she had missed two cycles of the moon.

She climbed off the bed, and then, standing before her maid, extended her hands above her head. Aloucca helped her pull off the light tunic she was wearing. She ran her hands over the flat of Devorra's belly, and down to her mound. "No signs of swelling yet," the slave observed, pushing a bit. Then she put her fingers on Devorra's round, pink nipples and the girl flinched. "Ahh, tenderness there," Aloucca hissed. "That's a sure sign."

Devorra felt a wave of nausea coming on. The room swayed a bit, but Aloucca caught her by the arm and sat her back down on the bed. Quick as a cat, she grasped the chamber pot beneath the bed and deftly brought it up under Devorra's chin just in time to catch the stream of vomit.

When the girl had finished, Aloucca brought her a cup of water to rinse her mouth, then clucked again, "Sickness in the morning. You are with child, mistress."

168

Devorra still did not feel right, and she lay back onto the covers of the bed. "I had hoped someday to bear Gabinier's child," she said sadly. "I cannot live in that dream any longer." Her thoughts turned to Caesar, and how she might tell him the news.

Aloucca climbed onto the bed beside her and took Devorra's hands in her own. "You must wait for the right time to tell him, perhaps after he's had some piece of good news, maybe another victory in battle."

Devorra closed her eyes and rubbed her temples. "Why is that?"

Aloucca replied in a conspiratorial tone, "Because if you catch him in a good mood, the chances are better that he will not cast you to the wolves."

Weary of the hectoring from her maid, Devorra said with a sigh, "I do not think he's likely to do that. Does this not ensure that Caesar will keep me with him?"

"Hardly," Aloucca said, as she fetched a bowl of water and a towel for her mistress. "Now that he has planted his seed, he will leave you to fend for yourself. These men are all beasts."

"Caesar is different," Devorra snapped, startling even herself. She was even more surprised to find that she almost believed it.

"Heed my words, mistress. Caesar, too, is a beast. A *Roman* beast!"

ONLY THE SLIGHTEST hint of dawn was showing in the night sky, but the Roman headquarters was a beehive of activity. The Twelfth Legion would accompany the engineers on the long trip to the new base at Corbilo. The engineering crew was assembled and ready to leave, and behind them, the Twelfth was formed up and awaiting the order to move out.

A small reviewing stand had been erected at the head of the long column so that the entire force could march by and be saluted by Caesar, Labienus, and the other legion commanders as they passed. Caesar summoned Brutus, Mamurra, and the tribune Hortensius, commander of the Twelfth, to meet him at the stand and receive his final instructions.

"We will come behind you when the fleet nears completion, which Mamurra assures me will be within a few months. We will plan to move out from Vesontio at the first thaw of the winter, and will join you by mid-spring," Caesar said. "It is essential that the fleet and the crews be ready by the time we arrive."

Brutus regarded Mamurra. "If your engineer can build the ships, I will have the men of the Twelfth sufficiently trained to fight on the water."

Mamurra took offense to Brutus's intimation that he might not be up to the challenge. He noticed that Curio shot him a look. Curio and Mamurra had privately discussed the plan for the project several times over the latrones board, and both agreed it would be a monumental task, but one that Mamurra could not avoid.

"The ships will be ready, sir," was all he said, his tone neutral.

Caesar put his hand on Mamurra's shoulder and said to the others, "I have complete confidence in him. He will not disappoint us." Caesar's tone carried the slightest trace of a rebuke to Brutus's doubts.

Mamurra's spirits soared, and he resolved to do everything he could to justify Caesar's faith. Curio had the slightest trace of a smile on his face.

Caesar then turned his attention to Hortensius. "When you arrive at Corbilo, your first priority must be to fortify the base with extra-strong battlements and stores of food. You must be prepared to withstand a siege until I arrive with the main body of the army in the spring. I doubt that the Veneti will assemble and offer battle, but if they do, you must not engage them. Withdraw into your camp and hunker down for the siege. Do not risk the entire legion on a major battle. If you stock enough food and water and your trenches are steep enough, you should be able to hold out until we get there to relieve you."

Hortensius struck his breast with his fist, signifying he understood the order.

"One other thing," Caesar said to the three of them. "Brutus is the commander of the ships, once they are built and at sea. Mamurra is responsible for getting them built, so his orders are to be respected in all matters regarding the construction, without question or argument. And Hortensius, you are responsible for the security of the entire operation, including the safety of the construction operations. Do I make myself clear?"

All three men struck their breasts this time.

"May the gods be with you," Caesar said. With that, the men turned to return to their posts, but Caesar took Mamurra's arm and said, "An additional word with you, please."

Once the others were safely out of earshot, Caesar tilted his head toward his engineer and asked in a low voice, "Who will be overseeing the bridge project while you're gone?"

Mamurra did not hesitate. "My best man, Giacomo."

"Good. He understands the importance I attach to this?"

"He does. You have made that abundantly clear to me, sir, and I have communicated your passion about it to Giacomo. I have left him here with my best bridge builders. They will get it done, and we will keep you advised on the progress of the planning effort."

Caesar thought for a moment, then slapped his engineer on the back. "They may plan it, but *we* will build it."

And he turned his attention to the parade that was already beginning to move out for Corbilo.

❧

CAESAR AND CURIO retired to their offices for a morning of scroll-pushing, sorting out the numerous details of the planned campaign against the Veneti.

"Our final count of the captives taken from the Nervii was a bit light," Curio said, scanning a report of the revenue received so far from the sale of the slaves captured at the Sabis.

"The Tenth got carried away on the battlefield. They should have allowed more of the barbarians to surrender instead of slaughtering them," Caesar replied.

"That, and we never took their camp, so there were no women to pad the numbers. The brothel owners are always calling for more supply. We must be more mercantile in our campaign against the Veneti," Curio cautioned. "The expense of building the fleet will be formidable."

"It's a necessary expense," Caesar said blithely, only half listening, clearly weary of this constant carping from Rome about costs. "I am conquering a whole country for Rome!"

Curio sighed. "At some point, we will have taken all the slaves to be had in Gaul. How will we keep the game going after that?"

Caesar was not perturbed. "I have been giving that considerable thought, Rio," was all he would say. "I intend to address that topic the next time I meet with the other triumvirs."

This was news. "When do you expect to see Pompey and Crassus?"

"In the early spring, before we leave to deal with the Veneti," was all Caesar would say.

Curio resumed his study of the accounting report. "This is most odd," he commented. "Mamurra has requisitioned huge amounts of lumber and iron, nails and rope, for which we are making procurements as we speak. I assume he wants it for the fleet he will build for Brutus. But he wants a significant portion of it brought here to Vesontio. And we will then have to move it to Corbilo. That makes no sense. We should send it there straightaway."

Finally, this caught Caesar's attention. "No," he said firmly, "Mamurra is doing this on my orders."

Curio was totally flummoxed. "Surely you don't mean . . ."

"Yes, Rio," he said acidly. "I have authorized preparations for the bridge I will build over the Rhine." In a few cursory comments, Caesar briefed his aide on the plan to fabricate and stockpile all the components for the bridge.

Curio remained silent.

"Just keep pushing the documentation," Caesar said. "If anybody starts raising questions, tell them it's been approved at the highest levels."

"But it *hasn't*," Curio objected.

Caesar rose. "I have given the order. That's all the approval needed."

Curio feared it was not so simple.

Around midday, Curio put his work aside. Normally, Molena would bring him a meal in his quarters. This day, however, he went directly to the kitchens, in the basement of the great fortress.

It was hellishly hot in there, with a considerable din from the clattering of cooking implements and pottery. The kitchen staff, a combination of slaves and professional army cooks, scurried about in no discernable pattern, preparing the noontime meal for the garrison troops and, of course, for Caesar himself.

The chief cook, seeing that Curio had entered his fiefdom, hurried over, alarmed at what business might bring Caesar's adjutant to the bowels of the fortress. But Curio's eye had already fallen upon Molena, standing at a long table, kneading dough for the evening's bread. She was absorbed in the task and did not hear him come into the kitchen. She wore a white linen shift—the common woolen tunic of the slaves would have been unbearable in the heat of the kitchen. Circles of sweat drenched her neck and armpits.

"Ah, Curio, welcome again to our lowly quarters," the cook said, the slightest obsequiousness in his voice. He pointed toward Molena. "We are training her in the art of breadmaking as you ordered, sir. When she has mastered it, we will move on to preparation of the meats."

"Well done," Curio replied. "I need to take her away for the afternoon."

The cook leered at Molena. "She is quite lovely. I am sure you will be pleased with her."

Curio could have demoted the man on the spot for this lascivious comment, but there was no point. He merely said, "Now, if you please."

The cook led him over to the table. Molena smiled when she looked up and saw Curio. Her hands were caked with flour.

Curio pointed at them and laughed. "Well, at least they aren't raw from washing dishes!"

"I am trying hard to make good bread," she said, happy to have a break in the monotony of the kitchen routine.

"I am sure your bread will be delicious. Now, go wash up and change into a clean dress," Curio said. "I'm taking you somewhere."

She looked at him with alarm, but her face softened when she saw his calm expression. She turned to the chief cook, to make sure he agreed with Curio's command.

The cook hastily said, "You heard the man. Do as he says."

Molena scurried away to obey.

In a coarse attempt to ingratiate himself with Curio, the cook remarked in a lascivious tone, "I'd like to take that wench somewhere myself!"

Curio had had enough. "Do you think the ability to taste your own cooking is important to how you do the job?"

The cook was confused. "Well, yes, of course."

"Another remark like that and I'll have your tongue cut out and nailed to the door," Curio said, turning to go. "I'll be waiting for her at the entrance to the fortress."

On the way out of the kitchen, he stole a glance back at the cook and was gratified to see the man still quaking.

CURIO TOOK MOLENA by the arm and escorted her through the gate and down a long gravel road, nearly a mile, to the encampment of the army hospital. As she got close enough to guess where he was taking her, she hastened her step in excitement, though still on guard against disappointment. She was afraid to believe she might actually see her brother at last.

Curio led her through a maze of tents. Men hobbled about on crutches, while others worked at exercises to regain their strength. As she passed the tents, she caught glimpses of other men still prone on cots, wrapped in bandages. The sight of these wounded men sent a shudder down her spine. *What had they done to Elliandro?*

They came into a small clearing, and suddenly she saw him. He was in iron shackles, hand and foot, and clad only in a gladiator's trunks, doing repetitions by hoisting a log. Her initial burst of joy evaporated like dew in the morning sun as she absorbed the awful stripes that crisscrossed his body. Even though the wounds had largely healed, the marks on his body were testament to the terrible punishment he'd suffered. Worse, he was gaunt and pale, having seen little sun during his recuperation. He was a shadow of his former robust self.

"Oh, Elliandro, what have they done to you?" she cried, running to him.

Stunned, Elliandro dropped the log. She reached for him, and he tried to wrap his arms about her as best he could, encumbered as he was by the shackles.

"Molena, Molena, is it really you? I thought I would never see you again!"

They stood in embrace, weeping with happiness and relief.

"Oh, how you have suffered!" Molena wailed, lightly tracing her fingers over his flayed body.

He smiled bravely. "The Roman doctor who has been caring for me says the scars will eventually fade." And then he saw Curio was there, watching the scene. Curio had been at Caesar's side that awful day they had pulled Molena out of the coffle and taken her away . . . before they had nearly killed him with the bullwhips.

"Has that man hurt you?" Elliandro demanded. He seemed ready to charge at the Roman, despite the fact that he could certainly not survive another beating like the last one.

Molena, fearful, reassured him. "No, no," she said urgently. "He has been kind to me. It was he who had you brought here and who made the doctors help you."

Elliandro became angry. "Has he taken advantage of you? Is that why he has saved me?"

Molena clutched her brother tightly. "No, please, you must not be angry with him. He works for Caesar, but he is not like the rest of them. He has not touched me, and he has protected me from the others, too."

They spoke in Germanic, so Molena assumed Curio could only understand snatches of it. But he looked tense and surely knew they were talking about him.

The shock of it all struck Elliandro, who, in his weakened state, sagged to the ground. Molena dropped to his side, still weeping and hugging him. She tried to coax him back to his feet, but he could not gather the strength.

Curio came over. Together, he and Molena helped him to stand.

"Let's take him back to his bed," Curio said. They supported him as he staggered to the tent that had been his home for the past weeks and settled him onto the cot.

Molena dropped to her knees at his side and stroked his face. "Oh, Elliandro, how they have hurt you," she whispered.

Vatteus appeared, winking a greeting at Curio. "You must let him rest," he told them. "He is still very weak."

"He is so thin!" Molena cried.

"Perhaps the next time you visit," Curio said softly, "you can bring him some of your bread."

Curio could see that Vatteus was studying Molena intently, as if he was trying to remember where he might have met her. "She is the slave you examined for Caesar," he said quietly. "I have taken an interest in her. Not a word of this to Caesar, understand?"

Then, after a pause, he said in his command tone of voice, "Increase his rations. Let's get some meat back on his bones."

Vatteus struck his breast in the customary salute, although Molena thought she detected a hint of a smirk on his face. The doctor excused himself to tend to other patients.

Elliandro's head lolled.

"Come, Molena," Curio said, "let him sleep."

Reluctantly, she stood and gingerly kissed her brother's forehead, then spread a blanket over him.

As they returned to the fortress, Molena had nothing to say. Her mind was a hopeless jumble of emotions. Hatred burned in her at the awful fate that had befallen them—herself a slave, her very body available for the taking at the whim of any who might be her master, her brother viciously beaten to within an inch of his life, perhaps marked forever.

But somehow, she could not hate this man walking beside her, who had protected her and even reunited her with Elliandro. He was a Roman; she *must* hate him! But she did not feel it, not at all. If anything, she felt . . .

"Time for you to return to the kitchens," he said as they neared the gate, interrupting her thoughts. "And if the chief cook so much as says a cross word to you, do tell me when you bring me my dinner."

"Thank you," was all she could say. Then, "May I see my brother again?"

"Of course you may," Curio replied easily. "I will keep an eye out for any opportunity."

THAT EVENING, Caesar took his supper with Devorra, as he had on numerous occasions since the first night she had let him have his way with her.

Devorra chatted pleasantly throughout the dinner about any number of inane subjects, wanting to give Caesar no sense of any anxiety on her part. He was in good spirits, the departure of his force heading for Corbilo having gone smoothly. She made no protest when he led her to the bedchamber, as had become their practice following their meal. She had time and again proved a worthy outlet for Caesar's ravenous carnal appetites.

Devorra had noted more than once that, unlike his office quarters, which were elaborately decorated with works of sculpture and art, Caesar's bedroom was relatively Spartan in comparison—a simple bed, a small writing desk and chair, and two trunks containing Caesar's clothing and other personal effects. The only noteworthy items were a golden locket on a long, thin chain, which Caesar kept draped over the headboard, and an ivory-handled dagger. Upon inquiry, she had learned the locket contained a wisp of his daughter Julia's hair. Caesar told her that in this way a part of her was always with him, which was of great importance to him.

Seeing the locket again, Devorra was reminded of her braided gift to Gabinier . . . *but no*. She must rein in her emotions.

She picked up the dagger, marveling at the precision of the eagle carved into the handle. "This is beautiful," she said, turning it over in her hands.

"Indeed," Caesar replied. "It was given to me by Julia. I carry it with me always, because it is so precious to me."

Devorra, who had known nothing but terror from her own father, was moved by this rare exhibit of sentimentality from a conqueror as mighty as Caesar.

They had already kissed for long minutes when Caesar reached to push the dress off her shoulders. After admiring the splendor of her bosom for a few moments, he began to pull down her dress. For the first time in their intimacy, Devorra pulled back.

Caesar asked, "What is wrong?"

She decided to strike straight at the matter. "You must be gentle with me," Devorra said lightly. "I'm going to have a child."

Caesar took this news stoically.

Dismayed by his lack of reaction, Devorra's face darkened. "I hoped you would be pleased," she whispered.

"A child. This *is* news," he said flatly. "When is the babe to be born?"

"In perhaps six months," she replied uneasily, fearful of his emotionless demeanor. "Possibly a bit more."

Caesar thought for a moment. "Well, we will be departing to deal with the Veneti in the spring," he said, noncommittally. "We will have to see how it all works out."

Devorra was not reassured. In the back of her mind, she could hear Aloucca's shrill warnings. Knowing she was on precarious ground, she said hesitantly, "It seems your campaign may be more important than the child."

"What will be, will be," he said.

Caesar's reply cut at her deeply, but Devorra was persistent. "What will become of me?"

"This is not the first time this has occurred," he said.

"What does that mean?" she asked, doubtful of the ways of the Romans.

Caesar reflected for a few long moments, then replied, "I have political enemies in Rome who would try to make a scandal out of this. It is imperative that we keep this news from reaching them. Curio will handle the details."

She was not assuaged. "I am carrying your child. What will happen to us?"

"I cannot have illegitimate heirs dotting the Roman landscape."

Devorra felt the bitter sting of disappointment but decided this was not the time to push her luck. She had other questions: "What about my father? What will he do when he finds out?"

Caesar laughed. "I have yet to encounter a father who wouldn't accept money to stay calm about it. And your father ought to be especially easy to deal with on that score."

Devorra felt no better.

"Now," he said, returning his hands to her bare belly, which did not yet show any sign of her new state. "Off with this dress."

She was hurt by his cold reaction and was in no mood to give herself over to him, as she had on all those other occasions. Caesar sensed her reluctance, but his passion was up, the potion having worked its wonders yet again, and he pressed ahead. He spent himself quickly after entering her.

After rolling off her, he stood and donned his toga while Devorra turned to her side and wiped silent tears from her face. Caesar briskly left the chamber without speaking another word, and when it became clear he would not return, Devorra dressed and hurried back to her own quarters.

Curio was buried in a morass of tedium when relief arrived in the shapely form of Molena, bearing dinner.

She was still in the same clothes she had worn to the hospital. This was pleasing to him, but he asked, "Didn't you change back to your other dress when you returned to work?"

"No," she said. "When I got back to the kitchen, the head cook said I need not work the rest of the day. He seemed to be afraid of me!"

"How odd," Curio said knowingly. He smiled at her as she put the food before him. A platter of roasted lamb, farro with a brown sauce, and boiled carrots, which smelled slightly of garlic. And, of course, a half loaf of bread.

"Your bread?" Curio asked lightly.

"Yes," she said. "I hope you like it."

"If the cook said you need not work more today, why then are you serving me?" he asked.

"I wanted to," she said softly. It sent a bolt of emotion through his body.

He motioned for her to be seated, and she eased herself onto the chair across from his desk. He tore off a piece of the crusty loaf, dabbed it in the sauce, and tasted it. "Marvelous," he said enthusiastically. Then he added, "You said the other night that you don't eat until after all the soldiers have been fed. Are you hungry now?"

She looked down, shaking her head slightly.

Curio tore off a piece of the bread and chewed it. "Mmm," he said encouragingly, "you have mastered the art."

This brought a satisfied smile to her face.

He rearranged the food on his plate, sliding some of it into the bowl of carrots. "Here," he said.

She did not move.

He was disappointed. "You are afraid to accept anything from me?"

She looked up at him. "I already owe you more than I can ever repay."

"Do not burden yourself with such thoughts," he said. "I help you because I care for you, not because I seek anything in exchange."

She seemed to be fighting back tears.

"Go ahead," he said. "I know you must be hungry." He poured some wine into a cup for her.

She took the cup carefully and lifted it to her lips, then made a sour face.

"Army wine," he explained. "Next time, I'll have something better for you."

She gave in and took a few bites of the lamb.

This pleased him. "Well, that's progress."

"You told me I may question you without asking permission," she said abruptly. "Is that still true?"

"Of course."

Molena chewed on her lower lip for a moment. "What will happen to my brother?"

Curio had not given it a moment's thought. "I don't know yet," he said. "But have peace of mind. We'll work something out."

"I am willing to give myself to you," she whispered.

Curio was unpersuaded. "You think that if you do that, you will entice me not to send your brother away?"

The astonishment on her face told him he was right.

"That will not be necessary," he said with a tone of command in his voice. "I will do what I can to keep you two together."

Now the tears spilled from her eyes.

He reached across the table and gently cupped her chin in his hands. "At some point, if you choose to be intimate with me, it should be what you want to do, not for what you hope to gain."

❦

THE NEXT MORNING, Caesar was at his desk, toiling over yet another stack of military documents, when Curio arrived.

Dispensing with niceties, Caesar told him the news about Devorra.

Curio was not surprised. The general had been spending a significant amount of time with the nubile wench. While it was good to hear that the apothecary's ministrations had worked and the old man was still potent, he feared for Devorra.

"You'll take care of it, I trust," Caesar said. "Perhaps you should see the apothecary?"

In the past, when Caesar had impregnated a slave girl, Curio had obtained a strong potion to be administered to the woman, causing a miscarriage, and then the slave could still be sold off. Curio did not particularly like this solution, however; the women usually hemorrhaged, and some did not survive.

"We have only done that with slave girls," Curio replied. "Devorra is a hostage, under our care. This could have severe consequences."

Caesar pondered this. "We would simply report that she died of a fever. Who would even notice? The girl has made it clear that her father has no interest in her well-being."

179

This was becoming increasingly disturbing to Curio, as he had sympathy for the girl. "Nonetheless, we are duty-bound to protect the hostages, not kill them."

Caesar looked at the ceiling, considering the problem.

"The critical thing is that no one know of her condition," Curio said. "You are at a delicate place in your discussions with Pompey and Crassus. We cannot hand your opponents a scandal to use against you."

"And they surely would not hesitate," Caesar said with a nod. "No one but you is to be aware of her condition, Rio," he continued. "My enemies have spies everywhere."

"Perhaps Vatteus should check in on her occasionally? He's eminently trustworthy."

Caesar was already losing interest in this situation. "He knows all my secrets," he said dismissively. "What's one more?"

"I will find a satisfactory resolution," Curio avowed.

"I have no doubt, my friend," Caesar replied, returning to his work. "I'm sure a few bags of gold will suffice to silence the wench."

XXVIII

IN THE TERRITORY OF THE NERVII

THE RUSTIC FARMER RABANUS bent over and pulled a carrot from the soil. He rubbed the moist black dirt between his fingers and was pleased—the growing season was progressing along with no hint of draught, well into the summer. He dropped the carrots into the oaken bucket he was carrying and continued through the modest garden just beyond the crude log hut he shared with his wife, Berhta, who would use the carrots to make a good stew.

As he made his way back to the cabin, Rabanus watched the stranger who had crawled out of the woods and into their lives after the battle with the Romans, barely alive. Rabanus, sick with worry over the fate of his own son in the battle, had carried the stranger to the safety of their home. The man was pale from the loss of blood and hardly breathing.

Just a few days later, they learned the magnitude of the Roman victory—thousands of Nervii warriors were dead or captured. Though overcome with grief and the awful uncertainty of not knowing what had happened to their boy, Rabanus and his wife patiently nursed the stranger back to health. And they had grown fond of him, perhaps seeing in him reminders of their own lost son.

Having made remarkable strides toward recovery, the man was now chopping relentlessly at a felled tree across the clearing from their homestead, piling up firewood for the home. His swing of the ax still retained a pronounced hitch—while he could hoist the heavy tool high above his head, he faltered a beat as he began the downstroke, his face contorting with pain each time. Still, he was improving daily as the healing process progressed.

"If you keep this up," Rabanus said as he drew near, the bucket of vegetables thumping against his thigh, "you will have us supplied with firewood for the whole winter."

The man idled his ax for a moment and gave Rabanus a hearty grin. "It's good for my recovery. Every day I feel more and more of my strength returning."

Rabanus reached out with his free hand and rubbed the man's shoulder. "The wound is fully closed. The joint seems to have knitted well. You'll be as good as new in a few more weeks."

The man shook his head. "I cannot tarry much longer. I must rejoin the tribe and continue the fight against the Romans." He raised the ax again for another swing at the dwindling log.

Rabanus sighed. He had explained many times during the man's convalescence that the battle against the Romans had turned into a shattering rout of the Nervii and their allies. He had heard that the Romans had offered peace terms and the Belgae had accepted. The war was over, and the Nervii had lost—badly.

The recovering warrior brought the ax down with a fierce strike, neatly splitting the log.

"You work with such intensity," Rabanus commented.

"It's easy," came the reply. "I pretend I am killing Romans."

The farmer, who hated the Romans himself for the loss of his son, still did not understand it. "If I had survived such a nightmare, I wouldn't want to go near them again," he said. "You are a better man than I am, Gabinier."

Gabinier gathered up the pieces of firewood and started stacking them. "There is no man better than you, dear Rabanus," he said. "This wood will feed your fire through the winter for you and Berhta, but my fire burns within. It burns for revenge."

SEVERAL WEEKS PASSED. Rabanus succeeded in convincing Gabinier that he should not leave the relative safety of the home until he could wield the ax in a smooth single stroke, without the pause at the apex of the swing. That, he insisted, would be the test of whether the shoulder was completely healed.

And the day finally came when Gabinier gathered Rabanus and his wife for a small demonstration. He chopped down a large oak tree from inside the forest and dragged it into the clearing, which had been much expanded by Gabinier's daily exercise routine. With little effort, he pared away the branches, leaving naught but the trunk itself. And in a series of rapid strikes, he reduced the huge trunk to yet another pile for the farmer's hearth.

"What say you, Rabanus?" Gabinier asked, barely winded from his exertions.

"We will miss you," Rabanus said. "Since you are so determined to make war against the Romans, I want to give you a gift."

Gabinier felt guilty. These people were peasants, scratching out a hard-scrabble existence from the soil. With no son left in the household, things would be hard for them in the years to come. They had nothing to give him, and he started to protest.

"No," Rabanus insisted, "take the ax with you. After all your work, we will have no need of it for months to come!"

They all laughed at that, and then Gabinier drew them each into a long embrace. "I owe you my life. I cannot say how, nor when, but I swear to you, someday I shall pay you back for your kindness to me."

IT WAS A TRADITION of the Nervii that any member of the tribe with a grievance could appear before the council of the clan leaders to air his complaint and seek redress for any wrongs done unto him. The council, though shrunk in size after the devastating loss to the Romans, had continued to gather at each lunar cycle, when the moon was at its fullest.

The council members sat cross-legged on the ground around a fire that had burned down to its still-glowing embers, crackling in the cool night air.

Boduognatus, not yet adjusted to his vastly reduced stature as leader of a much-diminished tribe, sat on one side of the fire, with only Pomorro at his side. The other leaders faced him in a semicircle. The men who by mere fortune had survived the debacle against the Romans were surly, blaming Boduognatus for bringing down catastrophe on them and their families. But they still feared him, and none had yet dared to challenge him for leadership of the tribe.

The council's business on this evening was mundane: a smattering of routine neighborly squabbles to be resolved. One fellow lost three sheep after his flock had been attacked by another tribesman's vicious dog. The dog's owner was directed to replace the sheep. Another man complained that his well had been fouled by the proximity of a new outhouse built by an adjoining owner, who denied there was any problem—until made to taste the water himself. The offending privy was ordered to be relocated.

A man who has dreamed of being a king does not appreciate being reduced to ruling on such trivial matters. Boduognatus mostly sat mute through the docket, occasionally tilting his head to indicate his assent or objection to the proceedings. Finally, they were done with their adjudicating, and Boduognatus wearily called out, "Does any member of the tribe have further matters for the council?"

From the darkness behind him, a clear, strong voice boomed out, "Aye."

Both Boduognatus and Pomorro recognized the voice in an instant. They jumped to their feet just as Gabinier stepped into the ocherous light thrown off by the dwindling fire.

"You!" Boduognatus could barely speak, so dumbfounded was he by the young warrior's sudden appearance. He turned to Pomorro and snarled, "You said you saw him fall!"

Pomorro, in his shock, wondered if they were seeing a ghost, come to haunt them as the gods' punishment for their folly against the Romans.

But Gabinier was no mere spirit, and all could see his face was contorted in anger.

"You *wished* for me to fail," Gabinier spat at them. "But the gods spared me, and I've come now to demand what we all know must be the wages of your failure against the Romans. Your leadership of the tribe is forfeited."

Boduognatus cast a glance at the men still seated opposite him. Their faces were grim. He could sense that the council was against him.

Boduognatus regarded Gabinier with disdain. "How dare you challenge my leadership of the Nervii, when it was *you* who failed to keep the Roman rear guard from reaching the field?" He made a sweeping gesture toward the others. "All of you were there—the battle at the Roman camp was won! We were plundering their baggage train! The Romans had formed a square in desperation against our final attack. Then their relief column arrived and struck us in the flank because *you* let them get away."

"We fought bravely against the Romans," Gabinier responded with not a trace of fear in his voice. "Pomorro here saw it himself. If you had but kept a force in reserve in the forest, you could have countered the Romans when they reached the field."

Several of the council members cocked their heads in agreement. Boduognatus could see he was losing them.

"The Atuatuci were to form the reserve, and they were late to arrive!" Boduognatus pleaded to the group, just a hint of a whine in his voice. "It was *they* who failed us!"

Gabinier gave him an icy stare. "If our forces were not fully ready, you should not have launched the attack."

The silence of the council was deafening.

Gabinier pulled back the deerskin shirt he was wearing and pointed to the jagged scar on his mended shoulder. "I myself nearly died in the battle. Where are *your* scars, Boduognatus?"

Boduognatus felt a familiar calm come over him. He placed his hand on the golden bear amulet that symbolized the tribe's leadership, then lifted it over his head and handed it to Pomorro. He stared unblinking at the young upstart brazenly challenging him. "I took leadership of this tribe by the strength of my arm. He who would take it from me must do the same."

Gabinier did not falter. "My shade has knocked on death's door before. It holds no fear for me."

Boduognatus was no stranger to facing death either, and he couldn't resist a taunt to his challenger. "Even if you prevail, boy, what you desire most is not here for you."

Gabinier's face screwed up in anguish. "What have you done with her?"

Pleased that he had wounded the lad with nothing but words, Boduognatus replied in his most insulting tone, "She is in the hands of the Romans, a hostage for life. She is the living bond of the Nervii to hold our faith to the treaty we made with them."

Gabinier face flushed with rage.

Boduognatus was enjoying his adversary's torment. "She thinks you are dead. She's probably forgotten you by now."

Gabinier trembled with white-hot anger; the men nearest him began to back away.

"And even if she were to return," Boduognatus went on, "she had sworn to me she would spread her legs for the prince of the Bellovaci. You'll never get into that honey pot of hers."

Gabinier erupted with a lightning blow to Boduognatus's chin, connecting squarely and sending the older man staggering backward. Before Boduognatus could gasp for breath, Gabinier was on him like a hawk on a field mouse, pummeling the tribal leader, out of his mind with fury.

But Boduognatus was immensely strong, and he righted himself with a rage borne of the humiliation he had endured at the hands of the Romans. The two skilled warriors traded punches, fighting only with their fists, giving no thought to other weapons. Their enmity was deep and personal— this would be decided with their own flesh, not the steel of their swords.

The council members and Pomorro watched in frightened awe as the fight raged. Both men were cut and bleeding from the power of their jabs, but neither showed any sign of retreat.

Boduognatus, though, was older and tiring quickly. He summoned all his strength for a mighty swing at his opponent's head, but Gabinier was just a touch quicker. The blow sailed harmlessly past his square jaw, leaving Boduognatus off balance and exposed. Gabinier saw the opening and struck with a thunderous punch to his adversary's ear, dropping the brute face-first onto the turf like a deer felled by an arrow. Boduognatus fought for consciousness, but vertigo from the terrible impact set in and he could not get to his feet. Gabinier launched a vicious kick with the heel of his boot at Boduognatus's head. The sheer force of this shot would have killed an ordinary man, but somehow Boduognatus groaned and clutched at the ground, still clinging to life.

As the stunned group looked on in silence, Gabinier, his rage unabated, dragged his adversary to the edge of the hot coals of the campfire. He grabbed the back of Boduognatus's head by his long locks, slimy now from the sweat and gore of the contest. He thrust Boduognatus's face into the coals, and despite his horrible screams, held him firmly there until the man moved no more.

Gabinier, panting from exhaustion, with blood dripping down his face, glared at Pomorro. "And you?"

Pomorro wanted no part of this man's rage. He handed the bear amulet to Gabinier. "You are now the leader of the Nervii," he said simply. "I swear my loyalty to you."

Gabinier turned to the others. One by one, they raised their hands in agreement.

"I do not care to lead the Nervii," he said, still gasping for breath from his exertion, "unless you will join with me to fight the Romans."

Now all the clansmen looked at their feet.

"It's out of the question," one of them said softly. "Some of us have given our sons as hostages. Even worse, there are too few of us left. We must keep the peace we have made and rebuild the tribe. It will be many years before we can multiply ourselves enough to threaten the Romans again."

Pomorro added, "And even if we did, the Romans would kill the hostages. Do you know how they kill hostages when a party has breached a treaty?"

Gabinier shook his head.

"They crucify them, and she shall not be spared," Pomorro said coldly. "They will flay the skin off her body with their scourges, then nail what's left of her to the cross. The insects, the birds, the dogs—all will have at her. She might suffer for days."

Gabinier said nothing. One of the clansmen brought forth a cool, wet cloth and Gabinier cleaned himself, doing his best to wipe the blood from the crevices of the braided leather bracelet he never removed from his wrist. When he was finished, he handed the golden bear back to Pomorro. "I will not wait for years to fight the Romans, and I will not put Devorra's life at risk."

Pomorro was befuddled. "But what can you do? All the tribes of the Belgae have joined in the peace. You have no army to challenge Caesar."

Gabinier did not hesitate. "I know where there is an army that will fight the Romans."

Taken aback, Pomorro asked, "And where is that?"

Gabinier tossed the grimy cloth into the last flickering flames.

"It is across the Rhine," he said simply. "I will join the one man who does not fear Caesar. His name is Ariovistus."

IN HIS ONLY OFFICIAL ACTS as the leader of the Nervii, Gabinier awarded himself a fast horse, a pack mule, and a large parcel of supplies for his journey into Germania to locate Ariovistus, and then he named Pomorro as his successor. He was packing the supplies when a group of three warriors approached him. He recognized them from the battle against the Romans in the forest.

"We want to go with you," one of them said. He was relatively short for a Nervii and more wiry than brawny, unusual for a warrior. But his gray eyes burned with intensity, and he spoke with a passion that could not be denied.

"Your name is Gustavus—do I remember correctly?" Gabinier asked, and the man gave a nod. "My journey is fraught with danger. Why would you want to join me?"

"We saw how you fought against the Romans. We want another shot at them." Gustavus introduced the other two men: Giovanus and Gregarus.

Gabinier looked quickly at one man, then the next, then back to the first—all surprisingly similar.

"We're brothers," said Gustavus, with a grin. "I am the oldest."

Gabinier was dubious. "I am honored, truly, that you want to come with me," he said slowly, "but this is a personal quest. I go to seek not just vengeance against the Romans, but, somehow, I must rescue the maiden Devorra from her captivity."

None of the men blinked.

"I cannot put your lives at risk for my own personal reasons," he insisted.

"We are free men, warriors of the Nervii," Gustavus responded. "Our subjugation to the terms the Romans have imposed is more than we can bear. Take us with you. Your chances of success in your cause will be improved by the addition of our strength, will they not?"

Gabinier could not deny it. "I cannot promise we will make it back here alive," he cautioned them. "You must say farewell to your families. This may be the last day you ever lay eyes on them."

The youngest of them, Gregarus, said, "Our parents are dead. None of us are married. We have responsibility to no one but ourselves."

"I am running out of objections," Gabinier said with a laugh.

"We saw you fall that day," said the middle brother, Giovanus. "None of us dreamed you could survive. Clearly, you are favored by the gods. Maybe some of that luck of yours will rub off on us!"

"So be it, then." Gabinier proceeded to clasp arms with each man in turn.

"Gather your gear," he told them. "We leave at sunrise."

XXIX

VESONTIO

GIACOMO WAS MASSIVELY ANNOYED to be interrupted in his work on the bridge plans by a summons to Curio's quarters, but orders were orders. He found the adjutant buried in a mountain of army make-work.

"Ah, Giacomo," Curio said, indicating for the engineer to sit. "How comes the work on the bridge plans?"

Giacomo's eyes grew large as saucers.

"Yes, of course I know about the bridge project," Curio said, with a bit of pique in his voice. He pointed at a huge stack of parchment on the corner of his desk. "Who do you think is handling the requisition of all the materials you are ordering?"

Giacomo had not given any thought to how the mountain of supplies they were stockpiling was being procured. "The project is going well," he replied assuredly. "We have a working design, which has been sent to Mamurra for review and approval. And the fieldwork is already underway. We believe we have found a suitable location."

Curio had reason to press further on this point. "How far away is the site?"

"Only a couple of miles," Giacomo responded. "It is ideal: the river is relatively narrow there—less bridge deck needed for the span."

"And the approaches?"

Giacomo smiled. "The bluffs are easily scaled at that point. The gods must have had a bridge site in mind for this spot when they carved out the river."

"Good. I may wish to ride out and inspect it myself before we leave for Corbilo," he told Giacomo. "Now, tell me the truth, Giacomo; I will share it with no one. What do you really think about this idea of Caesar's? Is it even remotely feasible?"

"With enough shovels and enough slaves, anything can be built, no matter how challenging the schedule," Giacomo replied.

Curio picked up a document, signaling the interview was finished. Giacomo stood and turned to leave when Curio said sharply, "Two weeks is better than three, in Caesar's eyes."

There was no point in disputing it, and Giacomo went on his way, already making new calculations.

❦

CURIO AROSE EARLY the next morning and rode out of Vesontio in the opposite direction from the bridge site Giacomo had indicated. He came upon a small farm and an unusually large stone cottage, a little more than a mile from Vesontio. It was perfectly situated on a gentle hill beside the Doubs River, surrounded by an overgrown fruit orchard.

As Curio approached the front door of the abode, a crooked, weathered old man emerged, warily observing his visitor.

"Greetings to you, sir," Curio said in the Gallic tongue. "Is this your farm?" he asked, hoping he had used the correct words.

In a few minutes of bargaining, Curio arranged a rental of the property for an indefinite time. He stressed to the owner, a farmer named Othon, the need for privacy for the residents, two women, and that he should discuss their presence with no one. Othon, having obtained what to him was a princely sum for the monthly rent, was happy to move himself to another cottage on the other side of the property.

Curio did not care where the man might go. "Let me see the inside."

They made a quick inspection of the stone farmhouse. Upon taking in the size of the place, he said, "Yes, this will do nicely." He took a bag of gold coins from his pocket. "And did I say two women? Forgive me; I should have said three."

For Curio had been struck with inspiration: If he moved Molena to the farm with Devorra and Aloucca, there was no chance that Caesar might again lay eyes on the slave who'd witnessed his impotence.

❦

CAESAR WAS JUST LEAVING his office when Curio stopped him with the news.

"I've taken measures to relocate the Nervii woman," he told him. "She should be of no further consequence to you."

190

"Good. I don't need to hear her whining any longer," the general replied. "Give her some gold and be done with her."

They agreed that it would fall to Curio to tell Devorra of her move, as Caesar wanted no further contact with her.

Later that day, Curio made his way to Devorra's quarters and announced his presence. He found her and her slave woman partaking of a modest meal at their small table. He noticed that Devorra had hardly touched the food, while the slave had all but licked her plate clean.

"Good evening, Adjutant," Aloucca said, rising to her feet.

Devorra remained seated but turned her head slowly, her steely eyes barely acknowledging him.

"I'm sorry to disturb your meal, but I have an urgent matter to discuss," he said. Devorra quickly stood to face him.

"Our general has made me aware of your condition, my lady, and I am here to advise you of highly favorable arrangements that have been made on your behalf."

"What arrangements?" Devorra asked, clearly suspicious.

The slave woman moved closer to her mistress and took her hand.

"A military headquarters is no place for a woman with child," Curio asserted in his most charming manner. "Too much noise and activity to disturb you, and if you do not get adequate rest, the delivery may be difficult."

Devorra said nothing.

Curio softened his manner. "Tomorrow I will take you and your companion to a special place I have found for you."

"We will be leaving?" the maid asked, alarmed. "How are we to manage on our own?"

Curio spoke directly to Devorra. "It's a lovely farm cottage only a mile or so from the fort, alongside the river. The elderly farmer who lives nearby is preparing it for you as we speak, and it will be comfortably furnished. You will have complete privacy and ample food and supplies to sustain you during the coming months."

Finally, Devorra spoke. "He's sending me away." It wasn't a question.

Curio knew she spoke the truth, but he did not confirm her conclusion. "This is strictly for your own good. You should understand that Caesar has powerful enemies, and they will stop at nothing to get at him. This puts both you and your child at considerable risk. The only way to protect you is to create distance between you and the general."

Devorra's glare was withering, but Curio went on. "I must also tell you that these enemies of Caesar are utterly ruthless, and it is very much in your best interest to share with no one the identity of the child's father."

Devorra's voice seethed with anger. "He will deny his own child?"

"No, no," Curio said soothingly. "His fondness for you is precisely why we are making these arrangements. I am merely advising you how best to protect your own safety."

Devorra pointed at her swelling belly and snarled, "How am I supposed to explain this?"

The adjutant thought for a moment. *Every lie should have a nugget of truth in it,* he thought. "I'm sorry to say it, but if you tell them you were violated by a Roman soldier, there are few who would not believe you."

Devorra's jaw shifted, her eyes narrowing in disgust.

"Better yet," Curio corrected himself, "tell them it was a Roman officer. That's more plausible. And tell them Caesar dealt with the perpetrator, but you don't know what happened to him."

Curio saw the tears welling in Devorra's eyes, though whether they stemmed from anger or despair he did not know. He wanted to be more re-assuring. "You will be provided with everything you need to be safe and comfortable. And your slave woman—she is a midwife, yes?—she will be with you through it all. We are so dedicated to your safe delivery, in fact, that we can make a Roman army doctor available for the delivery, if needed."

Devorra looked shocked. "You would have a doctor attend the birth?"

"Why not?"

"In our tribe, we have no doctors; the barbers handle whatever medical needs people might have."

Curio laughed at the thought of comparing the highly trained Vatteus with a tribal barber. "Well, our doctors are much more than mere barbers, as you will see."

His offer landed with a thud. She looked away, unwilling to maintain eye contact with him. Curio could see there was nothing to be gained by lingering further with them.

As he turned to leave, Curio addressed the slave. "I will be back early tomorrow morning to travel with you to the farm, and to help you get settled. Pack your possessions."

After Curio left, Devorra was feeling ill, and it had nothing to do with her pregnancy.

"I knew it!" Aloucca cackled. "I knew that once he had you heavy with child he'd move on to other morsels!"

192

Devorra shook her head. "I should never have given myself to him."

"Why did you do it?"

"I thought it would keep us safe!"

Aloucca reached out a bony hand and stroked her mistress's cheek. "Do not be hard on yourself," she told the girl. "Men and their animal appetites bring nothing but misery to women. You are neither the first nor will you be the last to fall prey to a man's craving."

Devorra set her jaw, determined to see this ordeal through to whatever outcome the conniving gods might have in store for her.

FOLLOWING HIS VISIT to Devorra, Curio went to see Molena's brother, Elliandro. Finally recovered from his horrible beating, the young man was in the hospital tent, busy rolling bandages for use on the next Roman campaign. Intent on his work, he suddenly realized he was not alone and looked up.

"Do you wish to see your sister again?" Curio asked.

Elliandro, who seemed to recognize Curio, regarded him cautiously. "Yes."

"I am going to assign her as a servant to one of the Nervii hostages we are holding," Curio told him. "The hostage and her slave woman are to be relocated to a cottage outside the camp. I require your assistance to move them there."

"And Molena?" Elliandro asked.

"First the hostage, and Molena soon after," Curio answered. "She will be completely safe. But let me be clear: If I take you there, and you ever try to escape, you will be captured with ease. We have five legions encamped in the vicinity, and they will hunt you down. Do you know the punishment for a slave who attempts to escape?"

Elliandro swallowed hard. "Crucifixion."

"Yes, but only after the condemned is thoroughly scourged. It would make what happened to you before seem like child's play," Curio said coldly. "Your sister will suffer the same fate—all the family members of a runaway slave are crucified as well. It won't matter whether you try to escape alone or bring her with you. Either way, I will not be able to save her."

The answer was obvious. "I understand, master. You will receive no reports about me."

"Good. I will come for you in the early morning. Say nothing of this to anyone. If I learn that you've spoken of it, Molena will remain here, and both of you will be shoveling manure out of the stables."

Curio turned his back on the slave and walked toward the fortress.

Having deftly maneuvered Elliandro and Molena safely out of the range of anyone's attention at Vesontio, he reflected on the dangerous game he was playing. *Why such risks to protect a mere slave?* he asked himself. But the truth was that his interest in Molena had grown into something far more than affection. Perhaps it was insanity; perhaps it was the gods playing some nefarious game with him. But there was no point in denying it: Curio was in love with her.

⌒⌒⌒⌒⌒

THE NEXT MORNING, just as the sun was breaking over the horizon, Curio arrived to escort Devorra to her new lodgings. The women were visibly anxious, still unsure of what lay ahead. He had commissioned a large wagon with a driver whose arms and neck were badly scarred. The wagon waited at the entrance to the fortress, together with Curio's own mount. Curio had reassigned the sentries at the gate so he and the women could depart unobserved.

They rode in silence through the forest, the only sounds coming from the horses' hooves on the hard clay path and the occasional call of a circling bird of prey. The trip was brief, and they soon emerged from the trees to take in their new home. Despite her misgivings, Devorra was pleased by the serene beauty of the place.

Devorra climbed down from the wagon and strolled over to the orchard, delighted to find at its edge bushes lush with juicy blackberries.

She returned to the little group carrying a handful of them. "Would you like some?" she said, offering them to the bemused Curio.

He graciously declined.

"I've always wanted to have a garden of my own. My father would not allow it."

"You may pursue your dream of a garden," Curio replied cheerfully.

"Oh, and there are chickens," Devorra said. "Aloucca, fresh eggs!"

The farmer greeted them and showed Devorra and Aloucca to the cottage. Aloucca objected that there was no furniture, until she looked back at the wagon and saw the driver unloading the parts for several beds, chairs, a table, and a large bureau. Curio had also packed an ample supply of food, beverages, and other necessities. Aloucca busied herself with directing the placement of the items.

Curio led Devorra to a small bench situated under a large tree. "I hope you are feeling more at ease now that you have seen where you'll be," he told her. "Living away from the army is the best situation for all of you, including your child."

Devorra nodded. She was surprisingly pleased by the farm, and besides, she had resolved to start fending for herself—there was no point in relying on the Romans.

But Curio said, "I'll be back soon, and I will be bringing you a gift."

Devorra was curious. "What might that be?"

Aloucca came outside to report on the progress with the rooms, and Curio told them both, "I am granting you another slave girl, to keep you company and help with cooking and such."

"We don't need any help," Devorra said. The last thing she needed was a spy reporting back to Caesar about her every move. Aloucca looked alarmed as well.

Curio seemed to understand Devorra's suspicion. "Have an open mind," he urged. "She is not here to spy on you. The girl is the sister of my driver, Elliandro. Her name is Molena. You will find her a very agreeable companion. And she is a capable baker and cook."

"Very well," Devorra said. "Perhaps she can teach me."

WHEN MOLENA BROUGHT Curio his lunch, he informed her that she would have a change in duties. She was surprised to find herself afraid that a new assignment might have her seeing less of him.

"This will be easy duty," Curio reassured her. "Your surroundings will be pleasant, and you need only to help care for the Lady Devorra during her pregnancy. She will rely primarily upon her own servant, I'm sure. Do whatever household chores they assign you, and bake them some of your wonderful bread," he added with a smile. "And you will have your own bedchamber."

Molena had lived her whole life in a one-room hut, never having a room to herself. She could barely imagine it.

Curio became serious. "There are two things I must warn you about."

She looked at him attentively.

"First, you must not venture away from the farm. We must make certain that Caesar never finds out that you are living with the woman Devorra. He believes you are dead."

"But my brother will wonder what has happened to me."

Curio smiled again. "Elliandro knows all about this change. He has already been to the farm with me, and I will have him accompany me whenever I bring supplies. You will see him regularly. He has fully recovered, and, in fact, I have asked the doctor to keep him at the hospital as an orderly. It's a relatively easy life for a male slave, and I have the authority to relieve him from time to time to assist me. This is a very comfortable situation for both of you."

Molena could hardly believe this news.

"Now," Curio said, "you will no doubt be wondering why the Lady Devorra is alone during her pregnancy, and how she came to be in that situation. The unfortunate fact is that she was violated by a Roman officer. Because she is under our care as a hostage, I feel a special responsibility to take good care of her during this trying time."

Molena felt immediate sympathy for her soon-to-be companion. She resolved not to bring it up unless the woman herself wanted to talk about it.

"Now, go and pack your things. And tell the head cook that he will need to find a replacement for you, as I have given you a new assignment. Tell him nothing more. If he has any questions, tell him to come to me directly."

Molena, her head still spinning, began to comprehend what Curio had done for her and Elliandro. She wondered if she might be more than a mere slave to him.

"I am most grateful for all of these changes. For me *and* for Elliandro," she said as she made to leave. But she lingered for a moment, and then stepped closer to Curio. Without giving it a further thought, she leaned forward and gave him a light kiss on the cheek, feeling the taut ripples of his scar on her lips.

He was too stunned to react, and she slipped out before he could say another word.

XXX

CORBILO, ON THE BRITTANY COAST

MAMURRA WAS PERPLEXED.

Seated at the end of a newly constructed pier extending out into the ocean, with Pompey's man Garibus at his side, the engineer was deep in thought, gazing at two ships moored just a short distance from his perch, swaying gently as the tide ebbed and flowed. The late autumn breeze was chilling, a harbinger of the harsh winter months that were only a few weeks away.

One of the ships was the first boat constructed by Mamurra's team shortly after their arrival at Corbilo. Once the staff had settled in and gotten their bearings, they had chopped and hammered and sawed night and day to produce a traditional Roman-style war galley, strictly by the book, right down to the last details specified in the naval engineering text Mamurra had toted with him all the way from Vesontio. The body was long and lean, with a deep and narrow keel, propelled by oars, built for speed on the Mediterranean, with a sharp brass point mounted on the bow for ramming the enemy. Mamurra was proud of it.

Alongside it was a hulking Veneti vessel. Mamurra had wanted to get a look at what his ships would be up against, so asked the legion commander to conduct a night raid against a lightly defended seaside village not far away, where the scouts had spotted an enemy ship at anchor. The raid was a success, and the captured Veneti sailors had been made to sail their ship to the burgeoning Roman port at Corbilo before they were sold into a lifetime of slavery. At first glance, Mamurra was disgusted by every aspect of the ship; if the Roman galleys were sleek, finely tuned instruments, this thing was a bludgeon. It was big and almost flat-bottomed, crafted out of solid oak, with much higher sides than the Roman vessel.

Upon further inspection, and to his alarm, Mamurra discovered that because the ship did not have a deep keel, it could easily traverse shallows or shoals—in fact, Mamurra had tested the boat and it could even rest on its bottom when the tide went out. This meant that the craft could escape to places that the Roman ships dared not enter. Even worse, the hull was so thick that in several tests, the prow-mounted Roman battering ram had merely bounced off. And the ship did not use oars for propulsion; it relied on large leather sails rigged from several masts. The Romans therefore could not employ one of their favorite maritime tactics: running alongside the enemy ships, shearing off their oars, and leaving them dead in the water.

"We are in trouble," Mamurra said to his subordinate.

"Without question," Garibus replied.

"Where is the admiral?"

Garibus thought for a moment and said, "He is drilling the legionaries on the tactics of sea warfare."

"Well, go and fetch him for me," Mamurra said. "His tactics must change."

Decimus Brutus, visibly upset at having been interrupted during a drill, stomped down the long pier to where Mamurra was still sitting, deep in thought.

In deference to the admiral's rank, Mamurra rose to his feet just as Brutus arrived at his side.

"Well, engineer, I hope this is important, to take me away from my plan for the day," Brutus grumbled.

Mamurra pointed at the Veneti boat. "What do you make of it, Admiral?"

Brutus studied the ship for a few moments and waved dismissively. "It is a barge. We will row circles around it."

The engineer stroked his chin, trying to think of the best way to make his points. Finally, he said, "Admiral, if we engage a fleet of these ships with our current tactics, we will lose."

Brutus bristled but asked, "Why do you say that?"

One by one, Mamurra pointed out the problems. "The walls of the ship are so high their men will be shooting down at us, whereas our missiles and catapults will barely carry over them. If they lead you into shallow waters, you will run aground and be stranded. And our rams are totally ineffective against their thick hulls—we have tested them several times."

Brutus looked unsettled. "What do you propose we do?" he demanded.

"I haven't worked that out yet," Mamurra replied.

"Well, then," the admiral said with a scowl, "work harder."

That evening, just as Mamurra was finishing his supper while Dominicus looked on, a courier arrived, bearing a bulging leather pouch. Mamurra was delighted to find it contained a thick roll of vellum drawings, wrapped in a crimson ribbon, the Roman color. He eagerly spread the drawings out on the plank that served as his table in the rough camp quarters.

A report from Giacomo was written on a wax tablet.

> *Sir:*
>
> *I am pleased to report we have made considerable progress with the plans for the bridge. We have identified an excellent site: the Rhine is relatively narrow at that place, the banks are not unduly steep, and there are broad plains on either side to afford suitable staging and encampment. We have laid out a road leading to the site, and we have taken readings across the entire span of the river, recording the river depth for each location at which we would expect to drive columns into the river bottom. These piles are already being cut and stacked, together with the beams to connect the columns and the planks that will form the bridge deck above the columns and beams. Caesar himself authorized these preparations. He asks me weekly for a status report.*
>
> *I have sent you a copy of the plans, and I anxiously await your comments. From all indications, Caesar will not tolerate delay.*
>
> *I trust all is progressing well with the construction of the fleet.*
>
> *Giacomo*

Mamurra set the tablet aside and leaned in to study the drawings. They were laboriously detailed, enabling him to see every aspect of the planned construction. It was an impressive effort. Mamurra was especially pleased to see that the design did not include any trusses between the columns—it would have taken days to place them. He knew that Caesar's entire plan required a rapid construction process. If the building of the bridge lagged, Ariovistus would have time to assemble a large force at the approaches to the bridge on the Germania side of the Rhine, rendering a crossing impossible.

Instead of trusses, the plan envisioned simply drilling a hole in each column and inserting an iron bar into the hole, perpendicular to the column; the beams could merely rest on the bar. A flange on the end of the bar would hold the beam in place. This process could be done in a matter of minutes! There would be hundreds of the columns, which meant hundreds of bars. *What a job for the blacksmiths! Nofio will complain to the heavens!*

Mamurra took up a piece of charcoal and made notes on the drawings, suggesting revisions and commenting on ways in which the construction methods might be accelerated. The lightning speed of construction that Caesar had demanded would require that the work be broken into a series of repetitive functions, with a dedicated crew assigned to each. He scribbled instructions to Giacomo for the formation of the assigned crews and how they were to be trained during the winter.

And it required testing, too—the size of the columns, the thickness of the iron bars, and so on. It would all need to be confirmed in advance; there would be no time for trial and error once the work was underway.

Finally, in the wee hours, Mamurra looked up from his work and across the room to his bed. Dominicus was sleeping, purring softly with each breath. Mamurra knew that under the blanket, the slave was naked.

Mamurra silently moved toward the bed, pausing only to remove his own garments. He eased himself down next to Dominicus and stroked the lad's backside. Dominicus awoke and pressed his hips against his master. As Mamurra began to lose himself in his pleasure, it dawned on him that he still had not solved the problem of what to do about the Veneti boats.

To Hades with Brutus, he thought. *That problem will hold until tomorrow.*

THE NEXT MORNING, Garibus found Dominicus drawing water for the day at the well that had been dug to supply the engineering staff. As he was turning the winch to lift the bucket from the depths, Garibus held out his own bucket.

"You do that so smoothly," Garibus said to the slave, "perhaps you might draw some water for me, too."

Despite the fact that Dominicus was assigned to Mamurra, no slave could deny an officer. "As you wish," the slave said. He put his own filled bucket on the ground and took up Garibus's empty pail.

"My friends here tell me that you are a talented valet," Garibus said.

Dominicus replied simply, "I have been well trained."

Garibus looked over the young man. He was quite handsome, yet seemed gently inclined. "Do you please your master in all respects?"

"No slave may speak for his master."

Garibus gave the slave a skeptical frown. "Do not be coy with me, slave. Perhaps I will ask your master to use you myself. And I am a demanding master."

"I am my master's property," Dominicus said. "If he wishes to give me to you, I will obey." He lifted the second bucket over the masonry ledge surrounding the well and handed it to Garibus. "Do you require anything further?" he asked.

"No," Garibus said.

Pleased by the exchange, he watched as Dominicus proceeded in the direction of Mamurra's cabin. *This,* he thought, *will make a juicy tidbit for my next letter to Pompey and Catullus.*

⚜

SEVERAL DAYS LATER, Mamurra summoned Decimus Brutus for another visit to the pier.

Upon his arrival, Brutus immediately noticed an odd contraption bolted onto the deck of the Roman galley. The base was a customary Roman catapult, but the lever normally used to fling flaming balls of naphtha against enemy ships had been removed. In its place was a long pole that extended far out over the side of the ship. A razor-sharp brass hook had been mounted at the very end of the pole. A crew of several engineers stood alongside the device, and below the main deck, a team of rowers awaited orders.

Another team of engineers had taken the Veneti craft out into the ocean a short distance, where it lay at anchor. Its sails were not rigged for movement.

Taking this in, Brutus gave a hearty laugh. "Mamurra, do you propose to turn our warships into a fishing fleet?" he joked.

Mamurra did not seem insulted by the admiral's chiding. "We thought you might appreciate a demonstration of our solution to the disparity in the vessels," he said. He motioned for the Roman ship to cast off from the pier, then waved at the crew of the Veneti vessel, who scurried about on the deck, unfurling the sails and turning the ship slightly to catch the wind. Slowly but surely, it began to move. As the wind gusted, it picked up speed.

By the time the Roman galley caught up with her lumbering prey, its sails were full and billowing. Mamurra gave another wave to the Roman crew on the deck of the galley, and the men sprang into action. They swung the long pole around as the galley maneuvered alongside the Veneti craft. This brought the pole within range of the lanyards rigging the sails. It was then that Brutus realized why the hooks had been sharpened by the engineers. The crew deftly sliced through the rigging, rope by rope, and the heavy leather sails came crashing to the deck. Within seconds, the Veneti boat was dead in the water.

Brutus was speechless. He now understood why Caesar had put such faith in this man.

"Well, Admiral, what do you think of our solution?" Mamurra asked with a self-satisfied smirk.

"I believe you may have found the key to our success," Brutus said grudgingly.

"Perhaps," Mamurra replied, "but we require some further experimentation to perfect the design. I want to put some shielding around the base of the device, to protect the operators from the arrows and javelins that will be thrown at them from the opposing ships."

Brutus thought for a moment, then said, "Yes, I quite agree."

"And no doubt the Veneti sailors will use spears or other implements to interfere with the action of the pole. Your men will need to throw everything they have over the sides of the Veneti ships to keep their sailors occupied."

Brutus, humbled now, merely sighed. "You are right again."

"You will have some training to do, Admiral," Mamurra said. "Each ship must have a team capable of operating the device while under fire, and all your other men will need instruction on how to suppress any interference with the poles."

Brutus extended his hand to the engineer, and Mamurra shook it.

"I will have the legionaries ready," Brutus said. "Can you deliver the ships?"

Mamurra tightened his grip on the admiral's meaty fist. "The fleet," he said with conviction, "will be ready."

XXXI

TERRITORY OF THE SUEBI, GERMANIA

As things turned out, finding Ariovistus was easier than Gabinier had imagined. The crisp fall air made the passage pleasant. They'd barely penetrated Suebi territory before they were intercepted by a force of scouts that Ariovistus continually kept on patrol as a precaution against a Roman raid. Once the Suebi fellows satisfied themselves that Gabinier and his crew were in fact Nervii warriors, several of the scouts were detached and tasked with leading Gabinier to Ariovistus's camp.

Ariovistus's main camp was established well east of the Rhine, deep enough into Germania to allow sufficient time to mobilize a defense if the Romans ever tried to invade. He had erected considerable fortifications as a further protective measure.

Ariovistus, like most of the Germanic warriors, was tall, muscular, and possessed of long blond hair and a thick beard of the same color. He was wearing the simple white shirt common to the Suebian farmers, wool britches cinched with a broad leather belt, and knee-high boots. His face was remarkably boyish for one who had carried the burdens of leadership for many years and showed no remnants of wounds from his many battles. Indeed, he had cultivated a belief among his followers that he could not be felled in combat.

Ariovistus greeted his visitors with courtesy. "What possible business of the Nervii would bring such powerful warriors to the land of the Suebi?"

"We have come to offer our services to your cause, mighty king," Gabinier replied. He related the story of the attempt by Boduognatus to rally the tribes of the Belgae and fight the Romans, only to lose in the climactic battle at the Sabis River.

ARIOVISTUS, OF COURSE, had heard all about the Roman intrusion into Belgic territory and the terms Caesar had imposed on the tribes after their catastrophic loss to him, but he listened sympathetically as this young man poured out his story. Ariovistus had initially thought that Caesar, having subjugated the Belgae to the north, would next turn his attention to Germania, especially after Ariovistus's provocative raids in the prior year. His informants, however, now told him that Caesar seemed to have focused on the northwest region of Gaul and would make the Veneti tribe in Brittany his next targets. Ariovistus considered this weakness on the part of the Romans—they feared another battle with him.

"If, as you say, the Nervii have made a treaty with Rome, why do you come to me?" Ariovistus asked, suspecting he already knew the answer.

Gabinier rubbed his thumb back and forth on his leather bracelet as he spoke. "I hate the Romans. They are holding the woman I love as hostage to bond the disgraceful peace treaty with the Nervii. I will not rest until I have recovered her. The Nervii will not fight Rome. I have heard that you do not fear the Romans. I am here to offer my services."

Ariovistus glanced at Gabinier's men. "And you?"

"We stand with Gabinier," one responded assuredly. The others agreed.

The king pulled on his yellow beard. He could see the intensity burning within this young buck. And the man was physically impressive, all bulging muscles and rugged good looks. But Ariovistus was concerned. *Will this young stud bull follow orders or go off on a frolic to chase after his lost love?*

Eager to impress the king, Gabinier told him about leading the attack on the Roman rear guard, and the wound he had suffered.

Now *this* was impressive. Ariovistus mulled it over a bit further.

"You said you were wounded. Are you capable of combat?"

The other Nervii all burst out laughing. "This man killed Boduognatus with his bare hands only a short time ago," one said. "He is more than a match for any mere Roman."

Ariovistus was wary. "Why did you kill him?"

"He was the father of the woman Devorra. He traded her to the Romans for that disgraceful peace." Gabinier pulled back his leather jacket, revealing his long, pink scar. "The spear caught me here," he said. "As you can see, I am fully recovered."

Ariovistus was still wavering. An idea entered his mind. "The Romans have been engaging in some type of reconnaissance along the Rhine River," he said. "Perhaps your first assignment in my service can be to ascertain their intentions."

Gabinier rose and stood before Ariovistus. The two men locked eyes upon each other. Gabinier slowly went down onto his knee. "I accept you as my king, and pledge to you my obedience and fealty," he said with deep solemnity.

Ariovistus's looked at the others. "And your men?"

They each stood and then went down to one knee. One by one, they repeated Gabinier's pledge.

Ariovistus himself got to his feet and gestured for Gabinier to stand.

"I accept your pledge," he said. The two men exchanged a firm handshake. "Together let us make life unpleasant for the Romans."

TWO DAYS LATER, Gabinier, accompanied by his Nervii squad and a handful of Suebi warriors who knew the territory, were squatting in a thick stand of trees near the banks of the Rhine. They looked out over a large area being cleared by a crew of ax-wielding Romans. The river, always sluggish just before the onset of winter, was more silver than blue in the afternoon sunlight. The woodcutters were accompanied by a small force of legionaries, who had been posted on a picket line just beyond the work zone, not far from where the scouts were hiding.

"What are they up to?" Gabinier whispered to his Suebian counterpart.

"I do not know," the man said. "We have seen them at other locations on this side of the Rhine over the summer. Ariovistus thinks they are looking for a place to make a ferry crossing over the river."

"Let them come," Gabinier said, itching for a fight.

"But," his companion added, "they have spent considerable time in boats on the river itself. They drop a line into the water over and over at various locations, but they never catch any fish. We've never seen anything like it."

"Look over there," Gabinier said, pointing at a small crew that was working separately from the ax carriers. "What is that?"

One of the men was standing by a tripod, which had a small rod atop it. He would hunch down and stare at the rod. Then he would turn and say something to another man who was standing beside him, who would then write on a scroll. The tripod man would then wave to another crew some distance away. This team had a bundle of iron bars and sledgehammers, and they would drive a bar into the ground, then attach a small cloth to it. There was no apparent consistency to the placement of the cloths—they were tied at varying places on the rods.

"Perhaps we should make a run at them," Gabinier suggested. "Maybe we could capture one of them and torture an explanation out of him."

The Suebian disagreed. "Ariovistus was quite clear. He wants no engagements with the Romans yet. He just wants to know what they are doing."

The scouts held their position for the balance of the afternoon, watching the Romans go about their work in methodical fashion. As the late afternoon sun dipped toward the horizon, the entire Roman troop packed up their gear, boarded a couple of boats, and rowed away.

When they were sure that no Romans were left on their side of the river, Gabinier led the men out onto the plain. They walked around the cleared area, marveling at the efficiency displayed by the Romans in chopping down trees, pulling out the stumps, and neatly stacking the timber.

Gabinier came upon one of the iron rods. He reached down and pulled it out of the ground. He gestured to Gustavus to do the same. Within minutes the whole day's work by the Romans had been put to waste.

Gabinier had all the rods laid on the ground and selected several that would demonstrate that the cloths were not tied uniformly—they were at different heights on each rod. "We will take these back to Ariovistus," he told his Suebian counterpart. "Maybe he can make something out of it."

In short order, the scouting team hurried back to the main Suebi camp, where Ariovistus was presiding over a vast celebratory feast in honor of the Germanic goddess Freyja, whose portfolio included love and magic. The Germani knew how to enjoy themselves; there was plenty of food of all types and the ale was flowing freely, served by lovely Germanic lasses.

Upon their arrival, Ariovistus excused himself from the festivities and led the group to a small meeting room. He immediately busied himself inspecting the rods, but held his questions until he heard their report.

Gabinier gave him a quick summary of what they had observed, taking care to point out that they had neither been seen by the Romans nor taken any action to initiate a confrontation.

Ariovistus seemed pleased that his instructions had been observed. He pointed to the rods. "What are those?"

Gabinier explained that the Romans had been driving these rods into the ground and tying cloths onto them, but they had been unable to ferret out their purpose.

Ariovistus's eyes narrowed, and for the first time, Gabinier saw the king's typically sunny disposition turn grave.

"I know what these are," he said. "They are stakes. What you saw was an engineering crew. They are getting ready to build something."

"A camp?" Gabinier asked.

"I think not," Ariovistus said. "See how these rags are tied at different places on the rods? That's how they mark the slope when they are planning to build a road."

The king's consternation now spread to the others. The implication was clear: If the Romans were laying out a road, then an invasion must be in the offing. But when?

"Let them come!" Gabinier said. "We will throw them back into the river, where they will drown like rats."

Ariovistus gave his new recruit a brief smile and put his arm around his good shoulder. "Perhaps," the king said. "But I am not inclined to wait for Caesar to ferry his army across the water to mount a campaign against us. Perhaps we will visit the Romans first."

"I would march tonight," Gabinier said eagerly.

"Patience, my young warrior, patience. Not while Caesar is at Vesontio. I am told he's preparing to move north, to Brittany, in the spring. We will strike at his base when he is gone."

XXXII

Outside Vesontio

AUTUMN GAVE WAY TO WINTER, but not before Devorra had brought order to the brambles and overgrowth of the orchard and laid out an area where she would put in her garden in the spring. Her pregnancy moved along without complications, under Curio's watchful eye. He and Elliandro visited weekly, bringing supplies to the little group.

Devorra, while busying herself with these domestic chores, fretted over what Caesar might do if she bore him a son. Would he take the child? Return her to her father? But as she became more settled in her new life, she resolved to banish these worries to a remote corner of her mind.

Perhaps because they both were young, Devorra and Molena quickly developed an easy friendship, notwithstanding the difference in their respective statuses. Devorra said nothing about how she'd gotten pregnant, and Molena did not ask. For her part, Aloucca was relieved to have someone with whom she could share the chores.

As time passed and they began to feel more like friends than servant and mistress, Devorra learned to help Molena with the cooking. She knew that she'd need the skill if she ever wound up truly on her own, and she learned to enjoy it, tinkering with the application of spices to produce variations in their meals. Molena praised Devorra's knack for making pies and other treats from the cornucopia of fruits available during the fall harvest season.

Molena had told Devorra that the situation was better than anything she might ever have imagined, either before her capture or since; she was especially grateful for the weekly visits with her brother. They shared only one complaint: the condition of the privy. Devorra pointed this out to Curio, who promised to make them something better.

ONE EVENING, after Devorra had retired for the night, Molena and Aloucca were washing the day's dishes when Molena found the courage to ask Aloucca about Devorra and herself. Up to this point, Molena had known only that they were of the Nervii people, made hostage to the Romans, but nothing had been said of their captivity nor of how Devorra came to be with child. She probed a bit.

"I am pleased to be here with you and our mistress," Molena began. "You have been so welcoming to me."

Aloucca raised her head and smiled at the girl. "We are grateful that Curio has brought you to us, Molena. I suspect we will rely on one another a great deal in the months to come."

"Yes, Curio, has been very kind to me and my brother. He is so unlike Caesar and most of the other Romans I have encountered," Molena offered. "He told me that you and our mistress were sent to Caesar by her father as hostages?"

"That devil, Boduognatus!" Aloucca spat. "Look what he has done to his own daughter—captive of the filthy Romans." She added quickly, "And now she has been made pregnant by one of them!"

Molena did not indicate she already knew the story. "How horrible," she said.

Aloucca softened her voice to a whisper. "I warned her to be careful, but she is strong-willed, and now she must bear the consequences."

Molena stifled a frown. Was Aloucca suggesting that Devorra had been a willing participant in the carnal act? This did not match up with the story she had been told.

"First her father tries to marry her off to gain an ally, then this miserable Roman plants his seed in her," Aloucca said, drying a plate. "And as soon it became known that she was with child, Caesar wanted to be rid of us. Curio is the only one who has shown any kindness."

Molena wanted to push for more details, but she said only, "He is a truly kind man."

"That girl has been like my own child, and yet I couldn't protect her," Aloucca whispered.

Molena asked, "How did you come to be with her?"

"I was taken into slavery by her grandfather when he raided the territory of the Bellovaci," Aloucca replied. "My parents were slaughtered in the attack. I was but a child, too young for much value on the slave blocks, so I was given to Devorra's mother as a companion. I learned the skills of a midwife but could not save her—she died giving birth to Devorra. I have been with our young mistress since the day she came into this world, and I will stay by her side through this difficult time."

⁂

THE SNOWS AROUND THE FORTRESS were deep, under yet another dreary afternoon of dark skies. There was little visible activity beyond the changing of the guard shifts at the entrance to the somber stone edifice. But inside, Caesar's office was humming as usual. Messengers came and went with information relating to the planning for the spring offensive against the Veneti. Caesar and his adjutant were also busy with preparations for the upcoming summit meeting with the other triumvirs, Pompey and Crassus.

Caesar was in a relaxed mood, pleased with the progress of the day's work. He also was satisfied with the latest account from Corbilo. "Mamurra reports that the shipbuilding is on schedule, and that Brutus is whipping the legion into an effective marine fighting force," he said, handing the scroll to Curio. "This should be a very lucrative campaign for us."

"We'll need a good result," he observed as he read. "The spending on the bridge is crimping our resources."

"Rio, you sound like a cranky senator," Caesar grumbled. "There will be an abundance of wealth. Keep your focus on the greatness of what we will achieve."

Curio was undisturbed by this mild rebuke.

"I need for you to visit the apothecary again," Caesar said lightly.

Alarmed, Curio thought of the potion for his seizures. "Have you experienced another spell?"

"No, I want the other potion. These winter nights in Gaul are long and cold," Caesar responded with a wolfish grin. "It's good to have a slave to keep me warm."

Another slave girl, Curio thought, unamused. *How soon before I will be cleaning up after him again?*

"I will get the elixir for you this afternoon," Curio said, and rose to go.

"Ask the apothecary if he can prolong the effect," Caesar said as Curio was heading out. "This mount demands more from her rider."

"Your wish," Curio said with resignation, "is a task for my hands." He turned his back on his general before allowing his eyes to roll toward the ceiling.

⁂

BEFORE VISITING THE APOTHECARY, Curio had other business. Accompanied by Elliandro and a donkey laden with foodstuffs and other supplies, Curio made a visit to the cottage. The deep snow made for slow going.

Molena was thrilled to see her brother again.

"And are you satisfied with the new privy?" Curio asked Molena.

"Yes!" she exclaimed. "The old one was horrible. Thank you for having Othon and Elliandro build us a new one."

They all laughed at that, and then the siblings were excused so they might have time together. Curio asked Aloucca to see if the hens had laid any fresh eggs that he might take back with them to the camp.

Now alone with Devorra, Curio made some small talk about the weather and the house. Then, he asked gently what was most on his mind. "All is well with your health, and that of the child?"

Devorra raised an eyebrow. "Surely you don't expect me to believe that you care."

"Whatever do you mean?" Curio was taken aback by her shift in mood.

"Come now, Curio. You pretend to be interested in our well-being, but all you've done is help Caesar be rid of me."

The truth in her accusation stung, but Curio kept his face placid. "I do care about you," he replied softly. "I am sorry that you are in this situation, and I am trying to help you make the best of it."

Devorra's face softened. "Yes, I suppose you are. And I am grateful. You are not Caesar, any more than I am my father."

He couldn't help chuckling at this. Then he asked, "Are you pleased with the servant girl, Molena?"

Devorra brightened considerably. "Oh, yes. She is pleasant to be around, a hard worker. We are getting along very well."

"I am pleased to hear that, my lady. I am sure she will be of great assistance when the time comes for the birth of your child. And, in that regard, it now appears that Caesar and the army will depart from Vesontio for the campaign against the Veneti before you are due to deliver," Curio told her. "I will make sure that you have abundant stores of supplies before I leave. Elliandro will be given special privileges so that he may return to check on you while I'm gone."

Devorra's eyes widened in surprise.

"Yes, as adjutant to Caesar, I am able to give him that freedom, as long as he reports back to camp at noon or at nightfall each day, depending on the time of his visit," Curio advised. "I am confident he will not try to escape, as he knows the deadly consequences of such an action."

"I am much more uneasy about what happens after the baby arrives," Devorra said.

"My lady, I have assured you many times, and there has been no change: we will make satisfactory arrangements for your comfort and future. Please trust me."

Though he was entirely sincere, it was easy for him to see why this woman might have difficulty trusting a Roman.

❧

MOLENA AND ELLIANDRO sat on the edge of her bed, happy to be together. Molena had baked him a loaf of bread, which he nibbled at between stories.

"Are they treating you well?" she asked him.

"Oh, yes," Elliandro said, "especially considering how they nearly killed me first."

The mere mention of his ordeal brought tears to Molena's eyes.

"Do not weep, sister," he said to her softly. "We are together, and our conditions are far better than most slaves experience."

He waited a few long moments before saying, "You have never told me what happened to you that day when we were separated, and I attacked the guard. What did they do to you that night?"

Molena looked away. "It was horrible. I can't talk about it."

Elliandro stroked her arm. "It is not good to keep this to yourself."

"I must," she said. "It is mine alone to bear."

Elliandro gave her a cold stare. "Was it Curio who pulled you out of the line? You told me he has not taken advantage of you. Is that the truth?"

She met his harsh expression with one of her own. "I have never lied to you, brother. I'm not lying now. He has been kind and gentle with me, always. I don't even know why. Do not think otherwise."

Elliandro's face relaxed. Then he asked, "Do you have feelings for him?"

Molena smiled. "And if I do?"

"He is a Roman!" Elliandro protested. "They have plundered our homes and made slaves of us." He lifted his tunic, exposing his scarred torso. "Even if you won't tell what was done to you, do not forget what they did to me!"

It was pointless for Molena to try to explain her conflicted feelings. Hatred of the Romans had been etched into her brother's skin with every stroke of the vicious whip. For the first time ever, she decided to lie to him.

"No, of course not," she said gently. "I have no feelings for him."

Just then, Curio knocked on the partly closed door, and Elliandro was

212

on his feet by the time he pushed it open.

"A moment with your sister, please," Curio said to the slave, and Elliandro stepped out.

When they were alone, Curio looked down at Molena, still seated on the bed, marveling at her unassuming beauty. He said, "I understand you are getting along well with the Lady Devorra."

"Oh, yes," she said easily. "I am very happy here on the farm."

"She is pleased with you, too. And the old hag?"

"We've had no disagreements," she laughed. "I have taken over all the things she hates to do."

Curio reached into a pocket of his tunic and withdrew an object. "I brought you something." It was a simple silver necklace, perfectly wrought.

Molena took it delicately and held it in front of her. "I've never had any jewelry."

He slipped it over her head.

"Its beauty suits you," he whispered to her, aware that her brother was just outside the room, well within earshot.

She stood so they were eye to eye. Curio turned his head slightly, as was his habit when near her.

"Why do you turn away from me?" she asked. "Do I displease you?"

Instinctively, he brought up his hand and covered his cheek. "It is I who wishes not to displease you."

She tenderly took his hand and looked into his eyes. "It does not matter. I don't even notice it anymore."

Curio could not speak, so jumbled were his feelings—shame over his disfigurement juxtaposed against hope that she might be telling the truth. She moved closer.

"I do not see it," she said firmly. "I see only a man who is kind when others show cruelty. I see only the gentleness in your heart."

This touched him deeply and he lowered their hands, still clasped. After a moment, Molena stepped back, and Curio turned to leave.

As he walked to his mount, with Elliandro following behind, the emotion of the encounter overtook him. Women had always been repulsed by his scar. Even pleasure slaves had turned their heads away. *But this girl . . . this beautiful girl . . . dare I believe that she cares for me? Or that someday she might love me?*

LATER THAT EVENING, after Aloucca had retreated to her bed, Devorra and Molena sat beside the fire sewing.

Molena took a deep breath and said, "May I ask you something?"

Devorra smiled. "Of course. And you don't have to ask if you can ask."

Molena returned her grin. "Curio said that to me once, when I was serving him a meal."

Devorra waited for Molena's question.

Molena fished the silver necklace from the pocket of her housedress. She held it up for Devorra to see. The light from the flames danced across the intricately worked silver chain.

"It's beautiful! " Devorra said. "Curio gave it to you?"

"Yes," she said, color spreading through her cheeks.

"It's easy to see that he's fond of you," Devorra said kindly. "What did you want to ask me?"

"My brother hates the Romans—with good reason, of course. He asked me if I have feelings for Curio."

"And what did you tell him?"

Molena bit her lower lip. "I told him no, of course not."

Devorra looked thoughtful. "And you are afraid of what your brother will say if he sees you wearing the necklace?"

"Yes, you see my dilemma. What can I do?"

Devorra lowered her voice to a conspiratorial tone. "Tell him I gave to it to you, as a gift for all you have done for me."

This was just the solution Molena had been hoping for. "Thank you! You are so good to me!"

Devorra shook her head. "You have done far more for me than I could ever do for you."

Molena lowered her eyes. "I am but a slave."

Devorra scoffed. "Were you a slave before the Romans took you from your life?" She took Molena's hand. "You are not a slave to me; you are like my sister."

This brought a flush a happiness to Molena's face. "I always wished I had a sister," she said.

"So did I," Devorra replied, smiling. "So, we have a plan. Of course, this story about the necklace will be the second lie you have told your brother."

Molena was confused.

"The first was that nonsense about you not having feelings for Curio."

Molena looked sheepishly at Devorra, then ripples of their laughter filled the room.

XXXIII

Lucca, Tuscany, 56 BC

T
HE SERCHIO RIVER CUT A CIRCUITOUS PATH through the sprawling
mountains of Tuscany, making its way south toward the Ligurian
Sea. The spring floods had washed out the closest bridge to the town of
Lucca, so Caesar and his entourage of trusted officers, including Curio,
Labienus, and Gordianus, were relegated to being ferried over the muddy
effluent in a scow piloted by an enterprising local merchant.

As the boat neared a makeshift dock on the south bank, just below the
main buildings of the town, Curio could see that there were two groups of
soldiers waiting. By prior agreement, none of them carried weapons. Caesar
had even left behind Julia's dagger. There was to be no treachery at this
rendezvous.

"Do you recognize any of them?" Gordianus asked.

The men were backlit by the sun, and Caesar had to squint. "The fellows
on the left are in Pompey's command. The others are with Crassus."

And then, after a pause, he added, "None of them can outfight the
Tenth."

The implications of this remark, and the tone with which he uttered it,
immediately registered with Caesar's team. Was he intimating that
someday they might be fighting their fellow Romans? It was unthinkable.

Much to Curio's chagrin, Caesar did nothing to disabuse them of such
suspicion. And the truth was, depending on the outcome of this meeting,
anything was possible.

The ferry tied up to the dock, and the groups exchanged greetings. After
a few minutes of these pleasantries, Caesar said, "Excuse me, gentlemen. I
need to relieve myself." He walked a short distance from the rest of the
group, turned his back to them, and made ready to urinate.

The rest of the military men gave it no thought and continued their conversations. Curio, however, kept a close watch on Caesar. In a quick motion that would have been imperceptible to anyone but Curio, the general pulled out a vial of the medicine for his spells and drained it.

Curio was shocked. This encounter with the other triumvirs was monumental, and Caesar had taken the medicine preventively, hoping to ensure that he would not experience a spell while meeting with the other titans. It was a dangerous new stage of Caesar's illness.

WITH THE WEATHER being pleasantly warm on this sunny spring day, the triumvirs held their meeting out in the peristyle, an open courtyard surrounded by a colonnade. Murals on the courtyard walls depicted scenes from Greek mythology, including a scandalous rendering of a phallic satyr having his way with a particularly voluptuous nymph, while Venus, goddess of love, looked on approvingly.

A round table had been placed on the portico under a scarlet canopy trimmed in gold—fitting for a meeting of equals. Pompey and Crassus were waiting for him at the table. This was undoubtedly Pompey's doing, Curio surmised—the older man would have wanted to work on Crassus before Caesar's arrival. Each of the men had selected a single advisor to sit in on the meeting as silent observers, and Curio took his place behind Caesar.

"Greetings, Caesar," Pompey said, rising stiffly to his feet. Curio noticed that the great man was pained by moving—the gout, perhaps? Curio could not help but wonder if there was any magic in the apothecary's jars that might help the old lion. Pompey was wearing a military-style wool tunic, a little too heavy for such a warm day, but no doubt chosen to show solidarity with the army attire in which Caesar was clad.

"My dear son-in-law," Caesar replied, clasping the larger man in a full embrace.

Caesar gave the third man at the table a hearty smile and extended his hand in greeting. "Crassus, you should be most proud of the great work young Crassus has done for Rome in Gaul."

Crassus, clad in a classic senatorial toga, was taller than Pompey, but shorter than Caesar. He kept himself trim and fit by means of regular exercises at the baths. He had the leonine features of classic Roman nobility, and wore his hair drenched with oil, slicked back on his head. The corners of Crassus's mouth were naturally downturned in a perpetual frown. His eyes had the darting nature of a man who, by guile and shrewd manipulation, had amassed the greatest fortune in all of Rome. But unlike Caesar and Pompey, who had acquired their money through military winnings, Crassus had accumulated his vast wealth by mercantile pursuits, which was frowned on by the Roman upper crust. Crassus chafed at this, of course; his sole military accomplishment had been crushing the slave revolt led by Spartacus, and it had caused no shortage of dispute between himself and Pompey over the fact that Pompey's army had contributed to the successful outcome.

"Young Crassus writes to me regularly of your great leadership in Gaul, from which he has learned much," Crassus said smoothly, in the most political of tones. "I am grateful for your tutelage."

When all were seated, Caesar hoisted a cup. "To our friendship and our partnership. Rome has prospered because of it."

"Before we turn to business," Pompey said, with a note of mischief in his voice, "I have some happy news for you, Caesar. Julia is with child, five months along. You are to be a grandfather."

Caesar rocked back in his chair and clapped his hands in delight. "Ah, dear Julia must be so pleased!"

"Congratulations, Caesar," Crassus said, offering up another toast. "May the child be healthy and prosperous." He did not, Curio noted, express the customary wish that the child be male.

"I wanted to tell you in person," Pompey explained. "I asked her to keep the news quiet until we could meet."

They all laughed at that, lessening the tension underlying the momentous nature of the meeting. This was followed by a few minutes of small talk, mostly Caesar telling Crassus about the exploits of his son in helping to subjugate the tribes of Gaul.

"Ah, Gaul," Pompey said, deftly turning to business. "Have you had quite enough of the wilderness and the barbarians, Caesar? Rome would benefit by your presence back in the Senate. Those rascals are always getting out of hand."

Crassus cracked a sly smile—no mean feat for that constantly scowling mouth—and said, "Indeed, neither Pompey nor I seem to be able to keep all the factions in line. But you, Caesar, you could bring them to heel."

Clearly, they wanted Caesar to give up command of his legions and return to Rome, where they could proceed to mire him in the intricacies of Senate politics and frustrate him in myriad ways. Caesar, like Curio, knew full well that real power in Rome flowed from command of an army.

"Crassus, surely your son has told you about the tribes of Gaul," he replied genially. "We have only begun to bring the country under Roman rule. At this very moment, Decimus Brutus is preparing a fleet that we will employ to subjugate the tribe in Brittany. My work in Gaul is hardly complete."

The two other leaders betrayed no hint of what they were thinking. Certainly, they expected that Caesar would want an extension of his command in Gaul. The question was, what could they extract from him in exchange?

Crassus took the first grab. "Pompey made great conquests for Rome in the east, taking Judea, Palestine, and part of Asia. But vast territory and riches lie beyond—all of Parthia. You are aware that our ally Mithridates has been displaced by one of his generals, a man named Suren. I wish to lead an army to restore Mithridates to his throne, for the benefits this will bring Rome."

The wealth of Parthia was immense, and the slave count would be enormous. Mithridates would reward his savior with riches beyond imagination—as if Crassus could even fathom the magnitude of the wealth he currently possessed!

Unfortunately, Crassus was hardly militarily qualified to lead such a complex campaign. But if Parthia was the price that Crassus would exact for the extension of Caesar's command in Gaul, Caesar was prepared to pay it.

"So," Caesar said, turning to Pompey, "if I am to take Gaul, and Crassus is to take Parthia, what can we do to ensure that you are happily occupied?"

Pompey considered the question, then said, "Rome continues to maintain our legions in Spain. You have your hands full in Gaul. Give me command of the Spanish legions, and all the legions of Italy."

Crassus must have been counting on pulling troops from Spain and Italy to form the core of the army he would take to Asia. Pompey's demand would require Crassus to recruit and train an entire army before disembarking.

Caesar, of course, understood this and spoke up before Crassus could object to Pompey's proposal. "Magnus," Caesar explained to his son-in-law, "Crassus will need some experienced soldiers in his army. Suppose we give him the legions stationed in Italy, but you keep command of all the garrisons protecting the cities? Might not that suit your purpose, Crassus?"

Crassus eagerly went along.

Pompey, ever planning several moves ahead, seemed reluctant. Curio suspected that he had designs on a ready army to counter his father-in-law, should he ever need it. But at last, he acquiesced. "Very well. Gaul to Caesar, Asia to Crassus, and I will keep an eye on Spain and Italy."

"Two small addenda," Caesar said softly. The other two men looked at him with cautious anticipation.

"A short distance across the ocean from Gaul lies the island territory of Britannia," he said. "I ask for the authority to mount an invasion of Britannia once the Gauls are completely under Roman dominion."

Crassus waved his hand dismissively. The talk around Rome was that the barbarians there were no more sophisticated than the Gauls. Crassus reasoned that if Caesar wanted to invest his energy in conquering them, let him.

Pompey, who did not care about money, was even less concerned. His position appeared to be that the farther away Caesar was from Rome, the better. "What is the second item?" he asked.

"The Germanic tribes under Ariovistus have been making raids into Gaul," Caesar said. "They hurry back to Germania whenever we take pursuit. I believe they do this because they know my imperium does not extend to their country. I want the authority to make a strike at Ariovistus if he is so impudent as to make another raid."

Curio, who had been following the discussion most intently, held his breath. The fate of the secret bridge project hung in the balance.

Crassus appeared to care even less about Germania than he did about Britannia. "I have no objection," he said lightly.

Pompey was more circumspect. "The Germanic tribes are even more warlike and vicious than the Gauls," he said delicately. "Be judicious in engaging them, Caesar."

"We beat Ariovistus at Vesontio." Caesar said, bristling a bit. He never liked being lectured to. "If necessary, we will do so again."

Pompey might easily have reminded Caesar that his troops had been surrounded by Ariovistus's army, but he refrained.

The men met through the rest of the day, breaking only to enjoy a bountiful buffet assembled in the atrium with their retainers. There were numerous offices to parcel out to the supporters of the three men, in order for them to maintain their control of the Senate and the offices of the government, including the courts. Artful cunning was on display as each man jockeyed for advantage in placing a supporter in this office or that, but the mood was cheerful now that the big prizes had been discussed and amicably divided.

"We shall have the Senate pass resolutions authorizing all of this,"

Pompey declared when all the horse trading was done, extending his right hand over the center of the table. Caesar and Crassus did the same.

And with a mutual clasp of hands, the known world was neatly carved up by the Triumvirate, much as a butcher might section a swine.

LATER, AS CAESAR'S PARTY was making their crossing back over the Serchio, the general briefed his men on the significance of having his authority over Gaul confirmed. Some of the officers were upset but dared not let it show; they had not been expecting to spend more years slogging about in that backward country. The prospect, however, of capturing thousands of new slaves meant considerable gold in their pockets, which softened the blow of their extended duty.

Curio was relieved that Caesar neglected to mention the agreements about Britannia or Germania.

Labienus put up his hands. "I am a soldier," he said. "I leave politics to you."

"Agreed," said Caesar. "Now, let us hope that Mamurra has the ships ready for Brutus."

XXXIV

Outside Vesontio

EVERYWHERE AROUND THE COTTAGE, signs of spring were abundant. The surrounding pastures and forest were suddenly verdant, and the farmer Othon and his two oxen were out every day, preparing his fields for the planting season. The women were happy to be able to enjoy the outdoors, even if there remained a chilly edge to the occasional breeze blowing off the river.

Devorra, heavy now with the baby she was carrying, was determined to spruce up their surroundings. She set about a vigorous program of pulling weeds and planting flowers, the seeds provided by Othon. Aloucca continually clucked at her about not overexerting herself, but after months of being shut in by the deep snows, Devorra reveled in the sunshine and fresh air, and Molena joined her outside whenever she could.

On this particular warm day, they were creating a flower bed along the pathway connecting the residence to the road to Vesontio. Molena set down her hoe to pull back her hair, which thankfully had grown out and returned to its natural deep brown.

Devorra, working to dig out a rock, paused to catch her breath. "I'm so glad Curio brought you here."

Molena smiled. "You have no idea how happy I am to be here," she said emphatically. "The kitchens at Vesontio were horrible, so hot and loud . . . and the men were always leering at me. I hate to think what they would have done to me if not for Curio's protection."

"Yes, he has been good to us," Devorra agreed. "So unlike Caesar."

Molena's ears perked up. Devorra had never mentioned him. "You met Caesar?" she asked.

"Oh, yes," Devorra replied, bitterness evident in her voice.

Molena recalled how vague Aloucca had been about the Roman who had

221

fathered Devorra's child. Could it have been Caesar himself? But how could that be, when the man had been unable to perform when she herself was naked and helpless before him? The contradiction made her certain that she must not tell Devorra about her own horrible experience with the Roman general.

"How did you come to know Curio?" Devorra asked casually.

Molena's heart skipped a beat. She could not tell Devorra the whole story of that night. "What flowers are you thinking about for this path?" she asked, trying to change the subject.

"We'll move some of the purple irises by the orchard," Devorra replied. And then, with a hint of teasing in her voice, she pressed, "You haven't answered my question."

Molena thought for a moment, then said, "After I was captured, I was sent to work in the kitchens. They made me deliver meals to the officers in their quarters. Curio was one of my stops. He was learning to speak our language. He liked to practice with me."

Devorra gave her an impish grin. "What else did you practice with him?"

Molena blushed. "Nothing. He has always been respectful to me."

"It is obvious that he cares about you," Devorra said, pointing to the silver necklace. "Slave owners do not usually present such gifts to their property."

Molena lay her hand on the chain. She wanted to confide in Devorra once more about the great conflict raging between her heart and her conscience. She felt terribly guilty about lying to Elliandro.

Devorra put her spade down and looked away. After several long moments, she said in a low voice, "I was in love with a man, a wonderful man who was gentle and kind, but my father didn't approve of him—he had other plans for me. We could have run off together. But I was too afraid—of the risks, of what my father might do. Now my love is gone, killed by the Romans in battle. I think about him constantly. I think about what we might have had together."

"How difficult that must be," Molena said softly.

"It tears at my heart every day," Devorra said. "Heed my lesson, Molena: If ever you have the chance to be with the man you love, throw caution to the wind. Seize him with every bit of energy you can muster. If the opportunity escapes, you may never retrieve it."

Molena lay her hand gently on Devorra's arm. "You are not alone," she said. "Soon, you will have the love of your child to sustain you. And I will stay with you, as long as you will have me."

Devorra pulled Molena into an embrace. "You have been a blessing from the gods, Molena—and I was certainly due!"

Molena laughed, then put her hands on Devorra's bulging belly. "*This* is your gift from the gods," she replied, "as you will soon enough discover!"

XXXV

VESONTIO

CAESAR'S ENTOURAGE ARRIVED at Vesontio with the general in good spirits. The meeting at Lucca had produced most of what he'd wanted from Pompey and Crassus, the weather was improving every day, and the latest report waiting for him from Mamurra was positive again. Construction of Brutus's ships was on schedule, and the fleet would be ready by the time Caesar arrived with the army on the march from Vesontio.

He brought Curio along on an impromptu tour of the camps of the legions to assess the state of their preparations for the upcoming campaign against the Veneti. On balance, the tour went well. They were pleased to find that the respective legion commanders had their gear and artillery packed and ready to move.

They paused to watch a drill of the reconstituted Twenty-Fourth Legion, complete now with new recruits. Lentulus, the officer whose hide Caesar had roasted in his office so many months ago, was the new legion commander. Nervous that the High Command himself was present, Lentulus called out, "Turtle!"

At this, the second and third ranks lifted their shields over their heads and pressed close against the first file, in effect creating an umbrella of cover protecting the entire assemblage. Arrows would have no effect against this formation.

Caesar clapped his hands in pleasure, "Beautifully executed. Your men have done well. You have proved yourself worthy of your new command of the legion."

With that, the tour moved on. Caesar eagerly anticipated seeing the vast storage yard established to hold the components and raw materials needed for his bridge over the Rhine. "Now, Rio," he said as they approached, "we shall see how Giacomo is coming with our great ambition!"

Curio only nodded, still somewhat skeptical of what seemed like little more than a great—and greatly expensive—folly.

Giacomo conducted the tour with some pride. The long, thick piles that would be driven at an angle into the river bottom to form the support piers for the bridge were all cut and stacked, each one precisely measured for the depth at which it would be placed and marked with a number to correspond to the location where it was to be driven according to the plan. Mamurra, after his sour experience with driving piles in the Doubs River, had insisted on a suitable store of backup piles, just in case the crews working in the river fumbled control of a column and lost it to the current.

Construction was well underway on dozens of huge rectangular wooden beams, made to stretch between the piles to create the structure on which the bridge deck would rest. The iron frames to be bolted to each pile to hold the horizontal beams were still being furiously fabricated by a team of blacksmiths, but a huge stockpile was already stacked and ready, along with a small mountain of nails. And perhaps most importantly, the mill was churning out hundreds of long planks that would be nailed to the horizontal beams to serve as the bridge deck.

At another location, a flotilla of flat-bottomed barges was being assembled, readying for deployment to the Rhine on Caesar's command to undertake the complex river work. At still another spot, a huge cache of tools had been accumulated: hammers, saws, cranes, pile drivers, and the like. And finally, a large area was set aside to hold the slaves who would provide the labor needed to erect the structure. It was replete with a whipping post and a high cross, a stark warning to any slave who might contemplate trying to make a break.

Overall, even Curio had to admit it was an amazing demonstration of organizational efficiency.

Caesar was delighted by the full-scale mockup of several sections of the bridge over a small channel that had been dug to provide a flow of river water. Mamurra had been adamant about constructing this prototype to ensure that the soldiers wouldn't fall through the deck, the deck wouldn't break the beams on which it rested, the iron frames wouldn't snap under the load, and the piles holding up the entire apparatus wouldn't give way. The timing of Caesar's visit was particularly opportune; an entire cohort of legionaries had been assembled with full marching pack and armor for a test. At a barked command, this hardy group tromped up an approach ramp, marched across the sample bridge section in good order, and trod back down an exit ramp on the other side. As each rank came off the structure, they scurried back over a second, smaller bridge to the approach ramp and marched across again, thus maintaining a continual flow of soldiers over the test structure. All the while, engineers were stationed at the several stress points under the bridge structure, watching sharply for cracks or design flaws.

"We want to see how the bridge will perform when the full army marches across, which will take some hours," Giacomo explained.

Caesar praised the planned testing, then asked, "What about the wagons of the baggage train? They are much heavier than the mass of soldiers marching across."

Giacomo could not hold back a satisfied grin. "Sir, we ran that test yesterday," he said. "There were no problems. Mamurra's design is sound. And just to be safe, we will run it again tomorrow, after the mockup has carried the load of the soldiers today."

Caesar extended his hand and congratulated his man. "Well done, Giacomo," he said. "Now, when will you begin drilling the construction crews? They must know what to do, down to the last detail, if we are to get this thing up and get the army across before Ariovistus can react."

"That training is already underway, sir," Giacomo said. Then he hesitated a bit, as if debating whether to tell Caesar something else.

"Out with it," Curio said. "Hold nothing back, man."

"I need to know of any problems," Caesar said, "so that I can help you solve them."

Giacomo replied, "We suspect the enemy knows we are up to something significant. Several times, our stakes and other preliminary layout work on the Germania side have been torn out by roaming bands of enemy scouts."

Caesar gave Curio a troubled look.

Giacomo offered, "We have to assume they are aware of our planned location now. But we don't believe they know just what we are planning to do. After all, who could imagine that anyone would try to build a bridge over the Rhine?"

At this, Caesar laughed. But before he could respond, Giacomo added, "As a precaution, we have undertaken similar preparations at nine different locations. They cannot know which one we will pick, even if they do guess what all this work signifies."

This was a clever ruse, and Curio chuckled, impressed, as Caesar himself saluted the engineer to signify his approval.

"We feel this sabotage of our work cannot be overlooked," Giacomo continued. "To prepare for the threat, we propose an adjustment of the deployment plan. We are asking for a full cohort of cavalry to be ferried across on the day before the construction begins to scout for any potential tribal movements against our work, and then for two full cohorts of infantry to be ferried across on the first day of the construction to establish a strong defensive perimeter on the Germania side. This force should be immediately increased to a full legion."

Caesar nodded. "You may write that into the orders for the deployment." A second later, he had another thought. "We have a considerable investment in work and materials here. I want all of this enclosed by a standard camp fortification, trench, and stockade. I will send you a legion tomorrow, and they can get started on it right away."

This time it was Curio and Giacomo who exchanged glances, each well aware of the cost of such precautions.

"As you wish, sir," Giacomo said dutifully.

XXXVI

VESONTIO

ETURNING TO CAESAR'S OFFICE in the Vesontio fortress, Caesar and Curio found the usual stack of routine military matters that had piled up during their trip to Lucca. With Curio seated opposite him at the desk, Caesar attacked this mountain with his customary gusto.

Upon opening one letter, Caesar leaned back in his chair, stroking his chin while he read. He grunted, then handed the parchment to Curio.

As Curio read, his heart pounded in his chest. "So Boduognatus is dead," he said flatly, though his mind was racing. *What if Caesar wants to break this news to Devorra himself? What if he goes out to the house and sees Molena? Will he recognize her?* "Shall I communicate the news to his daughter?" Curio tried to sound as disinterested as possible.

Caesar's attention had already drifted to other items in the pile. "I suppose she should be made aware, though I don't think she'll shed any tears over the man. Go out and see her; tell her the news. I rather think she'll be relieved."

In fact, it was Curio who was relieved. With a smart salute, he was gone.

THE THREE WOMEN were busy sewing—refitting Devorra's wardrobe to accommodate her ever-swelling belly and making items of clothing for the child, due to arrive soon. Devorra's pregnancy had progressed smoothly and uneventfully.

When a knock came at the door, Molena went to answer it. Her face lit up when she saw it was Curio who had come calling. He was carrying a burlap sack.

"Well, it smells like a feast for the gods in here!" he proclaimed, and his eyes fell upon a steaming hot meat pie, just out of the oven. It was a new dish for Devorra, and she was pleased that he'd noticed her efforts. Curio continued, "Molena, you have outdone yourself."

"Oh, no, Devorra made this herself," Molena said, proud of her pupil's progress.

Curio smiled with true affection. "Very nice." He turned to Devorra. "You are well, then? No issues with the pregnancy?"

"None at all. The child is well tempered." She ran her hands over her rounded belly.

"That's wonderful," he said with enthusiasm. Then, addressing the two slaves, he added, "I require privacy with your mistress, if you please."

Concern passed over their faces, but Molena and Aloucca quickly left the room. Curio and Devorra sat by the fireplace. He set the burlap sack on the floor between them, then reached out and took her hand.

"I have news for you," he said. At her frown, Curio hastened to add, "I doubt this news will distress you greatly."

Devorra took a deep breath and held it, waiting for him to speak again.

"We have received a report from the agent who is responsible for our dealings with your tribe. He informs us that your father is dead."

Devorra was duly shaken by this revelation, but she felt no sadness. Her father was a beast, and not even the fact of his death could diminish her hatred of him. "What happened?"

Curio answered with a sympathetic tone. "The report is short on details. The agent merely said that your father was challenged for the leadership of the tribe by one of the warriors and was killed in a fight between them."

This was surprising; she would not have thought any Nervii warrior capable of beating her father in a test of arms. "Who was it?"

"The report says only that the new leader of the Nervii is a man named Pomorro," Curio replied. He squeezed her hand gently in support. "So do you think this man, Pomorro, is any better than your father?"

Devorra thought for a moment. "I do not know," she finally replied. "He saved my life once, but is he capable of leading the Nervii after the horrible defeat you gave them? I really can't say."

Devorra fell into a deep silence, her eyes drifting to the orange flames dancing in the fireplace. She stared at them vacantly, her mind far, far away.

After a moment of silence, Curio asked, "What is troubling you, my lady?"

"If my father is dead, I presume I am no longer of any value to Rome as a hostage," she said. "What is to become of me?"

Curio smiled. "Fear not. Under Roman law, all issues involving hostages held by an army are within the discretion of the commanding general. That would be Caesar. I see no reason why your status as a hostage should be affected by the death of your father."

"But what is he going to do with me?" she asked. She was ready to get on with her life, preferably not at the mercy of the Romans.

"He hasn't made any decision yet," Curio replied earnestly. "I promise you, all will be well for you and the child. And your two housemates."

Devorra felt a jolt of hope. If he had not decided, then she—and her child—might still have the hope of freedom.

"I also want you to know that the army is departing very soon for Brittany. Caesar has business to conclude with the Veneti tribe," Curio said, seeing the hope in her eyes. "Elliandro will continue bringing you supplies, and I have made a hefty deposit with Othon, so you will not be hearing from him about rent. If you do, tell him that upon my return, he will answer to me."

He picked up the sack and handed it to her. "I want you to have gold available, should you encounter a need for funds. It is a substantial sum, more than enough to provide for your household for however long we are gone."

Devorra said nothing, but she could feel the weight of the coins and understood that even if Curio did not make it back from this campaign, she would be financially comfortable for years.

Before she could thank him, the infant brought forth a determined blow against her womb that left her gasping, then laughing.

Curio's eyes drifted over to the table, where the meat pie was still steaming. "Perhaps the child is anxious to partake of that beautiful dish," he joked.

"We are very grateful for all your kindness," Devorra said. "Would you stay and have a meal with us?"

Curio hesitated.

"I believe my teacher would be most interested in your opinion of her pupil's work," Devorra said.

Curio looked into the fire, making no comment.

"You have been kind to her and her brother," Devorra said. "Both she and I would be very happy if you graced us with your company for dinner."

Finally, he smiled. "Nothing would please me more, my lady."

LATER THAT DAY, Curio was alone in his office, wearily wading through yet another stack of army documentation, when there was a knock at his door.

"Come," Curio called out, glad for a break from the monotony. "Ahh, Vatteus, just the man I have been waiting for." He rose and shook hands with the doctor.

"What mischief have you been up to?" Vatteus asked, with a sly gleam in his eye. "Have you gotten that slave girl out in the country in trouble?"

"In your dreams you may wish to examine her body again," Curio said in riposte, "but otherwise, keep your hands away from her!"

They both laughed. Curio took his seat and motioned for his old friend to do the same, then said in a conspiratorial tone, "Before our meeting with Pompey and Crassus, I observed Caesar taking the potion, as if to protect himself from the spells. I have never seen him take it in such a manner."

Vatteus was alarmed. "These attacks now come without any warning symptoms, you say?"

"Yes," Curio said, throwing up his hands in despair. "Only the gods can know for certain. But we leave in three days for Brittany. You must have a large quantity of the potion prepared, and I will take it with us."

This was odd. "Can't I just have the apothecary make it as it is needed?" the doctor asked.

This brought a smile to Curio's face. "You are staying behind with the garrison at Vesontio," he said. "I want you to attend the Lady Devorra in her birthing of the child."

Vatteus was surprised. "Won't Caesar wonder why I am not with the army in the field?"

"I'll tell him that you injured your knee in a fall, and you should stay here to tend to the garrison guarding Vesontio while you recuperate."

"Won't he think that's peculiar?"

It was Curio's turn to make a joke. "I'll tell him you were drunk and chasing a slave girl. He'll believe that!"

Vatteus's argument was cursory; Curio knew the doctor was pleased with this assignment. Such easy duty suited him. Life on a campaign was hard, especially when attached to Caesar's army. The man was always on the move, making endless fast marches to gain advantage over an adversary, fighting battle after battle, and keeping the hospital tents full.

"As you wish," Vatteus replied. "What about the other potion?"

"Oh, *that*," Curio said, reflecting. "I don't expect that his current companion will accompany him on this campaign, but just in case, bring me some of that fluid as well when you deliver the treatment for his spells."

"Of course."

Curio added, "Write to me as soon as the infant arrives," Curio said. "As a precaution against the correspondence being intercepted, say only 'the package was delivered.'"

Vatteus scrunched up his face. "A male or female package?"

Curio gave him a dismissive wave with the back of his hand. "It will be a girl."

"But what if it isn't a girl?"

Curio did not want to contemplate Caesar's reaction if it was a boy. In the past, when his dalliances had produced a girl, Curio had settled the mother and child on a small estate somewhere safely under Roman control, leaving Caesar free to move on to his next conquest. That was probably how he would resolve the Devorra dilemma, although her circumstances were made more complex by her hostage status. A boy would be an infinitely more delicate problem—a nightmarish one, at that. But that was a bridge he did not expect to cross. "If it's a boy, I'll shine your boots," he said dismissively. "Don't tempt the gods or their ghastly humor."

"Aye," the doctor said. He stood up to leave.

"You do realize, Vatteus," Curio said in a low voice, "that sooner or later one of these spells is going to strike him in full view of the men, and I may not be able to revive him. I do wish you could come up with a cure."

"It's in the hands of gods," Vatteus replied. "And they have always favored Caesar."

Curio watched the doctor make his way out of the office. *Yes,* he thought ruefully, *the gods have always favored him . . . but why must he keep provoking them?*

XXXVII

AT THE FORTRESS OF ARIOVISTUS

GENTLE LILTING SOUNDS of flutes and stringed instruments wafted through the warm afternoon air. The fortress cast a cooling shade over the townspeople celebrating the feast of Sucellus, the god of farming, in the hope that he might favor the upcoming planting season with fair weather and a bountiful harvest. Food and beverages were plentiful. Children tussled and played while their parents tended to the preparation of the food offerings and rested in advance of undertaking the spring planting. It was a happy time for all in attendance.

Save one.

The warrior Gabinier stood at one of the crenels in the battlement wall atop the fortress, leaning against the merlon, brooding joylessly as he overlooked the festival. Pain was pressing upon him, but it was not the dull throb from his mended shoulder—it was far worse. Gabinier's heart was heavy with the ache of loneliness. The continued separation from his beloved Devorra was far worse than anything he had endured during the months spent recuperating from the wound he suffered in the battle with the Romans. He was wracked with worries over what had become of her and how she was being treated by her captors. *Was she in chains, locked away in some horrible dungeon?* He trembled at the thought. *How might I be able to spirit her away from under their noses?* His growing impatience with Ariovistus's caution in moving against the enemy was wearing on him, unceasing, unyielding, like continuous drops of rain eroding a stone.

A piercing blast from an alpenhorn jolted Gabinier from his reverie. He turned and saw a man standing at attention on the balcony outside the castle's great hall, holding the long wooden instrument. He blew the horn a second time, signaling that the meeting of the tribal council was about to begin.

Reminding himself of his pledge to obey Ariovistus, Gabinier descended the stone stairs alongside the battlement and made his way to the great hall.

Several large tables had been set in the shape of a large U. By tradition, only Ariovistus's seat, at the base of the U, was established—the balance of the seating order was settled by the drawing of lots, lest a chieftain with tender sensitivities feel slighted by his placement.

Ariovistus rose and held up his hand for silence, his face somber. An uneasy silence settled over the room.

"Much as I have wanted to leave you unburdened by concern," he began in a low tone, "I must lay before you the most worrisome of news."

There was considerable shifting on the hard seats as the chiefs perked up their ears.

Ariovistus gestured to an attendant, who left the great hall for a moment and then returned, pushing a large handcart. It was piled high with metal rods, each with a cloth tied to it, which Gabinier immediately recognized as the Roman stakes. But even Gabinier was stunned at the number of them—he had not been aware so many had been taken.

"My brothers," Ariovistus said as he picked up one of the shafts and held it before him, "these metal rods have been retrieved by my scouts at nine different locations along the Rhine."

Nine! Gabinier gawked at the pile in near disbelief. *How many roads were the Romans building?*

Ariovistus made a great show of turning the rod from side to side, affording the leaders on each side of the table a full view. "Do any of you know what they are?"

His question was met by a host of blank faces. The chiefs had clawed their way to the top of their clans by guts, cruelty, and guile. Mostly an unseemly, vulgar lot, they were not at all worldly. Ariovistus turned to Gabinier and said, "Our newest colleague, the great warrior Gabinier who has joined us from the Nervii, can tell you."

Gabinier rose to his full height and faced the men at the table, making eye contact with each of them in turn. He said in his most determined voice, "These rods are stakes, used by the Roman army. They drive them into the ground to lay out a path for their plank roads, over which their legions will march into Germania."

This brought a collective gasp from his audience. Even the slowest-witted man in the room knew this could only mean one thing.

Ariovistus gave them the conclusion: "The Romans are preparing to invade."

To a man, they sat back in their chairs as though someone had doused them with a bucket of cold water. Their minds were doubtless racing with the implications for themselves and their families.

One of the chiefs, a churlish-looking oaf, pointed at Ariovistus and hissed an accusation. "This is your fault," he said to Ariovistus. "Your raids against the Sequani have brought this down upon us."

Ariovistus remained calm. "It may be," he replied in a reasonable tone, "that we have poked the Roman bear in his cave. But who among us thinks that this bear has been merely in hibernation? Caesar is bent on conquest, my brothers. His history among the Gauls is proof of his motive. He has reduced them, tribe by tribe, to the status of mere serfs, toiling under the Roman yoke. And then what did he do? He moved against the Belgae last year. Gabinier here can give testimony to that outcome. After the Nervii were slaughtered, the other tribes knelt before him. Their grain now feeds the mouths of Romans on the Tiber."

He made a sweeping gesture in the direction of the still-standing Gabinier, who saluted to show his agreement. "We have sat and watched, drinking our mead and pleasuring our women, while the Romans have established themselves to our west and to our north. It is plain as the noses on your ugly faces: we are next!"

The chieftains sat aghast, until one broke the silence. "But what are we to do?"

This provoked a burst of animated conversation between clusters of the tribesmen around the table. Ariovistus let this disorganized chatter rumble on for a few minutes, then rapped the rod on the table for order.

"My spies inform me that Caesar's next move is not to the east, against us. He has marched west, into Brittany, to subjugate the Veneti tribe. With any luck at all, this will take up the full campaigning season. I believe he will not start a campaign against Germania going into the winter, so we should have a full year to make ourselves ready."

Ariovistus's eyes narrowed now as he let his message sink in. "We must do two things." He paused for dramatic effect and made a great show of pacing back and forth across the base of the table. "First, we must prepare our defenses. Every town must be fortified, ample stockpiles of food and water must be built, our blacksmiths must work night and day to produce arms, and most important, every able-bodied man must be trained to fight. We must be ready to repel the Romans if they dare to cross the Rhine!"

The chiefs shouted their approval and banged their cups on the table.

"The other thing we must do requires bold action on our part. Our mistake has been raiding the Roman allies, hoping to make them renounce their allegiance to their new partners. Enough of that nonsense. It is time to strike the Romans themselves."

Aside from Gabinier, who broke into a wide grin at this suggestion, the others were reserved. No one was eager to mount an attack against Caesar himself.

Ariovistus, seeing this hesitancy, now flushed hot with rage. "There are only two men in this room who have actually faced Roman steel," he roared. "I fought them at Vesontio, and very nearly prevailed, without the strength of all of you at my side. Gabinier fought them at the Sabis River, and would have won the day if his allies, the Atuatuci, had shown up on time. Dangerous as they are, the Romans can be beaten. I do not fear them. Do you, Gabinier?"

Gabinier pulled his tunic aside and pointed to his jagged scar. "The gods brought me through the battle and have given me life to fight again," he said with conviction. "I would lead the attack tomorrow."

One of the chiefs, shaggy with untamed hair and beard, asked, "But how, and where, are we to strike?"

"The spies say that Caesar will leave soon, with nearly his full army, and head to Brittany. He will leave only a small garrison at Vesontio. I say we strike him there and annihilate his base. We must ravage his stockpiles and his stores, leaving him no doubt of what awaits him if he dares to row across the Rhine and set foot on our soil."

The chiefs roared their approval.

Ariovistus waved for Gabinier to come to his side. Within moments, the two warriors locked their arms in a tight embrace.

Ariovistus asked Gabinier, "Will you lead the assault on Vesontio?"

Gabinier took up one of the metal rods and held it before him. "I will impale a Roman on every one of these."

And the room erupted in cheers.

LATER THAT EVENING, Gabinier was stretched out on a bed in a small room he had been given in the fortress, just down the hall from another chamber where his Nervii colleagues were quartered. His mind was not at rest, however; he was aflame with ideas for how best to strike at the Roman base at Vesontio.

It was a vexing problem. Ariovistus had built the place himself, so the stoutness of its defenses was well known. A direct assault had no chance of succeeding—they would have to come up with something else.

And then it struck him: *Why did Ariovistus choose me to lead the raid against Vesontio?*

The last time he had been chosen to lead, it was because Boduognatus wanted him out of the way. He could not help but wonder: *Is Ariovistus no better than Boduognatus?*

XXXVIII

Outside Vesontio

IN THE BEDROOM OF THE COTTAGE HIDEAWAY, Devorra lay on sheets drenched in sweat, propped up by goose-feather pillows. Two leather straps were tied to the bedposts. She wrapped them around her fists and pulled mightily during the contractions, which came with increasing frequency. On one side of her, Molena kept dipping a cloth in cool water and applying it to Devorra's forehead—a kind gesture, but one that offered little relief as she labored to birth the child.

Aloucca had repeatedly felt for the baby's progress. The child was not in the breech position, nor was the cord causing any issues. But the baby's head was facing the mother's abdomen, rather than her back, which would make delivery extremely difficult. And the infant was making agonizingly slow progress, probably attributable to what Aloucca observed to be an unusually large head. If the baby were to tear Devorra as it tried to enter the world, it would raise great risk of an uncontrollable hemorrhage.

Molena had just returned from the fortress, where she had gone to alert Vatteus that Devorra was in labor. There she learned the doctor had been called out to the camp near the Rhine to attend to a serious injury. Panicked, Molena had located her brother in the hospital tent and implored him to help. Once briefed, Elliandro swiftly left to retrieve Vatteus from the camp, urging Molena to return to Devorra's side. He knew nobody would dare to stop him, for the adjutant had given him privileges of passage.

But the baby wasn't going to wait for Vatteus. As an intense contraction gripped Devorra, she arched her back and cried out. She could feel her strength dwindling.

"Keep pushing through the pain," Aloucca urged. "Do not give up!"

Devorra was frightened now. She found it more and more difficult to beat back the feeling that she might share her own mother's fate.

Another contraction convulsed her, and Devorra nearly pulled the bedposts out of their brackets. "You have to do something," Molena cried to Aloucca. "She cannot take much more!"

Aloucca gasped. "There is blood now. That means the baby's head is too big to pass without tearing you apart," she told Devorra as calmly as she could. "I must cut you, and I will mend you once the child is out of your womb."

"Do it!" Devorra screamed, her eyes squeezed shut as another contraction overtook her.

"Quickly, Molena—the flaying knife and our sewing basket!" Aloucca directed. She placed a hardened piece of hide between Devorra's teeth. "The pain will be intense, mistress. You must bite down hard on this." To Molena, she said, "Hold her down, with all your strength."

Molena's arms shook as she wrestled to keep Devorra still through the ordeal. She leaned close to Devorra's ear, whispering encouragement, but Devorra felt as though her own will was no longer a factor in this delivery. Her body and her lifelong companion would do what they must to see her child into the world.

Devorra felt a sudden relief of pressure, and then all was still. A moment passed before she heard a smack, and a loud caterwaul penetrated the cottage. Devorra collapsed into tears of relief.

❧

AT LONG LAST, Vatteus arrived. The midwife explained that Devorra had lost consciousness after the birth while she'd worked to close the incision. She'd applied apple cider vinegar to ward off infection and dressed the wound in a clean cloth.

Vatteus carefully examined the new mother and commended the midwife on her handiwork. "I couldn't have stitched her better myself."

The old woman merely gave a modest nod.

The doctor then went to the slave girl's room and found her holding the newborn, wrapped snug in a light blanket. "Has Devorra awakened?" she asked him.

"No, but her breathing is steady, and her color has returned. I am hopeful." Vatteus took the infant and unraveled the blanket to make an examination, saying only, "All is well."

They went into Devorra's room and placed the infant on its mother's chest. As the child rooted for her nipple, Devorra stirred, and suddenly opened her eyes. It took her a few moments to focus, but once she saw the child, she smiled.

"Oh, Devorra!" Molena exclaimed. "The gods have brought you back to us."

But before they could tell her anything else, Devorra lapsed back into a deep sleep.

Since there was no further need for his services, Vatteus bade the household farewell, returned to Vesontio, and took up his stylus.

My dearest Curio,

Although the messenger nearly died in the effort, the package has been delivered. I expect the messenger to make a full recovery.

And I cannot wait to watch you polish my boots.

Vatteus

XXXIX

CORBILO

MAMURRA STOOD AT THE END of the long quay extending deep into the harbor, under an overcast sky that had the effect of making the harbor water seem more green than blue. He could not help but feel a sense of deep satisfaction as he gazed out at the fleet. Fifty-five gleaming new ships—five more than requested—had been built by his able team of engineers and craftsmen, rigged out for sailing, and fully provisioned for combat. Equally critical, the necessary port facilities to support the fleet—docks, cranes for loading and unloading the ships, and supply warehouses—had been erected along the waterfront. And it all had been completed and transferred to Decimus Brutus prior to the deadline!

Brutus, for his part, had made the most of Mamurra's efforts. Under his rigorous scrutiny, the Twelfth Legion had been converted to a fully effective marine fighting force. All preparations were in place for the arrival of Caesar and his army.

By prior arrangement, with Caesar's approval, Brutus had sortied out on several occasions with small squadrons of ships, usually in groups of five, to raid a number of the seaside towns of the Veneti. These raids had not only served to hasten the conversion of the legionaries into potent sea-borne warriors, but they also had produced the salutary effect of causing the Veneti to aggregate their fleet at their biggest port town, Darioritum. This was quite advantageous for the Romans, because it presented the opportunity to bring on a single decisive engagement. Everything on the line in one conclusive battle—that's how Caesar loved to operate. Significantly, in these minor skirmishes, Brutus did not unveil Mamurra's secret weapon; the turrets and long poles had not even been carried on any of these forays, lest a boat be captured by the enemy and the secret weapon revealed.

Caesar's march northwest into Brittany from Vesontio had been carried out with his usual alacrity, and the army had established a strong camp at a site selected to convince the Veneti that Caesar intended to join up with his fleet at Corbilo. Rumors to this effect were spread among the locals during the erection of the camp in the hope that word of such intent would reach the Veneti at Darioritum. Caesar's true intent, however, as Brutus had explained it to Mamurra, was to make a lightning march against Darioritum to cut off all overland routes of escape, while the fleet under Brutus would fall upon their harbor.

Before initiating this coordinated attack, Caesar sent word that he would leave the army at its base and travel to Corbilo for a planning conference. And, of course, to conduct an inspection of the fleet. This news sent everybody scrambling.

After one last look at the fleet to make sure all was in order, Mamurra, with his Pompeian assistant Garibus alongside, proceeded down the dock to the shore. Despite his early reservations about Garibus's true allegiances, Mamurra had to admit the man had performed admirably under the unrelenting stress of building the fleet and the port on Caesar's impossible timetable.

Once aground, Mamurra and Garibus joined the entire engineering staff assembled on the wharf awaiting Caesar's arrival. Brutus was not present; he had elected to join with the legion commander Hortensius in greeting Caesar at the camp gate and escorting him to the port. Mamurra suspected that Brutus had wanted the first opportunity to claim credit for all that had been accomplished at Corbilo in so little time. Mamurra told himself it did not matter—the achievement would speak for itself, and Caesar would know who had made it happen.

The wait was not long. A group of standard bearers came into view, followed by the drumbeat of hooves from Caesar's cavalry escort. Finally, the command group itself appeared and Mamurra spotted the general, clad as usual in common legionary's garb, save for the gold piping about the neck and arms of his long-sleeved tunic. Today he was riding a powerful stallion, black as coal.

Caesar waited for his staff officers, led by Curio, to dismount and form up before he climbed down from his own steed. Mamurra shouted an order and his men snapped to attention.

Caesar stepped forward and gave a hand signal for the men to stand at ease. He faced his engineer and said cheerfully, "Greetings, Mamurra. I am glad you found a way to keep yourself occupied over the winter."

Mamurra struck his breast in salute, and responded, "Aye, Caesar, we trust all will be to your satisfaction."

Brutus stepped forward to escort Caesar onto the wharf and lead him out to the moored ships, but Caesar gestured for Mamurra to come alongside them.

"How many?" Caesar asked when he reached the end of the dock, looking over the armada spread before him.

"Fifty-five ships," Brutus replied proudly, as though his very own hands had crafted the whole lot. "All built to the liburna-class military standard. One bank of rowers, forty oars on each side. Each ship is properly fitted and ready for battle."

"Well done" was Caesar's simple reply.

Then, to Mamurra's great surprise, Brutus made a broad, sweeping gesture toward the harbor and said, "Honor requires that I give credit where it is due, Caesar. When first we arrived, and absolutely no facilities were in place to produce what you now see before you, I despaired. I deemed the task impossible. But your man Mamurra here has pulled it off. He was the organizer and overseer of the success that will surely grant you a victory over the Veneti."

Mamurra, taken aback by this unexpected acknowledgment, hastened to say, "I thank the admiral for his praise, but all credit belongs to the men. They have worked tirelessly, night and day, to create this fleet for you."

Caesar slapped his engineer on the shoulder. "I expected nothing less." Then, turning to Brutus, he asked, "Now, what about these poles Mamurra has conjured up?"

Brutus gestured to a signalman waiting on the dock, who lifted a red flag and waved it in the direction of the captured Veneti vessel standing at anchor in the harbor. The crew jumped into action, hoisting the sails and rigging the ship to get underway. While this was in progress, a Roman galley approached at maximum speed and angled itself to ram the Veneti vessel.

Caesar was astonished when the ram merely glanced off the thick hull of the Veneti ship. "I read your report on the stoutness of their hulls," he said to Brutus, "but I could not imagine our rams being so ineffective."

Brutus grinned. "Fortunately, Mamurra has come up with a solution." He motioned again to the signalman, who this time picked up a black flag and waved it at the Roman galley, which had righted itself after the unsuccessful collision with its adversary.

On board the ship, the crew raised the turret onto the platform and locked it in place. Trained personnel climbed inside and were handed the long poles with their sharp hooks. The ship's captain directed his rowers to pull alongside the Veneti boat and, within moments, the rigging holding the Veneti sails was sliced to ribbons. The sails crashed down.

Once the Veneti craft was dead in the water, the Roman marines threw lines with grappling hooks across the short gap separating the two ships and lashed them together. Wooden planks were lifted into place, in effect making a bridge to carry boarding parties over to the enemy vessel. The men had been rigorously trained in this drill and carried it out with great efficiency. Within seconds, the Roman marines were in control of the enemy deck.

"Are all your crews as well trained as this one?" Caesar asked Brutus, accustomed to being shown only the best of everything during demonstrations.

"Sir, this crew was selected at random," Brutus replied with pride. Mamurra might have developed the strategy and built the fleet, but Brutus had given these landlubber infantrymen their sea legs.

"Very well," Caesar said simply. As he turned toward shore, he asked Mamurra, "What was the most challenging part?"

Mamurra did not hesitate. "The oars, sir, without question."

Caesar launched that intimidating flinty stare at him. "The oars?"

Mamurra let himself grin. "Sir, there are fifty-five ships. Each ship has eighty oars, with twenty in reserve under the deck. It takes two carpenters four hours to carve an oar and finish it."

He waited while Caesar worked out the calculations in his head.

Caesar finally seemed impressed, and with a twinkle in his eye he responded, "You show promise, Mamurra. We may yet make a serviceable engineer out of you."

∞

AT THE FORMAL LUNCHEON following Caesar's inspection of the fleet, the plan for the coming campaign against the Veneti was to be reviewed in detail. The senior commanders of all the legions in Caesar's army had accompanied him to Corbilo for this meeting, save for Gordianus, commander of the Tenth, who had been left in command with the main army back at the base should an emergency arise.

Brutus began the presentation standing next to a large map of Brittany stretched over a wooden frame. "Comrades," he said, pointing at the map, "the Veneti have committed a major blunder by clustering their fleet at

Darioritum. Not only does it provide us the opportunity for a decisive naval engagement, but the scouting reports say that a significant number of the population have fled to the town, thinking they will be safe there. This is utter folly—had they kept their population dispersed, forcing the army to lay siege on a town-by-town basis, they could have conducted guerilla warfare against us. By concentrating their ships and their people at a single location, they've made it so we can bag the entire lot in a single stroke."

He pointed out that Darioritum overlooked a natural harbor, known locally as the Gulf of Morbihan, which itself opened into the even larger Quiberon Bay. The Veneti fleet was stationed in the smaller Morbihan harbor, which meant the Roman fleet could maneuver to the mouth of the Quiberon Bay and bottle up the enemy fleet, permitting the naval engagement to be fought entirely within the confines of the bay.

He then proceeded to lay out the logistics of the plan: how many days it would take for Caesar and the main army to move to Darioritum, surround it, and establish siege operations there; when the fleet would need to leave Corbilo to set up the seaside blockade at the mouth of Quiberon Bay, just as Caesar arrived; and so on. A major issue was the limited storage space for food and water available on the Roman galleys—the ships' holds were not designed to allow the boats to remain at sea for days on end. It would be necessary to rotate the galleys to resupply them. A base for this purpose would be established as close as possible to Darioritum—a half-day's sail away. A portion of the army would be detached from the siege operation and moved to the base site to protect it. More significantly, the rotation meant that if the Veneti fleet could be induced to come out of their harbor and give battle, the full Roman fleet would not be in place at any given time. But Mamurra felt proud that the five extra ships he had demanded built would lessen the impact of this rotation.

A lengthy discussion of the details followed, through which Caesar sat rather quietly, only occasionally asking a pointed question or probing to make sure every aspect of the operation had been thoroughly vetted.

When it was over, he rose to address the group.

"Gentlemen," he said somberly, "allow me to commend you all for the dedicated effort you have put into the development of this plan. I am satisfied that you have anticipated every potential problem likely to arise and have made arrangements to deal with it. The gods delight in wreaking havoc upon us mere mortals. You may be assured that many things will go wrong. Some unexpected obstacle will undoubtedly arise, the enemy will make a sudden movement, the weather will not cooperate."

The assembly's attention turned to the map as Caesar studied it. "I must emphasize to you all that when the gods test us with unforeseen happenstance, you must improvise and exercise your judgment, but always keep in mind the overall plan and the impact your actions may have on what the rest of us are doing."

He picked up a cup. "A toast to your excellent work, and a prayer to the gods: May they bless our efforts with success!"

At the meeting's end, Caesar asked Mamurra to remain behind. The general described in glowing terms the great progress that Giacomo had made on the bridge and how well the demonstration crossing had been carried out. "You have overseen the simultaneous execution of two extremely complex projects while separated from them by a great distance. I will see that your efforts are richly rewarded," Caesar said.

Mamurra flushed with pride, not just from the praise he had received, but more importantly, from the fact that he had pleased Caesar. Over the months spent at Corbilo, separated from the high command at Vesontio, Mamurra had come to realize that Caesar was more to him than just a commanding officer, or even a father figure. Caesar was all that Mamurra wished he might be: decisive, insightful, accepting nothing but excellence, fearless, an amazing motivator of men. But that was not the real nub of it.

After months of nights spent with Dominicus, Mamurra knew now that he was a lover of men. Women did not arouse him at all. He had seen countless females taken as slaves and auctioned off naked—their bodies did nothing for him. But the men! So many shapes and sizes and characters— he had often looked at them, stripped and chained on the block, and lusted for them.

But Caesar? Was it even possible? He had heard the rumors, of course, and there was no question that Caesar favored certain handsome young officers over others. He had even heard gossip that Curio, flawed face and all, was secretly Caesar's lover, but now that Mamurra and Curio had become friends, he knew there was no truth to that. Many times Mamurra had thought back to that day when Caesar had suggested that Dominicus might be used for his pleasure. Had he been trying to get a read on Mamurra for his own purposes? Even now, months later, his spine tingled with the thought of it. He had even asked Dominicus what had happened between him and Caesar. "I would not tell anyone about what I do with you, Master," Dominicus had replied, and left it at that.

And now, here he was, alone with Caesar. But Mamurra dared not make a move.

Caesar, oblivious to Mamurra's musings, remarked, "I noticed Pompey's man Garibus at your side today. How has he performed?"

"I am aware of your issues regarding the man," Mamurra replied, "but I must be honest, sir. His work on the fleet has been outstanding."

Caesar stroked his chin in reflection. "Well, tell him we have a new task for him."

Mamurra felt a surge of dread. "How so?"

Caesar rose and walked over to the map of Brittany still standing at the front of the room. He pointed to the coast. "You are familiar with what is on the other side of this water?"

Mamurra replied, "Yes, of course. The territory of Britannia."

Caesar's eyes narrowed. "I intend to invade Britannia when we are done with Germania."

Mamurra was dutifully noncommittal. "An invasion of Britannia?"

Caesar's demeanor left no doubt; this was not conjecture but reality.

"We will need a fleet much larger than this one to make such a strike," Caesar said. "Tell Garibus he is to remain here until further notice. He is to busy himself with building the transport ships we will need for that invasion."

Mamurra mulled this over for a moment, then said softly, "But if you believe Garibus is keeping Pompey informed of your actions, putting him in charge of the shipbuilding operation will certainly tip off your adversary of your intentions."

Caesar smiled. "You are becoming astute at politics, my dear engineer. But be reassured. I have already discussed this plan with both Pompey and Crassus, and we have agreed upon it. Garibus cannot tell Pompey anything that Pompey does not already know."

Of course Caesar is one step ahead of those thieves and rascals, Mamurra thought.

Caesar gave him a sidelong look, as though he had been contemplating something for some time. "Why don't you join me for dinner this evening?" he said. "We can discuss the bridge in greater detail."

Mamurra's pulse quickened. "Of course; as you wish, sir. I am at your service, always."

"Indeed," Caesar said with a smile. "I expect great things from your service."

Caesar had been provided a suite of rooms in one of the barracks erected at Corbilo. There was a small fire smoldering in the hearth of his office, where Curio stood with a scroll in each hand, dreading the general's return.

Caesar strode in briskly, but stopped abruptly upon seeing Curio's ashen face. "What is it?"

"We have terrible tidings from Rome," Curio said, still staggered by the news. He lifted the opened scroll bearing Pompey's wax seal and handed it to Caesar as if it were a boulder. He had already read its grim message.

My dearest Caesar:

My heart is so heavy I can barely muster the energy to write this letter to you.

Our beloved Julia gave birth to a daughter, but the effort was too great, and she died from the loss of blood shortly after the child was placed in her arms. She passed away peacefully, smiling happily at the beautiful baby girl. I named the child Julia, for her mother. Most regrettably, the infant's lungs were not fully developed, and she survived for only two days.

They were given a proper Roman funeral, attended by all members of the Senate and the tribunes of the plebs. As a tribute to us both, by decree of the Senate, their ashes were placed on the Field of Mars. I am unaware of any woman ever having been thus honored. I was so overcome with grief, I could not rouse myself to speak. Your loving wife, Calpurnia, represented you nobly.

There are no words I can command to express my feeling of loss, and I cannot begin to imagine your own pain over this crushing news. Perhaps you may reconcile yourself with the knowledge that the gods favored her brief life with great beauty, warm kindness, loving charm, and a loyal daughter's tireless love for her father and her husband.

I remain,

Your loyal colleague,

Gnaeus Pompeius Magnus

Caesar's hands were trembling and his face contorted with grief. He slumped against his chair. Curio knew he could say nothing to ease this blow, so he stood in silent sorrow, awaiting whatever orders his general might make.

After several minutes, Caesar gathered himself and gave the parchment back to Curio.

"Put it in the fire," he said dully, as though all the life in him had been wrung out, like juice from a lemon. "I wish never to see it again."

Curio did as Caesar commanded. He returned to Caesar's side and prepared himself to deliver equally momentous news from the second scroll.

"There is . . . something else," Curio started hesitatingly.

Caesar shifted awkwardly to face Curio. The adjutant saw something he had never seen before: Caesar was weeping.

Curio held up the second scroll.

"It's from Vatteus," he said, his voice betraying no emotion. "The Lady Devorra delivered her child. The delivery was very difficult, but she has survived."

"Why do you bother me with this?" Caesar shouted. "My own beloved Julia is dead! I care nothing about the Nervii woman!"

"Fortify yourself, Caesar," Curio said softly, putting his hand gently on his friend's shoulder. "Devorra birthed a boy. You have a son."

The room was silent, save for the sound of Pompey's letter crackling in the fireplace.

"A son?" Caesar finally cried out. He fell back into the chair again. "I have a son?"

Caesar slammed his fist on the table, knocking a stack of reports onto the floor. "How fickle are the gods?" he exclaimed. "They pluck away my dear Julia, at the prime of her life, taking with her my grandchild, but then they grant me what I have most wanted, a son? They would not let me have both? Why do they torment me so?" He wrapped his hands about his head.

Curio had no answer for him. Long moments later, he asked, "What will you do?"

Caesar closed his eyes and rubbed his temples. "This changes everything," he said uncertainly.

"Well," Curio said, "you are hardly the first Roman of stature to sire an illegitimate son. I believe the Senate will barely notice."

"Pahh," Caesar hissed. "I care not what those windbags think. And they will do nothing, which is what they are best at."

Curio smiled, then ventured into more-sensitive territory. "If you wish to legitimize this son of yours, the path is complicated." Under Roman law, Caesar could not marry a foreigner without the official consent of the Senate. Although typically these consents were routinely granted, Caesar was hardly a routine individual. He was a clear-eyed elite Roman; marriages took place for political connections and money—love was irrelevant. Calpurnia was the daughter of the influential Senator Piso. If Caesar moved to divorce her, Piso and his faction could be counted on to oppose any bill seeking to authorize a marriage to Devorra.

Moreover, Curio knew that Caesar had neither desire to divorce Calpurnia nor to marry Devorra. Calpurnia had been faithful to him during his long absences from Rome, according to the reports he regularly received from the overseer of his household. And Caesar obviously had no attachment to Devorra; she had been merely a pleasurable distraction during the long months in Vesontio.

Curio could see the wheels turning in Caesar's mind. He had already worked through the analysis himself. "You could always adopt your son. That would make him a full Roman citizen. No action of the Senate is required for that." Calpurnia might balk at this, to be sure, but it was undeniable that she had not produced a child for him, despite regular efforts. This child was proof that the problem was not Caesar's seed.

Caesar seemed to consider this, then threw up his hands in exasperation. "There is no need to resolve this now," he said. "A son . . . a son." He buried his face in his hands, and when a few moments later he raised it again, it was dry of tears and void of emotion. "Let us turn our attention to Brittany."

"As you wish, sir," Curio said. "One question, if I may?"

"Always, Rio."

"In light of what has happened, should the Lady Devorra and her child remain outside the walls at Vesontio, or should we relocate them to the fort, where they would be protected by the garrison?"

Caesar looked appalled. "We don't need a bunch of nosy garrison officers spreading rumors. Let them remain where they are. No adversity can befall them in the countryside."

After Caesar left for his dinner with Mamurra, Curio did some calculating of his own. He cursed his luck—he had installed Molena in the cottage with Devorra, thinking this would put her safely beyond a chance meeting with Caesar. And even if Caesar unexpectedly did decide to visit Devorra, Curio suspected that Caesar had expunged the slave girl and his unhappy experience with her from his memory. Then again, there was always a chance he would remember her and demand to know why Curio had not merely had her killed. Curio could hardly tell Caesar it was because he himself was strongly attracted to her! Molena would take Caesar's visit to mean he must be the father—Caesar could have her killed for that reason alone. Curio's career—and his romance with Molena—would be over.

There was only one thing to do. Before the army returned to Vesontio, Curio would need to remove Molena from the cottage and out of harm's way. Thank the gods he had left Vatteus behind. With a plan forming, he relaxed a bit. There was plenty of time to send a message to Vatteus to arrange this.

༺❦༻

MAMURRA ARRIVED AT Caesar's quarters to find the general engaged in discussion with Brutus. He tried not to show his disappointment.

"Your man Mamurra is a miracle worker," Brutus said, as he took a seat opposite Caesar. "What do you have in store for him next?"

Mamurra knew better than to answer.

"Oh, nothing significant, for a while," Caesar replied in a matter-of-fact tone. "Now, Brutus, I have some routine personnel matters to take up with my engineer," Caesar said.

Taking the cue, Brutus dismissed himself from the room, much to Mamurra's satisfaction.

Caesar waited as the servers brought in a variety of offerings from the chefs. He showed little interest in the food.

"Personnel matters?" Mamurra asked.

Caesar gave him a dismissive flick of his wrist. "I just wanted privacy."

Mamurra's heart began to race, but then a sad look came over Caesar's face.

"I have had devastating news today, Mamurra."

Mamurra's first thought was that something had happened to the army. *Was there another surprise attack? But no, this seemed like true melancholy. Something personal, then?*

The general gave forth a heavy sigh. "My only child, my dear Julia, has died in childbirth. Nor did her offspring survive."

Mamurra was stunned. He groped for what to say. "Ah, Caesar; by the gods! This is so tragic. My deepest condolences."

Caesar picked up a dagger from the table. "This was her last gift to me," he said, his voice distant. "I shall keep it close to me always."

Mamurra felt guilty he'd dreamed for something more than a business meeting. He dropped his head in sympathy for Caesar's loss, then said, "Sir, if you would prefer to be alone, the bridge can wait."

The grief on Caesar's face turned in an instant to resolve.

"No, Mamurra," he said with conviction. "Duty first and always."

CAESAR LEFT THE NEXT MORNING to return to his camp. Shortly after his departure, Mamurra broke the news to Garibus about his new assignment.

When Garibus learned he was to be stranded indefinitely in Corbilo, building transport vessels for the Britannia excursion, he was quite unhappy. So, after Mamurra left, he took up a stylus and wrote a letter.

Pompey was far too clever to be taking reports from a subordinate under Caesar's direct command; instead, Garibus had been instructed to send his reports to Catullus, the senator in charge of monitoring Caesar's activities in Gaul. And Garibus had proved quite effective at monitoring all sorts of Caesar's activities. This time he wrote:

> *Caesar was here to inspect the fleet. He spent time alone with the engineer Mamurra, who, it is known, is a practitioner of the Greek habit. They dined together in Caesar's quarters. Can you guess what they might have discussed?*

XL

Outside Vesontio

EVORRA RECOVERED SLOWLY from the difficult birth, but several weeks later, with the aid of her companions and nourished by good food and fresh air, she and the child were thriving. Sadly, Aloucca had told her that the damage done during the delivery might have made her unable to bear more children. This was sobering, but she resigned herself to it, especially since she could not imagine ever loving a man other than Gabinier. It only made her more thankful for her son. Devorra had not yet given her child a formal name, but had taken to calling him Sonnig, meaning *sunny*, because of his cheerful disposition.

Devorra had lined the stone patio with an array of flowers, which were in full bloom now, adding bright color to the shade of the centuries-old oak tree. She found the fresh air so pleasing that she preferred to nurse her son while taking her leisure outside, often catching a soft breeze wafting up from the nearby river.

On this afternoon, Aloucca sat nearby in a rocking chair, knitting a swaddling blanket for the child, while Molena plucked at some small weeds between the stones.

"What are you making for supper tonight?" Devorra asked Molena.

"Lamb stew," Molena replied. "Tomorrow I want to make our favorite, the meat pie. But we are low on flour and we have no more grains. Elliandro is not expected for a while. Can Aloucca go into the town in the morning and buy what we need?"

Devorra, shifting the child to her other breast, gave it barely a thought. They had plenty of money.

"Yes, Aloucca will go," she said.

Aloucca smiled. She clearly enjoyed her shopping runs into Vesontio, always returning with proud tales of haggling with the merchants.

"Perhaps while you are there," Devorra mused, "you might look for some kind of plaything for the child. Something to occupy him during the day."

"I'm sure I can find something," Aloucca said. "I'll leave early. I want to return before it gets too hot."

Complacency is a terrible thing.

It is an especially terrible thing when it afflicts sentries. For as many days as Gabinier had had eyes on the fortress at Vesontio, the same two stodgy legionaries had been stationed at the entrance. It was their duty to inspect each wagon entering the fortress with supplies or produce, to make sure no treachery might be lurking beneath the tarps.

Presumably these inspections had never generated anything remarkable, and with human nature being what it is, these two guards had grown careless. They routinely waved wagoners through the gate without even inspecting their cargo. The legionaries were friendly with the rustic teamsters who drove the same wagons carrying the same supplies, day after day after day.

It had been laughably easy for Gabinier to buy his small force of raiders a ride hidden in the back of one of these wagons, which passed through the gates without so much as a flutter of the tarp.

Once the wagon was safely inside, the driver tapped the side of the wagon with his stick. Gabinier threw off the covering shroud and leaped from the wagon with his men. They killed the two lax guards before the stunned Romans could realize what was happening. Gustavus and Giovanus dashed up the steps to the watchtower, burst in with swords drawn, and stabbed the two guards inside, who were still half-asleep. Gustavus was toting an alpenhorn, slung over his shoulder. He gave it a long, hearty blast.

A large raiding party of Germanic warriors, all mounted on stallions, burst out of the forest and made straight for the fortress gate. They were inside before any of the garrison knew what was happening. The surprise was complete—as was the slaughter.

Gabinier knew that the fortress was lightly staffed. In making his reconnaissance, he had learned that the Romans had established a second camp between the Vesontio fortress and the Rhine. This establishment was a traditional Roman marching camp, staunchly protected by moat and stockade. No one seemed to know what was going on in there, just that it was much more heavily defended than Vesontio. Some of the raiders wanted to attack the camp itself and burn it to the ground, rather than assault the more daunting stone fortress at Vesontio. But Gabinier, having learned that the Belgae hostages were being held inside the fortress, had convinced the Germanic tribesmen that the other camp couldn't offer anything more than complications for the raid. He prevailed in convincing them to make their strike at the fortress instead.

The raiders wasted no time in launching their murderous orgy of raping, plundering, and burning. It would not be long before the Romans at the second camp saw the smoke billowing from the fortress and organized a rescue attempt.

Gabinier frantically set about searching for his beloved Devorra. He did not fear her falling victim to the raid since all the men had been given her description. If they came upon her, she was to be turned over immediately, unharmed, to Gabinier.

ALOUCCA HAD JUST FINISHED paying for the flour and farro in a small shop inside the fortress when she heard the horn blare from the watchtower. She gave it no thought—the Roman soldiers were probably running a drill. She stepped out into the square, thinking to make her way over to another merchant who she knew offered a small selection of hand-carved wooden toys.

But after only a few steps, it became clear that something was horribly wrong. Roman soldiers were running about frantically as a band of mounted raiders poured into the fortress.

Aloucca froze in place, watching in disbelief as the stampeding warriors cut down the handful of Roman soldiers feebly trying to mount a response. She soon gave way to panic, tossed her basket aside, and turned to run. But before she could make it even halfway across the square, a mounted warrior came up behind her and slashed her back, his sword carving a deep gash across her shoulder blades. With a shriek of agony, Aloucca tumbled to the grassy turf and sobbed as her life's blood flowed away.

GABINIER WAS FRANTIC. He had heard from his informers that the Nervii hostages were being held in a group of tents near the Romans' offices. He and many of the raiders had headed straight for this complex, figuring that the most valuable booty was sure to be held there. But the only treasure Gabinier sought was his woman. He scoured the Roman quarters and located several of the captives, but none of them knew what had happened to Devorra—only that she was not among them and had not been for some months.

Time was slipping away; he knew they could not stay much longer in the fortress before more Romans arrived. The recovery from his wound, the challenge to Boduognatus, the long trek to join Ariovistus, the sheer brazenness of this raid—it all seemed futile, yet he felt his determination to find her rise to manic levels.

Gabinier rushed to the town square, his sword dripping with the blood of Roman soldiers.

He saw an old woman lying face down on the ground, blood seeping from a deep wound in her back. As he hurried past her, the woman cried out in pain. Her voice stopped him in his tracks.

He whirled, bent down on one knee, and gently turned the woman over. *Aloucca!* He pushed her tangled hair from her face and wiped away the grime from the turf.

Aloucca, at the very edge of consciousness, stared at him wildly and whispered, "Gab . . . Gabinier?"

"Yes, Aloucca. I survived the battle with the Romans. I have come to rescue Devorra." He clutched her shoulders tightly. "Where is she?"

"S-s-sonnig."

"What are you saying, woman? Tell me where she is!" Gabinier shouted, shaking her shoulders.

Gasping for breath, Aloucca spoke. "Tell her . . . I loved . . ."

"No! No!" Gabinier screamed. "Where is Devorra?"

But Aloucca was gone. Gabinier sagged in despair. How would he ever find Devorra now?

He eased Aloucca back to the ground. There was a sudden clash of metal on metal, and he turned to look. A tall man dressed as a Roman slave was fighting against a small cordon of Roman soldiers who had formed up with their backs to the fortress wall. Gabinier leapt to his feet and threw himself into the fray, swinging his broad sword and hacking through the Romans.

"Who are you?" he asked the slave, panting from exertion, after the last Roman had fallen.

"My name is Elliandro," the man replied. "And by your accent, you must be Belgic."

"I am. My name is Gabinier."

"I am Belgic too," Elliandro said. "My sister and I were taken captive before the battle at the Sabis. Take me with you and I will help you fight the Romans."

"I cannot linger here," Gabinier said, sweat running down his face. "I must find a Nervii woman who was a hostage. I'm told she is no longer in the camp. That old woman was her companion, but she died before she could tell me where she has gone."

Elliandro looked at the crumpled body on the ground and drew a sharp breath as he recognized Aloucca. "Do you seek the Lady Devorra?"

"Yes!" Gabinier cried. "Do you know where she is?"

"My sister is with her!" Elliandro grabbed Gabinier by the arm. "I will take you there."

⸎

DEVORRA, TOO, thought nothing of it when she heard the horn from the fortress.

"They are at it early today," she purred to the bright-eyed Sonnig in his crib. "Aloucca will be back soon, and she will have a nice surprise for you."

Devorra savored the simple joy of watching her boy wiggle in his cradle. At times, she still marveled at the strange sequence of events that had brought her to this situation. What a path her life had taken! Finally, Sonnig made himself comfortable and dozed off.

Devorra went to the washbasin, where Molena was cleaning the dishes still piled up from last night's dinner. Their friendship had continued to grow, even more quickly since Sonnig's birth. More than ever, Devorra felt the bond of sisterhood with her.

"Aloucca must really be haggling with the merchants today," she said to Molena, who responded with a bright smile.

"I'm sure she's quite good at it," Molena said, pushing the last of the dishes through the soapy water.

Suddenly there was a powerful banging on the door. Devorra felt a bolt of panic rush over her. She grabbed a kitchen knife and moved to protect the crib. She gestured for Molena to do the same. They took up positions on either side of the child.

"Open this door!" a voice cried, in Devorra's native tongue.

Despite her blind panic, the voice sounded familiar to Devorra. But with her heart pounding wildly, she could not think clearly. *Who could it be, here in the wilderness of Gaul?*

With a great crash, the door gave way. A tall, bronzed warrior burst into the room, eyes bulging, his tunic spattered with blood.

When he saw her, he stopped. "Devorra!" He smiled broadly and took a step toward her.

His jubilance turned to confusion as he looked past her to the cradle, where Sonnig, incredibly, had not been roused by the racket.

Any confusion he might have felt, however, was nothing compared with Devorra's sheer inability to comprehend that it was truly Gabinier standing before her. *It can't be!* But then she saw it, still on his wrist, that simple bracelet that held a lock of her own hair. It really was Gabinier, her beloved Gabinier!

The shock was too great. She dropped the knife and sank to her knees.

MOLENA BRAVELY STEPPED between the bloody warrior and Devorra. "Away with you," she snarled, fire in her eyes, brandishing the knife. And then her brother stepped into the cottage, sword in hand.

"What . . . what is happening?" she asked, completely at a loss.

"Molena, this man has led an attack on the fortress," Elliandro replied. "They have killed all the Romans there. We have come to rescue you both."

Molena lowered the knife.

"We will be free again, Molena! Free!" Elliandro rushed to her, and the siblings clutched each other in a long embrace.

GABINIER STOOD STILL for a few moments, trying to comprehend what this infant was doing in the cottage. Perhaps it belonged to the slave girl. He quickly recovered his senses and knelt in front of Devorra. He reached out to stroke her face. She just stared into his eyes, unable to speak.

Gabinier took her in his arms and held her tight, and they wept for joy.

"But how?" Devorra finally managed. "They told me you were dead."

Gabinier ran his finger over the contours of her face. She was as lovely as ever, just as he had imagined her during all those nights of separation. "I was badly wounded, but I survived," he whispered. "I returned to the Nervii and challenged your father. He will never harm you again."

"It was you?" Devorra gasped. "They said it was Pomorro who killed my father."

Gabinier scoffed at that. "I became the leader of the Nervii. But they would not agree to fight the Romans. So I left the tribe in Pomorro's hands and went to join the Germani under Ariovistus. I led the attack on the fortress to rescue you."

Devorra, still weeping, pulled Gabinier closer and kissed him. It did not matter that he was soaked in the sweat of the day's exertions, or that the smell of blood was on him. It was like a dream. Gabinier was alive! And he had returned to her.

Sonnig's screech jarred them from their reverie.

Gabinier jumped to his feet and peered into the cradle.

"Is this your child?" he demanded, looking at Molena, whose terrified reaction made it clear the child was not hers.

A fresh wave of panic washed over Devorra as Gabinier grasped her tightly by the arm and jerked her to her feet. The force of his anger was overpowering. "Whose child is this?"

Devorra stammered, "I—I—I was raped by a Roman soldier," and burst into a new flood of tears.

Gabinier's face grew dark with rage. "Raped? By a Roman?" he bellowed. "I will slay every last one of the Roman scum!" And then he stopped. "This child is a Roman?"

"No, Gabinier," Devorra said, gathering her strength. "This is my son. He is innocent."

Gabinier's mouth fell open, but he was unable to find words. Devorra reached for his hand, but he pulled away. Reeling, he staggered out of the cottage.

Elliandro said urgently, "Pack only what you can carry. You will travel with us to Germania. And hurry—Roman patrols will be out soon."

Exhausted and bewildered, Devorra methodically gathered up what she and Sonnig would need. Her world, so serene and safe only minutes earlier, was now in turmoil. *My beloved Gabinier. Will he ever embrace me again?*

Molena placed her hand on Devorra's shoulder. "What about Aloucca?" she asked, turning to her brother. "We must wait for her to return."

"I am so sorry," Elliandro replied.

Devorra's head shot up, and with one look at Elliandro's face, she understood that Aloucca would never return. She and Molena cried out in unison one sharp, shared exclamation of grief. The two women clasped hands and tearfully brought their foreheads together for just a moment. Then, knowing that they must move quickly or risk their lives, they made ready to leave the farm that had become their home.

"I will look for Gabinier," Elliandro said, rushing from the cottage.

In the crazed bustle of the packing, Devorra noticed that Molena was standing still, gently running her fingertips over her necklace. "You are thinking about him, aren't you?"

"I'll never see him again," Molena said, her voice barely a whisper.

Devorra had no answer for her. The only other sound in the cottage was the soft whimpering of the son of Gaius Julius Caesar.

XLI

DARIORITUM

C AESAR'S OVERLAND MOVE to trap the Veneti at Darioritum was masterfully accomplished. The Roman cavalry first cut off all the roads leading to the city. Before the Veneti leaders could fully understand what was happening, Caesar's legions had moved up these roads and established a series of strongholds to ensure the Romans could hold them against any kind of foray in force by the Veneti. Then Caesar unleashed Mamurra, who, with the aid of thousands of legionaries wielding axes and shovels, swiftly erected a fortified wall that ran for miles, completely confining the Veneti to their coastal fortress. There would be no landward escape for them.

The tribal fathers, dazed by the speed of the Roman land-side deployment, must have been completely dumbfounded to discover one morning that a fleet of Roman warships had suddenly materialized at the mouth of the Quiberon Bay, in effect cutting off their access to the ocean. Caesar had hoped the realization that they were surrounded might induce them to capitulate without a fight. He sent several officers to meet with the Veneti under a flag of truce. But the Veneti clapped these officers into chains and offered to return them only if the Romans gave up their siege and withdrew. Enraged by this affront to the Roman notion of civilized warfare, Caesar stepped up his siege operations, putting even more pressure on the Veneti leadership.

In anticipation that the Veneti would likely draw upon their most potent weapon—their navy—to break free of their precarious situation, Caesar moved his headquarters to a high bluff on the edge of the Quiberon Bay so that he might be afforded a bird's-eye view of any ensuing engagement. He did not have long to wait.

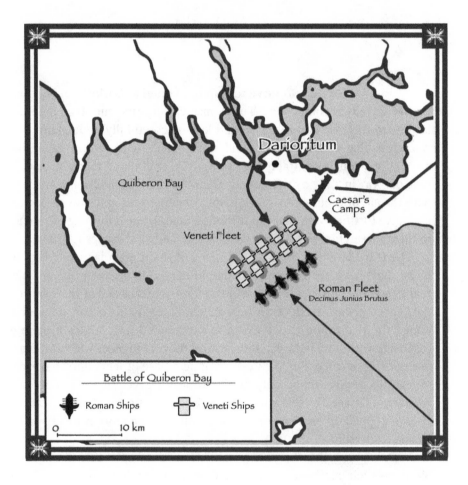

Darioritum

Quiberon Bay

Caesar's
Camps

Veneti Fleet

Roman Fleet
Decimus Junius Brutus

Battle of Quiberon Bay

Roman Ships   Veneti Ships

0   10 km

ONE BRIGHT MIDSUMMER DAY, Caesar and Mamurra were huddled over a map in Caesar's command tent, studying a plan for breaching the walls of Darioritum, when a breathless messenger interrupted their conversation. He brought news that the Veneti fleet in the harbor was rigging its sails and preparing to move out into the bay. They hurried to a high observation tower to watch the climactic confrontation.

Mamurra felt considerable anxiety about the pending engagement, not just because of the stakes, which were immense, but also because every one of the ships that the Romans were throwing into the fight had been built by his men. And even though Brutus had put the vessels through rigorous sea trials, Mamurra knew that if things went badly, it would be his own design for the hooks and protective turrets that would be faulted.

His anxiety was further exacerbated by the sheer number of Veneti craft at anchor in the harbor. The Romans had counted over two hundred ships at the disposal of the enemy, against which the Romans could only offer up forty-five in opposition, since at any given time ten ships in the fleet had rotated out for supply replenishment.

Caesar, however, remained remarkably calm as he and Mamurra briskly scaled the long series of ladders that transported them to the viewing platform. Mamurra, always squeamish about heights, appreciated the tall railing he'd designed for the platform. Caesar leaned against it, looking out over the glittering bay. They could tell from the configuration of the Roman fleet that Brutus had determined the Veneti were making ready to come out and engage them.

"Look there, Mamurra," Caesar said. "Brutus has installed the turrets, but he has not yet brought forth the poles."

Mamurra, as he had in the past, marveled at the acuity of Caesar's vision, particularly given the general's age. He himself had to squint mightily to make out the turrets, now mounted on the bows and the sterns of the Roman galleys.

Because the Veneti ships lacked oars, it took them some time to navigate into something resembling a formation and begin their advance against the Roman fleet. Struggling to maintain a line, they approached the waiting Roman navy in a haphazard manner.

Caesar gave a short laugh. "They have no organization. They are merely throwing all their power at us in blunt force. Brutus will make mincemeat of them."

"But their numbers are fearsome," Mamurra said worriedly. "Can Brutus cope with such an overwhelming force?"

Caesar gave him a confident smile. "Many times I have faced far superior numbers on the battlefield," he replied with the knowing tone of someone who had seen it all before. "Sheer numbers without structure, training, and discipline are nothing but a rabble. And no mere rabble can stand up to the organized ferocity of the Roman military."

A group of five Roman galleys pulled out from the main formation and rowed at maximum speed toward the leading elements of the advancing Veneti fleet, each boat approaching a specific enemy vessel head on, as if to ram it. As they drew within range of the enemy, the Romans unleashed their deck-mounted catapults, lofting burning mounds of highly flammable naphtha toward the lumbering Veneti ships. A sailing ship's crew has no greater fear than fire on board, and as these flaming bundles landed on the decks of their targets, the Veneti crews erupted in a frenzied disarray, scrambling to extinguish the flames.

The Veneti sailors were clearly expecting the onrushing Roman ships to ram them, and they crouched on their decks anticipating the force of direct collision. But the Romans had no such intention, and as the galleys drew near, their captains pulled hard on the rudders and the Roman warships glided past their heavy adversaries, so close that the tips of the Roman oars made scraping sounds against the Veneti hulls.

Hearing this, some of the Veneti leaped to their feet and attempted to rain down spears and pikes onto the much lower decks of the Roman galleys as they passed. However, the legionaries on the decks, now converted to marines by Brutus, formed a canopy of their shields above them, much like the turtle formation they had practiced so often on land. The bombardment of Veneti missiles bounced harmlessly away.

More significantly, the enemy sailors did not at all grasp the significance of the long, hooked poles that emerged from the turrets on the Roman ships. In the few seconds it took for the Romans to slip past their much bulkier adversaries, the razor-sharp hooks on the Roman poles sliced through the halyards and lanyards holding the leather Veneti sails in place. Mamurra breathed a sigh of relief as the sails crashed to the decks under their own weight, cords and leather entangling the Veneti crews in catastrophic confusion. Within moments, the Veneti ships lost their means of propulsion and were dead in the water, stuck in the relative calm of the bay, lush prey for the much faster Roman raiders.

The Roman galleys, now behind the victimized enemy ships, each made a sharp turn and pulled alongside their adversaries. The ships were quickly lashed together, footbridges lifted into place, and a contingent of Roman marines hurried across to wreak mayhem on the hapless Veneti. One by one, the commanders of the boarding parties signaled when an enemy ship was under control, her crew either slaughtered or surrendered, by raising a Roman flag on the main mast of the captured vessel. Upon seeing the signal, the galley captains cut the lines holding the ships together and rowed off in pursuit of other victims.

From high upon the observation tower, Caesar exulted in the success of Mamurra's poles. "See, Mamurra, they have no answer for your innovation! The day will be ours!" he crowed. Mamurra was overcome by a sweet rush of satisfaction—the plan was working!

Far out in the bay, Brutus saw the same progress and released more squadrons of his galleys to make their attacks. What little formation the Veneti had managed to assemble quickly dissipated under the stinging attacks of the Roman ships. As the engagement wore on, more and more of the enemy fleet were flying Roman flags. So far as Mamurra could tell from the observation tower, not a single Roman ship was sunk, or even seriously damaged. A stunning victory was in the making.

Somewhere in the midst of the naval chaos stood the admiral in charge of the Veneti fleet. Even he could see the day was lost. He ordered that a signal flag be raised, recalling what was left of his battered armada back into the safety of the harbor.

But disengagement was not so easy. The Veneti ships were strung out across the bay, and they were difficult to turn and maneuver. Many more of them fell victim to the ruthless Roman onslaught. By the end of the afternoon, of the two hundred proud warships that had ventured out to fight the Romans, fewer than fifty had made it back to their base. The Veneti fleet was now smaller than the opposing Roman force, which still controlled the bay and maintained the blockade of Darioritum.

AT DAWN THE NEXT DAY, the Roman emissaries who previously had been taken prisoner rode forth from the walls of Darioritum, now free of their shackles and carrying a message for Caesar: The Veneti were asking for the terms of surrender.

Caesar, whose rage at the Veneti treatment of his officers had hardly abated, sent back an icy reply, which he dictated to Curio. "The Veneti elders will present themselves before me at noon today and surrender. Following their capitulation, they will be informed of the terms. If they do not appear, there will be no further opportunity offered, and our siege will continue."

At noon, a procession of Veneti tribal and clan leaders emerged from the fortress, thirty or so in all, bereft of weapons. Each man was put into fetters, hands bound behind their backs, their ankles separated by a short chain, befitting the treatment they had inflicted upon the Roman officers. This sorry-looking group was brought before Caesar, who had donned the white-and-purple toga of a Roman consul. He sat in the same ivory curule chair from which he had presided over meetings of the Senate. He clutched an ivory baton capped with a golden Roman eagle, symbol of his authority as granted by the Senate. Curio and Labienus stood just behind his left shoulder.

Through an interpreter, Caesar asked the group if they were prepared to subject themselves and the Veneti people to the governance of Rome in all respects, and to accept without reservation any decrees Rome might issue. The group muttered their assent, but this was not enough. Caesar had each individual leader step forward and listen to the question. Each man was required to solemnly swear, in the presence of them all, and on the pain of affronting the Veneti gods, his agreement to the terms of the surrender, whatever they might be. Every man did just that.

Then Caesar had them draw lots, each man pulling a straw from a bundle. The three with the shortest straws were separated from the rest of the group. Expecting the worst, these three men fell to their knees, begging for mercy.

"You, whom fortune has favored with the shortest straws, will return to the Veneti and inform them of the terms that shall govern their fate," he said coldly to the trio. "The Veneti will surrender all their remaining ships, and their warriors shall turn over their weapons to a designated Roman officer. All the Veneti sailors, and one-third of the warriors, are hereby declared to be slaves of Rome. Lots will be drawn to determine the warriors to be enslaved."

Great cries of protest poured forth from the group.

"You shall also surrender a woman not older than twenty years for each male taken," he added.

Curio could not help but marvel at the haul Caesar was amassing. But he was not yet finished.

"One half of the lands of the Veneti are declared forfeit to the people of Rome. We will install a governor who will decree which lands will be taken in title by Rome and which may remain in the ownership of the Veneti."

Still more moaning erupted from the Veneti leaders. But in their bonds, and with the oaths they had just sworn, there was nothing they could do.

Yet another dazzling fortune to be distributed, Curio thought. They were all going to be rich beyond their wildest dreams.

And finally, Caesar pulled his dagger—Julia's dagger—from the folds of his toga. He pointed it at the large group of men who had been segregated from the other three. "As for you, you who captured the envoys who had approached under flag of truce and held them as hostage to your demands upon Rome, each of you shall bear the terrible penalty of the sword."

Amid the terrified silence of the group, Caesar turned to Labienus, who was standing at his side. "Remove the head of each of these men and post every head on a pike outside the walls of Darioritum, so that all may know the awful wages of treachery when dealing with the power of Rome."

He left as the men wept and pleaded for mercy. He gestured for Curio to come beside him as he walked away.

"Be certain," he said to his adjutant, "to include this episode in your chapter on our victory at Darioritum."

The next two days were spent dispensing with the gruesome work of posting the severed heads of the condemned Veneti leaders in easy view of the city walls as well as enslaving the young women and countless unfortunate sailors and warriors who had made war upon the Romans. Nofio's coffles were fully utilized. Some of these ill-fated men sought to resist; a number of them were killed outright, others whipped to within an inch of their lives and sent to live out their remaining days as galley slaves, devoid of hope, rowing Roman merchant ships.

Caesar decreed that a great feast of thanksgiving would be held to celebrate the astounding Roman victory. Curio transmitted word of this to the fleet, and the Roman ships were put into harbor so that the triumphant Brutus and his crews could partake in the momentous fete.

Each legion held a celebration at its own camp, and Caesar spent the afternoon touring the different venues to extend his congratulations to the men and assure them that all would receive shares from the sale of hordes of Veneti slaves.

The officers would be celebrating at a separate evening event. Under Curio's direction, the Romans commandeered a large villa, brilliantly sited on a promontory affording a spectacular view of the entire Quiberon Bay. The army's commissary crews worked frenetically to provide an abundance of delicacies, flavored with the wide variety of spices easily found in a large port city like Darioritum. Wine flowed in prodigious quantities. And plenty of nubile slave girls were made available for the carnal pleasure of the officers.

⌒∽৲∾⌒

THE REVELRY WAS WELL UNDERWAY, and some of the men were slipping off, many with one or more of the lovely slave girls at their side. It seemed nothing could hinder the joyous festivities. Then the sound of trumpets rent the air, signaling an approaching messenger.

The room fell silent as Caesar strode onto the balcony to learn what was happening. Curio and Mamurra, both still sober, accompanied him.

Gordianus, commander of the Tenth Legion, rode into view on horseback with a mud-splattered messenger at his side. Behind him, a bodyguard of cavalry escorts, including the trumpeter, fell into place in the courtyard facing the balcony. Gordianus's face was grim.

Caesar called out, "Gordianus, what has interrupted your celebration with the Tenth?"

"Tragic news, Caesar," Gordianus replied, loud enough for all to hear. He tilted his head toward the messenger.

The man, who looked exhausted, held up a leather pouch. "The garrison at Vesontio was attacked by Germanic raiders," he said. "I bring to you a complete report, issued by the engineer Giacomo."

Caesar gestured for the man to toss the pouch up to him on the balcony. He tore it open and pulled out a scroll. Finally, with a pained expression and sorrow in his voice, Caesar looked out onto the courtyard.

"Gordianus, spread the news to your fellow legion commanders. Our dear colleagues at Vesontio have been massacred. Not a man in the fortress was left alive."

He turned to Mamurra and Curio. "The camp and the garrison protecting the bridge site were not attacked," he said in a low voice.

"That is an oversight they will rue," Curio added through clenched teeth.

Caesar handed the second scroll from the packet to Curio, to whom it was addressed. Curio felt the color draining from his face as he read.

Curio:

Fortunately, I was not in Vesontio when the raid occurred—I was working at the camp. The bodies of some of the Nervii hostages were found in the ruins of Vesontio, including the

*body of the old slave woman who attended the Lady Devorra,
but the others presumably escaped. I assembled a cohort of
soldiers and immediately went to the cottage wherein the Lady
Devorra and her child were housed. There was no sign of
anyone present. The farmer told me he saw them riding away
with a Germanic warrior and the slave who had been bringing
them supplies. I must assume they were spirited away back to
Germania, with the rest of the raiders.*

Vatteus

Curio handed the scroll to Caesar, who read it quickly then crumpled
the message in his hand.

Mamurra did not have to wait for orders. "You will want the army to
leave for Vesontio as soon as possible. The staff will begin work tonight."

Caesar stared off into the distance for a long while, and Mamurra looked
to Curio, who signaled for the engineer to wait.

When Caesar spoke, his voice was colder than the winter snows atop
Vesuvius. "Not as soon as possible, engineer. We leave tomorrow."

In the frenzied preparations for departure, Curio barely had time to
breathe, let alone ponder the implications of the message from Vatteus.
There was much to do to break camp: voluminous records to be organized
and packed, furnishings to be safely wrapped and stored in the wagon train,
tents to be struck, provisions assembled, and so forth. It was especially
challenging given the fact that so many of the officers were either drunk or
freshly satiated by their slave girls, if not both. Yet finally, by the dead of
night, the situation was sufficiently under control to allow Curio some time
alone to sort through his thoughts.

Caesar was going to build the bridge over the Rhine or kill Mamurra in
the effort; that was a given. And he would march the entire Roman army
into Germania to take revenge for the massacre at Vesontio—there would
be no denying him. But revenge would merely be the cover story. Caesar
would spare no effort to retrieve his son, Curio was certain. It seemed
impossible, but Caesar was a master at making the impossible come to pass.

They did not even know for sure whether Devorra had gone back to
Germania with the raiders. Vatteus thankfully had omitted any reference
to Molena, but Curio had to assume she had joined Elliandro in the escape.
Perhaps they would try to make their way back to Nervii territory. But if
Devorra had indeed been spirited away by the Germanic raiders, could they

realistically hope to find her in the vastness of Germania? And if, by some intrigue of the gods, Devorra found herself under the control of Ariovistus, could they prevail upon the Germanic king to hand her child over?

Curio's gut churned with the possibility that mother and child might end up back in Roman custody, with Molena in tow. Somehow, he had to keep that from happening.

XLII

TERRITORY OF THE SUEBI, GERMANIA

D EVORRA STAGGERED OVER A WORN PATH toward the tiny hut that had become her home with Molena and Sonnig over the past days. She strained to keep the heavy bucket of water she carried from splashing out its contents, lest she need another trip to the well. As she had done many times during the days they had been installed in this shack, Devorra tried to accept the stunning reversal of her fortune.

The bottom plank of the door scraped the dirt floor as she shoved her way into the only room, lit by a solitary candle. Molena was holding Sonnig, rocking back on a small stool, trying to coax him to sleep.

Devorra crossed the room, still wrangling the awkward bucket. Her expensive Roman clothes, left behind in the race to escape Vesontio, had been replaced with the common peasant garb of the Suebian women. Her face was drawn and lined from the incessant worry that had beset her since that terrible day when Gabinier had burst into her comfortable home and turned her life upside down. She had relived the scene in her mind over and over: Gabinier alive and restored to her! But then the shattering realization when he saw her child. She could not put out of her mind the horrified look on his face as he dashed out of the cottage. It was like a nightmare, but one she had lived.

After Elliandro had told them to pack, he left the cottage, looking for Gabinier. Devorra and Molena had wrapped what they could carry in sheets and loaded everything onto Elliandro's wagon. Gabinier, still brooding, joined them but maintained a stony silence. With Molena's arm around her shoulders, Devorra wept at the loss of Aloucca, as well as in confusion over Gabinier's coldness. The acrid air was thick with smoke and ashes as the wagon made its way past the burning fortress and onto the path back to Germania.

271

It was all a delirious blur to Devorra, even now. They had hurried to the Rhine, taking great care to skirt the other Roman camp. Without another word to Devorra, Gabinier left the little group to rejoin the raiding party, which was on the alert for a sortie from the garrison at the camp. They crossed the broad river in a large scow in the company of cows and pigs that had been liberated from their Roman owners, as well as a number of the Nervii hostages who had survived the raid. Devorra spoke to no one.

Upon reaching Germanic territory, they were loaded onto another wagon and brought through the wilderness to a large town, wrapped around an imposing castle. Devorra later learned their new home was in the realm of Ariovistus, ruler of the Suebi. She clutched her child to her at all times, terrified that at any moment the tribesmen might rip him away.

Elliandro had obtained this humble shelter for the women and child and kept them supplied with food, meager though it might be.

There had been no sign of Gabinier. No one knew where he was. No one would tell her anything.

Devorra lowered her head into her hands. As she had done so many times in the past year, she gritted her teeth and resolved to stay strong, if for nothing but the sake of her child.

THE GRAY WATERS of the Rhine stretched endlessly into the distance. From a promontory overlooking the vast river, Gabinier watched as a ferryboat loaded with cargo downstream fought the strong current. The pilot's challenge, it occurred to him, was comparable to the conflict that had raged through his soul since the morning he had finally located Devorra at Vesontio, only to discover she was a vastly different woman from the ideal he had pined for through many long, lonely months of separation.

Gabinier knew it was his blind hatred of the Romans that had powered his recovery from his wound. That same hatred had fueled his relentless quest to find Ariovistus and enlist in the German's cause. But it was love, above all, that had driven him onward, and now here was his beloved Devorra—desecrated by some foul Roman, leaving a bastard Roman child nursing at her breast!

How many times had he fantasized about riding to her hut, tearing the Roman devil from her, and ending its existence? But the child was part of *her*, and he could no more kill her baby than he could slay Devorra herself.

Gabinier felt himself lost in a thicket of warring feelings. He ran his fingertips over the bracelet he had worn through every day of his long odyssey. He loved Devorra; there was no escaping that, regardless of how she might be shunned by others in the tribe. But could he marry her and live every day with that Roman child? He picked up a rock and with a great cry of anguish hurled it as far as he could, as if it might reach the far side of the river.

The sudden burst of energy seemed to clear his head. He knew what he had to do.

XLIII

VESONTIO

IN HIS HASTE TO RETURN TO VESONTIO, Caesar and his closest advisors rode ahead of the rest of the army, which would take at least two weeks to travel back to the shattered Roman headquarters from their camp at Darioritum. They sped across northern Gaul, the general exhausting everyone with his demanding pace. Even Curio, long accustomed to Caesar's proclivity for rapid movement, was painfully sore from the wear of the saddle upon his thighs during the long hours on horseback.

Caesar's demeanor throughout was somber, aloof, and relentlessly determined. Certainly he was angered by the knowledge that his main base had been destroyed and so many of his men brutally murdered, but only Curio knew the real reason their general hastened to return to Vesontio.

By the time they reached the fortress, Giacomo and his men had done a workmanlike job of restoring good Roman order to the devastated town. In that short span of time, not only had the bodies of the dead been respectfully burned, but the damage to the fortifications had been completely repaired, and even the fastidious rebuilding of the residential quarters was considerably advanced. Correctly anticipating that Caesar would return to his base just as soon as he learned the news, Giacomo had wisely made restoration of Caesar's own offices his top priority.

Curio was both pleased and relieved to find that an able team of clerks at the offices had begun the exacting work of reestablishing the sizeable bureaucratic apparatus needed to operate the army when it arrived. But to his dismay, it took only a few brief inquiries to confirm that Elliandro was indeed nowhere to be found. As Vatteus had reported, it was clear the man had fled along with the raiders, and that certainly meant that Molena had left with them as well. *The only woman I ever cared for is gone*, he thought morosely.

274

He was jolted from his musing by Caesar's sharp command. "Come, Rio. We must go join Mamurra and Giacomo now to make a tour of the bridge preparations."

EVEN THOUGH HE had been receiving regular reports on the progress of the project, Mamurra was overwhelmed upon seeing it all with his own two eyes: row upon row of assembled materials, every piece identified for the position in which it would be installed. The sheer vastness of the enterprise—the pilings, the connecting beams, the planks for the bridge deck, the iron brackets to hold the beams, great piles of nails, the boats and cranes all stacked and ready—finally struck home to him.

"And to think," he said to Caesar almost absentmindedly, "that the raiders bypassed all this to steal trinkets and slay the garrison at Vesontio. *This* was the real prize."

Caesar gave his engineer an icy stare. "They bypassed this because we had fortified it with moat and stockade, like a regular army camp. That was a clever move you made, Giacomo, wouldn't you say?"

Giacomo was not fooled. "Sir, you know very well that it was your own idea to fortify these assets. I claim no credit for your foresight."

Mamurra mulled that one a bit. Perhaps Caesar was testing Giacomo, to see if his judgment might be overcome by his ego? The engineer smiled. If that was what Caesar was wondering, it was pointless—Giacomo was completely self-effacing, always certain to recognize the effort of others, and never had he tried to aggrandize himself.

Their tour brought them to the mockup of the bridge, the same structure where Caesar had watched the training drill to ensure the deck and beams would withstand the load. Mamurra motioned for the team to halt.

Mamurra clambered through the underside of the test structure, almost like a child with a new toy, probing here, pushing there, climbing up on the pilings to examine the iron brackets for any sign of cracking under the stress. He had spent considerable time awake in his bed in the deep of the night, agonizing over these brackets. But seeing them now, and knowing how rigorously they had been tested, he knew his plan was sound.

"Come, Mamurra," Caesar called. "I want to see the approaches to the bridge."

With Caesar's ever-alert cavalry bodyguards close in tow, Giacomo led them over a well-prepared marching road toward the river. "We anticipate that each legion will remain in its own camp until just before the bridge is completed," he explained. "They will need to move with great speed to reach the bridge and cross over. Hence, we thought it wise to make a proper road, lest they get bogged down in the event of foul weather."

As they got closer to the Rhine, they noted the military presence was more pronounced. Sentries and checkpoints were in place, while several scouting teams were making the rounds in the thick woods adjoining the roadway.

"You have maintained proper surveillance, I see," Caesar noted with satisfaction.

Giacomo replied, "Aye, sir, especially after the raid. The raiders infiltrated the town by hiding in a delivery wagon. Our guards were not vigilant. They all paid with their lives. The same will not happen here."

When they reached the river, Caesar was especially pleased to see that a tall timber curtain wall had been erected along the waterfront to shield the work from any spying eyes lurking across the river. "This was not in the plan," he said to Giacomo, "but I am glad to see it. I rather imagine our friend Ariovistus is frantically wondering what we might be up to."

A catwalk had been built into the wall, just below the top, for lookouts and, if necessary, defenders. Caesar scrambled up a ladder attached to it, his engineers fast behind him. He proceeded to the center of the lengthy structure and stood there silently, gazing across the rushing river, deep into the heart of enemy territory.

Giacomo, having expended so much energy and dedicated effort over many months, could not help himself. "If I may, sir, we have done just about all that can be done in preparation. What is next?"

Caesar turned his back to the great river and faced his men. "I have ordered the Tenth to move by forced night march, at double time, to join us here as soon as they can. I estimate that will be in about three days. When they arrive, we will give them a day to rest. Then we will ferry them over to the other side at dawn to establish a camp so they can defend the bridge from the Germania side. While they are building that camp, you will begin work on the bridge."

Mamurra started figuring in his head, but Caesar was ahead of him. "Spare yourself the mental energy, Mamurra," he said, without a smile. "I foresee that the rest of the army will be at Vesontio ten days after that. And that is when the bridge must be finished."

Ten days? Mamurra stifled the astonished laugh that threatened to burst free. "Well, Caesar, we certainly will do everything we—"

Caesar grabbed the engineer by his tunic and pulled him close. "Ten days, Mamurra. You will build it for me in ten days."

"But Caesar, there are so many factors beyond our control—the wind, the current, the weather . . ."

Caesar pushed Mamurra back a bit and held him, teetering on the edge of the catwalk, high above the ground below. Mamurra's heart was pounding with fear.

"Build it for me and I will make both of you rich beyond your wildest dreams," he said with a snarl. "But if it is not ready in ten days, I'll have you both crucified."

And with that, he pushed Mamurra aside and headed for the ladder.

Mamurra and Giacomo stood there, mouths agape.

"He can't be serious," Giacomo finally said.

"Oh," Mamurra said wearily, "he's serious."

"He's insane," Giacomo dared to say.

"No," Mamurra said, his face grim. "He's obsessed."

BACK AT VESONTIO, alone with Curio, Caesar rallied. "My son—my only son—is somewhere out there in the wilderness of Germania. We will find him and restore him to his rightful place, here at my side."

Better that we never find the child. I should begin to soften his expectations, thought Curio. He said to his general, "It may be difficult to find him."

Caesar snapped. "The son of Caesar will not be raised by barbarians. We will do whatever it takes."

XLIV

TERRITORY OF THE SUEBI, GERMANIA

D EVORRA'S MOTHERLY INSTINCTS were correct: Sonnig had soiled himself yet again, judging from the familiar odor wafting from the crude wooden crate that had become his cradle. *The mighty Caesar's child is no different from any other*, she thought. *He smells just as awful.*

She lifted him out, set him down on the simple table in the center of their tiny cabin, and unwrapped the swaddling cloth bundled about the infant. Whether due to the contents he had deposited or the roughness of the table, Sonnig was cranky. Devorra dropped the foul-smelling cloth into a bucket of water that was kept available for just this purpose. Wearily, she saw that the bucket was nearly full.

Oh, Aloucca, she thought with sadness, *how I miss your help!*

Molena, stirring a pot of stew cooking over the hearth, saw her friend was deeply fatigued. "I'll take the bucket down to the river," she offered.

Devorra finished wrapping the child in a clean cloth as Molena hoisted the bucket and left the cabin. Devorra returned Sonnig to the cradle just as a knock came at the door.

Expecting that Elliandro might be calling, she hurried over and pulled the door open. And gasped.

Gabinier was standing there, in the midst of knocking again.

Devorra staggered back, speechless.

Gabinier followed her into the room.

Her heart pounding, Devorra picked up the baby and held him tightly to her chest.

Gabinier looked at her with gentle eyes. "I have not come to harm him."

His tone was reassuring. Devorra searched his expression, trying to divine his intentions. Slowly, deliberately, she placed her precious infant back into his bed.

There were only two plain wooden chairs in the cabin. Gabinier sat down. He said nothing, just looked at her.

Gabinier's gaze felt like a hot brand against Devorra's forehead. But she knew she must keep her composure. She sat opposite him and waited for him to speak.

"I have thought of little but you these many months," he said, finally. Managing a wan smile, he pointed to the bracelet on his wrist. "I never let this out of my sight. I imagined you were with me constantly."

She remained silent.

"I was badly wounded in the battle against the Romans." He tugged his jacket aside and pointed to the terrible jagged flesh of his shoulder, all pink and bulging.

She gasped, covering her mouth with her hand.

"I took a Roman spear in the shoulder," he continued, his tone calm. "I would have died but for a kindly farmer who found me in the field. He and his wife nursed me back to health."

Devorra willed herself to remain strong. "They told me you were killed in the battle," she said, barely above a whisper. "I wanted to die myself. When my father offered me as a hostage to the Romans, I did not resist. My life was over without you in it."

Gabinier's face remained passive. From his calm demeanor, she could get no sense of what he might be thinking.

"Have you wondered just why it was I killed your father?" he asked.

Devorra was dumbfounded by this question. She had no answer for him. The walls of the tiny room seemed to be closing in on her.

Gabinier looked away. "You were nothing to him. He was ready to marry you off to a life of misery in order to advance his own standing among the tribes. I know what he did to you, that night he tied you to the tree. He bragged to all the other chiefs about what a great sacrifice he made by giving you to the Romans. When I returned to the Belgae after my recovery and learned what he had done, I challenged him to a fight, and I killed him."

Devorra nodded slowly but said nothing.

"I did it for you," Gabinier said, his voice rich with sincerity. "I wanted nothing more than to be with you."

"And I was gone," she said, looking down.

"I wanted the Belgae to keep fighting the Romans," he continued, "so I could take you back. But the clans refused—they'd made a cowardly peace with the Romans. So, I gave up leadership and came to Germania to join

Ariovistus, who hates the Romans as much as I do. And he's not afraid to fight them. He allowed me to lead the raid at Vesontio. I planned every detail, killed many Roman soldiers with my own hands, just to find you."

"I never dreamed it was possible to see you again. If I had known you were alive . . ."

Gabinier's cool demeanor evaporated, and she could see he was deeply anguished. He grasped her by the arms. "I wanted you more than my own life!" he cried. "The thought of you kept me alive. Every day I worked so hard to recover my strength, thinking about nothing but you."

"And I mourned you night and day!" Devorra cried. "I could barely lift my chin from my breast, so heavy was my sorrow. And now the gods have given you back to me." She took his hand in hers.

Gabinier could not hold her gaze. He turned his head away and muttered in a flat tone, "It was a struggle for me to come here today."

"What is the struggle? We can have the life we always dreamed of! I love you, Gabinier. And I need you, now more than ever."

"But you nurse a Roman child."

Devorra pulled back. "I do. And it is not the life I wished for, but the child is mine, and I am his. His father is no better than a common criminal, but we cannot blame the child for that, nor is it something he ever needs to know. Can you not see that we can move past this?"

Gabinier looked at the baby in the cradle. He could see traces of his mother in his features. "To think what they have done to you!" He slumped back in his chair. So softly she could barely hear him, he said, "He is a Roman, and I have sworn to kill them all."

Devorra's love for Gabinier clashed against her instinct to protect her child. She too fell back onto her chair, exhausted by this emotional up-heaval. She said simply, "Only you can decide if your love for me can overcome your hatred for Rome."

His lifted his eyes to meet hers. "I have decided."

But before he could say more, there was a loud clang of metal against the door, and Elliandro burst into the hut. "Gabinier, you must come imme-diately. Ariovistus has summoned you with the most pressing urgency."

"Tell him I am otherwise engaged," Gabinier replied with a snarl.

"No, Gabinier," Elliandro insisted. "You must come now. The Romans are invading Germania."

Gabinier leapt to his feet, drawing Devorra up with him. His tortured eyes met hers, and he pulled her into a desperate kiss. Then he hurried from the room, leaving Devorra baffled by what was happening both inside and outside of her own little world. Why would he kiss her if he didn't want to be with her? How could the Romans be invading Germania?

As she sat there, trying to make sense of Gabinier's conflicting messages, the child cooed cheerfully, oblivious to it all. And suddenly Devorra knew why the Romans were invading. A new round had begun in this deadly game the gods were playing with her.

⁕

ARIOVISTUS, GABINIER, and a group of tribal chieftains stood on that same rocky promontory where Gabinier had spent time pondering his dilemma. From this vantage point, they could look down on the beehive of frantic activity as the Romans prepared to mount their attack. Ariovistus was livid.

Ariovistus pointed to the newly built Roman camp on the Germania side of the Rhine. "See there, how they have already established a legion on our territory and built a substantial camp to protect this work that is going on?" The fortifications were vigorous, bristling with artillery and archers. Even more discouraging, the Germani warily noted the banners of the Tenth Legion flying over the camp.

"The Tenth," Ariovistus grumbled. "Caesar's best fighters are the first to arrive and establish a beachhead on our soil."

"We should attack and drive them back into the river. Drown them like rats," one of the men said.

"It is only one legion," added another.

Ariovistus smirked and turned to Gabinier. "Didn't you tell me you fought against the Tenth?"

"I did," Gabinier said proudly.

"And what is your opinion of them?"

"They fought fiercely in a forest after being ambushed, taken completely by surprise," Gabinier said reluctantly. "They were too good for us. Behind those fortifications, with those soldiers, it would be futile to assault their breastworks."

"Agreed," Ariovistus said, seething.

"But what are they doing down there? What is all that activity in the river?" another chief asked. "I've never seen anything like it."

Boats equipped with cranes were pounding large logs into the water at an angle. On both sides of the river, hundreds of men were hurriedly digging and erecting what appeared to be large ramps.

"Caesar has gone mad," Ariovistus said.

"How so?" Gabinier asked.

"If I didn't know the impossibility of such a task, I'd say it looks like he's building a bridge," the king replied.

Several of the chiefs were in denial. "A bridge? Over the Rhine?" one of them asked, incredulous. "No one has ever built a bridge over the Rhine. It will take him years."

They all murmured their agreement; this could only be a colossal folly.

"See those ramps on both sides?" Ariovistus pointed. "See those pilings they are putting into the river between the ramps? The ramps would be the approaches to the bridge, and the pilings are going to carry the deck."

His men shifted uncomfortably. The Romans were highly organized, and almost by the minute, one could see a huge, long wooden structure beginning to take shape.

"I have an idea," another man said excitedly. "Let's put our fighters in boats and send them downriver. They can attack the men doing the construction—drive them off."

"I think not," Ariovistus said flatly. "Do you see those columns they are driving upstream from the base of the bridge?"

Everyone squinted.

"Those are intended to block any boats from getting to the bridge or any men working on it."

Ariovistus had learned the hard way not to take his adversary lightly. "Dispatch riders to all the tribes," he said after some thought. "Tell them to assemble all their men and gather at our castle with the utmost speed. And tell them to be ready for a fight."

Gabinier was more than ready to fight—he'd kill every last Roman if that's what it took. But there was something he had to take care of before he left.

DEVORRA HAD JUST put Sonnig down for a nap when someone banged on the door. When she opened it and saw Gabinier, her heart leaped, but when she noticed the murderous fire in his eyes, she backed away from him, spreading her arms in front of the baby's crib.

"What is it, Gabinier?" she demanded. "If you have come to harm my child, you'll have to kill me first."

Gabinier was incredulous. "What? Oh, no! Devorra, no, please." He fell to his knees, shaking his head before the bewildered Devorra. His voice turned gentle. "I didn't come here to hurt either of you—how could you think such a thing? I must return to the battlefield. But before I could go, I needed to come here."

Still wary, Devorra asked, "Why?"

"To tell you that I love you."

Devorra staggered back a bit, but her wits were keen.

"You cannot love me without loving my child."

"The child was brought forth by you," he replied. "I will love him as I love you, and raise him as my own, if you will have me."

"Truly?" she asked. "You still would marry me?"

Gabinier rose to his feet and took her face in his hands. "I would rather die than live my life without you."

Devorra fell against his chest. "I have prayed to the gods again and again to hear you say that," she whispered, lifting her face to kiss him.

"And you are the answer to all my prayers," he said. "I have pledged my service to Ariovistus, and I must carry out the mission he has set for me. But I promise we will wed as soon as we have dispatched the Romans to their side of the Rhine."

Devorra took both his hands in hers. "If waiting for you means a life without Romans, I will gladly summon all my patience."

"I must go now, but I will return as soon as I can," Gabinier vowed. He reached into the crib and stroked Sonnig's head, then kissed Devorra again and bade her farewell.

Only once the door was closed did she allow herself to collapse into a chair and weep in joyful relief.

XLV

ROME

POMPEY'S RESIDENCE IN ROME was, in the eyes of Catullus, even more opulent than his villa at Ostia. Majestically situated on the Palatine Hill, it directly faced the Forum, meeting place of the Senate, straight to the west on the Capitoline Hill. Every wall was frescoed, every floor was marble, and every room was decorated with exquisite furniture upholstered in the finest fabrics. Trophies of Pompey's many victories were on display throughout the sprawling home, perhaps none more stunning than the one Catullus was staring at, mouth agape, in Pompey's spacious den. Incredibly, the entire prow of a Cilician pirate ship had been cut out and installed on a broad wall opposite a massive fireplace.

"Amazing," he uttered, trying to take it in.

Pompey seemed barely to hear Catullus, so engaged was he in the document he was reading. He looked up and saw Catullus trying to absorb the magnificent trophy. "Oh, that?" he said, as if it were some mere bauble in a street market. "That was taken from the leader of the Cilician pirates after I defeated their fleet. It was disassembled piece by piece, brought here, and reassembled. Took months."

Pompey gestured for Catullus to take a seat alongside his delicately veneered teak desk, which featured a painstakingly etched Roman eagle on the front with gilding all around it. Catullus slipped a leather pouch from his shoulder and settled into the comfortable chair.

Pompey, all business, showed no signs of bereavement over the loss of his young wife. At a glance, Catullus saw that Pompey had been studying Caesar's report to the Senate on the remarkable naval victory over the Veneti at Darioritum. The great man appeared to be fuming about it, and Catullus was ready to stoke the flames.

"The impudence of the man, really," Pompey said, putting the vellum sheaves aside. "He proposes to reduce the share of the spoils allocated to the Roman treasury, and instead asks us to give shares equal to his own to his admiral and his engineer."

Catullus, well aware of the contents of the report, projected sympathy with Pompey's view. "Indeed," he said slyly, "he could have simply given them a share of his own reward."

"Fat chance of that," Pompey grumped. "Caesar has always taken great care to line his own purse."

Catullus had long sensed that the great Triumvirate might be fraying, made even less stable by the untimely demise of the fair Julia. He decided to press a bit further. "I should think you might be more charitable toward your father-in-law."

Pompey's icy glare set Catullus's teeth on edge. "He is my father-in-law no longer," he snapped.

"Ah, yes, Magnus, what a terrible tragedy," Catullus said in his most oily manner. "All of us in Rome were crushed by the news."

Pompey showed no sign of emotion. "She was a lovely girl," he said simply. "But this is business, and it is appalling to me."

Catullus greedily considered the implications of a rift among the triumvirs. It could open up many opportunities for bargaining and trading between the factions, and a savvy, well-placed broker might profit hand-somely from arranging such deals. "Well, Magnus, if you were to simply stand in the Senate and oppose this outrageous grab, surely it would fail completely."

A sour look crossed Pompey's weathered face. He scrunched up his nose as if he had gotten a whiff of something odious. "I think not," he replied. "An open break would have far too many repercussions. This issue is not worth such a momentous step."

Catullus felt suddenly uneasy, fearing his opportunity was slipping away. And then Pompey, having closed one door, opened another.

"Perhaps we need to foment some opposition to Caesar on this," Pompey said gently. He sat with his elbows on the gleaming desktop, his hands under his chin.

"How interesting you should say that," Catullus replied. "I myself have been giving some thought to just such an approach. Of course, I would never dream of launching any such effort on my own without at least your tacit approval."

Pompey's face was noncommittal, always the sign of a skilled negotiator. "How might you go about it?"

Catullus gave him a conspiratorial grin. "Caesar's base of support is in the masses, the common people. What if something were to circulate about him that most of those plain folks would find revolting?"

Pompey was tempted. "Go on."

Catullus opened the flap on his leather pouch and withdrew a sheet. Leering, he handed it to Pompey. "My latest poem," he said lightly.

Pompey was inscrutable. He had never shown any interest in Catullus's poetry. Still, he took the sheet and began to read.

> *Beautifully matched, the perverse buggers,*
> *Mamurra the catamite and Caesar.*
> *No wonder. Both equally spotted,*
> *one from Formia, the other the city,*
> *marks that remain, not to be lessened.*
> *Diseased the same, both of these twins,*
> *somewhat skilled in the selfsame couch,*
> *this one no greedier an adulterer than that,*
> *rivals in shared little boys.*
> *Beautifully matched, the perverse buggers.*

With a scowl, Pompey put it on the desk. "You're suggesting that Caesar has been intimate with his own engineer? Whatever gave you that idea?"

Catullus proceeded to tell him of the correspondence from Pompey's own man, the staff engineer Garibus, reporting that he suspected the two to be involved in a liaison. As he listened to this tale, disgust spread over Pompey's round face.

"I have heard these rumors for years," Pompey said. "You are aware that when Caesar was a young man, he was taken captive by pirates in the Aegean Sea? They demanded a ransom of twenty talents of silver for his release, and he was so insulted by this low amount that he insisted they demand fifty talents?"

Catullus, of course, knew the story. "And then after the ransom was paid and he was freed, he went back and captured them, even though the Roman governor of the province had refused him permission to do so. He had them all crucified, as I recall."

"Yes," Pompey agreed. "But you may not be aware of the rumor that while he was their captive, he was willingly used by the pirates for their carnal appetites. Caesar feared that they would tell the story of his captivity. That is the real reason he wanted them crucified."

Catullus sat back in the chair, astounded.

"But all these stories are mere rumors," Pompey said, dismissively.

"Magnus, we have this report from your own favored engineer. Why would he lie to us regarding something so serious?"

This struck home with Pompey. He knew the lad, Garibus, and had been most pleased with his work. He had no reason to doubt the report.

But this kind of tactic was unbecoming to a patrician like Pompey. "I don't know. This is gutter politics at its worst."

Catullus spoke sternly. "Do you want to be a gentleman, or do you want to win?"

Pompey still hesitated.

Catullus leaned forward again and went in for the kill. "Magnus, you are a great soldier. With you, it's all about honor and dignity. But this is politics, and Caesar is the greatest politician I have ever seen. If you are to best him at his own game, you must play in the same gutter he is in."

Now it was Pompey's turn to sit back in the chair. "I have been in that gutter for years," he said in a chilly tone. "I have had the good judgment to play through intermediaries, always publicly holding myself above such petty tactics."

At this, Catullus brightened and asked quietly, "Might not I be the intermediary for knocking Caesar off his pedestal?"

Pompey turned and studied the fireplace. Finally, he faced the senator and said, "Publish your poem, Catullus. Let's see if Caesar's greatness can withstand some tarnish."

XLVI

RHINE RIVER

OUR DAYS INTO THE CONSTRUCTION of the bridge, Mamurra was deeply depressed. Despite the Herculean efforts of the entire team, they were lagging behind the rigorous ten-day schedule. The culprit was the difficult task of driving piles at the angles contemplated by the design in the middle of the river. Mamurra remembered grimly when the crane at Vesontio had broken loose and crashed into the other boats, wiping out several days of work. Thankfully, nothing like that had happened on this project thus far, but the task was taking longer than anticipated. The depth of the water and the force of the current were unyielding—the columns had to be placed methodically or the whole structure could come crashing down. If he couldn't come up with something to make up for the lost time, they would miss the deadline.

Caesar is insane, Mamurra thought irritably. *Ten days for such an undertaking!*

The hour was late, and Mamurra had sent the engineering staff away for some badly needed rest. Feeling a sense of hopelessness, alone in the command tent, Mamurra sifted through the plans yet again, looking for some way they could compress the construction timeline. The bridge was a huge, interdependent thing—each element supporting the next, each feature critical in its own way. If they cut corners, it could result in a catastrophic failure. He would not countenance it. Better to be executed by Caesar than to preside over an engineering debacle that would ruin his reputation for all time!

The ever-diligent Giacomo, spattered in mud from tireless close inspection of the ongoing work, trudged into the tent and dropped like a dead weight onto a stool in front of Mamurra's desk.

"We aren't going to make it, are we?" Mamurra asked.

Giacomo picked up a decanter of sour wine sitting on the desk and pulled out the stopper. He poured a stiff shot into a cup and drank it down without pause. "I'm afraid not," he answered, wiping a few drops from his lips with the back of his gnarled hand. "The whole thing was folly from the outset."

"We are so close!" Mamurra cried in frustration, banging his fist on the desk. The force of the blow knocked a burning candle onto a metal plate. A brief flare brightened the tent before Giacomo grabbed the candle and set it upright.

"Burning down the command tent will not advance the project," Giacomo said dryly.

Mamurra was mesmerized. He picked up the plate and held it behind the candle. This had the effect of brightening the desk. He rotated the plate, changing the angle, noting the way the light reflected.

Could it work? he wondered. *Maybe . . . just maybe . . .*

Giacomo asked, "What are you thinking, Mamurra?"

Mamurra put the plate down.

"Rouse everyone from bed. Assemble them at the river right away. We have some experimenting to do."

ALWAYS AN EARLY RISER, Caesar was up and at his desk well before dawn, churning through correspondence and assorted reports. Curio, fully aware of Caesar's tense mood, kept the paperwork moving with as little comment as possible.

A knock came at the door, and Curio went to answer it. He pulled a sheet of vellum from the messenger's pouch and glanced over the communication. "It's from Mamurra," he said, and began reading aloud. "'Noble Caesar, your presence is urgently needed at the construction site.'" He looked at Caesar, clueless.

"That's all?" Caesar asked, irritably.

Curio held up the message so Caesar could see for himself that there was but a single line of text.

"This had better be important," Caesar muttered, getting to his feet. "Summon my escort."

THE MORNING WAS STILL BLACK AS PITCH when Caesar and Curio arrived at the bridge site. Mamurra, Giacomo, and a cordon of tired-looking engineers were grouped near a large burning torch mounted atop a tripod. They were engaged in an animated argument with the head blacksmith of the army. Mamurra beckoned Caesar to him.

Caesar reined his horse to a halt but did not bother to dismount. The arguing parties fell silent in the presence of the commanding general. The torch cast the entire complement in an orange hue.

"Well, Mamurra, what issue is so pressing that my presence is required at this hour?"

"Greetings," Mamurra replied, thumping his breast with his fist. "Sir, you want your bridge in ten days. Today is day five and we are behind. To make it in time, we must work at night. We have something to show you."

Mamurra pointed toward an object covered in canvas behind the torch. Several men pulled off the tarp to reveal a large, curved sheet of metal, somewhat resembling the shape and design of the shield carried by the common legionary. At a wave of Mamurra's hand, the men lifted the curved metal object and hoisted it behind the blazing torch. The brightness of the flames against the metal cast out a reflection over a large area, amplifying the torch's effect.

"With more of these devices," Mamurra explained, "we can illuminate enough of the river to enable us to work in the water throughout the night. We have tested it already, Caesar, and it will work."

Caesar was impatient. "Why am I needed at this meeting?"

Nofio stepped forward and sputtered, "They dragged me and several of my best men out of bed to make this crazy thing. Now they want ten of them. And they want them today!"

"Actually, ten today, ten tomorrow, and ten the day after that," Mamurra clarified.

Nofio erupted like Vesuvius. "My men are exhausted! You want to treat them like pack animals, working them to death! They are men, and soldiers, too. Caesar, they have a right to be fairly treated, same as any soldier!"

Caesar cut him off by raising his hands, palms facing the quarreling officers. He swung one leg over the saddle and lowered himself to the ground. He went over to Nofio, put his arm around the irate fellow, and walked him away from the others. They all stood and watched, wondering what this private conference might be about.

Within a few minutes, they made their way back to the group. Nofio looked sullen but mollified.

"I believe Nofio now understands the significance of these devices to what we are all to accomplish here," Caesar said amiably. "Nofio, will your men deliver the devices Mamurra needs, starting today?"

Nofio held up his hand. "I swear on the Roman eagle that is our sacred standard," he said solemnly, "if the bridge is not finished on time, it will not be my men who have failed."

Caesar tilted his head slightly toward Mamurra. "You have what you need," he said. "Perhaps next time you will be able to resolve your problems without my intervention."

Mamurra accepted this rebuke without comment.

Caesar remounted, wheeled his horse about, and rode off, his escort trailing behind.

Curio brought his horse up alongside Caesar's as the first traces of daylight cut across the sky.

"How did you do it?" he asked.

Caesar did not turn his head to his aide. "Well, there are two options. Do you think I won him over by threat, or by incentive?"

"Nofio is dumber than an ox," Curio replied, "but I don't believe you would have threatened him."

Caesar laughed. "Your intellect never disappoints me, Rio," he said jovially. "When you want men to do impossible things, you cannot get them to do it by threats. You must offer them money, a sum so vast they cannot imagine it."

Curio, interested by this tutorial, dared to ask, "How much did you offer him?"

"One hundred times the daily wage of each man working for him."

Curio was taken aback.

"It is a pittance," Caesar said dismissively. "If we conquer Germania, no one will care what we paid the blacksmiths."

XLVII

GERMANIA

THE MOOD WAS GRIM at Ariovistus's camp, where the tribal chiefs had gathered to plot a strategy to meet the threat of the imminent Roman invasion.

When the king was satisfied that all the desired participants were in place, he rose to his feet. "My brothers," he began in a low tone, "all of you are aware of what is taking place at the river. The Tenth Legion has crossed the Rhine and established an impregnable camp in our territory. To attack it would be suicide."

He surveyed the shaggy heads nodding in agreement.

Ariovistus continued, "I must tell you, however, the bridge the camp is protecting is being erected at an unimaginable pace. Our scouts bring me reports every four hours. In only eight days, they have completed the approaches, the columns have been driven into the riverbed to carry the weight of the deck, and the planks for the deck are being placed even as we meet. The scouts estimate that the bridge will be finished in a matter of days."

The group seemed thunderstruck by this prediction. In their chatter about the imminent invasion and what to do about it, all had assumed they had months before the Romans could finish so monumental an undertaking as a bridge across the mighty Rhine. They had been expecting to complete the fall harvest and remove the bounty to stockpiles to be established deep in the vast forests of Germania. If the Romans were forced to rely on a slender line of supplies from Vesontio, they would give up and return to Gaul before the harsh winter weather set in. But now the Romans would be upon them within the week? It was unthinkable!

"How can this be?" one of the fellows shouted. "How can they build a bridge to withstand the current of the Rhine in only a few days?"

Ariovistus let the crowd rumble for a few moments, then held up his hand for silence. "The Romans have been working day and night on the construction. It also appears," he said caustically, "that the Romans have been fabricating the components of the bridge for a great many months." He spoke directly to Gabinier. "Our recent raid on Vesontio did not detect these preparations, and so we did nothing to prevent their being put into use against us."

This brought another outburst of chatter from the chiefs. One of them rose and pointed at Ariovistus. "That raid was foolish," the man accused. "We tickled the nose of the sleeping Roman bear, and now he is roused against us, to take vengeance for the massacre. And what do we have to show for it?"

"Nothing of any apparent value," Ariovistus said simply.

Gabinier felt his blood run cold. *Is he blaming me for urging the strike against Vesontio? How could I have known what the Romans were doing in that camp near the river?* With a jolt, Gabinier realized why Vesontio had been so easily breached—the real prize was there, at the river! It was all he could do not to show his distress amid the tumult of the chiefs.

Ariovistus held up his hands and said, "There is nothing to be gained by squabbling among ourselves like a bunch of old women while the Roman army is about to invade our soil. What do you suggest we do about it?"

This brought another eruption of rage from the assemblage—everyone had an opinion. Gabinier thought this was most odd. *Wasn't the king supposed to lead them? Why would he let them waste time arguing over alternative courses of action?*

The answer became clear soon enough.

Ariovistus shouted, "All of you are wrong! Caesar *wants* us to amass all our men to fight him as soon as he gets his army over the river. He craves a decisive engagement in a set-piece battle on an open plain where he has all the advantages. The Romans fight in a tightly organized and disciplined order, while we merely line up all our men and charge at them. We have no formations, no coordination, and little communication between the tribes. We hit them with brute force. So they maintain their shield wall; they do not break their ranks for anything. If a man falls, they close the gap and keep fighting. They chop and they hack with their short swords until their opponents break from fatigue or panic. Gabinier, is this not so?"

Gabinier, still wallowing in the shame of what he now considered the debacle of Vesontio, was roused from his doldrums by this question. "Yes, my lord," he answered quietly.

"But what would you have us do?" one of the chiefs shouted. "Run away?"

Ariovistus gave them a wry smile. "I would prefer to call it a planned withdrawal."

Another chief, outraged, spluttered, "But with all our tribes combined, we will far outnumber them!"

Ariovistus sighed. "Throughout Gaul, Caesar has often been up against far greater numbers. Both Gabinier and I have tried to slug it out with them, each time with the advantage of superior numbers, and have failed, even with the benefit of total surprise. They are too good for that."

The men shifted uneasily in their chairs.

"We must withdraw all our people, deep into the forests, and adopt hit-and-run tactics against them," Ariovistus continued, getting passionate now. "We must burn all the crops, take all the livestock with us. Everything! Let Caesar find not even a single apple to feed his troops or his horses. The deeper he advances in pursuit of our people, the easier it will be to raid his rear from the forests. When he realizes he cannot bring about an all-out pitched battle, he'll give up and go back to Gaul."

Several of them still seemed dubious.

"There is one additional benefit of this approach," Ariovistus said. "The Romans finance these military campaigns by capturing natives and selling them into slavery. If we deprive them of the opportunity to take captives, they will quickly find the business unprofitable and give up."

This made sense, and murmurs of agreement rippled around the table.

Ariovistus made each man stand and pledge to keep to the strategy. He admonished them with a stern warning that if any of them were foolish enough to stand and fight the Romans, none of the rest of the tribes would come to their aid.

As the group filed out, somewhat sullen and sobered by the unhappy choice that had been made, Ariovistus pulled Gabinier aside.

"So, warrior, what do you think of my strategy?" Ariovistus asked him, almost in a conspiratorial tone.

Gabinier was in fact disappointed. He hated the Romans and wanted to fight them. But he remembered his bitter experience on the field, when the element of surprise and the burning desire of his men to fight had fallen short against the superior discipline and training of the Roman soldiers. And so he merely said, "You are right about the fighting quality of the Romans. But what if Caesar does not withdraw? We cannot retreat forever—sooner or later we will have to fight."

Ariovistus reflected on that. "You may be right. Perhaps you should use this time to start organizing our tribes into a better fighting force."

"I am yours to command," Gabinier said dutifully.

"And perhaps it will get your mind off this girl," Ariovistus said sharply.

His mind was already made up, but Gabinier saw no reason to tell him what he had decided. "My mind is dedicated only to serving you, my king."

"Very well, then. Make yourself busy," he told Gabinier. "We will need all the preparation you can give us."

XLVIII

RHINE RIVER

NEAR SUNSET ON THE TENTH DAY, **Mamurra** stood at the western edge of the structure, in front of thirty supply wagons crammed with the heaviest cargo that could be assembled—armor, missile bolts for the artillery, and the like. He intended to lead them across for this test. If the bridge failed, his career and life were forfeited anyway, so he figured he might as well go down with the bridge if such was the will of the gods.

Others, however, were not so fatalistic. Boats were stationed just outside the columns in the river to fish out any survivors if the whole thing collapsed.

There was still a great deal of finishing work to do, of course—the railings had to be placed and additional brackets had to be installed to further strengthen the structure, among other tasks—but the basic elements were in place. It was time to put it all on the line.

Caesar, Labienus, and Curio were assembled at a viewing stand that had been erected for the occasion on the Gaul shoreline. The general's battle standard was flapping in the breeze, and his ever-present cavalry escort was lined up, dressed in their parade uniforms. On the far side of the bridge, Mamurra could make out Gordianus and his command group, flags flying, waiting for the test group to make it across. It was a magnificent sight.

Mamurra's thoughts flashed back to that day Gordianus and his officers were laughing at him as the piling gave way on the Vesontio bridge. *By the gods, I hope they will have no reason to laugh today.*

He motioned to Giacomo, who was holding the reins of his horse. Giacomo handed him the reins and began to move away. They had agreed that Giacomo would not make the crossing—if disaster were to befall them, someone would have to pick up the pieces and try again—assuming Caesar did not have the entire engineering corps beheaded.

Mamurra took Giacomo by the sleeve of his tunic. "I have something for you," he told his subordinate.

Mamurra pulled two letters from a pocket in his tunic and gave them to Giacomo. "If the gods should curse this crossing and I do not survive," he said to the man, "please deliver these letters."

Giacomo glanced at them. One was addressed to Mamurra's parents, the other to Caesar. Giacomo said, "Of course, Mamurra. But this will not be necessary. The bridge will stand."

Mamurra mounted the horse and looked out at the assemblage of wagoners. "I hope all you bastards know how to swim!" he shouted, drawing a hearty laugh. Then he turned the animal about and started across.

Mamurra's heart beat much faster than the steady *clop-clop-clop* as the horse moved off the approach ramp and onto the bridge deck. Mamurra had decided not to look at or think about the swirling water flowing beneath the deck. He kept his eyes locked on the men waiting on the other side.

His ears, however, were keenly tuned to the sounds of the wagons, three abreast, filling the width of the thick planks of the bridge. He was expecting to hear creaking, but praying not to hear cracking.

The chosen site for the bridge was at a relatively narrow spot in the river, but the span, including the expansive approaches over the wide bluffs, still measured more than a quarter of a mile in length. The design had called for waypoint markers to be installed along the bridge deck. Mamurra held his breath until he passed the first marker. Upon reaching the second marker, he began to relax just a bit. But he knew the deepest part of the river was coming up. The little cavalcade rolled on, passing the third waypoint—the midpoint of the bridge. Mamurra allowed himself to begin believing they might actually make it.

As they approached the fourth marker, the soldiers on both sides of the bridge were cheering and waving their banners exultantly.

And then they were across. Gordianus and his officers crowded around Mamurra, congratulating him loudly and slapping him on the back. Mamurra waited until the final row of three wagons rolled off the deck and onto the land-anchored approach ramp before jumping from his horse and acknowledging the cheers of the Tenth by raising his clenched fist triumphantly into the air.

Gordianus bent his head toward Mamurra's ear, and whispered, "I told Caesar it couldn't be done. You have made a liar out of me, you bastard, but I am proud of you all the same!"

After a bit of this celebration, Mamurra rode back across the bridge, this time accompanied by a squad of empty wagons from the Tenth, which would be restocked at the base camp. He received another rousing ovation as he approached the Gaul shoreline. He was especially pleased to see that Caesar and his staff were waiting for him.

But before he reached Caesar, he dismounted and hugged Giacomo and the other members of the engineering staff who had toiled so furiously over the last ten days to meet the impossible deadline.

Finally, he turned his full attention to the general, who was waiting patiently.

"Greetings, Caesar," he said cheerfully and saluted. "Are you satisfied with your bridge?"

Caesar returned the salute. "Well done, Mamurra," he said. "Your name will live on in the annals of engineering for all time because of this great achievement."

"All the credit goes to the staff, Caesar," Mamurra said, his stock response to praise. "They have labored tirelessly to bring forth this amazing structure."

Caesar smiled. "You are humble, Mamurra, and it is fitting that a leader recognizes those who have contributed to his success. And all will share in the reward, as I have promised."

Mamurra bowed his head in gratitude.

Caesar turned to Labienus and Curio. "Alert the legion commanders," he said. "I will lead the army across the bridge tomorrow, starting at dawn."

Later, when Mamurra and Giacomo were alone in the project office after sending all the men to get some badly needed rest, Giacomo put the two letters on the table. "I return these to you happily," he said.

Mamurra reached to pick them up.

"I can understand a letter to your parents in the event of your demise," Giacomo said, "but Caesar? What would you have said to him if the bridge had collapsed?"

Mamurra smiled and handed the letter to him. "Read it."

Giacomo opened the scroll.

Mighty Caesar:

If you are reading this, it is because the bridge has failed, and I have gone down with the structure.

I must tell you that the men of my staff truly did all that was humanly possible to ensure this project would be a success. Any blame attached to its failure is mine and mine alone.

I particularly urge you to spare Giacomo. In fact, you should promote him to be the new prefect of engineers. There is no more loyal officer in the Roman army, and no better engineer.

Marcus Vitruvius Mamurra

Giacomo grinned. "You are an ass, Mamurra."

Mamurra returned the grin.

Giacomo crumpled the document and tossed it into a nearby brazier. "How many times must I tell you? I don't want the job!"

XLIX

GERMANIA

GABINIER WAS AGAIN LODGED on that same promontory from which he had first glimpsed the Romans building their extraordinary bridge. He watched in grim fascination as row after row of Roman soldiers marched across the massive structure, with standards and battle flags waving, trumpets blaring, and drums thumping. Each legion was followed by hundreds of loaded wagons, many of which towed artillery pieces. There seemed to be no end to them! Gabinier had counted six legions already across—over thirty thousand men.

"Clearly, Caesar is bringing his whole army into Germania," he said to Elliandro, who stood nearby, mouth agape. "As much as I hate the Romans, I must concede: this spectacle is remarkable."

As each legion cleared the long ramp leading down from the bridge onto the riverbank, they moved with methodical precision into a line that stretched from the water's edge all the way to the walls of the camp stockade erected by the Tenth. Caesar apparently intended to move deeper into Germanic territory that very day.

A few minutes later, the gates of the camp swung open and the first legion in the line—the Tenth, of course—moved out onto a plank road that had been laid in anticipation of this march. Gabinier had been told by other scouts that the Romans had been building this road and placing sites for camps in a direction that led straight to Ariovistus's fortress. *The Roman scouts are better than we thought*, he mused.

Gabinier had seen enough. He needed to get back to Ariovistus to tell him that the entire Roman army was now in the field and beginning to move against the tribes of Germania. He gestured to Elliandro and Gustavus. "Stay here with your comrades, and keep an eye on the Romans," he said. "The rest of us will report back to Ariovistus." He motioned to the other men to make their way to their horses, tethered to a stand of trees nearby.

Gabinier's scouting team was moving along a narrow path through the dense forest, alert for any signs of the enemy, but not unduly fearful. There was no reason to believe that the Roman cavalry would be screening this far in advance of the oncoming legions.

As the horses made their way over the path, Gabinier's thoughts turned to Devorra and her child. His mind was at peace. He wished he'd been able to visit her again, and perhaps even be wed, but the uproar and preparations for the imminent Roman invasion had taken precedence over all else.

Along with these scouting missions, he had been working nonstop to force the people from hundreds of farms and villages to uproot their families and their livestock and retreat to the east. This took some doing—many resisted the move and had to be forcibly sent packing. And when the villagers and farmers were well to the rear, Gabinier's men took the hardest step of all—they torched the abandoned houses and crops to deprive the oncoming Romans of food and shelter for themselves and fodder for their animals.

As the group rounded a bend in the path, they heard a clanking sound. Before Gabinier understood what was happening, they came into a small clearing and found themselves face-to-face with a mounted squadron of Roman cavalry. The nimble Roman commander immediately put his men into a charge directly at the smaller Germanic party.

The engagement was short but sharp. His group was outnumbered, but Gabinier and his men fought savagely.

I cannot let them take me alive, he thought, trying to keep from panicking. *Better to die here than rowing some Roman galley!*

Remaining steady on his mount, Gabinier took on a young cavalryman who looked even more frightened than he was himself. The Roman swung his sword wildly, leaving himself open for a counterthrust. Gabinier drove his sword deep into the man's chest, toppling him backward off his frenzied animal. But the force of the blow and the fall of his enemy pulled the sword out of his hand. Gabinier looked dazedly at his empty hand.

In combat, even momentary lapses can be deadly. From behind, another Roman landed a blow to the back of Gabinier's head with the butt of his spear, and everything went black.

GABINIER FORCED HIS EYES OPEN but had difficulty focusing them. All he could see was light brown canvas above his head. For a few seconds, he wondered whether it was his funeral shroud.

But then he became vaguely aware that his arms were causing him pain.

Gabinier slowly came to realize he was lying on a cot in a tent. His head pounding, he tried to push himself up with his right arm only to discover that both his arms were tightly bound to the sides of the cot. Although he could not see them very well, he could tell that his feet were in iron fetters. His mind was still muddled, and he thought for a moment that he might be in the custody of his own people.

Soon a man clad in a Roman military tunic came up to him. "Congratulations. You are still alive," the fellow said in the Germanic tongue. "I am Vatteus, a doctor serving in the Roman army."

The realization that he was now a Roman prisoner hit Gabinier nearly as hard as the blow to his head. "How long have I been out?" he asked.

"Since yesterday," the doctor replied.

"What happened to my men?" Gabinier asked, feeling the exhaustion overtaking him again.

"All were killed but two."

"Where are they?" he asked.

The doctor frowned. "I'm afraid they're being tortured for information."

Gabinier pressed against his bonds.

"Spare yourself the effort," the doctor admonished him. "There is nothing you can do for them. Just pray that Caesar has something else in store for you."

WHEN GABINIER AWOKE NEXT, the pain in his skull had lessened considerably. He smelled broth and felt a pang of hunger.

The doctor came into his range of view. "Well," Vatteus said lightly, "you have slept most of the day away. Are you ready to rejoin the world of the living?"

Gabinier blinked his eyes to sharpen his focus. "Is there anything worth living for?"

Vatteus stepped away but returned in a few moments with a steaming bowl. "When you work in the medical tents, you learn how fleeting life is," he said in response to the warrior's question. "So yes, I say every single day of life is precious."

Bound as he was, Gabinier could not feed himself. The doctor held the bowl to his lips and let him take a sip of the hot concoction. Gabinier leaned in for more, but Vatteus pulled the bowl back.

"Just a little at first," he said. "Too much will make you sick." He put the bowl down and brought a mug of water to Gabinier's lips. "You are dehydrated," he explained. "You must drink some water."

Gabinier was in fact feeling a ravenous thirst, and he tried to take a deep draw, but again the doctor withdrew the mug after only a few swallows.

Gabinier put his head back on the cot. "Where are we?"

"The medical corps moves with the army, fortunately always in the rear echelon of each legion," Vatteus explained, moving out of Gabinier's sight again as he put the water away. "So we are somewhere in the vast expanse of Germania."

"What has been happening?"

The doctor brought the broth bowl back and let him take another sip, longer this time. "Not much at all," he said. "We have fought no significant engagements. The tribes have retreated to the east, and they have burned everything that might be of use to us."

"Have you taken many captives?"

"Not many, no."

Gabinier smiled; Ariovistus's strategy might be working. Then he remembered his two comrades. "What happened to my men?"

"They both died under the hot irons," the doctor said. "But they identified you as their leader. Caesar wants to talk to you."

Gabinier was astounded. "Me?"

The doctor again moved out of his line of sight. He was gone for a few minutes, leaving the Nervii warrior to puzzle over why Caesar might want to see him.

Vatteus returned with two legionaries, who put Gabinier's wrists into iron fetters and ran a chain connecting his wrists to his feet before they removed the bonds holding him to the cot. He was filled with dread as they led him out of the tent.

As they moved toward a wagon, he saw the sky was thick with smoke. He smiled again, pleased that Ariovistus was continuing to burn the fields and the forests in front of the oncoming Roman horde.

They reached a wagon. He was loaded onto it, then one of the soldiers produced a black cloth and blindfolded him. With a grunt to the wagoner, they were off.

Sightless, Gabinier could smell meat cooking and could hear all kinds of talk, though he could not understand any of the Latin conversations. Considerable clanking of metal suggested that the Romans were keeping their armor and weapons ready for combat.

At length, the wagon came to a stop. Gabinier, still blindfolded, was lifted from the wagon and put on his feet. He felt himself being prodded forward, then heard the snap of a canvas tent flap being pulled back. He heard more conversation in Latin, and abruptly the blindfold was removed.

He blinked a few times and found himself in the tent of what obviously was a Roman commander, given the ornate furnishings and the generous space. And then he saw it, mounted on the side of the tent, big as life: Caesar's own battle standard, white with the golden eagle of Rome emblazoned on it. He gasped; the lanky man standing before him must be Caesar himself! Gabinier staggered a bit and would have fallen but for the two soldiers still flanking him.

When Gabinier had gotten his bearings, Caesar spoke to another Roman officer standing in the room. While Caesar was speaking, Gabinier could not help but gawk at the second man's badly scarred face. When Caesar was finished, the officer turned to Gabinier and said in Germanic, "I am Curio, adjutant to the command of Gaius Julius Caesar, Proconsul of Rome, who stands before you."

Gabinier remained silent.

"You have the profound misfortune of having become a prisoner of the Roman army," the man continued. "Do you understand the implications of that?"

Gabinier continued to stare straight ahead. He wanted to give them no satisfaction at his plight.

"I shall take your silence as a yes. Caesar is prepared to release you if you agree to carry a message to Ariovistus."

Freedom? From the Romans?

"If you decline this offer," the officer continued, "you will be taken to the docks and sold into service as a galley slave. You will never wear clothing again, you will never see the sun again, and you will die there, chained to an oar, standing in your own waste, under the lash, probably within a year."

Gabinier scowled at the man, radiating hatred.

"I can see you understand," the officer said with satisfaction. He turned to take up a scroll. "Can you read?"

Gabinier held his silence.

Curio sighed.

"We are aware that Ariovistus or someone in his tribe can read Latin, based on his prior negotiations with Rome, which resulted in his being recognized as king by our Senate," Curio said. He unrolled the scroll. "'Gaius Julius Caesar, Proconsul of Rome and Commander of the Roman army of Greater Gaul, sends greetings to the King of the Suebi, Ariovistus. The Roman army has entered the territory of Germania to redress the recent insult perpetrated upon the arms of Rome by the raid of Germanic warriors at the Roman camp at Vesontio. The determination of Rome to have justice for this brazen criminal act is demonstrated by the speed with which Rome erected a bridge over the Rhine River, in only ten days. It is the intention of Caesar to burn every town, village, and homestead in Germania, and to enslave every man, woman, and child we encounter. Rome will not relent in this effort until the following terms are met.'"

Curio looked at Gabinier, as if to make sure he was absorbing every word, and then he continued. "'First, Rome demands all the lands of the Suebi located in Gaul be forfeited to Roman ownership. The Suebi tribe members living on such lands will be permitted to remain as tenant farmers, on the same terms Rome has accepted from the other tribes in Gaul. Henceforth, however, no part of any proceeds of such land shall be paid to the Suebi tribe or its king.'"

Gabinier swallowed hard. So many Suebi had settled in Gaul—and they had purchased their farms from the tribe. The funds, of course, had ended up in Ariovistus's own purse. Would he possibly agree to submit all these tribesmen to Roman rule and the loss of their freeholds?

Seeing that this term had registered, Curio moved on. "'Second, Ariovistus must swear a solemn vow and sign a pledge, on behalf of all the people of the Suebi and its affiliated tribes and clans, never again to attack the Roman army or any Roman interests. Such pledge is to be signed in Ariovistus's own blood.'"

Gabinier did not think much of this. Vows were merely words, and words could be renounced.

"'Third, Ariovistus must hand over to the Roman army his own firstborn son, and the firstborn sons of the leaders of the ten largest clans in the Suebi Tribe, to be held as hostages for ten years to secure the performance of Ariovistus to these terms, with such hostages to be subjected to the penalty of death upon any breach.'"

At this, Gabinier reeled. Ariovistus was known to be very fond of his eldest son. He would never give the boy up to be a Roman hostage for ten years.

"'And finally, the Roman army believes that Nervii hostages being held at Vesontio were kidnapped during the raid and are in the custody of Ariovistus. All of these hostages and their offspring must be returned to the custody of the Roman army immediately.'"

This was too much. Gabinier's blood ran hot. "Why, so she can be raped again by some pig of a Roman soldier?" he asked sharply. He did not miss the glance that shot between Curio and Caesar.

"If any hostage of Rome was raped," Curio said, "Caesar regrets such unfortunate circumstance, but the demand must be met nonetheless."

"I will never let her fall prey to a Roman again," Gabinier cried.

Caesar said nothing, but Curio snapped, "You have Caesar's terms. If Ariovistus wants to save his homeland, this is what he must do." He rolled up the scroll and handed it to Gabinier, then gestured for the two guards to take the man away.

Just as they were about to leave, Curio grabbed Gabinier by the arm. "Caesar assures Ariovistus," he said quietly, "that he will burn every bit of this worthless wilderness to the ground and enslave every person we find if these demands are not met. Be certain to tell him this."

Gabinier was taken from Caesar's headquarters, blindfolded again, put onto the wagon, and taken over a smooth plank road to the outermost edge of the Roman position. There he was given a mount and sent out into the wilderness.

L

ROMAN CAMP, GERMANIA

CURIO WAITED UNTIL THE BARBARIAN WARRIOR was well away from the command tent, then turned to Caesar.

"Well?" he asked nervously. "What do you make of that?"

Caesar had sat down in the chair behind his desk and was looking over the pile of orders, reports, letters, and other items, as though disinterested in Curio's question.

Curio knew better, and he waited patiently.

Finally, Caesar spoke. "Are you aware of any other Nervii hostage being with child while in our captivity?" Caesar didn't wait for an answer. "Obviously," he said, "Devorra told them she was raped in order to explain the existence of the child. This is a good thing. We had been worried that she might have returned to the Nervii. Instead, he has confirmed that she is held by the Germanic king, and she has not revealed to Ariovistus the value of what he is holding."

"I must wonder," Curio said insightfully, "if we haven't tipped him off by demanding her return."

"We asked for *all* the Nervii hostages," Caesar said.

"And their offspring," Curio noted.

"It is a risk," Caesar acknowledged, "but we placed that demand at the end, after the more substantial items. Ariovistus will certainly try to negotiate the earlier points. Under these circumstances, we must hope he will view the girl and her infant as incidental."

"Take a look at these," Caesar said, handing Curio a stack of reports. "Dispatch with them in the customary manner."

Curio sifted through the documents, noting a recurring theme in the reports. They were less than a week into the campaign, and already the legion commanders were grumbling that the scorched-earth tactics being utilized by their adversary were causing all sorts of problems with keeping the men and horses properly fed. Making things worse, the natives were beginning to mount nettlesome raids on the wagon trains hauling the needed supplies over the ever-lengthening trail to the front, as the Roman incursion plunged deeper and deeper into Germania. Caesar's standard response to such complaints was simply, "Make do."

Despite his misgivings, Curio dutifully took the reports and put them on his own much smaller desk, only a few feet from Caesar's.

"One other thing," Curio mentioned. "Mamurra is urgently asking to see you."

Caesar by now was absorbed in reading a communication from one of his political operatives in Rome. He lifted his head and asked, "What does he want?"

Curio shrugged. "He would not say. He said he would only talk to you about it."

Irritated, Caesar gave a dismissive wave of his hand. "Well, then, fetch our engineer. Let us hear what is on his mind."

❧

A SHORT WHILE LATER, Mamurra was standing in front of the general. Caesar sat back in his chair and crossed his arms, a sure sign that his patience was likely to be short.

But Mamurra was accustomed to keeping his reports succinct. "Mighty Caesar, I must tell you of my concern with the manner in which the campaign is progressing."

Caesar interrupted him harshly. "You are my engineer, not my senior tactician. What engineering matter brings you here today?"

Mamurra was undeterred. "The circumstances we are encountering in the field are placing great stress on the supply chain. Rather than living off the land, we are required to keep an almost continuous flow of wagons moving over the entire route to Vesontio."

"Is that not a matter for the master of supply?"

"Mighty Caesar, all those loaded wagons, rolling night and day, are crossing your bridge. The strain is enormous."

"Was the bridge not designed to carry a great load?" Caesar demanded.

"It was," Mamurra agreed, "but not for the intensity and duration of use that is being placed upon it. And that, sir, *is* an engineering matter."

Caesar reflected on this for a few moments, then declared in his most imperious manner, "If the bridge requires further reinforcement, you are directed to make it so."

Mamurra was firm. "We have already begun such improvements, sir, but I must also warn you, we are getting into the fall season now, and foul weather will soon be upon us. I cannot guarantee what will happen if the bridge is barraged with heavy storms while straining under this greater-than-anticipated load."

Caesar laughed. "I have priests attached to the army making sacrifices daily so that the gods will favor us with fair weather. What are they telling us about the auspices, Curio?"

Curio fished about on his cluttered desk and found a report. "They are unanimous in their findings—the entrails of the sacrificed beasts are uniformly good. The prospects for continued fair weather are outstanding."

Mamurra kept a straight face. He did not believe in any of this nonsense and doubted that Caesar did either, despite the general's public posture of giving great deference to the gods. "I am grateful for that information, sir. My duty is to advise you about the engineering issues associated with overreliance on the bridge to maintain the line of supply."

"Thank you for the advice, prefect," Caesar said coldly. He picked up the letter he had been reading before Mamurra had interrupted him.

Mamurra saluted. "Thank you for the audience, sir," he said crisply, and turned to go.

He had taken only a few steps when Caesar said, "Mamurra, perhaps you might be interested to hear what they are saying about you in Rome."

Mamurra faced his general again. "About me? In Rome? Whatever could that be?"

"I recently received a letter from one of my operatives in the Senate. It appears that you have come to the attention of that louse Catullus," Caesar said, disgust evident in his voice. "Surely you remember meeting him, back when you were first installed as our prefect?"

Mamurra had to think for a few moments before recalling the day that the oily senator had grilled him in Caesar's office. "Yes, certainly, Caesar. But me? How could I possibly be a subject of his interest?"

Caesar, expressionless, handed the engineer the letter.

Mamurra's hands began shaking and he felt his face flushing more and more deeply as he read its contents.

"Caesar, it's vile! How horrible! This . . . this . . . 'poem,' as he calls it—it is scandalous," Mamurra spluttered, unable to control his disbelief and anger. "What will my parents think?"

Caesar stood up and came around his desk. He put his arm around Mamurra for reassurance. "If you wish, I will write to them, and assure them it is all lies, the dastardly work of craven and corrupt men in Rome who envy your success in the army and hate me for my victories."

Mamurra was aghast, his eyes locked on a single phrase: *Mamurra the catamite.*

"Caesar, he calls me your boy, used for your sexual pleasure! We must do something!"

Caesar patted his engineer on the shoulder and walked him toward the exit. "We are, we are. My supporters in Rome are issuing the appropriate denials."

But Mamurra was not assuaged. "Denials? I must demand a duel!"

"I have already instructed my operatives to resolve this matter," Caesar said as they reached the exit. "For now, try to concentrate on strengthening the bridge. It must hold up until our business here is finished."

Mamurra waited until he was past the guards outside Caesar's tent before he wiped away his angry tears.

ONCE MAMURRA WAS GONE, Caesar turned to Curio. "Welcome to Roman politics, Mamurra."

Curio rubbed his forehead with the palm of his hand. He was a jaded veteran of such dastardly political attacks on Caesar, although this one was remarkable for its outrageousness.

"It was wise to keep the information about Devorra's pregnancy tightly held," Caesar said. "Imagine what that snake Catullus would have written about that!"

Caesar again settled himself into his chair. "Mamurra's right about the bridge, you know."

Curio put up his hands. "What can we do? The gods control the weather."

Caesar sat quietly for a few moments, then said, "Send a confidential order to the commander at Vesontio. Strict secrecy, for his eyes only. Tell him to commandeer every boat and barge he can lay his hands on. Let us have a fleet ready in case we need to ferry the supplies over here."

Curio was afraid that if Devorra were returned to the Roman camp, Molena might come with her. Much as he wanted to be reunited with Molena, he did not like the risk inherent in having her anywhere near

Caesar. He offered, "Caesar, the effort would be enormous. If the Germans will not fight us, would it not be better to withdraw now, while we can?"

Caesar did not hesitate. "Withdrawal without my son is out of the question. Banish all such thoughts from your mind, Curio."

With a weary sigh, Curio picked up his stylus and scratched out a message to the man in charge at Vesontio. He knew that tone in Caesar's voice; further debate on the topic was closed.

LI

FORTRESS OF ARIOVISTUS

AFTER HOURS OF HARD RIDING, Gabinier arrived at Ariovistus's fortress headquarters. He was sickened by the barren landscape he had traversed—the occupants were nowhere to be found, and their farms had been stripped and burned. The smell of smoke was heavy in his nostrils, and everything was coated with ash.

Once inside the imposing stone structure, Gabinier became even more alarmed. Wagons, lined up end to end through the narrow streets, were hastily being loaded with all manner of possessions. Clearly Ariovistus had decided to abandon his fortress rather than try to defend it against a Roman siege.

With little effort, Gabinier was ushered into Ariovistus's quarters.

The king was seated behind a large oak table serving as a desk, studying several parchment maps. Upon seeing Gabinier, he broke into a wide grin, clambered down from the high stool, and hurried over to greet his scout.

"Gabinier! We feared we'd never see you again!" the king exclaimed, pulling the warrior into an embrace. "A few of your men escaped from that skirmish and said they saw you taken captive. How did you ever get away?"

Gabinier stepped back from the king and handed him the Roman scroll. "They released me so that I could bring this to you."

Ariovistus took the document gingerly and saw the crimson wax seal. "Caesar has sent me a message?"

"Yes," Gabinier confirmed.

"Did he give it to you himself?"

"I met with him," Gabinier replied. "But his junior officer did all the talking."

Ariovistus pulled on his yellow beard. "Did he say what this contains?"

Gabinier said simply, "Yes. He has laid out the terms on which the Romans are willing to leave Germania."

313

The king narrowed his eyes in disbelief. "Caesar is offering to leave?" He pulled away the wax seal and unrolled the document. He read silently, then looked up at Gabinier.

"You are aware of the terms of this letter?" he asked.

Gabinier had been anticipating this question and had his answer ready. "They told me they want you to surrender all the Suebi lands in Gaul, and to swear with your own blood you will not attack them again. They want your son as a hostage to secure your vow."

"Nothing else?"

"That is all they told me."

Ariovistus reflected on this for several moments. "Yes, there's nothing else of consequence," he said at last.

Gabinier's instinct had proved correct. *Not only was Ariovistus a liar, but he cares nothing for the hostages. He considers Devorra to be nobody of consequence!*

"That is all?" the king asked.

Gabinier did not hesitate. "They said that Caesar is determined to burn everything in Germania to the ground if you do not agree to these terms."

"Well, he won't find much left to burn," Ariovistus replied. Finally, he put his hand on Gabinier's good shoulder. "You look like you need some hot food and some rest. I am grateful for your effort in bringing me this most important message."

ARIOVISTUS SAT ON HIS STOOL, reading the letter again now that he was alone. He put it down, and a smile spread across his face.

Two of the terms—the lands and his son as hostage—were obviously out of the question. The other two—a mere promise of no further attacks and return of the captives—were nothing to him.

He called for one of his attendants. "Have all the Nervii hostages taken at Vesontio brought into the fortress. Keep them under guard. Let them have no visitors."

Ariovistus watched as the man hurried out of his presence. He was perfectly glad to bargain away the hostages—never mind that Gabinier would be quite unhappy about the departure of one of them. He wasn't going to let his lovesick young scout ruin the deal.

GABINIER DID NOT NEED an order from the king to know he was hungry. There was a large kitchen in the cellar beneath Ariovistus's quarters, fully staffed. Within minutes, the kitchen workers had placed bread, wine, and platters of roasted meat before him.

Gabinier ate ravenously. And he drank a little too much, too quickly, and without regard to the fact that he still was recovering from a severe blow to the head. Much to the amusement of the kitchen staff, he passed out, his head plopping onto the table.

When he woke hours later, he found himself in a bunk in one of the barracks. Elliandro, Gustavus, and the others were staring down at him.

"How long have I been out?" he asked, rubbing his eyes as he sat up.

"Most of the day," Elliandro responded with a grin. He placed a large fired-clay bowl on a table beside the bed and poured water from a metal pitcher into it.

Gabinier splashed the cool water onto his face. The chill was bracing and helped him clear his mind.

"Do we have orders from Ariovistus to go back out?" he asked, reaching for a nearby cloth.

"No," his companion replied. "After what we've been through, we're due for a break."

"No breaks while the Romans are ravaging our country," Gabinier replied, drying his face. "But while Ariovistus is coming up with something for us to do, I'm going for a walk."

Though he felt lightheaded, he was determined to see Devorra. He left the barracks and made his way to her little hut.

His knock on the creaky door was answered by a frantic Molena. "Oh, Gabinier, thank the gods you have returned! They've taken her, they've taken her!"

Gabinier was still thinking slowly due to his injury and the after-effects of too much wine. "Calm down, Molena," he said gently. "What has happened?"

"A group of armed men came and took Devorra away, with the child."

"But who were these men? What reason did they give?"

"They said the king wanted all the Nervii hostages removed to the castle. Why?" Molena moaned. "What could the king want with her?"

"I don't know," Gabinier said. But he had a strong suspicion, and he knew where he had to go.

ARIOVISTUS WAS ONCE AGAIN studying his maps, which were continually being updated by the latest scouting reports. The Romans were only a few days' march away from the fortress now, and all preparations had been made to withdraw farther to the east. But the menacing army seemed to have slowed its approach—perhaps to give him time to receive Caesar's offer and respond to it? Caesar's letter had changed his strategy. He intended to reply, offering to negotiate the terms if Caesar would halt his advance into Germania. This would buy time for the tribes to continue to prepare for battle, if it came to that.

Just then, one of the attendants stepped in and announced that the warrior Gabinier was outside and asking for an audience with the king. Ariovistus knew this was coming and gave his consent.

"Well, Gabinier, you look much better than when you first returned," the king said genially. "What brings you to see me?"

"My lord," Gabinier began, "I'm told you have brought the Lady Devorra here to the fortress. Is that true?"

"I have brought *all* the hostages here."

"May I ask the reason?"

Ariovistus bristled at this. He was not accustomed to explaining himself to his warriors, but he kept his temper and replied simply, "I am expecting that the Romans may want the Nervii hostages returned. I want to keep them here with me at the fortress, where they will be safe."

Gabinier spoke slowly. "Before the Romans began building their bridge, you asked me to make up my mind about the Lady Devorra."

The king nodded, feigning interest. "And what have you decided?"

Gabinier's stare was steely. "I have decided that I love her and would take her for my wife, with your permission."

"And the child? You can be at peace with raising a son who is Roman?"

"You yourself said it: no one, including the child, need ever know of his true heritage," Gabinier said. "We will raise the boy as if he were our own. And," he said, smiling, "I anticipate giving him siblings."

Ariovistus laughed at this. "Well, then, of course you have my permission, but I must ask you to delay the wedding until after we have resolved our business with Caesar. I need your keen eyes and ears as a scout. In fact, I was about to ask you to take your leave of us today and head east. I want you to check on the status of our preparations for battle should the negotiations fail."

Gabinier was in turmoil. "May I see her?"

Ariovistus knew full well this could bring nothing but complications.

"Certainly," he said. "But prepare for your mission first. Go gather your men and make ready to leave. Then I will allow you to see her."

Gabinier stifled his urge to protest, instead asking simply, "One other small item, my lord?"

Ariovistus was losing patience. "Yes?"

"The Lady Devorra was accompanied by a slave girl who was left behind when she was brought to the castle. Might they be reunited?"

Ariovistus could not have cared less. "Consider it done. Now get on with your duty."

A few minutes after he was gone, the king summoned his attendant again.

"Send someone to the hut where the hostage Devorra was living and have them bring her slave woman here to join her."

The attendant bowed deeply from the waist, but before he could leave, the king added, "One other thing. Send my captain of the guard to me. I need his assistance in the arrangements for Gabinier's mission."

The king gave a wry chuckle as the attendant ran off to do his bidding.

GABINIER WENT TO THE BARRACKS and roused his men. He led them to the stables where their horses had been groomed and reshod, ready for action at a moment's notice. He needed to get through this quickly; he was anxious to see Devorra.

The crew was in the process of saddling their mounts and packing their gear when the captain of the guard approached. He was a portly fellow with a neatly trimmed beard, clearly not having suffered from the burning of farms in the path of the Roman advance.

"Gabinier," he said easily, "the king has additional instructions for you. He asks that you rejoin him in his quarters."

Gabinier handed his travel bundle to one of his men and followed the officer back toward the citadel within the fortress. The two men entered through a side door and proceeded down one of the innumerable narrow stone corridors that laced throughout the larger structure, with Gabinier in the lead. They rounded a sharp bend and Gabinier pulled to a sudden halt.

Six of the king's strongest warriors were blocking their path, swords drawn.

Before Gabinier could fully comprehend what was happening, he felt the sharp tip of a blade pressing against the small of his back. The captain held a sword against his spine, just firmly enough that Gabinier knew resistance was futile.

One of the warriors produced a set of shackles, and within moments Gabinier was in chains, bound hand and foot. "What is the meaning of this?" he cried angrily.

The men pushed him roughly along the corridor, but not in the direction of the king's rooms. Instead, they made their way down a long circular staircase. His heart pounding madly, Gabinier realized they were heading for the dungeon.

Within minutes, they were met by a rancid-smelling fellow bearing a large wooden mallet. By the dim torchlight, Gabinier could make out a handful of fearsome-looking torture devices. The man, obviously the jailer, pointed to one of a line of small doors, and Gabinier was pushed toward it. The jailer used the mallet to knock an iron bar out of its wooden loops, which enabled him to shove open the door. The warriors roughly prodded Gabinier into the cramped, black cell. He was nearly overcome by the stench.

"Why am I a prisoner?" he cried out as the door slammed, leaving him in total darkness.

He heard the iron rod being pounded into place.

Through the small opening in the door, the captain of the guard explained. "The king may return the Nervii hostages to the Romans. All of them," he said sadistically. "In here, you won't be able to make any trouble for him."

ALONE WITH NOTHING but Sonnig and a few belongings, Devorra was wrought with apprehension. She had been transported to the castle with the other hostages, and then lodged in a small, sparsely furnished room. The guard posted outside the door left no room for doubt: she was a prisoner.

Sonnig was fussy, and Devorra busied herself changing his wrapping, then settled onto a chair to nurse him. She fretted over her situation, trying to conceive of something—anything—she might do to improve her prospects. Could she somehow get word to Gabinier? Just when she had thought they had a future together, at long last, this happens. How could they ever be wed if she was locked away? Devorra felt truly helpless, completely at the mercy of the Germanic king.

Why would he bring us here? she asked herself again and again.

But she knew the answer. *Only if he felt it would be to his advantage.*

ARIOVISTUS WAS STILL PERCHED on his tall stool, laboring over the text of a response to Caesar, when he was interrupted by yet another attendant, with an unfamiliar man in tow.

"Well?"

The attendant pointed at the visitor. "This fellow is one of the Nervii hostages. He told me something I thought you should hear for yourself."

Ariovistus put down the stylus he was using to mark the wax tablet and studied the frail man standing before him.

"Go ahead," the attendant said to the man. "Tell him what you told me."

"Well, my lord," the man said nervously, "the Lady Devorra was always kept apart from the rest of us hostages, from the very first day we arrived."

Ariovistus was impatient. "And?"

"She had an old slave woman," the man continued, "and she gossiped to us that the general himself was wooing the Lady Devorra."

Ariovistus nearly fell off his stool. He bolted to his feet. "Caesar? Did she say any more?"

"No," the man replied. "But the Lady Devorra and her other slave were taken away from Vesontio. We never saw them again until we arrived here."

Ariovistus laced his fingers together and put them under his chin. *Caesar himself? How could he have been courting a Nervii hostage? Could Caesar be the father of that bastard child?*

"That is all," he said dismissively to the hostage, but he asked the attendant to wait.

Ariovistus gave the attendant a blazing glower. "It would be most unfortunate for that man to go around spreading rumors like that," the king said. He did not want the other tribal chiefs getting wind of this tale and trying to interfere in his negotiations with Caesar. "Take him to the dungeon and lock him away. Nobody in the cell with him. If the jailer lost the key, it wouldn't sadden me."

The attendant bowed his head and hurried away.

Ariovistus picked up Caesar's list of demands and studied it yet again. As the last provision, Caesar had demanded the return of all Nervii hostages—and their offspring. Clever man, making that the last item on the list.

Ariovistus could not say for sure what had really happened to Devorra, nor did he much care. Even if Caesar had fathered the child, it mattered not to Ariovistus. He wanted Caesar gone from Germania, and exchanging the hostages cost him nothing—but it might just be the most valuable thing to Caesar.

He took up the stylus and finished his letter to the Roman commander. He would counter Caesar's bid by offering to give up the hostages . . . and nothing else.

LII

ROMAN CAMP, GERMANIA

TWELVE DAYS INTO THE INVASION, Curio looked in vain for any good news among the reports piled on his small desk in Caesar's command tent. All the legion commanders wrote that morale was sinking; little in the way of food was being found during the continuous foraging raids on the countryside. The tenuous supply line back to Vesontio was barely transporting enough to provide minimal rations of porridge and bread for the men. The cavalry commanders reported that their mounts were suffering and growing weak from insufficient fodder. And a baleful report from Mamurra related that a storm two days earlier had damaged several support columns of the bridge. Repairs were being made, but the army could not make a crossing until they were complete.

Curio normally might have dismissed much of this grousing—after all, it was the inherent right of every soldier to grumble. These reports were different, however; they were not so much a compilation of complaints as they were a series of warnings that the army was in a precarious position. And Caesar seemed indifferent to it all.

Curio was placing the reports on the general's desk when Caesar strode in, looking serene.

"Anything noteworthy?" he asked, settling into his seat.

"The usual," Curio said. "Bad morale, insufficient food, starving horses, and Mamurra says the bridge was damaged in the storm, but repairs are underway."

Caesar said nothing.

"You have a letter from your nephew in Rome," Curio added.

"Young Octavius?" Caesar asked.

"Aye," Curio said, handing over the scroll.

Caesar opened it and read it through. "He writes well for such a young boy. He tells me he has heard about our great naval victory over the Veneti, and he dreams of joining us when he's old enough to serve in the army."

Curio smiled at this. "He hasn't experienced army food yet."

Caesar did not laugh. "We shall see what he is made of, in good time. In the meantime, send him a token from our great victory, perhaps an amulet taken from the neck of one of the Veneti leaders, before it was disconnected from his head?"

"As you wish, sir," Curio replied, jotting himself a note.

Curio knew he was about to tread on thin ice, but the negotiations with Ariovistus had been dragging on too long. They had exchanged proposals and counterproposals, slowly inching toward a meeting of the minds. The Suebi king had already conceded the return of the hostages and in subsequent bargaining agreed to a solemn vow never to raid Gaul again, which both sides regarded as mere window dressing. But not even Caesar's extensive political influence could justify all this effort and cost solely to recover Caesar's illegitimate son—they had to obtain something meaningful for the army and the Senate. Caesar knew he could not exit Germania without significant financial benefits—the men would not stand for it. At the very least, the costs of the entire undertaking had to be recouped, including the vast sums expended on the bridge.

"Ariovistus has consistently refused to turn over his lands in Gaul. If he does not come off this position," Curio said gently, "perhaps we should terminate the discussions and move against his fortress."

This was not at all what Curio wanted, but he had learned that often the best way to manage Caesar was to first offer to do something that Caesar might pretend to want.

Caesar reflected on this suggestion. "I am reluctant to undertake a siege with the current challenges to the supply chain," he said finally. "A siege can take weeks. I would rather bypass that stronghold, leave a garrison there to keep them from raiding us, and move farther into the countryside."

Curio stifled a groan. Moving deeper into Germania was the last thing he thought they should do. "If they continue to scorch the earth in front of our advance, I do not see how we can sustain the march," he pointed out. "We are having to bring in everything we consume by wagon. The bridge is fragile; we know that. The better course may be to announce that we have proved the prowess of the Roman army by making this foray, and go back."

Caesar did not respond. He pretended to be absorbed in reading some piece of correspondence from Rome. Curio interpreted this silence as a rejection.

Finally, Caesar handed the letter over. "Give this to Mamurra."

Curio skimmed it. "So that despicable cur Catullus has renounced what he wrote about you and Mamurra?"

Caesar gave him a satisfied smile.

"How did you bring that about?"

"How do things usually get done in Rome?"

Curio was appalled. "You *paid* him to renounce the vile trash he published?"

"He settled for less than it would have cost to have him killed," Caesar said, as if tutoring a schoolboy. "It was an easy business decision."

Curio rolled up the letter and tied a ribbon around it. He would take it to Mamurra himself and get a firsthand report on the bridge.

"Well, what about our situation?" he asked the general.

Caesar did not look up from whatever he was working on. "One more day," he said simply. "If we do not hear from Ariovistus today, we will break camp and march on his fortress tomorrow."

MUCH TO CURIO'S GREAT RELIEF, only a couple of hours after Caesar uttered his ultimatum, a pair of riders appeared at the front lines carrying a white flag and a wax tablet from Ariovistus.

Once the tablet was delivered, Curio scanned it first. Elated, he passed it over to Caesar.

Caesar read it, then set it on his desk. "Well, Rio, what do you make of it?"

"This is a huge concession on his part!" Ariovistus had countered their demand for all the Suebi lands in Gaul by offering to pay to Rome all his rents from Suebi farmers for five years. "We can parcel out that rent to the army—with a hefty share for the Roman Treasury, of course. That ought to satisfy the Senate."

Caesar was stirred by the idea. "We've also gotten his solemn vow to never again raid Gaul. That will be seen as something of value to our friends back in Rome, even if we know Ariovistus's word is worthless."

Curio studied the letter again. "The only thing he has not given us is his son as a hostage. We never thought we'd get that."

Caesar's eyes twinkled. "Five years of rent is not enough, Rio. Let us demand thirty."

Curio drew in a deep breath, lest he shout at his general. "That will involve another round of discussions," he said, trying to keep his voice level, "adding days to our highly precarious position. I say we should take his offer and get out of Germania."

But Caesar was a gambler. "Let us cast the die," he said. "Write back and tell him twenty years. And that is our final offer. If he rejects it, we will be at his doorstep the next day."

LIII

FORTRESS OF ARIOVISTUS

RIOVISTUS WAS THRILLED to receive Caesar's letter. He had expected a counteroffer, probably for thirty years, so twenty was tolerable. As much as he hated to give up the lucrative rents for so long, he preferred a known cost to the gamble of a pitched battle with the Romans.

The next round of correspondence established the details for the transfer of the Nervii hostages, which would occur at an agreed-upon location midway between the Roman advance positions and Ariovistus's fortress. This diplomacy took two more days, during which Ariovistus ordered the hostages to be made ready for transit.

FOR GABINIER, locked in complete darkness in the bowels of Ariovistus's fortress, rage had given way to despondency. In his first hours of captivity, he had cursed Ariovistus and banged his still-shackled fists on the unyielding door for hours, to no avail. Occasionally he felt something at his boot, and in a fit of revolt finally realized it must be a rat, trying to gnaw at the leather. He instinctively flung the chain binding his wrists to his feet. There was a soft thud, and the sensation stopped. For a while, at least, he had driven it away.

Though the cell was barely big enough to move a few steps back and forth, Gabinier began to pace. On one of his first passes, he stumbled over what he guessed was a wooden bucket, surely intended for bodily waste considering its smell. He prowled back and forth, over and over, seething not only at his own plight but also at the treachery of the king, who had decided to bargain with the Romans rather than fight them. And most crushing of all was the thought of Devorra, lost to him yet again, perhaps forever. He vowed that someday, somehow, he would escape from this hole and take vengeance on the king.

But the hours passed slowly, and then the days, until his sense of time was irretrievably lost. His strength and vitality gave way to fatigue and the complete hopelessness of his situation. There was no way out.

Periodically, the small slot at the bottom of the door would open, and a stripe of light would fall upon the floor. A platter of bread and a cup of water were then pushed into the cell.

Each time, Gabinier would plead, "Wait! Please wait! Help me, please!"

But the slot always snapped shut, plunging him into total darkness once more.

Gabinier would grope about to locate the bread and water, his chains clanking against the floor as he probed.

The bread was always hard and moldy, barely edible. And the water was stale.

Gabinier fought to keep his wits about him. He knew that to give up was to die. But the silence of the cell was overpowering. He could do nothing but sink to the cool stone floor once again, pull his knees up under his chin, and pray to the gods to rescue him.

❦

DEVORRA WAS SOUND ASLEEP when she was harshly awakened long before dawn by a pounding at the door to their little apartment. She stumbled from her cot to the door, with Molena trailing behind her, both rubbing sleep from their eyes. Several strapping thugs muscled their way into the dark room. The first man to enter was carrying a small torch, which cast a pale light across the tiny quarters.

Another man, apparently the leader, leered at the women in their simple sleeping garments. "Get dressed, now!" he shouted at them.

Devorra protested, "Who are you to come in here and disturb my child's sleep?"

The leader continued to gawk at Devorra's figure. His haughty attitude sent a shiver through her, but she planted her bare feet firmly on the cold stone floor and gave him her fiercest stare.

Finally, he spoke. "The king is sending all the hostages back to the Romans. There is a cart waiting outside. Make yourselves ready." He gestured for his crew to step out of the chamber, leaving Devorra and Molena alone, astounded by this sudden turn of events.

"Back to the Romans?" Devorra asked.

Molena, panic evident on her face, cried out, "No, no! I will not go back to a life of slavery. The guards can kill me first."

Devorra tried to reassure her friend. "Molena, don't talk like that."

But Molena was nearly hysterical. "Forgive me, but you have no idea what that life is like. You've been treated as a hostage, given fine clothes and jewelry, put up in a comfortable country cottage—and I am grateful to have lived that life with you these many months. But I haven't forgotten what it means to work your fingers to the bone from dawn to dusk."

Devorra knew they had but one asset among the Roman army. "When we get back, we will ask Curio to set you free. I'm certain he will allow you to return to your tribe."

Molena was not convinced. "Why would he do that?"

"Because he's in love with you. It's as plain as the nose on your face."

"But why would he give me freedom when he can have me as a slave?"

Devorra smiled at her friend. "When you were with me at the cottage, did he treat you as a slave?"

In response, Molena took a deep breath and blew it out forcefully. Devorra knew Molena could make no argument against Curio's kindness toward her and her brother.

"And you know you have feelings for him too," Devorra said. "Molena, I am terrified to go back alone. I beg of you, please come with me."

Molena looked from Devorra to the stirring infant.

"Please, Molena. We need you. Curio will do whatever you ask him to. I know he will," Devorra said, praying it was not a lie.

After several moments, Molena gave in. "Come, let us get packed before they come back."

The hubbub in the room had, of course, awakened Sonnig, and he was screeching now. Devorra took him up in her arms and bared her breast.

"There, there, my little one," she said softly. As she nursed the hungry child, Devorra could only think about Gabinier. She believed that he wanted to be with her, and she still hoped that someday they would finally be together. But she had heard nothing from him for days. And now that she was to be returned to the Romans, she feared they would never be reunited.

Before long, the trio were collected and led to a covered oxcart, one of a long line assembled to transport the Nervii hostages. A cadre of warriors were lined up on their horses to accompany them, and the journey toward the Roman camp began.

Seeing dark clouds on the horizon, Devorra asked the driver whether they might be delayed by the storm.

The man studied the sky. "Hard to say, but if it's bad, we might have to stop for a day, at least."

Devorra regarded him stoically. "Very well. We are in no hurry to get back to the Romans."

⌘

THE JAILER MADE HIS RESIDENCE in the awful dungeon, sleeping on a cot in a side chamber. As a sharp blade pressed against his throat, he woke with a start. The blade cut slightly into his skin, and blood dripped onto his blanket. Elliandro clamped a hand over the man's mouth.

"We are Gabinier's men," Elliandro hissed in the jailer's ear. "Show us where he is and we will spare your life."

The men followed the jailer into the section of the dungeon where the cell doors were all held closed with the iron bars. With only a little prodding, he brought them to the cell they wanted and showed them how to use the mallet to remove the bar.

When the door swung open, Gabinier was already on his feet. Though the torchlight in the outer chamber was dim, he threw an arm across his eyes at its sudden onslaught.

Elliandro pulled Gabinier out of the cell and waited for him to regain his vision. While he was rubbing his eyes, his men forced the jailer to remove his shackles. With a rush of gratitude, Gabinier warmly greeted each man in turn.

"It took us a while to figure out where you'd gone," Elliandro told him. "We came for you as soon as we found out."

Gabinier cast a murderous look upon the jailer, who by now was white with fear.

"Wait," said Gustavus. "We also heard that the king locked up one of our comrades." He put the dagger to the jailer's neck again. "Where is he?"

In a matter of moments, the Nervii hostage was liberated. He had been imprisoned for nearly as long as Gabinier, with nary a word of explanation. The man was so emaciated he could barely stand.

Gabinier pushed the jailer into the just-vacated cell and pulled the door shut. In a single motion he grabbed the iron bar and pounded it into place.

"Are you just going to leave him in there?" Gustavus asked. "How long do you think it will take them to find him?"

"With any luck," Gabinier said with venom, "they never will. Now tell me: What has happened to Devorra?"

Elliandro felt his face flush with anger. "Ariovistus has sent all the hostages back to the Romans. My sister included."

Gabinier slapped him on the shoulder. "We must leave at once if we are going to intercept them."

⁓⁓⁓

GIOVANUS HAD THEIR HORSES at the ready just outside the fortress gates. He had managed to steal four pack animals as well, which were now heavily laden with large canvas panniers.

They had been riding for over an hour when Gabinier signaled for them to stop at a small stream.

"The horses need a rest," he told the men.

As they watered the horses, Gabinier jumped into the stream to rid himself of the stench from his imprisonment. Elliandro watched and was about to say something when Gabinier stopped him. "I know, I know. Even *I* couldn't stand myself," he growled.

Serious now, he said to his men, "Once we've thwarted the hostage exchange, let us meet where the river splits to the north."

Elliandro looked dubious. "How are we going to stop them?"

Gabinier gave him a determined look. "This will be much easier than Vesontio," he said with firmness. "I have a plan."

LIV

ROMAN CAMP, GERMANIA

CURIO BROUGHT ONLY A SMALL SQUAD of Caesar's most loyal staff officers to the clearing in the woods where the hostages would be turned over. Vatteus came along to attend to any hostages who might be in poor health.

They pitched tents atop a broad hill, planning to stay overnight and begin the journey back to the Roman camp the next morning.

The hostage party reached the clearing at dusk. The first Germanic warrior came to a halt a short distance into the clearing and hoisted a white flag of truce. The Romans were obliged to ride out and meet them.

Curio watched the scene from his horse on top of the hill, greatly relieved that his instincts had proved correct—Molena was with Devorra and the child. *Now I am in a position to keep her well out of Caesar's sight*, he thought.

He sent the Roman team out to meet the group. Vatteus rode with them should he be needed.

As the Germanic warrior waved for the drivers to bring the wagons bearing the hostages forward, Curio noticed a sudden blur of activity. An instant later, his brain registered what he was seeing, as a shower of deadly arrows slammed into the Germanic warrior and Vatteus, knocking them from their horses. Horrified, Curio watched as his lifelong friend hit the ground.

Arrows flew through the air, targeting the other Germanic guards. The Roman contingent leapt from their horses and banded together, shields overhead in a turtle formation.

Before Curio could move, he saw two men on horseback break from the woods and make a furious charge toward the wagon train of hostages, now bereft of their wounded and dying Germanic guards.

Stunned, Curio realized the two raiders were heading for the cart carrying the women and child. One of them pulled the teamster off the seat and took up the reins. He turned the cart back to the forest, accompanied by the other raider, but they took a path considerably away from the source of the arrows, as though not wanting to block the archers' line of fire.

They'll keep the soldiers pinned down while they make their escape, Curio thought, his military mind starting to function over the shock. *If they get away, I will never see Molena again.*

He gave his mount a hard kick in the ribs and took off in pursuit.

ON THE CART, Molena grasped her brother's arm with both hands.

"Elliandro!" she cried. "What is this?"

Elliandro grunted through clenched teeth, "Did you think we'd let the Romans take you back?"

Devorra called out, "Gabinier, my love!"

Gabinier, turning to see if they were being pursued, flashed her a smile. "We have to hurry. Hold fast!"

The little group plodded along at the oxen's top speed toward a steep rise. The men hidden in the forest continued to rain arrows down on the Romans. Huddled under shields riddled with arrows, the group looked like a giant thistle.

As they passed over the top of the rise, Molena let out a sigh of relief, but then Elliandro yanked hard on the reins.

In front of them, armor gleaming in the fading sun, was a single Roman, mounted on horseback, sword drawn.

CURIO WAS STARTLED to recognize the raider on horseback as the same man who had stood before Caesar to hear the terms the Romans proposed to Ariovistus. It was the very same fellow who had been outraged by Caesar's demand for the return of the hostages—and suddenly this made all the sense in the world.

Curio looked to Molena and found her seated on the cart by the man holding the reins. *Elliandro? By Jupiter, what is he doing here?*

Curio laughed aloud. "Allow me to guess," he said to Gabinier. "You led the raid on Vesontio to rescue her the first time?"

Gabinier's silence served as an admission.

Curio rubbed his eyes with his free hand. He could fight this man, but the warrior was powerfully built; Curio did not like his chances.

If I allow them to escape, the headache of what to do about the child will simply vanish—no scandal for Caesar in Rome. And it will put an end to this disastrous expedition into Germania.

In the few seconds it took for all this to pass through Curio's mind, Gabinier acted. He plunged his horse toward Curio, knocking the Roman out of the saddle. Curio slammed into the ground, sword flying.

Gabinier jumped from his mount and lunged for Curio.

"Now, Roman," he cried, "you, who would have sent me to die in the galleys, will perish yourself!" He reared back with his sword, ready to strike at Curio's chest.

"No!" Molena cried. She jumped onto Gabinier's back, knocking him off balance. Gabinier threw her to the ground, but Molena grabbed at his ankles. "No, no!" she pleaded. "You must spare him, I beg you!"

Before Gabinier could shake free of her, Devorra stepped forward. "This Roman is not like the rest," she asserted. "He was kind to us."

Gabinier hesitated, sword still at the ready.

Elliandro approached. "Devorra speaks the truth," he said. "I would be dead if not for this man."

"He saved my life, too," Molena added, getting to her feet and wiping away the mud.

Gabinier looked at each of them in turn, slowing his breath, then spoke to Curio. "If you send anyone after us, I will come back and kill you myself." Curio gave an almost imperceptible nod, and Gabinier backed away, keeping his sword level. "Quickly," he said to Devorra, taking her by the arm and leading her back to the cart.

But Molena did not follow. She reached out to Curio and helped him to his feet. She did not release his hand.

"Come, Molena," Elliandro urged. "Freedom awaits us."

"I am free now," Molena said to her brother, then turned to lock eyes with Curio. "Is this not true? I may choose as I wish?"

Curio tilted his head a bit. "You may," he said, feeling a smile tugging at the corners of his mouth. "And I ask you, as a free woman, to choose to stay with me."

Elliandro began to protest, but Molena raised her hand to silence him.

"He could have sold me as a slave a hundred times at Vesontio," she said. She turned back to Curio. "Why didn't you?"

Curio took a step closer to her. "Because I love you."

Molena looked at Devorra. "Do you remember telling me that if ever I had the chance to be with the man I love, I should seize it while I can?"

Devorra's smile spread wide, and she grasped Gabinier's hand. Sonnig cooed, as if to endorse the proposition.

Molena turned and embraced her brother. "May the gods bring us back together again someday," she said, her voice breaking. After a few long moments, she released him and returned to Curio's side, wiping away her tears.

Elliandro, clearly overcome with emotion himself, staggered to the cart and silently climbed aboard. Devorra and her son soon joined him, and with one last wave to Molena, they followed Gabinier into the abyss of the forest.

"You saved my life," Curio whispered to Molena.

"You *are* my life," she replied.

WHEN CURIO AND MOLENA arrived at the camp, they found the other Romans had already returned. One of the junior officers explained that when the blizzard of arrows had finally stopped, they had been able to retrieve Vatteus's body and collect the rest of the hostages, who were baffled by the odd turn of events. None of them had any useful information about the attackers. The officer gave Molena a lascivious look. "Where did this morsel come from?"

"I gave chase to the group that broke away from the rest," Curio replied. "I could not catch them, but I found her. They evidently threw her aside to lighten the load."

The fellow smirked. "She'll bring a fine price on the blocks."

Curio gave him a cold stare. "I think I'll keep this one for myself. Now get about the business of preparing a funeral pyre for poor Vatteus. We'll honor him in the morning."

AS CURIO SETTLED MOLENA in his tent before heading out to check on the other hostages, he asked her, "So, who is that warrior who has made a career out of spiriting Devorra away from the Roman army?"

Molena laughed. "His name is Gabinier. There is much to tell you about him."

Curio gave a rueful laugh. "We will have time soon enough, assuming Caesar doesn't have my head for what happened here!"

⁕

LATER, SATISFIED THAT THE ATTACKERS were not likely to strike again, and having attended to the preparations for Vatteus's funeral, an exhausted Curio forced himself to a hard decision: he dispatched a courier to Caesar with a terse message reporting the raid. *He will be angry, to be sure, but I will tell him there was nothing we could do—the warrior disappeared with Devorra and his son.*

As he made his way back to his tent, he put all thoughts of Caesar out of his mind.

The single candle on the table cast a pale amber hue across the canvas walls. Molena lay on the cot under a rough army blanket, her back to the entrance.

Not wanting to disturb her slumber, Curio turned to leave.

"Don't go," she said.

He pivoted and saw she had turned, only her face showing above the blanket, her lustrous hair splayed about her head. Even in this dim light, her aura was overpowering.

"When the raid began, I—well, I feared I would never see you again," he said softly. "I have no words to tell you how happy I am you chose to stay."

"I stayed only to be with you," she said, sitting up.

Molena pushed the blanket away and motioned for him to join her on the cot. She had nothing on but the necklace he had given her. Her body was just as he remembered it, full and ripe.

He became fully aroused and wanted her more than any woman he had ever seen. Yet he hesitated. All his life, he had lived with rejection, believeing himself undesirable. He was helpless, gripped by the fear of it.

Molena sensed his discomfort. She took his hand into her own and placed it on her heart.

Curio stroked her hair and gently kissed her eager lips.

She lay back on the cot, offering herself to him. "When you truly love someone," she whispered, "you love them as they are."

It took but a breath for Curio to shed his tunic and come to her.

LV

GERMANIA

EVORRA AND SONNIG SPENT THE NIGHT jostling along in the back of
the cart, as Gabinier and Elliandro negotiated the narrow path
through the otherwise impenetrable forest. In the darkness, shrouded by
thick foliage, Devorra could not fathom where they were or where they
were headed. Not that she was concerned—she and Gabinier were finally
together, and he was accepting her child as his own. Nothing else mattered.

They came into a little clearing and saw a small group of men gathered
about a fire, a rabbit roasting on the spit. They were laughing and joking, in
the best of spirits. Devorra recognized them—somehow, despite the gloom
of the night and the immensity of the endless forest, Gabinier had found
his squad.

They all gave a cheer when Gabinier's steed drew near to the fire's glow,
and then cheered again when they saw that his mission had been successful—once again he had stolen Devorra and the child away from under
the Romans' noses!

Devorra handed Sonnig to Elliandro as one of the men helped her from
the back of the cart. She hobbled around for a bit, stiff from having sat on
the hard boards for so many hours. Gabinier's feet barely touched the
ground before he swept her into his arms. They kissed passionately, lingering in their embrace. He whispered, "I'll never leave your side again. We
shall never be apart!"

When the lovers finally separated, Devorra found a quiet place to nurse
Sonnig and change him, then she rejoined the group. One of the brothers
handed her a cup of warm wine. Another was waiting with slices of roasted
rabbit, apparently taken as a hunting prize while the group was waiting for
their leader's return. Gustavus offered to hold the baby, and since Sonnig
seemed perfectly happy in his arms, she took a moment to eat and drink.

Seated now by the fire with the group, and beginning to feel the effects of the wine, Devorra shook her head and said to Gabinier, "I'm still in disbelief. First, I'm told you are dead, then you appear out of nowhere and save me, the next thing I know you're taken away and I'm being sent back to the Romans—oh, and then you appear out of the trees to rescue us *again!* Are you flesh or are you a spirit?"

This brought a round of laughter.

"Best you tell all," Gustavus chimed in, "or you'll never hear the end of it."

Gabinier proceeded to relate the harrowing stories of his battles with the Romans, of Ariovistus's treachery, his own nightmarish imprisonment, and the bold strike by his loyal men to rescue him. Devorra joined them in another round of laughter when Gabinier got to the part about locking the jailer in his own cell.

After several more flasks of wine and more stories, the fire was beginning to fade. As the brothers began to drift toward their sleeping areas, Gabinier rose and said, a little too loudly, "Rest well, my friends. And may the god Sucellus deliver you from the pain of overindulgence!"

"It's too late for that!" Gustavus said, hooting and stumbling away.

But Devorra noticed that Elliandro's laugh was quickly replaced by a melancholy look and she reached out for his hand.

"Try to be happy for Molena," she said gently. "Her dream was to be free and to be able to choose her own path in life. She has done that, and I know she will be content."

Elliandro sighed. "I will try to draw comfort from your kind words. But I know I will never see her again."

Gabinier put his hand on Elliandro's shoulder. "Do not try to predict what the gods will do; they love to play with us. Who could have believed they would save me from death on that battlefield, or bring me back to my true love, again and again?"

Devorra looked at Gabinier and embraced him once again. Then she said, "Well, this is all lovely, but I'm fearful. Even if Curio can hold them off for a while, the Romans will be searching for us, and I imagine Ariovistus won't be pleased to find out what has happened either. What are we to do?"

"We shall return to the territory of the Nervii," Gabinier responded with confidence. "But I will not reclaim leadership of the tribe, or the Romans would be on us like a fox on a rabbit. We will take up residence in the countryside near the farmer Rabanus and his wife, who nursed me back to health when I was wounded. I intend to repay them for their kindness."

"And I shall go with you," Elliandro said, drawing a smile from Gabinier.

"We have the means to reward them generously for what they did for me, and more than enough to live well for the rest of our lives. Right, Elliandro?"

"Come with me," Gabinier said, and led her over to the packhorses that were part of their little entourage. Elliandro pulled back the covering on one of the panniers, enough for her to see the treasures within.

"Booty from Vesontio," Elliandro told her, his mood better now.

Devorra began to laugh in delight. Gabinier took her in his arms, and they kissed again.

Finally, Devorra broke away, saying, "I am impressed by your trove of plunder. However, I wish to contribute as well."

Devorra placed the sleeping Sonnig in the wagon and retrieved the bundle she had so diligently kept with her from Vesontio to the fortress of Ariovistus, to the rendezvous with the Romans, and with her through the night to this meeting place. Gabinier watched with interest as she gingerly untied the knot and spread open the sheet. Triumphant, she hoisted the hefty burlap sack of coins that Curio had provided her back in Vesontio in the spring. "I did some plundering of my own! Roman sesterces, and plenty of them," she announced.

Gabinier applauded her. Then he took her hand and said to Elliandro, "Keep an eye on the babe for us, will you, my friend?"

"Where are you going?" Elliandro asked.

It was Devorra who answered. "I am certain Gabinier has much more to tell me," she said with a wink.

⁂

AS THE SUN was beginning its ascent, Gabinier started a fire and went around the camp rousing his comrades. There was much groaning and spitting as the men gathered around the morning fire.

"We need to make quick work of breaking camp now," Elliandro said. "Ariovistus and the Romans will already be looking for us."

"You are all more than welcome to make a home with us at Rabanus's farm," Gabinier offered. "And we need never say another word about all we have done."

The brothers talked quietly among themselves, and after a moment Gustavus spoke up.

"Your offer is generous, Gabinier, but we are soldiers, not farmers," he said slowly. We joined you to fight the Romans, and we want to continue the fight until all Romans are dust."

Gabinier frowned. "But how . . . and where? Ariovistus has made a treaty with them, worse even than that of the Nervii."

Gustavus gave Gabinier a slap on his good shoulder. "You know Caesar won't stop until Rome controls all of Gaul. There are still many tribes in need of our services."

Gabinier nodded and swallowed hard. "Then this may be the last time we're all together," he said with a wistful tone in his voice. "I'm honored to have fought with you. I have known no warriors more courageous, nor better men than you."

He embraced each man, and Elliandro stepped forward.

Gesturing to the pack animals, he said, "Take your shares of the Roman plunder. May we live long enough to be reunited someday."

Devorra had been watching from the wagon. She came into the circle, wiping her eyes. "There are not enough riches in the world to repay you for what you have done for us. Without your bravery, I would not have my love, and our son would not have his father. May the gods protect you always."

LVI

The Roman Camp, Germania

THEY BURNED VATTEUS ON HIS PYRE AT DAWN, but it took some work to get the caravan assembled and on its way. During this time, Curio dispatched search parties to look for Devorra, knowing this was futile; the effort was mere window dressing for what he knew would be a difficult meeting with Caesar. The old man was likely to have Curio skinned alive.

The trip to Caesar's camp consumed the rest of the day. Curio agonized throughout the return trip over the tirade that might await him, but the journey was made considerably more tolerable by his blossoming relationship with Molena.

Still, Curio knew anything could happen.

He arrived at Caesar's quarters to find him in conference with Mamurra and several of the legion commanders, all stone-faced. Curio drew himself to full attention, gave his report on the events of the attack, and waited to be roasted.

Caesar looked at him coolly. "When the arrows began to strike our men, they took proper defensive measures?"

"Absolutely, sir."

Caesar sternly pursed his lips. "How is it that two warriors were able to get away with some of the hostages?"

Curio was calm. "The barrage from the forest was formidable, sir. Our men were pinned down."

Caesar's jaw twitched, only slightly. "And you undertook a vigorous search effort to recover the kidnapped hostages? Are you satisfied that everything possible was done?"

"No effort was spared, sir."

"And you have no reason to believe that this raid was organized or endorsed by Ariovistus?"

Curios kept his eyes straight ahead. "I have no reason. He did return the other hostages to us. Why would he have singled out this one? I believe this was an independent action by a group of rebels."

Caesar looked around the tent. "Well, gentlemen," he said after a long moment of reflection, "I would say that the commander of the mission observed all proper military procedures and, under the circumstances of the attack, did all that could be expected of him to save his force. In fact, he is to be commended for maintaining the cohesion of his command, notwithstanding the unfortunate loss of these hostages. Is there anyone who disagrees?"

There was no one.

"At ease," Caesar said to Curio, who heaved a sigh of relief. He had escaped official censure for the disaster; at least his military record would be clear. Then Caesar asked the others to leave him alone with his adjutant.

When the last of the officers had left the tent, Caesar stepped close to Curio and whispered desperately, "It was Devorra and the child who were taken, yes?"

Curio could only nod.

"And we have no way of knowing who took her, nor where they've gone?"

"I have done everything possible to find out, but no."

Caesar's face darkened toward purple as he growled like a caged beast. He spun on his heel and gave the side of his desk a brutal kick. "By the gods!" he shouted, then collapsed into his chair. Caesar closed his eyes and held his head in his hands for several long minutes, until Curio began to fear he was slipping into yet another seizure.

Finally Caesar looked up between his fingers, his hands still clutching the sides of his face. "How can it be, Curio, that the gods favor me in so many ways, and yet keep conspiring to deprive me of a son?" He slammed his fist into the palm of his hand. "For all my power, there is nothing more to be done? Nothing?"

"All that can be done, I have done already," Curio assured him.

Like Curio, Caesar was a clear-eyed realist. It was one of the things Curio liked best about the man. They both knew they would never find the child in the vast expanse of Germania.

Caesar threw up his hands in despair. "So the gods have played out their little drama, with me as their foil. At least we know that I am capable of producing a son, eh, Rio? And if all else fails, I suppose there is always Octavian."

"Indeed." Curio felt his chest tighten as he prepared to deliver his final piece of bad news. "Caesar, there is one more difficult thing I must tell you."

"How can it be worse than the news you have already brought?"

"I'm afraid that one of the casualties of the attack was our old friend the physician."

"Not dear Vatteus! Oh, Rio." The general shook his head and blew out a long breath. "It's down to just you and me now, then."

"It is." Ever practical, Curio wondered where he would find another doctor he could trust to be discreet with Caesar's many private needs. But he would have to figure that out on his own time. For now, Caesar appeared to be channeling his grief toward the battlefield, calling for a messenger to summon Mamurra and the legion commanders.

⌘

MAMURRA HAD BARELY sat down at his desk when he was called back to Caesar's quarters. Once the group had reassembled, Caesar asked each legion commander to give a brief report. It was all bad—they were nearly out of food, the men had begun slaughtering the pack animals because there was no fodder for them, and nothing could be found in the countryside.

"Mamurra?" Caesar asked.

"All of you are aware of the most recent storm," Mamurra said. "More of the pilings were damaged. The weather grows more treacherous by the day. If the campaign is to continue, I cannot be responsible for the integrity of the bridge."

"Curio?"

Curio faced his general. He had been rehearsing this carefully. "Sir, we are eighteen days into this campaign. Respectfully, we agreed that if Ariovistus consented to the twenty-year lease, returned the hostages, and took a solemn vow never to attack Gaul again, we would withdraw. He did those things. I submit that we are honor bound to keep our word."

Caesar thought for a moment, then said, "This campaign had two goals. First, we wanted to show Germania, and indeed the whole world, what the Roman army can do. By building a bridge over the Rhine in ten days, we accomplished just that."

He shot a wink at Curio, who understood the gesture in an instant. Caesar wanted that explanation in the chapter about the invasion of Germania in his book about the war in Gaul.

Then the general looked proudly at his prefect of engineers. "Well done,

Mamurra." Turning back to the rest of the group, he said, "The second goal was to obtain control over the Germanic settlers in Gaul and obtain assurances that the raids from Germania will cease. We have accomplished those goals, as well. The rents from the twenty-year lease will be lucrative, and each of you shall receive your rightful share."

They all grunted approval to that.

Continuing, Caesar said, "Curio is correct in his assessment of our situation. Orders will be issued this afternoon confirming that we are to break camp and begin the return to Gaul immediately."

The relief on every face was palpable.

Caesar dismissed the group, but Mamurra remained behind.

"Yes, Mamurra?" Caesar asked when all the men but Curio were gone.

Mamurra had been mulling a question for several days, and now he had to ask it: "Caesar, what are we to do with the bridge once the army is back in Gaul?"

Caesar's expression was inscrutable. He tilted his head toward his adjutant. "What say you, Curio?"

Curio did not hesitate. "With all due respect to our masterful engineer, sir, we must burn it. The enemy must not be allowed to make use of it against us."

Mamurra sagged a bit. This was what he had been expecting, but so much of his heart and soul had been invested into the structure, he could not bear to put it to the torch.

Caesar was not insensitive to the engineer's reaction. "I have a different idea," he said, glancing briefly at Curio, who nodded slightly. "I think we should disassemble the bridge, rather than burn it. We will put as much of it as we can salvage into storage."

"Storage, sir?" Mamurra asked. "Whatever for?"

Caesar picked up his dagger from the desk and twirled it lightly between his fingers.

"Because," he said with a wistful look, "I just may return to Germania someday."

Epilogue

Rome, 41 BC

MAMURRA, RESTORED TO HIS FABULOUS MANSION on the Caelian Hill after the victory of Antony and Octavius over Caesar's assassins at Philippi, sat on a comfortable chair on the veranda, pitting dates. He could have asked any of the servants to do it, of course, but he was constantly finding little tasks to keep himself busy. It passed the time, it wasn't taxing, and if he made a mistake, nothing was going to collapse and kill somebody. It was enough at this point in his life. The breeze was pleasant, and Mamurra had not a care in the world. The epic power struggle that had gripped the Roman world for the three years following Caesar's murder had largely passed him by . . . and he was glad of it.

Dominicus approached.

"Yes?" Mamurra asked his servant and companion.

"Curio is at the gate with two other gentlemen. They say they have an appointment with you," Dominicus said.

"Yes." Mamurra dropped his knife, then handed the dates to Dominicus and rinsed his fingers in a bowl of water. "Show them in."

Within minutes, two young men, accompanied by the much older Curio, made their way onto the veranda. One of them was slim, almost frail, with sandy hair, and walked with a commanding air about him. The other youth was stout, with a block-like jaw and dark hair styled in the traditional Roman manner. He carried a valise of fine Spanish leather.

Mamurra shook hands with his old friend. He gestured for the men to sit.

Curio handled the introductions. Pointing to the slender fellow, he said, "This is Octavius, the adopted son and legal heir of Gaius Julius Caesar. Hence his new name, Octavius Caesar."

Mamurra knew him by reputation, and he bowed his head respectfully.

"And this," Curio said, "is Octavius's most trusted colleague and commander of all his military forces, Marcus Agrippa."

It was Agrippa who bowed his head now, to Mamurra. "It is an honor, sir, to meet the greatest engineer in the history of the Roman army."

Mamurra, ever self-deprecating, gave him a dismissive wave. "No, that would be a man named Trolianus, who taught me everything I ever knew," he said with a laugh. "What brings such eminent men to visit a broken-down old donkey like me?"

Octavius got right to the point. "I assume you are familiar with the tribulations we have been experiencing in Rome."

Mamurra lifted his hands sympathetically. Caesar's heir had claimed his rightful inheritance over the jealous and ambitious Marc Antony. Octavius and Antony cobbled together an uneasy alliance and vanquished Caesar's assassins in a cataclysmic battle at Philippi in Macedonia. They then proceeded to rule Rome jointly.

"Antony has left Rome for Egypt," Octavius said, with apparent disgust. "He has taken up relations with Cleopatra. He needs her money. And I am sure he's promised to help her advance the career of her son, Caesarion."

Mamurra kept silent, knowing full well that Caesar had traveled to Egypt after defeating Pompey in the civil war, and while there dallied with Cleopatra, producing the male heir he had always wanted, Caesarion. But Caesar had left everything to Octavius, and Cleopatra was said to be furious.

Octavius perceived the boy as a threat to his own inheritance. Rumors swirled that Octavius and Antony would turn on each other for yet another round of bloody competition to rule all of Rome and her empire. Mamurra had studiously kept a low profile in all this intrigue. He'd had his fill of Roman politics during that disgraceful incident with Catullus and his libelous poem.

"I have followed your great success," Mamurra said. "But how can that involve me? Certainly I can be of no value to you in such matters."

"My father told me repeatedly you were the best engineer he ever had. In particular, he told me many times about the fabulous bridge you built for him over the Rhine."

Mamurra felt a twitch of gratitude from this praise—and a twitch of disdain at the young leader's blithe reference to Caesar as his father. "Well," he said artfully, "I had the high privilege of serving your father during the campaign in Gaul, the invasion of Britannia, and the civil war with Pompey. After the great victory at Pharsalus over the Pompeians, when Caesar went off to see the pyramids, I retired."

Octavius made a great effort to give him a friendly smile. "Yes, that is what my father told me. But I came here to see if you might help us with something."

Mamurra shifted uneasily on his chair. "No, no," he said. "I am retired, and much too old to even remotely consider taking the field with an army."

Octavius's determined look made it clear: this was a young man who did not take no for an answer. He stroked the amulet on a chain around his neck, then gave a little laugh and reached out to touch Mamurra's shoulder. It was an endearing gesture.

Perhaps this clammy, seemingly aloof person might have the makings of a politician after all, Mamurra thought.

"We don't want you to take the field. We want to build a temple after we are successful against Antony, to celebrate our triumph. I told Agrippa here that you are the only man who could bring it off."

Mamurra was taken aback. "Oh no," he said. "I have forgotten everything I ever knew about structure and construction. Surely there are others far more capable."

"Perhaps not," said Agrippa, speaking up for the first time. He opened the valise and withdrew several sheets of vellum. "Our idea is to build something the likes of which has never been seen before."

Mamurra felt the familiar flame of ambition licking at the challenge as Agrippa spread the drawings on the small table. "The building will have a rectangular portico of stone masonry, but behind it will be a massive brick rotunda with a concrete domed ceiling."

"Domes have been built before," Mamurra said dismissively. "The techniques are well known. You don't need me for that."

"Not like this," Octavius said confidently. "We want no columns in the building underneath, supporting the dome. It should appear to be free-standing."

This boggled the mind. The structural implications were immense.

"And," Agrippa continued, pointing to another sheet, "the dome will be open at the top, so that the building can commune with the spirits and the elements."

Mamurra scratched his head. "But rain will get into the building."

"Yes, of course," Agrippa said, pulling out yet another sheet. "The drain will be in the floor, directly under the opening, which we call the oculus."

Almost against his will, Mamurra had to admire the design elements. The portico was classic, with eight huge Corinthian-style columns in the front and two sets of four columns behind, holding up a massive triangular pediment bearing the building's inscription. But, as they'd said, no support columns within. It would be a marvel, if it could somehow be built. As he studied the drawings, he found the design truly exquisite—the dimensions perfectly proportioned, the dome elegantly curved. And then one of the dimensions caught his trained eye: the height of the dome at its peak was exactly equal to the diameter of the circle it formed. It was stunning.

"Easy to draw," he muttered, "impossible to build."

"And that, old friend, is exactly why I have brought them to you," Curio said cheerfully. "You always specialized in the impossible."

Mamurra stroked his chin. "This is going to cost a fortune."

Octavius waved his hand. "Money is no object."

Mamurra remembered Caesar's similar attitude when the bridge was being planned. He mused for several moments.

Agrippa added, "We have also talked to the only other engineer in Italy who has the skill and experience to undertake the project. He refused to do it unless he's working under you."

Mamurra gave them a blank stare. "Who could that possibly be?"

Agrippa laughed. "Why, your old sidekick, Giacomo. He said that the bridge over the Rhine was child's play compared to the challenges of this structure!"

"You will have plenty of time to work out all the details," Octavius said.

Mamurra ran his eyes over the drawings again. It was tempting . . .

Agrippa saw him wavering and went in for the kill. "We will call it the Pantheon," he said, "and we will put your name on the cornerstone. It will be there for all time."

Mamurra had become putty in their hands. "Very well," he said. "Leave the drawings. Let me give you my thoughts."

"You may name whatever fee you think is fair," Octavius said. "The magnitude of the task requires your talent. Cost is of no concern to me."

For a fleeting moment, Mamurra again heard the echo of Octavius's uncle—or father, as he now put it.

"Let me see what I can do."

Octavius seemed satisfied. "Very well, then, my dear Mamurra. Perhaps you will serve me as loyally as you served my father."

The group rose to go and as Mamurra was shaking hands with them, Curio asked, "Will I see you for our regular game?"

"Yes, of course," Mamurra huffed. "Someday I will prevail against you."

Mamurra watched the two young men as they left. He could not help but notice how they walked with a certain bearing, almost a swagger, a gait he remembered all too well. It was the distinct mannerism of one Gaius Julius Caesar.

"IT'S YOUR MOVE, PAPA."

Snapped out of his daydreaming by the remark, Curio smiled at his son.

"Well, Marcus, you've certainly got me in a predicament," he said, focusing on the game board. "Your namesake would be proud of you."

The towheaded boy flashed his father a wide grin, revealing his missing front teeth. "Do you really think so, Papa?"

"Oh yes," Curio replied. "Mamurra may be the greatest engineer who ever lived, but he has never beaten me at latrones. You're on the verge of it now."

They were playing the game in the sitting room of Curio's relatively modest manor house, located on the back side of the Aventine Hill. He had chosen a spot with a view over the Tiber, rather than one facing the Capitol and the Forum. He had had enough of dealing with the scoundrels in the Senate—he couldn't bear to look at that den of thieves from his home every day. That, and he wanted to keep a low profile. Too many enemies of Caesar were still lurking.

The sitting room was comfortably furnished, with upholstered chairs and couches flanking a handsome fireplace. On the mantel was one of the few mementos from his time with Caesar that Molena had allowed in her home: the wine decanter made of cut Egyptian glass that Caesar had kept in his office all those years.

Curio reached down and moved a stone, exposing his position to catastrophe. It was a reckless move, of course; he was letting the boy win.

Curio glanced across the sitting room at his wife, who was helping their daughter with a weaving project. He loved Molena even more now than he had that evening when she'd saved him from the bloodthirsty warrior Gabinier. How devoted she had been in the years since! To keep her safely out of Caesar's line of sight, Curio had sent her from the camp at Vesontio back to Rome. She had patiently waited there for him while he toiled loyally for Caesar. They'd finished the campaign in Gaul and the invasion of Britannia, and then fought through the tumultuous years of the civil war between Caesar and Pompey.

Through all those years, Curio and Molena had treasured their precious time together upon the fleeting occasions when Caesar and his entourage would sweep through Rome during the whirlwind of his ambitious climb to domination of the Roman Empire. They'd even conceived their two children during these interludes. But Curio had never allowed Caesar to come into contact with Molena nor did he mention their relationship to him, lest Caesar recall that shameful experience with her in his tent and take retribution on them both. More importantly, Curio kept it quiet out of respect for Molena. They were formally married only after Caesar's assassination.

Curio's dreams of a quiet and happy life with his wife had fallen by the wayside in the three years since Caesar's death, as he'd become caught up with helping Octavius in the struggle first against Caesar's assassins and then against Marc Antony. Curio knew the alliance was doomed—it was only a matter of time before there would be a fateful showdown between Octavius and Antony. Fortunately, after the battle at Philippi, Curio had limited himself to overseeing Octavius's interests in Rome; Octavius had recruited Agrippa as his chief military advisor.

Young Marcus picked up a stone and placed it just where it was needed to capture several of Curio's pieces. "I've won!" he cried. "Mama, I've finally beaten Papa at latrones!"

Molena gave them a sweet smile. "That's wonderful, Marcus! I always told you that if you kept trying, someday you would win!"

Curio had begun resetting the pieces for another match when one of the house staff came into the room. The servants were all free men and women who were paid for their labor—Molena would not tolerate the keeping of any slaves.

"There are two visitors," the man said. "A man and a boy. They are waiting in the tablinum."

Curio and Molena exchanged glances. They had nothing planned for the morning.

"Who is it?" he asked.

"They would not tell me. They said only that both of you would be glad to see them."

"Stay with the children," Curio told the servant. "Come, Molena; let us see what this mystery involves."

They made their way down a long corridor, frescoed with images of Caesar's great victories, including a depiction of Mamurra's galleys with the turrets and poles. Entering the tablinum, they saw the adult had his back turned, studying a mural portraying the great bridge across the Rhine. But the boy was facing them. And upon seeing him, Curio gasped.

The youth was the spitting image of a young Caesar, exactly as Curio remembered him from the day they had burned down the Julian family barn. He would have recognized that square jaw and prominent chin anywhere. Molena, observing her husband's reaction, narrowed her eyes and studied the boy.

The adult turned. The years had changed him, of course, but there was no mistaking the man.

"Elliandro," Curio said, astonished.

Molena staggered back a few steps, and then, with a whoop of joy, ran to her brother. "After all these years! I thought I'd never see you again!"

The siblings held each other in a long embrace, during which Curio could do nothing but try to calculate what this reunion might portend.

"I see you are still wearing that necklace," Elliandro said.

Molena laughed. "Yes, Curio has given me many other pieces of jewelry, but I still wear this daily as a reminder of our humble origins!" Molena finally released her brother and turned to the boy. "And who is this young man?"

"This is Sonnig," Elliandro said.

"Sonnig!" she said. "My goodness, how big you have grown!" Molena widened her eyes at her husband, and Curio could read it on her face: she had suspected all along that Sonnig was Caesar's child. He had never said a word about it to her, and she had never asked him, but there was certainly no denying the resemblance was strong.

"The last time I saw you," she said to the lad, gently grasping his hands, "I could hold you in one arm!"

Sonnig blushed, turning his eyes to the floor.

"But where are his parents?" Curio asked Elliandro.

At the mention of his parents, Sonnig stifled a sob, and Molena pulled him into a motherly embrace.

"They died this past winter," Elliandro said, his own tears erupting. "Gabinier took sick and was gone before we knew it. And then Devorra fell prey to the illness."

"My condolences," Curio said, a little more frostily than might have been appropriate. But his agile mind was already beginning to play through the implications of the presence of this boy in Rome, and none of them were good. "What brings you to us?"

"I have missed my sister dearly all these years, and I regret not having come sooner," Elliandro explained. "After all, none of us are getting any younger," he laughed. "And Sonnig would hear nothing of staying behind, as he was eager to meet the Roman who had been so kind to his mother."

"My mother told me all about you, sir," Sonnig added, looking directly at Curio.

Curio's eyes narrowed, then brightened. "You must be famished," he said amiably. "Molena, why don't you take young Sonnig here to get some refreshment? I would like a few private moments with Elliandro."

Molena took the boy by the hand and walked toward the kitchen. Curio directed Elliandro through a corridor to his office, littered with stacks of scrolls and documents.

Curio motioned Elliandro to a Greek-style klismos chair, settling himself into a matching chair. "What a journey you must have had to get to Rome!"

"It was an adventure," Elliandro agreed. "But fortunately, as you know, Rome has built very good roads."

"Yes, but how did you find us?"

"It wasn't hard—we just asked for the location of the man who had served as Caesar's adjutant."

Curio was not surprised. The city was full of people who had served in the army; any one of them would have known him. "I cannot believe you came all this way just to see your sister. What is the real reason you have sought me out?"

Elliandro leaned toward Curio. "Before she died, Devorra told me the truth about what happened when she was a hostage at Vesontio," he started slowly.

Curio's heart was racing, but he kept his face placid. "Before you say more, I must tell you that Caesar legally adopted Octavius and named him in his will," he explained. "And Caesarion is not only Caesar's son by blood, but he is the successor to the throne of Egypt, making him a formidable adversary to Octavius."

"I understand this," Elliandro retorted, "but I remember Caesar from that day he pulled Molena out of the coffle. I can see him in this boy already. As he grows, he will more and more resemble his true father."

"Even more reason to keep him away from Rome," Curio asserted.

Elliandro's jaw tightened.

Curio spoke bluntly. "Does Sonnig know his true lineage?"

The former slave shook his head. "Gabinier and Devorra raised him to believe he is the son of Gabinier. Devorra never told him the truth, out of respect for her husband."

Curio touched his chin. "And there are no siblings?"

"No," he answered sadly. "She was unable to conceive again due to the trauma of his birth."

"Elliandro, you must return to the forests of Belgae and never speak of any of this again," Curio said firmly. "Octavius walks around calling himself Caesar's son. He has cloaked himself in the legitimacy of Caesar's will. Like many people I have known who acquired their wealth by inheritance rather than by earning it themselves, he suffers from a great sense of insecurity. Should he get wind that some new young fellow is being recognized as Caesar's blood son, Octavius will find him and have him killed."

Elliandro was skeptical. "That seems rather extreme."

Curio gripped Elliandro's hand like an iron vise. "Caesar had you flogged to within an inch of your life for coming to your own sister's defense. You think he was a ruthless bastard? This young Octavius puts Caesar to shame in that regard!"

Elliandro was still not entirely convinced.

Curio rolled his eyes in exasperation. "It has already happened with others. Octavius has hunted down every one of them, and they have vanished. Do you know how I know this to be true?"

"No."

Curio drew in a deep breath, and then let it out. "Because," he said simply, "I am the one who arranged it all for him."

⁓⁓⁓

A SHORT WHILE LATER, Curio and Elliandro rejoined the others, who had enjoyed a hastily assembled lunch. The children had already gone outside to play.

"Elliandro," Molena said eagerly, "you must tell us what happened after the attack in the field. What did you do? Where did you go?"

Curio refilled their glasses as Elliandro began.

"After we rescued Devorra and Sonnig from the Romans that evening, Gabinier led us back to the territory of the Nervii. He took us to the farmer and his wife who had nursed him back to health after he was wounded."

Molena gave her brother a sweet smile.

"We had riches from the raid at Vesontio," he continued, "and Gabinier had promised someday he would pay them back for saving him. They would not accept any reward, but welcomed us all into their home. We bought the neighboring land, then built a house for Gabinier and Devorra and a smaller one for me. The farmer and his wife became like grandparents to young Sonnig."

"Your farm?" Molena said. "Tell me about it."

"It's a beautiful place, with plentiful water and game. It produces ample crops every season. We give the Roman governor his share, and no one bothers us," Elliandro said with a satisfied grin.

"Sonnig has stepped right into the shoes of his father," he continued. "He will be able to run the farm himself soon."

"And you never married?" Molena asked.

Her brother laughed. "I never found a father I could stand enough to bargain with for a daughter's hand."

"Very prudent," Curio said, but he could not withstand this small talk any longer. "What are your plans?"

Elliandro gave his brother-in-law a long look, then relaxed his shoulders. "Sonnig and I must return to the farm in time for the harvest. We leave at first light."

"Surely you can stay with us a few days before you return," Molena implored. "You have come such a long way for so short a visit."

Looking at Elliandro, Curio said, "Molena is right. We would be happy to accommodate you and Sonnig."

"And the children would love to get to know their only uncle," Molena added.

"Very well. We shall stay a day or two, then be on our way," Elliandro said. "But I promise you this, dear sister," he continued. "As soon as Sonnig is able to run the farm on his own, I will come back to Rome to be with you and to watch your children grow."

With a nod, Curio extended his hand to Elliandro.

AS SCHEDULED, Mamurra appeared at Curio's home for their weekly latrones game. Curio brought him into his study and began setting the pieces upon the game board.

Mamurra noticed a lacquered ebony box sitting atop Curio's ornate mahogany desk. "I see you have added a new artifact to your collection," he remarked when Curio returned.

"The artisan Morelli just completed the box for me," Curio replied.

Mamurra opened the lid. He removed a worn-looking dagger, embossed with an ivory eagle inlaid in the handle and bearing a razor-sharp edge.

"Caesar's dagger," he said. "You took it on the day he was murdered."

"Yes," Curio replied. "It was a gift from his Julia, whom I believe he loved more than anyone or anything. Perhaps even more than power."

"He died trying to defend himself that day in the Senate," Mamurra said.

"I think otherwise," Curio stated.

This was news to Mamurra. "What do you think?"

Curio grew wistful. "I believe," he said quietly, "that his last thoughts were of Julia."

Mamurra contemplated this for a moment, then ran his fingers over the weathered ivory eagle and reverently returned the dagger to the box. As he placed the box on the desk, he noticed a hefty sheaf of papers.

Mamurra squinted at the cover sheet, and focused on the title:

Caesar Obsessed

"What's this," he asked, "another book? Are you feeling guilty because you didn't give me any credit in *Bellum Gallicum*?"

"That was Caesar's book," Curio protested. "I was the mere scrivener."

"Pahh," Mamurra said with a huff, knowing better. "What's this one about?"

"This, my friend, is the story of the Gaius Julius Caesar *I* knew."

Mamurra grinned, then pointed to the game board.

"It's your move, Curio."

AFTERWORD

As I wrote in the Afterword of my first book, *Hannibal's Niece*, an historical novel "takes a series of established historical events involving actual individuals and spins a story for which there is no established documentary record." So too with *Caesar Obsessed*.

The most frequently asked questions I receive from readers are (1) How did you get the idea for the book?, (2) Did that really happen?, and (3) Who was real and who was fictional? My responses follow.

My dear father was a civil engineer, and while growing up I often spent time with him visiting construction sites. That's the source of my interest in bridge building. Later in life, as an avid reader of Roman history, I learned about Caesar's astounding feat of building a bridge over the Rhine in only ten days. After traveling to Germania and seeing the Rhine for myself, I kept wondering how he could possibly have spanned that great river in so short a time. And why? There had to have been something else going on! That's how I came up with the main plot line for this book.

A secondary consideration driving the book was the realization I've gained of the role of slavery and land confiscation as the financial underpinnings of the Roman empire. I've taken a clear-eyed view of how the Romans actually financed their military campaigns and the building of their empire—they did it by brutally enslaving the people they conquered and ruthlessly confiscating their property.

The major events of *Caesar Obsessed* are factual. Caesar survived a deadly battle in Gaul against Germanic tribes led by Ariovistus, established his headquarters at Vesontio, invaded Belgae, narrowly won the battle at the River Sabis against the tribes led by the Nervii, returned to Vesontio to refit his army, then invaded Brittany and defeated the hapless Veneti tribe in the great sea battle at Quiberon Bay. The actual historical events leading up to the invasion of Germania were much more complicated than I have related, involving minor battles I've omitted, complex tribal intrigue, and a raid (although not against Vesontio, as I have imagined it), which provoked Caesar into famously building the bridge over the Rhine in ten days. The historical accounts make no mention of the time spent in drawing up plans for the bridge and compiling and preparing the materials needed to build it. In my treatment, those plans and preparations are initiated considerably in advance of the actual construction. It had to have been that way.

The phrasing of the various missives found in the story is mine, although many of these letters and orders are based on historical events. However, Catullus's infamous poem as presented in the book is translated nearly verbatim from his original text, with only a slight adjustment for consistency with the story.

I confess to having taken liberties with a number of historical facts. For example, Caesar's daughter, Julia, died at a later time than what I've depicted in this book. And Caesar did not return from Germania with a new treaty to pump money into the Roman purse. Other anomalies are sprinkled throughout the book, all in the name of making a better story.

In this book, the main characters of Caesar, Julia, Pompey, Labienus, Mamurra, Catullus, Crassus, Decimus Brutus, Ariovistus, and Boduognatus are all historical figures, although they've been embellished considerably. Curio, Molena, Elliandro, Devorra, and the brave and hopelessly lovestruck Gabinier are all imagined. Mamurra's great staff engineer, Giacomo, is fictional, and is named in honor of my father, Jack.

I relied on a number of sources in crafting the novel. Caesar's own account, aptly titled *Commentarii de Bello Gallico* or *The Gallic War*, is a primary source. (In my version, however, the loyal Curio is the actual author of this book.) I found *Caesar: A Biography* by Christian Meier to be an extremely helpful and readable source. A relatively short book by Trevor Nevitt Dupuy, *The Military Life of Julius Caesar: Imperator*, does a great job of boiling down all the minutia of the tribes and the battles into an easier-to-understand summary of the military events.

I always strive to include a lot of visual imagery in my text, and in that regard, Virginia L. Campbell's book *Ancient Rome* is a fabulous collection of images of artifacts that helped fuel some of my descriptions. When it comes to descriptions of the city of Rome and its architecture during that era, nothing matches the scale, scope, and detail of *The Atlas of Ancient Rome*, edited by Andrea Carandini and Paolo Carafa. (That said, historians will spot many deviations from fact. My descriptions of certain buildings, ships, weapons, clothing, and foods come largely from sources detailing these items from periods later in time.) Finally, I must give a shout-out to the ubiquitous online resource Wikipedia. It makes a vast array of mostly well-researched information available to all, and I found it valuable for locating source materials and basic facts.

ACKNOWLEDGMENTS

Writing an historical novel is a humbling experience. What begins with a passionate idea inevitably turns into a long and grueling slog of endless research, first checking facts and accurate use of terminology and then listening to countless opinions on how to make the story even better. No author is an island when it comes to the book-writing process, and I am no exception.

First and foremost, as noted in my Special Dedication, G. A. Beller and Vivian Craig of G. Anton were tireless in pushing for more depth to the story and making literally scores of suggestions that enriched the plot and helped to create some unforgettable characters. We very quickly pressed the redoubtable Maya Myers into service as our primary editor. The talented Jim Swanson agreed to provide multiple iterations of the maps and other illustrations. Having thus resurrected the team that produced my first novel, *Hannibal's Niece*, we worked doggedly through draft after draft before finally emerging with a solid manuscript. My deepest thanks to all of you.

Many others helped out along the way. I'm especially grateful to Susan Licata, who patiently reviewed several drafts and with her usual eagle eye caught numerous details needing attention. Additional vital comments came from Michele Lomax, a gifted attorney and accomplished speaker and consultant on diversity, equity, and inclusion. I found her input on the book to be quite insightful. Special thanks also to Stephanie Rocha, who demonstrated great skill and tolerance in responding to all our input on the cover design.

I was also fortunate to recruit a former colleague, Beverly Loder, who drew upon her extensive background in book publishing to jump in and assist with final editing, production management, and more. She was manna from heaven. She painstakingly guided us through multiple sets of revised page proofs, working to bring to fruition a top quality book of which we can all be proud. If the final version in any way falls short of that goal, the responsibility is mine and mine alone.

Gathering reader feedback is invaluable in shaping the final draft, and I was gratified to find willing reviewers in nearly twenty friends who had enjoyed *Hannibal's Niece* and were continually asking, "When's the next book coming out?" They generously agreed to review the page proofs and share their reactions, providing not only helpful input but encouragement.

Finally, I must acknowledge the tremendous loving support of my significant other, Christina Michael. She, too, read multiple drafts, made numerous suggestions, helped with the cover design and the website marketing effort, and generally kept me from chucking the whole project at several critical junctions. Special thanks to her for believing in me.

I'm profoundly grateful to all of these folks.

About The Author

A graduate of Harvard Law School, Anthony "Tony" Licata has built a long and illustrious career as a highly regarded Chicago attorney specializing in commercial real estate and family office clients. Widely known to clients and peers for his legal acumen and civic contributions, few were aware of Tony's knack for crafting epic tales set in ancient times, far removed from legal briefs and contracts. The publication of his first historical novel in 2017 changed that.

Inspired by the movie *Spartacus* as a young child in rural Illinois, Tony has long been an avid devotee of the Roman Empire and a committed student of Roman and European history through research and writing as well as international travel with his beloved daughter, Haley. This lifelong passion culminated in the publication of his debut book set in ancient Rome, *Hannibal's Niece*, which earned high praise from professional reviewers and fans of the genre alike. Its enthusiastic reception prompted Tony to create another sweeping saga based on historical fact, *Caesar Obsessed*.

When he's not counseling clients or outlining plot twists for his next book, Tony has been methodically working through his bucket list by visiting every major Civil War battlefield and many of the major battlefields of Europe.

For more information, please visit www.anthonyrlicata.com.

Also by Anthony R. Licata

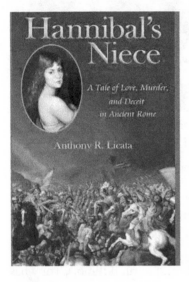

Hannibal's Niece transports readers to the battlefields of Europe and Africa in a riveting tale of love and war, alliance and betrayal, political machinations and intrigue, bringing history to life with unforgettable grandeur.

Hannibal, the fearsome champion of Carthage, has been marauding through Roman territory behind his trained war elephants for many years. Scipio, a handsome young Roman general, takes up the fight against Hannibal's brother, Hasdrubal, in Spain. Employing dramatic new tactics, Scipio purges the Carthaginians from the field.

When the Romans seize Hasdrubal's harem, Scipio claims the finest woman for himself. The stunning Vibiana, however, turns out to be no mere harem girl—she is Hannibal's own niece! Scipio soon finds himself bewitched by her charm and beauty, which may lead to his undoing.

While Scipio makes treaties with African kings and executes innovative strategies on the battlefield, his love for Hannibal's niece will come to drive his decisions in ways that threaten to rock the very foundation of Roman society.

Praise for *Hannibal's Niece*

Named a Distinguished Favorite in the New York City Big Book Awards for 2018

Recognized during the Chicago Public Library Foundation's 2017 Carl Sandburg Literary Awards

"From the sensation of a slave girl's silk gown to the strategies of a master general, Hannibal's Niece *engages all your senses as it provides an authentic and captivating look at love, war, and politics in Ancient Rome."*
—**Lori Andrews, Author of the Dr. Alexandra Blake Mystery Series**

"An extraordinary first book and a pleasant surprise with well-crafted plot, unforgettable characters, and superior writing."
—**Meghna Hulsure, *Manhattan Book Review***

"A moving story of blood and war and love told with a skillful hand."
—**Alex C. Telander, *San Francisco Book Review***

"A must-read historical novel. Licata's knowledge of this period in time and his attention to detail are masterful and brilliantly demonstrated in his exceptional writing and storytelling."
—**G. A. Beller, Author of *Not Black and White: From the Very Windy City to 1600 Pennsylvania Avenue***

CPSIA information can be obtained
at www.ICGtesting.com
Printed in the USA
LVHW102313020722
722641LV00004B/93